Khisanth rose to her feet. "I've spoken many times of my amazement that humans rule the world while dragons live in the shadows. I couldn't understand how such a thing was possible. After today, I begin to comprehend."

Anger squeezed Khisanth in its enormous grip. She tipped her head back, raised a bloodied claw to the skies, and howled, "Takhisis, I've called you my queen! Can treachery be your plan?" The black dragon blasted her fury and frustration into the sky, exhaling a cloud of acid that rocketed upward. Spraying out, it rained back down in sizzling droplets and gobs. Ogres, men, even Jahet and Maldeev, scrambled out of the burning mist.

Only Khisanth did not emerge, for she was no longer on the Prime Material plane.

Saga

From the Creators of the DRAGONLANCE® Saga

VILLAINS

Before the Mask
Volume One—Verminaard
Michael and Teri Williams

The Black Wing
Volume Two—Khisanth
Mary Kirchoff

Emperor of Ansalon
Volume Three—Ariakas
Douglas Niles
Available in December, 1993

Hederick the Theocrat
Volume Four—Seeker Hederick
Ellen Dodge Severson
Available Winter, 1994

Lord Toede
Volume Five—Fewmaster Toede
Jeff Grubb
Available Summer, 1994

DragonLance® Saga

VILLAINS
Volume Two

The Black Wing

Mary Kirchoff

DRAGONLANCE® VILLAINS SERIES
Volume Two

THE BLACK WING

©1993 TSR, Inc.
All Rights Reserved.

Random House and its affiliate companies have worldwide distribution rights in the book trade for English language products of TSR, Inc.

Distributed to the book and hobby trade in the United Kingdom by TSR Ltd.

Distributed to the toy and hobby trade by regional distributors.

DRAGONLANCE is a registered trademark owned by TSR, Inc. The TSR logo is a trademark owned by TSR, Inc.

Cover art by Jeff Easley.

Interior art by Karl Waller and Jeffrey Butler.

First Printing: September 1993
Printed in the United States of America
Library of Congress Catalog Card Number: 92-61098

9 8 7 6 5 4 3 2 1

ISBN: 1-56076-650-6

TSR, Inc.
P.O. Box 756
Lake Geneva, WI 53147
United States of America

TSR Ltd.
120 Church End, Cherry Hinton
Cambridge CB1 3LB
United Kingdom

Acknowledgments

I must thank Jim Lowder for his enthusiastic encouragement and for his honest friendship beyond the convenience of proximity; Harold Johnson for his sourcebooks and accessibility; Karen Boomgarden and Barbara Young for their thought-provoking discussion of "badgerness"; and Joan Cooper for the patient flexibility that gave me peace of mind, as well as stretches of blessed silence.

And, as always, Steve Winter, for the late-night discussions and tinkering without which I would never be able to successfully complete these soul-taxing tomes.

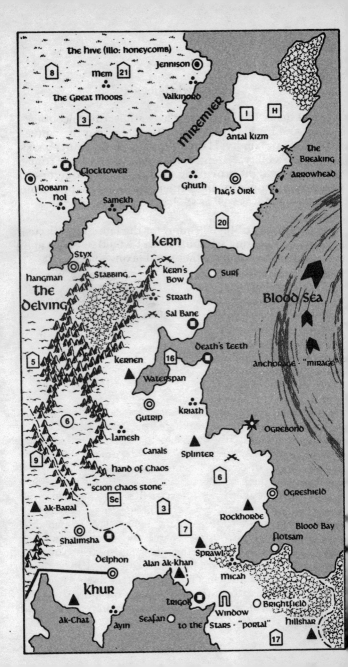

Prologue

Like switchblades snapping open one by one, the black dragon's pearly talons flexed. Khisanth's foreclaws lingered on the tooled leather binding of the spellbook she'd found in the ruins that were Xak Tsaroth. Sighing, the dragon slapped the tome shut; she couldn't bear to memorize another spell today. She set the book at her horned feet and hopped down from the stone altar. The dragon's wings stretched open with a muffled sound, leathery sheets billowing in the wind.

Khisanth's eyes had aged from tawny yellow to angry red in the dark confines of the sunken city. Her orders were to guard a staff she was to neither touch nor see. Unbeknownst to Highlord Verminaard of the Green Wing, Khisanth *had* seen the staff. More than a little curious, the dragon had once shapechanged into a mouse and taken the gully dwarves' odd lift to the upper level of the ruins. No draconians would report to Verminaard that a mouse had slipped through the golden doors to the Hall of Ancestors. Inside, Khisanth had found a statue of a woman. Held in her marble arms was a staff of plain, unimpressive wood. Some sense had stayed Khisanth's hand from touching it. She had no desire to add a stick to her hoard, anyway.

What a waste of time and talent this assignment is, she fumed.

Khisanth had once led the infamous Black Wing, but her time in the Dark Queen's army was a distant memory, before her reassignment to this hole. In fact, it was the reason for it. Her demotion was just another indignity in a long life that deserved greatness, but had received only betrayal and deception.

Khisanth was bored enough to contemplate walking from the huge, domed chamber that was her underground lair to engage one of her draconian minions in conversation. But she spotted in the dim light a filthy gully dwarf. The witless creature in the floppy shoes was getting dangerously close to the shiny piles of gems and other treasures. Khisanth lashed out with a claw and snapped up the wide-eyed creature before it even knew the dragon was near. Popping the morsel into her jaws, Khisanth closed her eyes languorously as she savored the crunch of moist bones.

The dragon spit out the shoes. Underground there were only shoes. No hooves of wildebeests. No elk horns. Khisanth's ever-hungry stomach growled, as if it, too, remembered when the dragon had freely hunted the forests of Endscape. The entire Khalkist Mountain range had been her larder. Then, with one swipe of the mightiest hand, her rank, her freedom—everything—had been taken away.

The black dragon's mind frequently wandered to the people and events that had led her to this low point. It comforted her to realize that she'd slain nearly everyone who had ever thwarted her. Khisanth had high hopes for getting revenge on the ones who had eluded her grasp in recent years. A dragon's life was long, and one day, she would claw her way out of this predicament, too.

In her time, Khisanth had known the innermost thoughts of only three other beings: a dragon and two odd little creatures, whose lives she had valued. And one other, the dragon amended: a human knight named Tate. She had killed him, too. All of them were dead now. . . .

Strangely, their deaths were tied to the destiny that the goddess Takhisis herself had laid on Khisanth, a destiny that had yet to be realized.

And never will be, the dragon told herself sullenly. Here I am, confined to Xak Tsaroth, while the war is just beginning to rage across the world. Nothing interesting will ever happen here.

Khisanth pushed aside the bitter thoughts. She'd been trapped underground once before. Then, too, she'd thought she would never see the light of day again. It had been a time long ago, even before Takhisis had pronounced her destiny. . . .

PART ONE

Chapter 1

The gossamer wings of the tiny nyphids fluttered in silent syncopation as they hovered above the sleeping dragon's broad, curved spine. The darkness of the small pit was illuminated by the melon-sized maynus that floated between them, blue lightning streaking within the glassy orb. Kadagan, the younger of the two nyphids, arched one dark, delicately curved eyebrow in surprise at the creature.

"We were right, Joad," he breathed softly to his elder, glancing down the length of the black-scaled dragon beneath him. The beast's ribs, as wide as the hull of a ship, gently rose and fell. "It *is* a dragon. The rumors of their return are true. I thought they were but stories told to children . . . like me."

"What's that?" Kadagan asked suddenly, tilting his head toward Joad. His luxurious mane of dark hair bounced on his slight shoulders. Listening to Joad's silent conversation,

Kadagan's expression grew dark. "Yes, I know we've got to hurry. How dost thou propose we wake it up?"

Shrugging, Joad reached down with his slim index finger and lightly touched the dragon's spine. Like flint on steel, the touch caused blue sparks to zag crazily in the blackness of the stony pit. The dragon's limp body jumped once off the dirt floor, as if struck by a thunderbolt, then settled back down with a loud *wumppph*. The nyphids winged their way upward to the safety of a ledge, dimmed the maynus globe, and watched with stunned fascination as the dragon awoke.

Khisanth opened one enormous golden eye in confusion. Drawing their first conscious breath in centuries, her lungs nearly exploded in a great, barking cough from the acrid taste of scorched flesh and sulfur. The movement brought her sensitive snout scraping against rough stone. She opened her other eye and looked around.

Where am I? her sleep-fogged brain demanded. Water dripped and echoed hollowly nearby. What did I do to land myself in such an impossibly small cave? she thought, taking rueful note of the damp, stone walls just inches away on all sides. Her last memory came back slowly, murky and distant and dreamlike.

The *geetna* had brought her mountains of food in a similar chamber. Khisanth's crimson tongue slithered greedily over knifelike teeth as she remembered the way she had gorged. The *geetna*, a snaggle-toothed matron of the lizardlike bakali race, had encouraged her.

"Eat, eat, Khisanth," she'd said in the odd hisses, growls, and smacks that were the bakali language. Khisanth had always found its timbre oddly soothing, though she had only half heard the ancient one over her own noisy gulping of raw rodents. "It will be many centuries before you feast again."

Where was her old *geetna* now? The tumble of memories continued.

"I am too old for the Sleep," the bakali had said, "and I would be of little use to our queen when she returns to raise her legions, as she has promised. But you, Khisanth, you are more cunning and perceptive than the other young dragons.

7

You will see greatness done in her name."

Khisanth had understood little of what her *geetna* was saying, until she saw the old bakali's withered, leathery arm, more like a human's than a dragon's, lift high and sprinkle Khisanth's snakelike head with a glittering, silvery substance. The dust had tickled her nostrils.

"There, I have done my last magic," the elder bakali had sighed. "Sleep now, as it is ordered, until Takhisis awakens you." Soothed and sated, Khisanth had drifted into slumber.

The black dragon's eyes opened wide now in wonder. The Dark Queen herself had awakened her! The *geetna* had said it would be so. That must mean Takhisis was raising her legions. But why? Khisanth had been young before the Sleep, had known little of the world beyond the warren. How long had she slept?

Khisanth's stomach rumbled, finally awakened by the memory of her last gorge. The gnawing hunger drove all other thoughts from the black dragon's mind. Her flared nostrils detected the meaty scent of rats. Rats and worms. Something nibbled at her tail. She wriggled on her belly to thrash it away, but she discovered again that she could barely move in the confines of the cave. The cavern of her memory was roomy; if, as she suspected, this was that same cave of long ago, she had grown at least four-fold while she slept.

Khisanth felt the persistent nibbling again. The dragon snaked a claw arm along her right side, absently noting the tightly folded, leathery wings on her back. Snatching at the offending rodent, she held it up at eye's height for inspection, taking pleasure in the stunned and terrified gleam in the rat's orbs.

"How long have you been chewing on me?" she asked aloud, surprised by the dark timbre of her own voice.

She tossed the rat into her waiting jaws, eyes closing as her senses delighted in the taste of flesh. But the morsel only whetted her appetite. Blood pounded in her head, and she could think of nothing but gorging.

Still lying, curled, on the cool cave floor, Khisanth rose slowly, carefully, onto her massive elbows and tried to turn her whole body about. But her new size would allow no shifting in the egg-shaped cave, just long enough and wide enough to contain her. The long, sloping tunnel to the surface was blocked by new, jagged projections of rock, shiny with dripping water. They rose from the floor and ceiling like teeth in an ancient dragon's slathering maw. She would not be leaving by the same route she had arrived.

Driven by hunger, Khisanth let loose a horrific, braying wail of frustration that rent the still air. Her mouth was filled with a hot, acidic-tasting liquid that roared past her teeth in a powerful stream, splashing the cave wall before her.

The dragon felt a slow, painful warmth spreading on her right claw arm and looked down, where green, glowing droplets sizzled through the dusty black scales to the flesh beneath. Angry at herself for forgetting her ability to breathe acid, she snatched up a claw full of sand and rubbed it on the wounds. The sizzling stopped, replaced by numbness both there and in her head.

There has to be another way out of here, she told herself stubbornly.

Khisanth's great, golden eyes turned upward for the first time. Expecting a rocky dome, she was surprised to see no ceiling at all. Her cave stretched upward like a chute beyond her field of vision. The air above lightened gradually, giving Khisanth hope for an opening to the surface.

Suddenly, the dragon's sensitive eyes and ears perked up. To her surprise, she both saw and heard movement on a rocky ledge above.

"Is that you, Dark Queen?" Khisanth gulped with a shaky voice. She instantly wished she sounded more reverent and less timorous.

"Thou must be speaking Dragon with that deep voice, because I cannot understand," someone said casually, the words floating down to the dragon's ears. "It is too much to hope thou understands Nyphid. Wouldst thou know the Old Common tongue?"

Khisanth understood the speaker's formal, stilted words, but she had never heard the language called anything but

Common. When had it become old? Craning her heavy head back, Khisanth squinted upward, straining for a view of the voice's owner. A ball of bright white light stabbed her in the eyes. The dragon slammed her leathery lids shut against the pain and tore her gaze away.

"Thou shouldst not look into the maynus globe," said the voice from above, now closer.

When at last the burning light disappeared from her mind's eye, Khisanth opened her lids, searching about with an angry squint for the speaker. Her expression softened slightly to surprise.

Hovering above her just beyond the reach of her claw arm were not one, but two small creatures, sheer wings fluttering like thin crystal between their shoulder blades. Belted green tunics covered their slight frames down to their deeply tanned calves. Poking from their cuffs were slender hands with tapered fingers. Their hair, one's chestnut, the other's silver-gray, seemed to glow around the edges as if lit from behind. Their faces were an even deeper bronze and filled with gentle grace.

Their most remarkable and riveting features, though, were their piercing blue eyes. The color of lightning, thought Khisanth.

"What are you?" she breathed, not quite in awe, but distracted by their aura nonetheless. "Pixies?"

The chestnut-haired one scoffed and rolled his blue eyes. "Pixies! Humph. They are pointless and flighty." His chest swelled. "We are nyphids. I am known as Kadagan, and he"— the young one pointed to his elder —"is Joad. Our full designations would be indecipherable to thine ears. Hast thou a title?"

"You mean a name?" the dragon asked, mildly perplexed. When Kadagan nodded, Khisanth became downright confused. "I'm called Khisanth. Didn't she give you my name?"

Kadagan and Joad exchanged puzzled looks of their own.

"Aren't you agents of the Dark Queen?"

Kadagan's vivid blue eyes clouded over, and he shook his head. "We serve no queen."

"Then who are you?" Khisanth demanded, her voice rising in pitch and intensity at the same time that her eyes flattened into suspicious slits. The feeling of wonder the nyphids had first inspired quickly dissolved into vexation. Even the nyphid's awkward speech was beginning to grate on Khisanth's nerves.

"As I said, we are nyphids," Kadagan supplied again, oblivious to the dragon's irritation. He looked at the other of his kind, dark head tilted as if listening; Khisanth heard nothing, though. "Yes, I believe that is the proper way to approach her." He turned his blue eyes on Khisanth. "We woke thee for a business proposition."

Khisanth froze momentarily, then slowly tilted her head back to consider the nyphid. "*You* woke me? Then the queen had nothing to do with that either?"

"Joad jolted thee awake with his finger," Kadagan offered.

Khisanth closed her eyes and tried to still the anger that was rising with each word the nyphid spoke. She felt choked —by chatter, by questions, by this pit. Nothing was turning out as promised by her *geetna*. Nothing that had happened since she'd awakened made sense. Except the rat. She understood gorging. The hunger flared in her stomach, making it difficult to concentrate on anything else.

"Listen," she growled, squinting against the soft light of the glowing globe. "We are both victims of some cosmic case of mistaken identity. You're not who I thought you were, and I'm definitely not interested in any business deal with pixies. Get away from me now, and I'll overlook the trouble you've caused me."

"Nyphids," Kadagan corrected. "And thou shouldst hear our proposition first." His soft features were pulled into a frown. "We would like thee to rescue Dela."

Khisanth shook her head like a dog with a burr in its ear. "Huh?"

"Dela. My betrothed, the daughter of Joad. The last female of our race. She—" The nyphid's voice caught in his throat. "She was captured by humans, and—"

"That's all very interesting to *you*, I'm sure," cut in

Khisanth. "But as you might have noticed, I'm having difficulties of my own." She looked up, considering the climb before her. The nyphids' glowing globe allowed her to see farther into the gloom, but she still could not detect any opening.

The nyphid followed her gaze, then took quick stock of her size. "How didst thou come to be in such a tight spot?" he asked artlessly. Without waiting for an answer, he added, "Joad and I could assist—"

Khisanth cut him off with a raw, vicious chuckle. "You can't retrieve this pixie friend of yours from some humans, but you think you can help me climb out of this pit?" Laughing humorlessly, the dragon dipped her head to look for toeholds in the base of the rocky walls.

"We would not have awakened thee if we could not help thee from this pit."

"You'd be better off not to mention waking me!" growled Khisanth. Blood boiled at her temples, and she flexed her foreclaws. "There is only one thing of interest to me at this moment: getting out of this hole so I can gorge." Khisanth's leathery lips pulled back in a threatening sneer. "In fact, if I could reach either of you now, I would eat you. You'd scarcely be a mouthful," she said archly, "but if you don't cease your chatter, get away from me, and take that blasted, blinding ball with you, I'd settle for a snack."

The nyphids fluttered up and away from the angry dragon, drawing the maynus globe with them. "Yes, she is most excitable and stubborn," said the dark-haired one to his companion. "Fare-thee-well, then," he called. With a silent fluttering of wings, the pair rose together through the still air, beyond Khisanth's sight. "Call and we will assist thee."

"Never!" she growled, her own throaty, guttural word nearly deafening in the confines of the cave. Instead of their departure calming her, it made Khisanth livid. She was a member of the most powerful race that ever lived, and she couldn't get away as easily as two puny pixies—nyphids. Whatever! She would die before she called for their help, as if they had any to give!

She would claw her way to the top, if she had to. Rage born of desperation made the dragon lash out wildly, wings straining upward, rocks tearing at the tough leather webbing. Her claws raked uselessly at the walls, the dirt-and-sand floor, until her own dark blood ran freely from countless cuts and abrasions.

The smell of the blood jolted Khisanth's rumbling stomach. She licked her bleeding cuticles, savoring the meaty taste. It calmed her nerves.

Think. Turn your energies from rage to survival, Khisanth told herself. If you continue as you are, you'll surely die.

Taking the smallest outcroppings of rock into her talons, the young dragon pulled herself up with her short forearms. But her appendages, grown during centuries of sleep, were as atrophied and undisciplined as the flabby, humanlike arms of her old bakali nursemaid. More often than not, her grip faltered, and she caught short her fall by digging her hind feet into the walls. She progressed by sheer force of will, two steps taken for every one secured.

Khisanth had no concept of time. Having slept underground for most of her life, she was unaware that the dim light from above waxed and waned in a regular cycle. Moments were measured in steps taken, brief rests stolen, feedings missed. She could have been dragging herself upward for as little or as much time as she'd slept, for all she knew or cared.

The dragon fed herself on the blood that oozed from her wounds; it slaked her hunger somewhat, though it gave her no energy. She bled mightily from a host of large wounds and broad scratches. Every part of her huge, unfamiliar body ached. Her massive head felt heavy, yet strangely light and dizzy at the same time.

Stopping to rest for a moment on a large, jutting rock ledge, Khisanth allowed herself to look up at last. The light from above was noticeably brighter. She could scarcely believe it. The opening had to be near, perhaps not even as far as the length of her own body, a mere thirty feet.

If only I were a bit closer, she thought blearily, I could

stand on my haunches and pull myself up. But she knew there wasn't enough strength in her claw arms for that. If only I could eat. Or sleep. . . . Her lids—her whole cumbersome body—felt heavy and lifeless. Just a few moments of rest, she thought, and I'll be able to make it.

Khisanth struggled to curl her bulk up on the narrow ledge. Pressing her neck and spine into the stone wall, she tried to settle on her right side, but her long, heavy tail slipped over the edge. Its great weight dragged her down, hind feet scrabbling futilely. Suspended for a moment in midair, Khisanth flapped instinctively. She heard a snap in one of her wings as it caught on the walls.

She fell, plummeting, spiraling head over tail, every part of her scraping and slamming into the rough stone walls. In her descent, she became aware of a regular pulse of light, dim at first, then bright and hot like blue-veined lightning. Takhisis's evil realm would be filled with fire and lightning, the dragon thought distantly. Perhaps the Dark Queen has summoned me, and I am on my way to her side.

Khisanth could barely keep her enormous, golden eyes open. She struggled against unconsciousness, wanting to witness her first journey into the Abyss, the plane where the evil goddess made her domain. Yet the dragon lost the battle, even as she felt the strange surge of energy pulse through her body.

Chapter 2

"The sun will energize thee, Joad," Kadagan said kindly. He brushed the silvery hair from his elder's shoulders to make way for the beloved sunshine, which cut through the canopy of trees just beyond the mouth of the pit. Truth to tell, Kadagan doubted anything but Dela's return would restore Joad's vitality.

Joad's well-being was but one of countless reasons Khisanth had to help them rescue Dela. Time was running out, and Kadagan knew the dragon was their last hope. Secretly, the nyphid had grave doubts that the quick-tempered dragon would ever cooperate with them.

Kadagan and Joad stood watching the bands of blue-white lightning illuminate the darkness of the pit, lifting the unconscious dragon like a gigantic sling. Just ten more feet and the creature would be aboveground.

In anticipation of her arrival, the nyphids had cleared the passage of rock and dirt days before, when they had left the stubborn dragon below to begin her climb. The opening had been little more than a gopher hole when Joad had first sensed the strong, magical life-force far underground. At Joad's insistence, they had widened the abandoned burrow to a mere two feet to permit their own passage. It was now a crater vast enough to accommodate the dragon.

Kadagan and Joad jumped back as the sizzling, buzzing bands of electrical energy bearing the dragon rose past the mouth of the pit, then levitated her to the side. Waggling a tapered digit, Kadagan commanded the lightning to follow him and Joad as they set off into a shadowy forest. The trail was not nearly large enough to accommodate the passage of a dragon, but the white-hot energy carrying the comatose creature singed a wide swath through the undergrowth. Large trees toppled left and right, severed from their now-smoldering stumps.

A half-league from the pit, the nyphids led their burden through the last dense ring of pines in the darkened wood. The sun pounded a grassy field that stretched as far as the eye could see, the horizon broken only by the occasional cottonwood tree jutting skyward. Goldenrod, purple bull thistles, and lacy wild carrot swayed in the breezes above the tall grasses. Grasshoppers and yellow-breasted meadowlarks sprang from the path. Well into the grasslands, Joad and Kadagan stopped. The dragon-bearing lightning hovered momentarily, then gently lowered the body into the stiff, late-summer grass. Abruptly, the fingers of lightning disappeared into the maynus globe which hung, imperceptible in daylight, at Joad's side.

"She is gravely injured," observed Kadagan, walking a path through the head-high weeds around the dragon's crumpled form. Crimson trails of blood cut the dust on Khisanth's black scales. The pink flesh of one nostril was split all the way to her thick lips, which were pulled back in a wide grimace that exposed a broken incisor among the jagged teeth. Many of the claws on the dragon's forearms were torn off at the cuticles. Worst of all, her right wing bent backward, obviously broken.

"Will she live?" Kadagan asked Joad.

The elder bent over the dragon, pressing to her wounds fresh leaves of the lady's mantle plant. The astringent juices of the circular, blue-green leaves helped to stanch the flow of blood. Kadagan knew that if the elder nyphid was trying to save the dragon with his herbal skills, there was still hope.

When Joad finished, the small nyphids struggled to straighten the dragon's bent wing into proper position. Kadagan was glad the creature remained unconscious through what had to be excruciating pain.

Suddenly, Kadagan felt something squeeze him around the chest and hoist him from the ground. Legs dangling, gasping for breath against the ragged black claw that constricted him and made his rough-spun tunic chafe, he looked over his shoulder and saw the dragon's golden eyes regarding him accusingly.

Khisanth suddenly became aware of a dull ache that grew sharp in the claw that held the nyphid. She dropped the green-clad creature as if burned.

"Are you pixies trying to kill me?" Struggling to keep her head off the ground, Khisanth looked to the gray-haired nyphid. He was busily attempting to secure a straight, thick branch to her wing with a length of vine. Though Joad frequently tossed a concerned glance over his shoulder, he did not stop his ministrations. Khisanth winced from the stinging pain beneath Joad's hands, but did not try to stop the creature.

"We are trying—to set—thy wing," Kadagan gasped. "Thou must have broken it trying to climb to the surface."

"The surface," Khisanth repeated in wonder. Her expression turned abruptly stormy when she realized she hadn't arrived there on her own. Her last memory was of falling headlong from the ledge. She'd seen a light, lightning. . . . She'd thought it was Takhisis calling her. "How did you bring me up?" she demanded.

Kadagan nodded toward the glowing ball hovering at

Joad's shoulder. "We are unsure of the physics involved, but we simply told the maynus globe to catch thee, and—"

"You should have commanded it to leave me in darkness," Khisanth interrupted harshly, unimpressed. Her sensitive eyes, long accustomed to the darkness of sleep underground, squinted against the bright sunshine in the field.

"The light of the sun is healing. Shadows foster infection," stated the nyphid emphatically. His companion bobbed his gray head in agreement.

The creature's confident tone reminded Khisanth of their conversation below ground. Her eyes narrowed. "I presume you believe I am indebted to you now and will feel compelled to rescue your friend?"

"Actually, we—"

"I didn't call for your help or ask you to tend my wounds," the dragon snarled. "I especially didn't ask you to wake me before it was time. You may have ruined my chances to aid my queen. For that alone I should kill you." Her leathery eyelids opened wide in an expression of mock tolerance. "However, I will acknowledge your aid, although unwanted and unwarranted, by letting you live."

Expecting a show of gratitude, or at least fear, Khisanth was surprised to feel Joad still wrapping her wing, the chestnut-haired nyphid silently watching, arms crossed, expression unconcerned.

Irritated, Khisanth snapped both wings painfully to her sides, sending the elder nyphid flying. She tried to pull herself to her feet. Clenching the muscles in her mighty jaws, the dragon summoned the last of her strength, more determination than power. She pushed her head and chest off the ground with her claw arms and rolled from her side. Resting for just a moment, Khisanth then planted her horned hind feet under her broad belly. Driving her legs up and locking them, the dragon managed to stand briefly. Her lips drew back in a mocking smile. Then she teetered and wobbled and crashed back down on her chest, setting the ground shaking.

Khisanth sucked in shuddering breaths through nostrils pressed to the sun-warmed dirt. Reluctantly opening her golden eyes, she saw pity on the faces of the nyphids. "Get away from me!" she bellowed, then weakly scraped her arms over the grass, as if to bat the nyphids away.

"Thou hast brought on the bleeding again," scolded Kadagan. When the silent, elder nyphid began applying more leaves, Khisanth did not protest. Instead, she closed her eyes and tried to listen to the noises around her: locusts buzzing, birds singing, wind rustling through leaves. The sounds were neither familiar nor unfamiliar. She vaguely remembered hearing the combined din as a young dragon, but had never paid much attention to it. Now she focused on it, used it to drown out everything else in her muddled, starved brain. Maybe if she kept her eyes closed long enough, all of it—the nyphids, the elements that had conspired to trap and weaken her—would disappear, and she would not feel so . . . defenseless. That realization made her want to lash out again, but she knew she hadn't the energy.

"Food will restore thy strength." Kadagan pulled several worms from the humus underfoot and laid them proudly before the starving dragon. "Here, I've found thee something to eat."

The scent at her nostrils brought Khisanth's red, forked tongue from between her sharp teeth. She lassoed the two tiny worms, pulled them back into her jaws, and let them slide down her throat without chewing. Opening her eyes, she looked around greedily for more.

"Were the worms not enough?" Kadagan asked in surprise.

"I'm not a bird," grumbled Khisanth, her senses awakened by this merest nibble. "I need meat!" She paused and eyed the creature warily. "But I don't need to owe you for anything else. I can hunt for myself." Khisanth tried to pull herself to her feet again, but she couldn't even manage to squat on her haunches.

Kadagan saw exhaustion in the droop of the dragon's head. "We can discuss the details after thou hast feasted," he suggested. "What dost thou require?"

Khisanth sighed inwardly. Since it was obvious she

couldn't hunt for herself, she might as well test the limits of
their skills.

"A moose or other large creature would do nicely," she said
artlessly, smothering a smug grin as the younger nyphid's
flickering blue eyes grew as large as fists. How these tiny
creatures would go about slaying a moose, so many times
their size, was not her problem. The ludicrous vision gave
her the first amusement she'd felt since waking. They
shouldn't make promises they can't keep, she told herself.

Kadagan was, indeed, in a quandary. Nyphids derived
most of their energy from sunlight, but they needed water
and ate fruits and vegetables because they tasted good, and
because they, too, needed sunlight to flourish.

But a moose?

Joad touched Kadagan on the shoulder and suggested the
obvious solution. Tucking the maynus globe into the neck of
his tunic, the elder hefted a tiny sack woven of spiderwebs
and led them on a moose hunt. No longer encumbered by the
slow-moving lightning sling, the nyphids moved swiftly
over the shady forest floor, headed southwest toward higher
elevations. They scampered up trees and slid down sun-
beams. The forest gave way to pine-covered foothills, and the
nyphids' bare feet sent the dried needles snapping. Past the
foothills, among low scrub and decaying pines, they saw
badgers, mountain goats, and wolverines. They left the
beasts alone, though, considering them too small to meet the
dragon's needs.

At last the nyphids spotted their prey, lazy-lidded, loung-
ing on a knoll in the last rays of day. Placing a finger to his
lips to keep Kadagan silent, Joad slipped his hand under the
lump inside his tunic and removed the large globe, letting it
hover at his shoulder. The maynus made no sound and cast a
dull yellow glow in broad daylight; the small bolts of lightning within were gone. The elder nyphid then reached into
his spiderweb sack and removed some crumbled, pungent
herbs. Joad sprinkled them atop the globe. Soundlessly, he
bade the maynus to float until it was over the unsuspecting
moose's fuzzy, oak-leaf-shaped antlers. The globe reached

the beast and slowly rotated, spilling the herbs bit by bit. Nearly invisible, the dust sifted down through the air to settle on the animal's head and shoulders.

The natural sedative properties of wood betony, chamomile leaves, cowslip petals, and valerian root put the already drowsy moose to sleep. At Joad's wordless command, the bands of lightning formed within the maynus, then encircled the moose. The creature snorted and twitched from the movement, but did not awaken. The lightning was benevolent and didn't set the moose's hair afire any more than it had singed the dragon's scales.

Their captive in tow, the nyphids headed back downhill to their hamlet in the grasslands and the hungry waiting dragon.

* * * * *

Darkness had descended, and Khisanth was sleeping fitfully by the time Kadagan and Joad returned. The glowing bands deposited the moose before her. As the scent penetrated her dreams of food, the dragon's red-rimmed eyes popped open in disbelief.

Khisanth vaguely heard a sound—a voice—but she was beyond hearing, beyond caring. Her jaws stretched wide, and her daggerlike teeth pierced the creature's rib cage. The moose awoke, screaming with surprise and pain and rage, and tried to scramble away from the dragon. Blood sprayed and gushed across the ground. The moose thrashed until Khisanth, strengthened by every grisly bite, slashed and severed its head with her mighty tail, silencing its death cries.

Kadagan and Joad watched, both repulsed and mesmerized. The nighttime sounds of the forest were drowned out by the clamor of crunching bones and slurping. In barely the time it had taken Joad's herbs to put the moose to sleep, the ravenous dragon had consumed the entire corpse, spitting out only the hooves in distaste.

Kadagan stared mutely at the gory remains.

"The hooves are too bitter and tough," Khisanth explained, "not moist on the inside like bones." With that, a great belch

21

ruffled the dragon's blood-flecked lips. She sighed happily, deeply, then picked at a pearly tooth with a razor-tip claw.

"More."

Beyond amazement, the nyphids delivered two beavers, a goat, and four long-eared hares before Khisanth's gluttony was slaked that night.

"Art thou fit enough to speak now?" asked Kadagan after a time. He sat cross-legged in the center of an unusually large, three-foot-wide seed pod, low enough to the ground to be obscured by the surrounding tall grasses. Its soft, waxy sections fanned in a circle around him. Joad was similarly perched in the open center of another of the pale green plants. Khisanth was curled before a fire Joad had made for her. The yellow glow of fireflies blinked on and off across the field, and a small benign swarm even clustered on the fringes of their camp.

"I'm feeling generous," said the dragon, leaning back on an elbow lazily, still picking her teeth. "Go ahead and name the price for your unwanted aid, and I'll consider it."

Kadagan looked mildly surprised by her attitude. "Nyphids do not embrace the concept of indebtedness," he said. "We helped thee because it was mutually beneficial."

Self-interest. Here, at last, was a concept Khisanth could understand.

"We intend to pay *thee* for thy services."

Khisanth's brows raised in surprise. She could not think of anything they could pay her that she would value . . . gems, perhaps, but unadorned as the nyphids were, jewels seemed unlikely.

"Art thou interested?" pressed Kadagan

"You don't waste much time, do you?" asked the dragon.

"We have none to waste," Kadagan said, suddenly grim-faced. "Dela is dying."

Khisanth sat up. "I'm listening."

"First, watch the maynus," said Kadagan, then nodded to Joad. The gray-haired nyphid stepped up before the dragon and cupped his slender hands. The bright globe slipped between them. As Khisanth watched, a moving picture began to form where before small bolts of lightning had danced.

The image of a nyphid in a white tunic appeared, curvy and golden-haired, obviously female, with the same backlit glow of the others. There was an etherealness about her that instantly engendered in the dragon a notable urge to touch the globe. Khisanth looked at Kadagan.

"Dela," the dark-haired nyphid supplied. "My betrothed. Watch closely," he commanded with an insistent gesture toward the globe.

Dela knelt at the bank of a stream that appeared to cut through the grassy plain. Lying on its side in one of her tiny hands was a hummingbird. Its head sagged as it gamely sipped water Dela had scooped into the other palm. With the maynus a barely visible glow at her shoulder in daylight, Dela touched her finger to the bird's diminutive, iridescent breast. Sparks flew. Khisanth thought Dela had killed the thing. But the creature, more butterfly than bird, sprang up, and its wings began to beat so swiftly they blurred.

"Dela heals animals. That is her gift, as herbs are Joad's," explained Kadagan.

Khisanth's eyes remained on the maynus. In the globe, a smiling Dela tossed the rejuvenated hummingbird into the sky, and it flew away. The nyphid pulled herself up to her bare feet and turned away from the creek.

Four creatures sat above her on horseback.

"Human males," supplied Kadagan, noting the dragon's puzzled look. Khisanth had seen all forms of animals as a young dragon before the Sleep, but never a human. She was not particularly impressed.

The men were obviously impressed with Dela, though, their stares entranced, covetous. Dela blanched, flabbergasted by their unexpected and unwanted presence. Diaphanous wings sprang from between her shoulder blades. She had cleared the grass on the bank when a fine net dropped upon her. Its weight knocked the nyphid back to the ground. Two of the men slid from their horses and reached for her, to secure the net and simply to touch. The two still on horseback closed in on either side and waited.

The men's hands fell upon the two-foot nyphid crouched under the net. Dela's mouth opened in a shriek, though the image in the maynus was silent. Two bolts of blue-edged lightning shot from Dela's body. The flashes slammed into the chests of the men who'd touched her, tearing a huge, black-rimmed hole in each and tossing them high into the air.

Their comrades on horseback looked stunned but unafraid. One had vivid green eyes and shoulder-length brown hair. Lashed across the rump of his horse was another human, his hands and feet bound. The other horseman was small and wiry with slanted eyes. They pulled their horses back just slightly. The green-eyed one waved and pointed toward Dela. Abruptly, a number of oddly colored creatures, much taller than the humans, streamed into the maynus's field of vision for the first time and rushed the netted nyphid.

"Ogres," said Kadagan.

"Why doesn't she stand and use the lightning bolt again?" demanded Khisanth as Dela collapsed under the net.

"Dela did not do it intentionally the first time. The electrical bolt is our involuntary response to contact with humans and others like them. Thou art not like them, which is why we sought thee. Humans cannot help but touch nyphids when they see us, and we cannot help but harm them when they do. The contact with them so drained Dela's energy that she fell unconscious herself."

Khisanth remembered the tingling she felt whenever the nyphids touched her. Shuddering, she looked back into the maynus, where a large drawstring sack of rough weave was being lowered over Dela. The nyphid was carefully hauled up by the strings of the sack. With that, the green-eyed human put two fingers in his mouth, blew, and the entourage set off toward the south, horsemen in the lead. One ogre carried the sack at arm's length. Then the picture in the globe blurred to the usual yellow glow.

Watching his daughter's kidnapping in her maynus globe had etched deep lines of worry into the elder nyphid's face, cold determination into Kadagan's eyes. "We had heard that humans, ogres, and even red dragons were rising up in the region, but we did not realize they had encroached so far into our forests." Kadagan sighed raggedly. "Had we known, we would not have left Dela even for the few moments it took to gather berries and water for the morning meal."

"I don't get it," said Khisanth. "Why did the picture stop?"

Kadagan shrugged. "The maynus is not sentient. Dela was unconscious, and it had no direction. Nor did we. Joad and I searched for Dela all that day. Finally, when darkness fell, we sighted her maynus glowing across the field where she had been kidnapped. It was several more days before we realized it had recorded her capture."

Kadagan could see that while the dragon found the globe's ability to project pictures fascinating, she had not been persuaded to help them.

"We do not ask thee to rescue Dela simply because she is Joad's daughter and my betrothed." Kadagan paused, as if he, too, were just fully understanding the impact of what he was about to say. "We are the last of our kind. Without Dela, nyphids will die off entirely."

"Why don't you use the maynus to find out where she is and rescue her yourself?"

Joad colored noticeably at the question, but remained silent as always.

"We know where she is." Kadagan struggled with the words to explain. "Dela sends . . . *feelings*, for lack of a better word, to Joad. These feelings led us to a village in the south." His brow furrowed. "When I was sleeping, he slipped into the town to free her."

"What went wrong?"

Knowing the subject was painful to Joad, Kadagan searched for gentle words. "In his desperation to free his daughter, Joad walked into the human settlement unmasked. Thou canst guess, from seeing Dela's capture, the impact Joad's presence had on the humans there. When I realized where he'd gone, I covered myself with clothing I borrowed from a farmer's wash line. I managed to find him, but not before he, too, had been surrounded and rendered unconscious. That energy drain, as well as his sadness over losing Dela, has brought on his muteness."

Kadagan saw the dragon's disgust at their ineffectual attempt at rescue. "We are neither warriors nor mages, nor are we physically strong. Thou art all of these things."

Khisanth stood and stretched her muscles, then resettled into a comfortable position that resembled an enormous black ball with a head. "Let's assume that I'm interested in rescuing Dela," she mused. Her long snout was perched on her claw arms as she regarded the nyphids with heavy-lidded eyes and asked, "What could you possibly possess that I would value as payment?"

"We can give thee something that will grant thee unparalleled strength and wisdom."

The horns on Khisanth's head shifted as her eyebrows rose with undisguised interest. Kadagan had to be talking about a very powerful artifact. The maynus globe, perhaps? Its powers were certainly impressive enough for it to be the first item in her dragon hoard. At the thought, the salivary glands in the pink folds of flesh next to her second row of teeth sprang into action.

"We can teach thee the discipline of qhen."

Khisanth blinked in disbelief, and her images of a dragon hoard vanished. "You think a tiny creature made extinct by *humans*," she spat the word in distaste, "has anything to teach a member of the mightiest race ever to exist on Krynn?"

"It is true that nyphids are on the brink of extinction because of humans. They kill us or display us as possessions because what they do not understand frightens and intrigues them. Yet those are also the reasons that dragons have nearly perished."

Khisanth pushed herself up to her haunches and gave Kadagan an indignant poke in the chest that sent him reeling. "We haven't. . . .'nearly perished'! We were ordered to go underground and sleep until . . ." Her voice trailed off weakly, and Khisanth felt foolish as she realized how slim the dividing line was between extinction and the eternal dormancy the Sleep might have become if the nyphids had not awakened her. The notion made her feel foolish, and black dragons did not like to feel foolish.

Through her angry musings Khisanth became aware of the nyphid's innocent, expectant stare; it did nothing to pacify her. "What has any of that to do with payment for retrieving this lost female of yours?" Khisanth snapped peevishly. Leering down at the slight fellow, she enjoyed the feeling of power her size alone bestowed.

Kadagan, however, was not intimidated. "Nothing—and everything—when thou art truly qhen." But the nyphid could see that he was losing the dragon's attention to wounded pride and mounting frustration. "Thou couldst use qhen to assume different body shapes."

This time Khisanth's horns shifted with cynical curiosity. She had been learning her first spells, those that extinguish light and create thick fog, before the *geetna* put her to sleep. But shapechanging, that was a difficult and highly unusual skill.

Khisanth donned a mask of indifference, but the fact that she sat down again indicated her interest. "What makes you certain I don't already know how to shapechange?"

Kadagan's slight shoulders lifted in a shrug. "Thou wouldst have done so to escape the pit."

Khisanth inwardly cursed the nyphid's faultless logic. Still, she gave the young creature a skeptical glance. "Give me some proof of your own ability to shapechange," she challenged. "Change into a—" She looked around the field and spotted a creature even smaller than the nyphids on a distant cottonwood. "Change into a sparrow."

"I cannot," said Kadagan simply.

"You propose to instruct me in something you don't know yourself?" Khisanth stood again and looked about for the best direction in which to depart. "Obviously you've wasted my time, so I'll be go—"

"Male nyphids are the teachers of the race. We are not magical beings, like thee," Kadagan cut in, his voice still composed. "Only the females of our race are magical. Only Dela."

Khisanth did not take a step, but her gaze remained on the

forest across the field. "But what about the maynus? You use that."

"Only on a rudimentary level," Kadagan admitted. "It is like having a sword capable of slaying an entire clan of fire giants with one stroke, yet only having the strength of arm to peel apples with it."

Khisanth was satisfied with the explanation. If the nyphid spoke truly and could give her the skills to alter shape, her power would be unequalled. Besides, she reasoned, if the lessons proved to be a bore or a ruse, she could leave at any time.

Still, she had questions. Keeping her broad back to Kadagan, she asked, "If Dela's so magical and you've taught her to shapechange, then why doesn't she do so and free herself?"

Joad hung his head sadly. Kadagan's lips pressed together into a pale, thin line. "She cannot employ her skills to escape because the maynus is the source of her magic, and she does not possess it. I fear that even if she had it, she no longer has the physical or spiritual energy to use it. Her captors have kept her covered to prevent the compulsion to touch her. Dela has not felt sunlight for too long. She is despondent. . . ."

"This qhen thing," Khisanth mumbled, turning around at last, "will it take long to learn?"

Kadagan and Joad exchanged hopeful glances. "That is entirely dependent upon thine ability to learn."

Khisanth smirked. "If that's true," she said, "then we'll be on our way before two moons rise." With that, she circled the fire twice and settled down for a night's sleep under twinkling stars, her first in centuries.

The nyphids sealed themselves up in their green pods to protect against predators. In their silent, moonlightless berths, they, too, looked forward to a good night's sleep, their first since Dela's disappearance.

Chapter 3

Sultry summer rain came down in a slanted curtain on the rocks and brown pine needles outside Khisanth's lair. The damp feeling should have been as tranquilizing to the dragon's dark soul as a warm-blooded meal. But today, there was little that would soothe her hot temper.

Khisanth was seriously contemplating reneging on her deal with Kadagan and Joad. The nyphids had already violated their agreement as far as she was concerned. The yellow sun had risen and set countless times, and still they'd taught her nothing, not one single incantation. They'd kept her so busy doing pointless things that she hadn't even had time to work toward recalling those few minor spells she'd known before the Sleep.

Counting the petals of a wild rose, she fumed, viciously plucking out the stamen of the fuchsia-colored one she held in her left claw. Inanity! A thorn found its way to the tender flesh between two scales, and she flung the denuded flower from her angrily.

Kadagan had left her the prickly pile of blooms with instructions to contemplate the essence of a rose.

"What in the Abyss does that mean?" she'd ground out.

"Thou must discover what makes a rose a rose."

"That's obvious. It looks like one."

Kadagan had smiled indulgently and said as he left, "That would be the conclusion of one who is not qhen."

At first, Khisanth had swallowed her annoyance and risen to the challenge Kadagan had flung at her. Her immense claws were clumsy tools for plucking fragile, pale pink petals, as futile an exercise as using a broadsword to find the wishbone in a tiny sparrow. Yet Khisanth was determined to prove to Kadagan that she had as much patience as he, and so she'd concentrated on separating the velvet-soft petals with the pointed tips of her claws. She held handfuls of petals to her flared nostrils and inhaled until the spicy fragrance was as familiar to her as rats or moist earth. Her long crimson tongue sampled both petals and stems until they no longer tasted bitter. But as time passed, measured by the number of petals Khisanth had plucked, her forced patience waned, then died.

Khisanth slowly paced the confines of the small cave Joad had found for her. It was not what the black dragon would have chosen for a lair. Her horns scraped the arched ceiling when she stood up straight in the regal, threatening pose she liked best; thus, when not asleep, she was forced to either stand with her long neck hunkered over, or sit on her haunches like some eager giant hound. She wouldn't be able to stretch and flex her wings here when the nyphids removed the annoying splint on her right wing.

Bats and small birds had called the cave home before Khisanth had arrived, but she had already consumed those she had not frightened away. A large, stagnant puddle of water in the farthest corner of the cave was the only source of pleasure for Khisanth in the lair. After meals on hot summer days and nights, the dragon liked to splash the fetid water up to her neck with her tail, then lie on the cool, dark stone-and-dirt floor.

At least it was dim inside the cave. Khisanth pondered the nyphid's adoration of light. They needed sunshine; she sought the solitude of darkness. Why had she agreed to follow the training of creatures so opposite to her own nature and needs? Greed, of course. The answer didn't shame her. Instead, it supported her decision to force them to teach her as promised.

Just then Khisanth froze and cocked her head to the side. Someone or something was approaching her lair. The underside of her long tail made a soft scraping sound as she scuttled to within twenty feet of the opening, where the shadows would still conceal her. She pressed her bulk up against the left wall. The burning green acid that constantly roiled in her stomach stood waiting in the back of her throat.

Kadagan bounded through the opening to the lair. Shaking rain droplets from his luxurious hair, the nyphid took one look at the scattered remains of roses. "Thou hast been busy," he said, oblivious to Khisanth's threatening posture.

The dragon stepped from the shadows in the foulest of moods, one eye half-closed in a furious squint. "Don't you know better than to approach a dragon's lair unannounced? I nearly boiled you in acid."

The nyphid looked neither concerned nor surprised. "I was aware of thee. Besides, I do not fear my own death."

"Not fearing it and walking foolishly into it are two different things," growled the dragon.

"Come, Khisanth," said Kadagan as if she'd not spoken. He stepped from the cave. "The rain has stopped." Still grumbling under her breath, the dragon followed the nyphid to the ridge of trees downhill from the lair, where Joad waited cross-legged on the ground. "Let us see what thou hast learned."

"I've learned that I'm sick and tired of your games." Khisanth impulsively snatched Kadagan up by the front of his green tunic and raised him a dozen feet from the ground.

"Either you teach me to shapechange right this minute, as we agreed, or you can pull some other hapless creature from the bowels of the earth to smell flowers."

"Does a rose look like a badger?" Kadagan rasped from the pressure on his chest. His expression was strangely serene. Joad had not moved.

"Of course not!" snorted Khisanth at the improbable question.

"So, it is not a badger. Does it have the flavor of a moose?"

"No, it tastes like a rose!"

"And how is that?"

Drawn into the line of questioning despite herself, Khisanth set the nyphid down on the still-damp pine needles. "The wooden stem is acrid, and the center is sweet, compared to the rest."

"Wouldst that not describe an orange or an apple?"

"No—" The dragon paused and thought for a moment. "Yes, it would." She grew frustrated at this realization. "What's the point of all this?"

Kadagan looked at her straight-faced and said, "I think thou knowest, even if thou dost not yet understand it completely."

Khisanth's eyes narrowed. "Are you trying to say that there is a commonality between all things, and that the differences are but nuance?"

Kadagan looked impressed. "Thou hast learned more than expected. All I hoped for was recognition of the distinctions." Adjusting his tunic back into place, the nyphid settled onto a rotted tree stump and wrapped his slender arms around his knees.

"Any magical creature can learn the rudiments of shapechanging," he continued. "But a master of the skill brings all of his other . . . . 'essences' to his new shape, combines it with complete understanding of the creature whose shape he would take." Kadagan paused. "The result is a magical creature superior to the natural one. Anything less is simply a magically animated shell, no better than a golem." He nodded solemnly. "Thou art becoming qhen, Khisanth."

Khisanth was moved to silence. She could feel an almost physical transformation overtaking her body as she began to understand. The dragon shivered in the oppressive heat of the rain-dampened forest.

"I believe thou art ready to try thy wings."

Surprised, Khisanth looked back over her shoulder eagerly. Joad was unleashing the vines and slipping the splint from her damaged limb. "It's all right, Joad?" she asked, not waiting for an answer as she gingerly flexed her wing. "I've thought for several days that it was healed." The joint felt stiff, but not sore. She stretched it farther, opening the wing to full extension. The pearl-white, razor-sharp claw at the tip pierced the treetops.

Khisanth tucked the wing back to her right side. Her heart pounded wildly with anticipation. Raising up on her hind legs she stretched both wings in unison toward the sky, furling and unfurling them with a rhythmic snapping.

Kadagan's soft, even voice said, "Canst thou launch thyself here?" His gaze traveled up to consider the tall canopy of trees that grew some distance before them and afforded protection for Khisanth's lair in the hillside.

"I'm . . . not sure," muttered the dragon.

Frowning, Khisanth searched her mind for memories of flight. All she could unlock was the still image of a tightly packed herd of extremely young dragons, barely distinguishable among the clouds of red dust they kicked up as they pushed their way toward a distant precipice. She wasn't even certain she'd been among the wyrmlings-turned-dragons, or if she'd just heard about them."

"I think I need a ledge," she mumbled at last.

"Is the one above thy lair of sufficient size?"

Khisanth looked over her shoulder at the shelf of rocks that formed a hood over the opening to her lair. It was not overly high, perhaps twenty-five feet above the ground, but it might be adequate. The rocky shelf continued up the face of the steep hillside, interrupted only by the occasional low shrub. Below her lair, the ground dropped away sharply; the line of trees under which they now stood lay at least one length of the dragon's thirty-foot body from the cave.

"We'll see if it's high enough," the dragon said at last.

Anxious to test her wings in flight, Khisanth stepped from the protection of the trees and into the sunlight that had chased the rain clouds away. How the nyphids could enjoy the sun's blinding light, she would never understand. Squinting, she lumbered past her lair and continued upward some distance on the shelf.

That should give me enough room for a running start, Khisanth reasoned. She raised herself high and extended her wings, once, twice, as a test. Drawing in a deep breath to concentrate, she tucked her wings tightly to her sides. Leading with her right foot, she took elongated strides, gaining great speed as she approached the precipice. The ground shook beneath her; rocks tumbled away. The clawed toes of her right foot met the edge first, as she had planned. Then Khisanth pushed herself up with all her great strength, drawing her wings out and driving them first down, then up.

She plummeted like a rock.

For five heartbeats, she scrabbled and clawed and flapped to no avail. Then she met the moist ground and tumbled head over wings.

Breathing heavily, Khisanth let her face remain covered by her left wing as it had fallen. She could feel Joad at her side, silently examining her right wing. She didn't stop him, though she knew she wasn't hurt.

"Thou wast trying too hard."

Khisanth's head snapped up from under her wing. She glared at the nyphid, who was hovering above her left shoulder blade, his own little wings fluttering effortlessly. "How can I try . . . . 'too hard' to learn to do something I don't know?"

"Thou dost not need to be taught to use thy wings—dragons fly naturally. Didst thou need to be taught to walk before the Sleep?"

In truth, Khisanth could not recall.

"Thou likely took stumbling steps at first. But thou assumed upon waking that thou couldst walk, and thou didst."

"Are you saying I should just assume I can fly, and I will?" Khisanth scoffed. Standing, she brushed damp pine needles from her chest and tail and affected a look of disinterest. Still, she waited for the nyphid's response.

"No." Kadagan shook his head as he alighted to the ground. "Though the skill is natural, the knowledge is not. Thou needs to practice, but effortlessly, like a leaf falls from a tree. Thou must stop caring about flying and just do it. After thou hast practiced, it will become second nature." Kadagan could see that she was trying to absorb his words, yet her natural hostility had wrinkled her brow into a scowl.

"Stop thinking about being a dragon, and just be a dragon."

Khisanth's thick lips ruffled contemptuously. The nyphid's gall was limitless! "If there's anything I know more about than *you*," she stormed, "it's how to be a dragon!" With that, she spun her snout around and thundered off again toward the shelf above her lair.

The indignant dragon posed herself as before and prepared to sprint down the hill toward the ledge. But at the last second, she caught a glimpse of Kadagan, standing far below, arms crossed expectantly, face tilted up to catch the sun as he watched her. Whether from spite, or some emotion far more powerful, Khisanth abruptly conjured a brief mental picture of herself flying above the earth. She stopped thinking of every step she would take, of leading with her right foot so she could push off with the same. She commanded herself to move, to run, and when her toes touched the edge, she sent no conscious message to her wings.

She was over the brink. Her wings snapped up, then out. The dragon's horned head jutted forward, and her four wingless limbs stretched backward beneath her expanding chest, in starched, straight lines, parallel to the ground.

Khisanth was gliding. She saw the tree line fast approaching and tensed for a moment, then remembered to simply be a dragon. Her wings angled slightly on their own, and she rose sharply above the thick green leaves and into the waiting blue sky. Coming at last out of the glide, her long, leathery wings folded, then sprang open again with a snap. Wind currents tugged at her, jostling her as she soared. She let the wind take her where it willed.

Khisanth saw the whole of the world as the gods had created it—rugged land, shifting water, turbulent air—and she thought what a loss it would have been to sleep through her entire life beneath it all. Looking back, she saw herself with an admiring detachment. The scales above her rippling muscles were sleek and black like polished onyx. What perfect creations are dragons, Khisanth thought. Surely as god-touched as the land itself.

Ah, flying. . . . The blood-rush it inspired was akin to that of gorging, especially when a tail wind helped her cruise with impossible swiftness. She pushed herself on this maiden flight, past the first ache of her wing muscles, until the legs that would help her land cramped as well. She located the edge of forest that shielded her lair and let her body take care of the details of returning to earth.

Either she had flown too long, or her body had little practical knowledge of landing, because her legs buckled upon contact with the ground. Khisanth tumbled head-over-tail, losing count after the tenth rotation. At last her tail met with a stout tree trunk and she stopped, unable to tell up from down.

"Not bad," said Kadagan, as ever at her shoulder. "Not good, but not bad. Next time thou wilt know not to fly beyond thine endurance."

* * * * *

Khisanth was still smarting from Kadagan's chastisement when she awoke the next day. She had wanted to make him choke on the smug look he maintained during his insufferable preaching about qhen. Khisanth had proven that she could fly, and the greatest compliment he could offer was "not bad." She'd asked him about it, challenged him. The nyphid had said with maddening serenity, "Thou canst fly. So can a mosquito." She'd cast him a scorching look that made her golden eyes look like burned amber. He'd been unmoved. Then he'd left her for the night. Before following the younger nyphid, Joad had handed her some herbal liniments with the unspoken understanding that she should apply them to her stiffening muscles.

Stretching painfully now, Khisanth was sorry that she had defiantly flung the small, unused pots of balm across her lair the night before. Spotting the cracked vessels of ointment, she dabbed the fleshy ball beneath one claw into a partially dried puddle and touched it to the sorest muscles in her wings. To her surprise, the goo provided instant, if not total, relief. The dragon reached down for more and was dismayed to realize that she could not salvage enough from the sandy floor to apply to her whole body. It enraged her to think that her anger had cost her the cure to her ills. Her tail lashed out, and she sent the shards of the crude ceramic pots flying through the lair's opening.

"Anger will defeat thee in battle as well as in life," said Kadagan, calmly dodging the flying fragments as he fluttered into the cave. "An old nyphid maxim."

"Does nothing enrage you? Aren't you furious those humans took Dela?"

"Anger is energy spent foolishly."

Khisanth's eyes rolled up in exasperation. "It never ceases to amaze me that such a wise and all-knowing race has come to the brink of extinction," she stabbed.

As usual, Kadagan did not rise to the bait. "A cruel trick of nature hast given nyphids wisdom without the physical strength to defend it. Thou hast the opportunity for both." Kadagan settled himself, pulling up his tunic slightly to sit cross-legged on the dirt floor. "Art thou prepared for the next lesson in qhen?"

"Qhen?" snorted Khisanth. "I intend to fly today."

Kadagan watched the dragon's stiff, jerky movements as she shuffled around the cave.

"I feel fine! I'll have no problem flying," Khisanth croaked defensively at the nyphid's cool gaze. "Besides"— she whirled on the small creature —"I thought you and Joad were in a hurry for me to rescue your Dela. I'm just trying to oblige you." She crossed her claw arms in a challenging pose.

"So let's skip these fascinating lectures of yours and get on with teaching me to shapechange."

"I am more than anxious to rescue Dela," said Kadagan evenly. "But thou wilt surely fail in the task if thou dost not moderate thy temper. How canst thou hope to control an enemy without first controlling thyself?"

"Is that why you're always so maddeningly calm?" Khisanth snapped

They both knew the question needed no answer. In a strange way, she was beginning to understand the nyphid's logic. Besides, she was tired of looking foolish in contrast to the nyphid's unshakable tranquility. "How long will it take to learn what you want me to know?"

"As I said before, that depends on thee," said the nyphid. "I cannot hurry and teach thee patience." Sensing the circular course this topic could take, Kadagan noted, "The males of my race pass down a tale that might help thee:

The time came for a young nyphid to develop her magical nature and learn qhen. She walked to the pod of her teacher uncle and said, "It is time for me to become the finest nyphid qhen. How long must I study?"

"Ten years at least," her teacher uncle said.

"Ten years is a long time," said the young female. "What if I studied twice as hard as all thine other students?"

"Twenty years," replied her teacher uncle.

"Twenty years! What if I practice day and night with all my effort?"

"Thirty years."

"How is it that each time I say I will work harder, thou tells me that it will take that much longer?"

"The answer is clear. When one eye is fixed upon thy destination, there is only one eye left with which to see the way there."

The thick, scaly skin above Khisanth's brow bones drew up in understanding. She heaved a rumbling sigh of surrender. For a hot-tempered dragon, grasping qhen was going to be a lot more difficult than learning to walk or fly.

Chapter 4

Under cover of darkness, Khisanth, with Kadagan clinging to her neck, soared over the eastern cliffs of the bay known as the Miremier. Guided by the nyphid, the dragon was learning the names of the lands over which they flew.

The terrain just south of the long narrow forest of End-scape was unremarkable for anything but its rugged coasts on both the east and west sides of the peninsula. Impossibly long stretches of flat, unforested land continued south until, abruptly and without foothills or even forest, the easternmost ridges of the Khalkist Mountains jutted out of the earth like jagged fangs.

The flat land might have made for good farming, if any humans cared to go into the far northern reaches of the Ogre-lands, to face the isolation of life beyond the populated villages of either Kernen or Ogrebond. It was a strange and silent stretch of land, surrounded by lonely rain-washed cliffs.

The nyphid and the dragon shared a new spirit of, if not mutual respect, common purpose. Khisanth was learning qhen even more quickly than Kadagan had hoped, for the dragon was a very bright student and was learning, above all, to control her ever-ready temper. Her muscles were toned by long daily flights. With a little more practice, she would be able to master the rudiments of shapechanging. With a little more mental discipline, both teacher and student knew that Khisanth would be ready to fulfill her end of the bargain.

In light of this fact, Khisanth had persuaded Kadagan that she was ready to begin shapechanging. Kadagan himself had said she must see, firsthand, a human female in order to assume its shape. It would also be helpful, Khisanth had reasoned, for her to see the village where Dela was being held. The young nyphid had given a fairly detailed description of Styx from his own journey there with Joad, but Khisanth had a difficult time envisioning it. She'd never seen human dwellings before.

"Something puzzles me mightily, Kadagan," said Khisanth now. "How have these humans come to govern the world? By your own words, they are weakly built, to the point of perishing from simple indigestion. They aren't the least magical by nature. Only after a lifetime's study can a very few of them wield even paltry spells.

"You've said they can do almost nothing for themselves," the dragon continued. "Beasts of burden plow their fields and pull their wagons. They use bows and arrows to bring down prey larger than the smallest rodent, and even those they will not kill with their bare hands or teeth."

"That's all true," noted Kadagan. "Yet they can walk freely, while nyphids and dragons must hover in shadows, for fear of retribution."

The dragon shook her head vigorously. Kadagan clutched her neck more tightly against the sudden turbulence. "Tell me, how have they subordinated so many more powerful races?" Khisanth demanded. "Why would anything but a worm fear them? They aren't nearly as strong as dragons. They can't even fly! I will hate being one of them!"

The nyphid's expression softened at the dragon's plight, and he added with gentle confidence, "Thou wilt understand their crude power after thou hast been one. They are emotionally complex. Their many facets make some weak and small, but give others a fire that inspires followers."

"I will never follow or fear them," said Khisanth, scowling. "As dragon or human, I will bow only to the Dark Queen." She snapped her head up, to punctuate the end of the discussion.

Recalling Kadagan's qhen teachings to live the moment, the dragon concentrated on something more pleasing. She watched the ground below with vain pleasure, catching glimpses of her graceful, menacing, moonlit shadow as it skimmed from cliff face to dusky bay and back. At full extension, she was the most beautiful creature of her limited memory—powerful, gliding silently over the unsuspecting land. What a world it must have been when those of her kind had traveled wingtip to wingtip in the skies—but that had been long ago, before the banishment known as the Sleep.

"There is Styx," Kadagan said abruptly into the dragon's ear. Khisanth followed the line from the nyphid's tapered finger to a dimly glowing collection of lights in the distant southwest. The village was cupped around a calm, indigo blue bay, and its back was pressed against a low ridge of mountains.

"Remember to keep thy distance," warned Kadagan. "For Dela's sake, we cannot risk detection."

"Why would they assume a dragon flying overhead was looking for a kidnapped nyphid?"

"After the disturbance Joad and I caused, they will be suspicious of anything unusual. But thy presence is nothing compared to thy nature. Lest thou forget, the return of dragons is still just rumor to much of the world. The villagers of Styx would be most surprised and alarmed to sight one of your kind."

"No one will see me," Khisanth said confidently.

41

Taking in the dark ridge of mountains at Styx's back, Khisanth banked and flew southeast, paralleling the far northeast edge of the village. "I should be able to see what I need from the foothills above Styx," she explained. Reaching the northernmost peak, Khisanth slowed her speed, dropped her elevation to just above the tree line, and lowered her right wing ever so slightly to swing westward.

The dragon became aware of a dim, flickering glow from the forested foothills below. Curious, cautious, Khisanth dropped back behind a spiky pine and fluttered her wings just enough to remain aloft. Kadagan clung to her craning neck as she peered down into a small glade that would have gone unnoticed if not for the firelight illuminating it. A dozen or more creatures were reclining around a small campfire. The flames made the orange tusks that protruded from their jowly mouths glow like hot coals.

"What are they?" breathed Khisanth.

"Ogres."

Khisanth vaguely remembered them from the maynus, lurking in the background at Dela's capture. By comparison to the two-foot-high nyphids, ogres were huge, perhaps ten feet tall, with sloping foreheads that made them look witless. The warty yellow, brown, and violet flesh beneath their green hair was covered with torn scraps of animal fur that stank even at a distance. Despite the foul stench, Khisanth found the underlying scent of living flesh inviting.

If thoughts of their taste weren't invitation enough to strike, Khisanth spied gem-studded swords near each creature, the precious stones winking at the dragon in the firelight. Picking their teeth with the bones of their recent dinner, the sleepy ogres did not notice the threat that hovered in the shadows beyond the trees.

"Thou art planning to attack."

Khisanth had to force herself to think enough to respond. "Instinct tells me to, yes." Spittle flooded her maw in anticipation of the feast. Blood hammered at her temples and burned in her veins at the thought of the treasure.

"It is most unwise—"

The pounding in Khisanth's head prevented her from hearing anything but her own blood-thirst. She didn't even notice when, sighing, the nyphid extended his gossamer wings and fluttered earthward into the protection of the leafy branches beyond the glade.

Unable to contain her hunger for another second, Khisanth spiraled downward like a black tornado. She only distantly heard the ogres' screams as they spotted her circling in the dimness above. They panicked, and every ogre jumped to its feet. Thinking only of running away, they slammed into each other and fell back down in a tangled pile. Several stumbled and landed in the fire, setting their greasy hair and clothing aflame.

Pulling up short just eight feet off the ground, Khisanth snatched up an ogre by the chest. The creature's purple eyes flew wide open before Khisanth's fangs cut through the flesh and laid its chest bare. The dragon landed with a hop, looked inside the cavity to the heaving heart, and sighed. That delicacy would have to wait until she had dealt with the others.

Khisanth whirled to find a second ogre brandishing a thick branch in its talons, slashing the air before the black dragon. Khisanth bit through the club with a satisfying snap, then tore off the ogre's arm. She thrilled to the unaccustomed texture of the limb sliding down her long throat.

In the fighting that followed, Khisanth was aware of only her own sound and speed, the ogres' fear and blood. She simply acted and reacted. As with flight, the dragon discovered that she instinctively knew what to do. Her entire body was a weapon, effective beyond anything these ogres could imagine. Her talons slashed like sabers, her teeth impaled like spears, her tail whipped and smashed like a battering ram, her wings beat and buffeted like windstorms. There was no escape for the ogres, and turning to fight was hopeless. One after another they died, screaming, stumbling in their own gore.

The campsite was strewn with torn bodies, blood still pumping from dying hearts. Khisanth's red-flecked face looked up sharply from the last kill and saw that only one more ogre stood between her and the treasure.

Khisanth paused to consider the last ogre. Its cured-hide loincloth was of high-quality deer instead of bear, and much less moth-eaten than the others, suggesting some care. This ogre was noticeably bigger than its comrades, its dusty, sweat-streaked forehead a little less sloped. Something about its heavily scarred face suggested enough intelligence for the creature to realize that this was its dying day. Yet there was an absence of fear in this one, too. Khisanth noted that the ogre's eyes still gleamed with a feral light as she slithered over the corpses, preparing her attack.

"You dragon?"

Khisanth stopped short. "You know what I am?"

"Hear stories."

"What have you heard?"

The ogre drew back warily. A weak, threatening growl rumbled through its filed orange teeth, as if warning her to keep her distance while it thought.

"Tell me what you know, or I'll kill you slowly," Khisanth growled, leaning in.

The creature had been chieftain of this small band of ogres and had killed enough foes to realize that mercy in exchange for information was unlikely. The ogre's eyes shifted from side to side, looking for something to help it. Bursting into motion, the tall warty creature stooped and snatched up a sword lying in the dust. The chieftain's attack was straight-forward and ferocious, wasting nothing on cleverness. The ogre simply lunged and drove the point of its sword toward Khisanth's breast.

Ever wary, the black dragon lashed out with her right claw. The dusty sword was torn from the ogre's hand, sent spinning across the clearing until it disappeared in the darkness among the trees. The ogre's eyes hopelessly followed the weapon for only a moment. It looked back again quickly, hatefully, at Khisanth.

She threw back her head and opened her toothy jaws in laughter at the creature's impotent rage, displaying slimy chains of pink-tinged slaver.

The ogre's scarred face testified to countless scrapes with

death, and it called upon that hoarded experience for another ploy. Keeping its eyes locked on Khisanth, the ogre reached down again and snatched up the torn corpse of a fallen comrade, holding it by its ankles. A rake of Khisanth's claws had ripped away the creature's shoulders and head just moments before. The chieftain swung the gruesome torso in a circle overhead and launched it at Khisanth before she could dodge away. The gory bulk slapped her in the left eye, a broken rib slashing across her leathery eyelid. Her own blood streamed from the gash and mingled with the corpse's.

Squeezing the throbbing eye shut, Khisanth could see the desperate ogre scramble over broken weapons and dead bodies. If the creature reached the woods, she would be unable to follow.

Khisanth pulled back her thick lips and constricted her abdomen. The black dragon's gorge rose, and she felt the hot, salty acid race up her long throat, storm over her crimson tongue, and roar through her tightly drawn lips. As it hit the air, the steaming bile exploded into a shimmering mist and blasted across the clearing in a five-foot-wide stream of ruin. Plants withered and dissolved in the awful vapor. Droplets fell and sizzled upon the remains of bodies in the path of the blast, filling the air with a noxious green fog and the scent of burning blood.

In less than a heartbeat the full force of the blast slammed into the back of the fleeing ogre. The corrosive river splashed around the beast's shoulders and head, eating through its deerskin clothing and past to its flesh. The chieftain's death scream pierced the air for a second before fading into a strangled gurgle. Then the forsaken creature fell forward on the hideous remains of its face.

The only sound in the still clearing was the hungry sizzle of acid burning through bone. When it had finished its meal, the darkened liquid bubbled and soaked into the dirt and ashes, burying itself.

An eerie, whispering wind rose to fill the silence in the clearing. Khisanth stood among the wreckage, her hind legs a bit shaky. The bloodlust that had driven her was gone, leaving her weak and light-headed. The blast of acid had left a sour taste in her mouth. She bent her head to feast on the corpses, if only to cover up the bitter taste in her mouth and renew her strength.

A beam of light suddenly sliced across her path. Khisanth's gore-covered face popped up and looked toward the night sky. The moon had cut through the clouds, and the angled beams of bluish light provided a pathway for Kadagan. He slid along the moonlight and landed soundlessly at the dragon's hind feet.

"Did you see the battle?" she asked the nyphid eagerly.

Kadagan nodded. "Thou fought brilliantly, striking with the power and unpredictability of lightning."

Khisanth's brows raised at the pleasing comparison. Resuming her feast, she spoke only between gulps. "I used the qhen technique and fought on instinct. You would have been proud of how I just let myself be a dragon. Nothing can stand up to the power of a dragon who knows qhen."

"Thou knowest nothing of qhen," said Kadagan, his voice and bright blue eyes as cold as ice.

Khisanth's head snapped up. "How can you say that?" she gasped. "You've seen how I've studied and practiced."

"It is not a skill to employ when it suits thee," said the nyphid with silent fury. "It is a way of living."

"How can you say in one breath that I was brilliant, and in the next say I know nothing?"

"Greed blinded thee to thy goal. Qhen is focus, and patience, among other things. What hast thou accomplished, and what not?"

Chortling, Khisanth puffed out her chest. "I knew I could overpower fifteen ogres, and I proved it!"

"To whom hast thou proven what thou already knew?"

The dragon bristled. "I also have a full belly, and gem-studded weapons with which to line my cave."

"Was thy goal to slaughter a band of ogres?"

"No, but—"

"Hast thou furthered thy goal to study Styx or sight a human female?"

"No, but—"

"Could the ogre thou spoke with, undoubtedly their leader, have furthered either goal if thou hadst not killed it in anger and lust?"

"No!" Khisanth snapped defensively. Frowning, she thought for a moment, then had to mumble, "How do you mean?"

"Perhaps, living so close to Styx, it knew something of the village, or even of Dela."

Khisanth thought about that for a moment. "The ogre was not going to tell me anything."

The nyphid surveyed the stinking goo that was once the chieftain. "Thou hast ensured that with thy thoughtlessness."

Khisanth looked up with angry eyes. "Have a care, little creature," she muttered, her tone low and threatening. "I tolerate you when you are useful. When you are not—"

The little nyphid was not cowed. "Thou cannot control me in a meaningful way, if thou cannot control thyself."

Khisanth's first instinct was to pluck off the nyphid's wings, but on some level she realized she would only be proving him right. The dragon turned away from her teacher in frustration. Hoping to calm herself, she ran her long, moist tongue over a small abrasion on her left foreleg.

Khisanth stopped abruptly. Kadagan's displeasure had soured her mood so that she found even the taste of blood was dulled. Moving clumsily over the mounds of bodies in the small glade, Khisanth thoughtfully hooked her claw into another ogre corpse and dragged it to the growing pile of bones in front of her. The task of separating ogre bodies from their treasure was tedious with her large claws, which were not suited to such fine work. She neither wanted nor expected the help of Kadagan's slender fingers. His silent observation of her work made her burn with unspoken fury, yet she did not express it, would not give him the satisfaction of proving she couldn't control her temper.

Kadagan surveyed the wreckage around the campsite, then looked to the moon traveling across the night sky. "It is late," he muttered. "We will return to thy lair."

"What about Styx?" Khisanth asked. "We still have time to observe, and perhaps spot a human woman."

"We will return to thy lair," Kadagan repeated firmly. "Only dogs are about at this late hour. Further, after tonight's display, I would not allow thee near Dela." Before Khisanth could fire off an angry defense, the nyphid issued an order. "Use thy acid to destroy the evidence of thy folly." Snatching up a loincloth from a dead ogre, he darted out of the way.

Startled by the tone that brooked no insolence, Khisanth obeyed. When she finished, she saw that Kadagan had fashioned the filthy loincloth into a sling that accommodated the swords she'd pilfered from the dead ogres. His thoughtful acknowledgment of her desire for treasure angered her since it engendered the first pangs of guilt she had ever experienced.

"Canst thou fly?" Kadagan asked, considering her wounds. "I did not expect to need Joad's services on this trip."

Khisanth stood slowly and stretched her wings high. There was some stiffness. The descending moon shone as a fuzzy blotch through the translucent, leathery membranes, except in a few places where it streamed through jagged tears in the flesh. She would be sore for several days, but Khisanth was certain she could make the flight back.

Taking three powerful, rabbitlike hops she sprang into the air. Then the dragon dipped her left wing to pivot north toward her lair in Endscape.

* * * * *

Summer gave way to autumn while Khisanth applied herself to her studies. The leaves turned golden and tumbled from the trees. Ambling in the form of a white-striped badger through grasslands gone stiff and brown, Khisanth was contemplating the stride and stance that made her form uniquely that of a badger. She had long sharp claws like a dragon, but—

Khisanth's head jerked up. She heard soft rustling ahead in the tall grass, coming toward her. She stood only half as high as the weeds, so she could not see what approached. Baring her teeth against possible predators, she waited.

Joad popped through the grass and waved her on. "Come," he said, his voice old and scratchy from lack of use.

Khisanth's badger body nearly fell over with surprise. "You talked!" she rumbled.

"Of course," Joad said simply, as if his speaking were nothing unusual. "Thy progress has renewed my strength. I am grateful." His old gray head bowed.

Khisanth had thought of late that the elder nyphid looked better, not so sad, his lightning-blue eyes less hollow. She was strangely gratified.

"And now I have a surprise for thee in the forest," he rasped. "Come." Seeing the badger's eyes focusing, he reached down and laid a soft hand on her head. "Do not change—a dragon would be far too large to follow where I lead thee."

Thrilled at the change in Joad, intrigued by the mystery of his surprise, Khisanth followed, past the pods the nyphids would soon have to abandon when the grasses died entirely. Nyphid and badger entered the trees, tiny booted feet and splayed claws crunching over mounds of fallen brown leaves. The forest looked more spacious to Khisanth than when she'd first seen it, but she wasn't certain if that was because the leaves had dropped from their branches or because, as a badger, she was so much farther from the canopy.

Cresting the near side of a hillock, Joad turned left and followed a narrow, twisting gully downhill. Rounding a sharp corner, the gully joined with a trickle of water, scarcely a stream since it came only to where the fur on Khisanth's badger legs gave way to paws. As she splashed in the cool water behind the mysterious nyphid, Khisanth's curiosity grew with each step.

Joad stopped so suddenly, Khisanth's pointed snout met with the back of his legs. He jumped to one side of the gully and gave her a clear view of an abrupt drop, the small stream of water forming a narrow waterfall. Joad leaned over and looked down, waving Khisanth to do the same.

Creeping forward cautiously on the opposite bank, the badger peered over the edge and was amazed. The drop was short, perhaps one and a half times the nyphid's height. But that was not what amazed Khisanth. Like a furry blanket, lush green moss covered every dead branch and rock below in a six-by-six-foot swatch. Somehow it had sustained its rich emerald color long after the underbrush around it had turned brown. The forest seemed to be holding its breath; a damp green scent filled the air.

"It remains green year-round," said Joad.

"How? The stream?"

Joad bobbed his head toward the center of the collection of mossy rocks. "Their energy," he said mysteriously. "Look, they know we're here."

Squinting, Khisanth saw thousands of the yellow-tailed glowbugs that often hovered near the nyphids at night. The insects crawled through the green cracks between the rocks. She could hear the faint sound of tiny, fluttering wings. "Why are they all gathered here?"

"They always return here to pass the daylight hours. Each spends its lifetime gathering energy. They give it back to us by illuminating the night." Joad paused, then gave a happy sigh. "That is a life well spent, I think."

With that, the nyphid led the way back up the ravine. Khisanth was silent, pondering the great wisdom she was certain she'd just witnessed. But like most of the nyphids' lessons in qhen, Khisanth did not immediately understand the message.

The difference now was that she was content to wait, for Khisanth knew that one day Joad's message would be clear to her.

Chapter 5

Autumn had given way to an early and unseasonably cold winter in the Khalkist Mountains, bringing snow to the higher elevations, which Khisanth was now approaching by wing. A shadowy form against the night sky, the black dragon sliced through the pearly flakes, silent, steadfast.

Khisanth could scarcely remember her first stumbling attempts at flight, just a few months past. The activity was now as much a part of her spirit, as important to her vitality, as eating. Where once she had to concentrate to counter the effects of even the smallest air currents, her body now utilized them without conscious thought. Khisanth remembered hearing before the Sleep stories of dragons who'd been permanently grounded by wing damage. She knew she would commit keptu, ritual dragon suicide, before she would live without flying.

Solinari, the white moon, had made two full revolutions around Krynn since Khisanth had last flown this route to Styx. The days since the encounter with the band of ogres had been overfilled with silent study, deprivation to promote patience, deep breathing to foster concentration and strength. Each day Khisanth grew closer to achieving the heightened sense of awareness, of qhen, that Kadagan taught in his mysterious, sometimes nonsensical, way. She suffered occasional feelings of foolishness and humiliation because she had seen the positive effect of every single exercise, no matter how odious. She felt less the ignorant child, more the admiring student. Best of all, whenever she was able to demonstrate true patience or unique observations, Kadagan rewarded her with time to develop her natural spellcasting abilities.

Khisanth knew from the pace they set, never Kadagan's composure, that the nyphids were increasingly anxious to complete her training. Whenever she inquired about Dela's health, Kadagan calmly informed her to focus on her studies.

Until this morning. Waiting for Kadagan to arrive for the daily lessons, Khisanth had been on her haunches in the tiny cave, tinkering with the effects of a simple cantrip. She could create and hold a healthy spark on the tip of her claw, but had difficulty turning it to flame. Summoning her energy, she'd channeled it down her right claw arm and focused it on the index talon, banishing all other thoughts. A tiny, flickering yellow flame leaped to life. Khisanth's lips drew back in a smile of triumph.

Suddenly the usually serene and nimble nyphid stormed into her lair. Startled, Khisanth's concentration wavered, and the flame extinguished. The dragon glared at Kadagan through a thin trail of smoke.

"It is time," the nyphid had said, out of breath. His glowing golden hair was disheveled, his green tunic twisted, his soft skin flushed. "Get ready to depart before the sun climbs to midday."

Khisanth stood up, bumping her horns on the ceiling. "What's happened?"

"Dela's signal to Joad has been weakening," the nyphid

explained hastily. "It has become erratic. Joad thinks they are moving her . . . or something worse." Kadagan's expression became sadder than Khisanth had ever seen. "I had hoped to give thee more time for study, but we dare not wait another moment. We may lose her if we do. . . ."

One way or another, Khisanth had thought inwardly. "I'm ready," was the reply she voiced.

"Perhaps," the nyphid said before departing again to make his own preparations.

Khisanth had only one thing to prepare; a way to transport her small treasure hoard. She was determined not to return to the tiny cave, no matter the outcome in Styx. The sling Kadagan had fashioned before had been utilitarian, but too cumbersome to carry as a human. She needed something that would free her hands and be unobtrusive, if ever a dozen swords could be. She'd settled on stringing the hilts of the weapons through a length of soft vine and tying the unusual necklace tightly around her throat. She could use a spell to shrink the choker later.

Now, many hours after leaving her lair, Kadagan's finger was aimed ahead of them in the twilight sky, toward the dull glow rising up from the lantern-lit village. "There it is," he said from behind her head.

Both nyphids, wearing furry vests over their usual green tunics, rode between Khisanth's wings and neck. Joad sat behind Kadagan, clutching the younger nyphid. Slung over the elder nyphid's shoulder was a sack of dried curative herbs.

Joad's spirits had picked up considerably in the past month, as Khisanth's qhen skills increased. The elder nyphid had begun to believe that the dragon might be able to rescue his daughter. After the trip to the moss garden, when he'd first spoken, she found she pushed herself even harder, seeking the silent wise one's praise.

As he peered toward the village where his daughter was held, however, concern filled Joad's eyes. He alone knew the depth of Dela's despair, how little time was left.

Khisanth would have recognized the village without the

nyphid's help. Under her now, the rolling farmlands on the north edge of Styx were tilled and dotted with snow-covered hayricks, harvested since her last trip. Just ahead, trails of smoke rose from the chimneys that poked through the thatch roofs on the buildings clustered around Miremier Bay. One street followed the curve of the bay, its dirt turned to slushy mud by the snow. At regular intervals, impossibly narrow cobblestone walkways passed between the closely placed buildings, like the spokes of half a wheel.

Wasting no time, Khisanth tipped her wings and spiraled earthward. She lowered her hind feet, clutched in flight to her belly, and landed gracefully on a snowy path. Kadagan and Joad slipped off her back, their soft booted feet dropping silently into the frigid powder. The three stood where the tree line met the mountains, just beyond the light from the covered lanterns on the town wall.

"Thou knowest what to do?" asked Kadagan. Arms crossed tightly before him, he began to pace, kicking up the fluffy snow, which came to the top of his boots.

"Find, then free Dela," said the dragon in a monotone, as if it were a mantra.

"Locate the human thou saw in the globe, and thou wilt find Dela. Remember to keep her covered in the presence of humans. Revert to dragon form only if necessary for ye both to break free."

The dragon patted the tense nyphid's shoulder. "I'll remember everything, Kadagan," she said softly. "I'll be as quick as I can, but I don't know how long it will take," she warned.

Kadagan's face looked pinched. "We will wait in the forest as long as necessary."

Joad nodded agreement, then reached into the bell-shaped cuff of his green tunic; the glowing globe overfilled his aged hand. "Take the maynus," he said, holding it out. "Dela will need it when thou rescues her."

Khisanth hesitated. "Won't you need it?"

Joad raised the globe over his head and pushed it insistently toward the dragon's claw. "I will know if thou hast found her. Perhaps, with thy magical nature, it will help thee as well."

"Slip it onto thy necklace," suggested Kadagan.

Humbly Khisanth untied the vine around her neck and threaded it through the center of the glowing orb. To her surprise, the small ball caught hold and continued to glow softly between the swords on the thick string. She refastened the vine around her scaly neck and adjusted it so that the maynus hung just above her breastbone.

"Someone comes!" hissed Kadagan.

Khisanth's glanced up from her necklace to see a shrouded form emerging from the unguarded gates of Styx, its head bent against the early snow and unseasonably cold winds. Khisanth dropped to a crouch to make herself smaller against the backdrop of the black trees. Squinting, she focused her sharp dragon sight on the creature.

The person looked up suddenly, as if it felt the dragon's gaze. It peered into the darkness beyond the torchlight, but its limited human vision revealed nothing.

Khisanth's eyes allowed her a clear view. Heavily bundled against the elements, the form lacked definition. Its features, swathed in a tattered blue scarf, were something like an ogre's, but softer, much more pleasing to the eye. A narrow strip of soft brown fur arched over each of its eyes, which were shaped more like Kadagan's than Khisanth's, but not so impossibly bright as the nyphid's. It had plump pink cheeks that curved, then hollowed abruptly. The mouth between them was too small to be of use in tearing apart food, Khisanth thought disdainfully.

"It is a human woman," said Kadagan. "She seems nervous about the weather."

Aggis Mickflori was indeed worried. Her trip to Styx for much-needed supplies had taken longer than usual. Now she was terribly afraid of traveling back to her small shack during a snowstorm on a moonless night, but her children were little and her lame husband was nearly as helpless as they. In truth, with rumors of ogres in the hills of late, she was more afraid of what she would find at the shack if she did not hasten her steps, storm or no.

Dragon and nyphids watched the woman adjust her scarf lower over her determined face, hug her packages closer to her chest, and set off. Head bent to the storm, she was oblivious to the presence of the black dragon lurking in the darkness ahead.

Annoyed that the woman should pick the path that led to her hiding place, Khisanth's first instinct was to ready her breath weapon. She wondered absently what human flesh would taste like.

"No!" Kadagan hissed softly, sensing her thoughts.

The dragon shook away the urge to attack. "I remember the ogres," she whispered. Khisanth focused on her breathing, envisioned the steady rise and fall of her own chest to slow the pounding of her blood. In time, it thrummed peacefully through her veins. The woman was almost close enough to see Khisanth, if she looked up.

"Now thou hast seen a human. Change form, before she discovers us," urged Kadagan.

The dragon closed her eyes and concentrated on an image of the woman: hair under the scarf, plump cheeks, softly curved jawbone, arms to the narrow waist, the stride of legs that were half the height of the body. She held tight to the vision in her mind, blocking out all other sensations.

Suddenly the black dragon's snout began to tingle. Then through her body a hot flash raced like mercury, ending at the very tip of her tail. Her entire frame convulsed as her bones constricted. Khisanth could hear strange pops and clicks, and then only the eerie wind that accompanies a snowstorm.

The dragon nearly staggered from the enormous weight that suddenly pulled at her neck, dragging her to her knees. Looking down, she saw that the sword choker that before had seemed so tight now dangled to the ground, the maynus casting a soft yellow glow from under snow that was quickly covering it. Closing her eyes again, Khisanth formed a mental picture of the choker reduced to about the size of the human woman's neck. Tinkling together gently like bells in the wind, the swords and globe shrank until the vine was snug, the snow-covered swords and globe unexpectedly cold against the skin of her neck.

"Goodness, child, what are you doing out in this storm? And as naked as the day you were born. Did you think that ugly necklace would keep you warm?"

Khisanth's eyes popped open at the insult to her hoard. She looked into the woman's clear brown eyes. The young dragon's mind was a tumble of conflicting sensations, not the least of which was a new and unpleasant vulnerability to the elements. She glanced around furtively for Joad and Kadagan, but the nyphids were gone.

"Look at those goose bumps! You must be freezing!" cried the woman, dropping her packages in the snow. She shrugged off her shawl and draped it around Khisanth's naked, dark-skinned shoulders.

So this is what cold feels like, the black dragon-turned-young-woman thought. She looked down at her new, shivering form, barely covered by the shawl. Soft flakes of snow drifted onto her warm brown skin and melted into rivulets.

The woman ripped the ratty blue scarf in two and handed both halves to Khisanth. "Wrap your feet in these until we can get you inside and find you proper shoes." She tucked her packages under one arm and put the other around Khisanth's slight but muscular waist in support.

"Were you robbed?" the woman asked, turning Khisanth toward the gates. "Or worse?" She dropped her tone to a horrified whisper. "Did someone—" she stumbled over the distasteful word "—*molest* you, dear?"

Khisanth didn't know how to respond, so she said nothing.

"Are you touched, dear, or just mute?"

The words were unfamiliar to her, but Khisanth was somehow certain she had been called stupid. She was conjuring up a fiery response when her training in patience came unbidden to mind.

"I can speak," Khisanth managed to moan, her human voice unfamiliar to her own ears. It was surprisingly soft and pleasant. "I was robbed—by ogres," she added.

"Oh, you poor thing," cooed the woman. "Styx isn't the

same place, now that the mercenaries and their filthy bands of ogres have found us. No one feels safe anymore." She clucked her tongue. "Strange that they took your clothing, but left this necklace," she said. Her hands, swollen and red-tipped, touched the tiny swords that lay against the smooth skin of Khisanth's human neck. The disguised dragon jerked her hoard from the human's touch.

The older woman looked surprised but compassionate. "Don't you worry, hon. You're safe with Aggis. I'll help you back to your home."

"I—I don't live in Styx," said Khisanth. "I was just passing through."

"If this is how the city treats its visitors, then I'm glad I live in the hills!" she spat. Aggis patted Khisanth's hand, and the dragon had to force herself not to pull away. "Not to worry. I know an innkeeper near the city's edge who'll help you. We'll slip in the back way, through the kitchen, to spare you the embarrassment of prying eyes." With undisguised envy, she glanced again at Khisanth's barely covered form. Her own figure had not looked half so feminine even before children, she thought wistfully.

As they walked to the town gates and into the city, Khisanth listened only enough to respond when necessary. She was caught up in her own thoughts and had no concept of human embarrassment, especially about nudity, having never worn clothing.

With one arm draped around Khisanth's shoulders and the other steadying her elbow, Aggis led the disguised dragon through the narrow alleys. In places, the thatched peaks of the buildings leaned so close together the falling snow scarcely reached the ground. Yellow light from candles bled through oiled parchment windows, keeping the darkness of night from the walkways. A bull-necked youth cut across their path, struggling under the weight of two buckets on a yoke. Dogs ran, barking, between the legs of villagers hurrying home. Women leaned from second-story windows and called their children to the evening meal.

Finally Aggis rapped on a battered wooden door that was

nearly hidden between piles of empty crates and small barrels. A fat, balding man with saggy cheeks opened the door, permitting a wave of warm air to escape and surround the two women. The innkeeper gawked in surprise for a moment at Khisanth's naked body, but he came to his senses when he heard his kitchen help whistling appreciatively behind him.

"Slice them stew potatoes and mind yer own businesses," he growled. Quickly he helped Aggis hustle Khisanth up a narrow set of stairs just off the kitchen.

The innkeeper waved them into an unheated room, lit only by the light streaming in from the hallway. The sloping, thatched roof of the building formed two walls. Rough whitewash covered the other two. The room held a trunk, a narrow rope bed, and a cane-backed chair. Dry rushes on the floor crunched softly beneath the women's feet. Snow was piled against the outside of the windowpane in the back wall. Another, similar room could be seen across the hall through the open doorway.

Aggis and the innkeeper spoke in whispers for a few moments. Finally the old woman nodded, and the man left, stealing one last, red-faced, admiring peek at Khisanth before lumbering down the staircase.

After using her teeth to pull the fingerless woolen gloves from her hands, Aggis turned to the chest and began sorting through the clothing. "Bert says to apologize, but he's only got men's clothes. He doesn't get too many ladies passing through, leaving frilly dresses behind." She pulled out a dark purple drawstring tunic and handed it to Khisanth.

"Here, this will do for now." Jamming her hands on her hips, Aggis stood back and peered at Khisanth. "You've got the blackest hair I've ever seen, as black and smooth as polished onyx." When Khisanth didn't reply, Aggis tried another tack. "What's your name, child?"

Khisanth was about to respond honestly, but something inside warned her to protect her dragon name.

"You've guessed it," she said. "Onyx. For my hair."

"Isn't that pretty?" Aggis handed her leggings, pantaloons, and thick-heeled, cuffed boots. Khisanth looked in puzzlement at the collection of clothing, unsure of where she should don any of it. Fortunately, Aggis attributed her confusion to the garment's being men's clothing.

"You must be used to dresses. Here, Onyx," she said, standing on her tiptoes to hold the tunic above the girl. "Slip this over your head. My goodness, you're a tall girl. You remind me of a black oak tree, with that dark hair and milk-in-coffee skin of yours," she muttered.

Seeing Khisanth's dark hands fumbling next with the pantaloons, Aggis took the russet-colored leathers from her and turned them around so the girl could slip them on. "Of course, you know how pants go on—your fingers must be stiff from the cold. Tuck in the tunic like this." She stuffed the hem of the purple top into the waistband and stood back to examine her charge. The waist was loose, but the legs fit the young woman's muscular frame like a second skin. "You'll have to cinch in the top with some rope."

After Onyx slipped her feet into the boots, Aggis held up one last, fringed garment. Backing into it, Onyx slipped her arms into the sleeves. "This buckskin jacket'll keep out the cold," Aggis pronounced.

"Th—thank you, Aggis," the young woman stumbled over the unfamiliar words.

Aggis shook her head, and her careworn face broadened into a smile. "It was nothing." Glancing to the small glass window, where frost was quickly climbing, she saw that the snowfall had stopped. "We must be good luck for each other. You're safe and dry now, and I won't have to travel in a snowstorm." Aggis stepped to the window and closed the shutters against the weather.

"That should warm it up in here a little," she declared, tugging her gloves back on. Turning, she clasped Onyx's icy hands and frowned. "You must have cold blood." Onyx sniggered inwardly at the truth of it. "You'll warm up soon enough. I wish I could stay, but I must get home, or my man will give me an earful!" Chuckling, the older woman shuffled in her heavy skirts toward the light in the hallway.

Not knowing what else to do, Onyx followed.

In the doorway Aggis turned, her gloved hand on the copper knob. "Bert says you should stay the night here, after your ordeal. In any case, don't leave without letting him give you a warm meal and a few steel pieces to get you started again. He's a good man, Bert." She wagged a finger at Onyx. "Mind you, be more careful from now on. A young woman who looks as you do shouldn't travel alone. You should find yourself a man to protect you if you've got the wanderlust." She pressed her lips to Onyx's dark cheek, squeezed her hand once more, and then was gone, pulling the door shut behind her.

For some time, Onyx stared at the door, not knowing what to do with herself. Blinking, she became aware of her surroundings and turned to walk across the rushes. She lowered herself to the floor and tried to curl into the position most comfortable to her as a dragon, but her spine wouldn't curve sufficiently. Spotting the cane-backed chair, she settled her slim form into it with a sigh. Much better.

In the quiet dark of the room, Onyx became aware of the warmth of the maynus against her neck. She untied the vine and slipped the choker from under her tunic. The room was suddenly awash with the globe's light, reflected off the chipped green shutters. She remembered Kadagan's explanation of the magical globe's origin:

Handed from mother to daughter since the gods created nyphids, the maynus is a source of great magic. It receives its energy from the elemental plane of lightning. Dela believes it was crafted there.

Kadagan might as well have been speaking another language, Onyx thought now, gazing into her only material reminder of the nyphids. Instantly, small bolts of lightning leaped within the glass. She saw something that made her press her nose closer. Were there yellow eyes and mouths on the flickering blue zags of energy? Were electrical genies the source of Dela's magic? Tying the sword choker about her neck again, she resolved to ask Kadagan about it when next she saw him, when her thoughts had cleared after the shape-change.

Onyx was experiencing the same eerie sensation she felt whenever she transformed; hyena or human, after the change she felt as if she were outside the form, watching herself, controlling from a distance. Previously, the blending into the adopted form had taken only moments, since the most obvious difference between a dragon and a badger was size. But the human form was very different from her own or any other she'd experienced, the body so much more complex. It was clear now that adopting this form, however inferior she believed it to be to a dragon's, would always pose a great challenge to her abilities.

To accelerate the merging of mind and body, Khisanth meditated on the differences between humans and dragons. She had certainly lost the sheer power she derived from her weight as a dragon, but there were benefits she gained, as well.

"I feel lighter, freer," she said aloud, standing and stretching luxuriously, "and, well, slender." That was a word she would never have used to describe her dragon form.

Yet for each benefit there were limitations. Without her protective scales, she felt as vulnerable as she had when naked in the snow. Her eyesight was not as keen as a dragon's, and her close-set eyes narrowed her peripheral vision. Yet she could more easily turn her head or body to see behind her. Something of her sharp dragon hearing remained, for she could detect tiny creatures skittering around in the walls, but in her new form, she wasn't particularly interested in devouring them.

Onyx's stomach rumbled abruptly. "I wonder what humans eat?" She caught the scent of roasting meat floating up the stairs from the kitchen. Without thought, she started toward the source of the aroma.

Standing in the cold hallway at the top of the stairs, Onyx was about to descend to the kitchen when she heard the crackle of flames and a mingle of loud voices coming from a staircase at the end of the hallway. Intrigued by the unfamiliar sounds and scents, Onyx strode slowly toward the noise, her thick-heeled boots hammering against the plank flooring.

Onyx came to the end of the hallway, which led to an open-sided staircase. Through the carved spindles, Onyx could see that the steps descended into the center of a large, crowded taproom and led to the inn's front door. She came to the bottom of the stairs facing the entrance, with her back to the room. But before she could even finish turning, the room had fallen silent. All eyes were upon her. Men sat with mugs of foaming ale poised before whiskered lips.

They must be staring because I'm a stranger, she thought. Analyzing their bold, gaping glances, she realized she was wrong: they were staring because she was a woman. Apparently her form was appealing to humans of the opposite sex. The realization amused her. Spotting Bert behind a wooden counter, she smiled in recognition. His face reddened. She made a step toward him, and the tightly packed, still silent throng of men rippled back like a wave to let her pass.

"Come now, boys. We've all seen a woman who weighs under ten stone before!"

Onyx glanced over her shoulder and located the speaker, a round, blotchy-faced woman whose long dark skirt was stretched to the limit of its gathers. The woman slammed large mugs of ale down on a table, foam splashing her filthy apron. "Looks scrawny to me," she muttered.

The taproom exploded with laughter at the woman's scornful observation. One man seated before the angry serving woman gave her thick waist a reassuring squeeze, then said something Onyx couldn't make out. Smiling triumphantly, the woman looked up and scowled at the lovely, raven-haired stranger. Onyx simply smiled back. The other woman's smirk dissolved into puzzlement.

"We don't see too many young women here in Styx," a voice explained kindly behind her. Onyx swung around to see Bert's sweaty, sagging face. The innkeeper's expression as he contemplated her attire was more fatherly than the other looks she'd received. "I'm glad you was able to find some gear that fit."

Taking her elbow, Bert steered her toward the long, gleaming wooden bar and onto a stool. He held a mug beneath the tap of a keg, waited while the golden ale splashed forth, then pushed it over the counter toward Onyx. "You could probably use a drink, after the night you've had. Did you lose much?"

"Lose much?"

Bert looked puzzled. "Aggis said you was robbed by ogres."

"Oh, yes—uh, no," Onyx sputtered, remembering her story to the older woman. "I mean they didn't get much. Just my clothes."

"Filthy creatures, them," spat Bert. "We don't let 'em in here." He frowned suddenly. "Strange that ogres would want your clothes. Didn't you have no steel on you?"

"Steel?"

"Coin," prompted the innkeeper. "Money."

Onyx saw a man down the bar toss back the contents of his drink and push a round piece of steel across the wooden tabletop.

"Ah, money . . . I didn't have much," Onyx said. "I was just passing through town," she added, in case he, too, inquired about family.

"What do you do?"

"Do?"

She's as simple as Aggis said, Bert thought. "How do you earn your money?" he asked slowly, careful to enunciate.

"I—I'm a good fighter and hunter."

"So you're a mercenary, eh?" He looked dubiously at her slight form. Perhaps looks were deceiving.

"I'm pretty good with my, er, hands," Onyx said to the innkeeper with a sly wink. She downed the bitter-tasting ale with several long gulps, wiping the foam away on her buckskin-covered arm—as she would have on her dragon scales. The amber liquid tasted strangely refreshing.

Bert wasn't sure what to make of that comment, or her hearty display of drinking. Something about the beautiful stranger made him uncomfortable. Almost grateful that he had other customers to attend to, he pushed a small mound of round steel pieces toward her. "Here. Take these to get back on your feet," he said. "If you're hungry, I'll get a boy to bring you food."

"Thanks," she said, placing the steel pieces in her trouser pocket. "I'm starving." The ale had warmed her belly in a pleasant way. She saw Bert signal to a whey-faced boy with badly chopped, ashen hair. The boy disappeared behind a swinging door, only to reappear within moments carrying a rough-cut square board covered with steaming food. Nervously averting his eyes from the pretty woman, he set the board on the counter before her.

Onyx frowned at the ridiculously small portion. "I'll need more," she ordered. Then, with her hands on the counter, she bent forward to sink perfect white teeth into the juicy drumstick of a small bird. Some instinct stopped her. Hardly lifting her face from the platter, the dragon-turned-woman looked quickly from left to right. The other diners at the bar were watching her strangely. Some held odd, pointed pieces of metal poised above their food.

Leaning back slowly, self-consciously, Onyx tried to emulate the actions of the humans around her. Though she found the practice slow and cumbersome, she managed at last to spear a piece of potato on the point of the metal stick and placed it into her waiting mouth. Hot! Her tongue leaped back in her throat, and she spit the offending potato back onto her plate. More foolishness! Humans heated their food!

Onyx impatiently allowed the potato to cool and placed it back into her mouth. It had been spiced. She had to admit that it tasted better than she would have expected from a root.

Onyx waited for the steam to dissipate from the drumstick before taking a bite. It, too, had been heavily seasoned and was far superior to the raw, cold meat that had been her daily diet. Onyx cleaned the food from her plate. Then, taking a cue from her fellow diners, she licked the board clean. She was surprised to feel a familiar tightening in her stomach. She felt as full as if she'd eaten a moose.

Groaning, Onyx pushed the empty board back, as well as the second full one the bewildered boy had placed before her. She had eaten—now what? Perhaps someone here had information about Dela, or even knew the man from the maynus. With that thought in mind, Onyx spun around on her seat and contemplated the occupants of the room over the rim of her second mug of ale.

Many of the patrons still eyed the pretty young woman now and then, but for the most part they had returned to their conversations. Onyx looked toward the hearth on the short wall to the right of the taproom door. Seated before the roaring fire, at a large round table, were a number of toothless, paunchy men. After pushing coins toward the center of the table, they would roll some polished white cubes with black dots on each side. Every now and again one of them would leap back, yelp victoriously—as if he had just killed something—then scoop up the coins.

At another long, narrow table, more than a handful of men were holding small, thick pieces of paper inscribed with pictures and words, which they would occasionally throw toward the center. After a number of these pictures had accumulated, someone would collect the money, while the others looked on grimly.

Was this how humans "earned their money"?

"Do you like to roll the bones?" said a honeyed voice at her elbow.

Onyx turned to look at the speaker, then caught her bottom lip between her small human teeth in a slight gasp. Dark tendrils of shiny hair curled around his face and dropped to rest on broad shoulders. The cheekbones beneath his wide-set emerald eyes were high and arched above smooth, weathered skin. His full, almost purple lips, inside a short-clipped beard and mustache, pulled up into a smile that brought out crease lines around his eyes.

Something about him looked strangely familiar. The green eyes . . . Onyx gasped again. The man from the globe.

"I usually kill anyone who stares at me for so long," he said, "especially with such penetrating eyes. You remind me of Vil, a snake I once kept as a pet." He looked almost coy. "Are you as sly as a snake?"

"Huh?" Onyx tossed her hair back from her face, and the room tilted crazily. Keeping one hand on her mug, she grabbed her stool to stop the spinning in her head. What was wrong with her? Perhaps the food had been tainted. . . .

Grinning, the man took the mug of ale from her hands and pushed it down the polished length of the bar. "It is also my policy to encourage women to drink until they're well past dizzy, but for some reason you inspire chivalry in me."

The ale had made her light-headed? Too bad, she thought, it had tasted good.

"The name's Led."

Onyx squinted up into his face, her expression blank.

"It's customary to respond with your name." The man gave her a penetrating look. "Unless there's some reason you don't want me to know it."

"No!" she said almost too quickly. Onyx touched her head. "The ale has made me a touch slow-witted, is all," she managed, borrowing from Aggis. "My name is Onyx."

"How appropriate." Led lifted a hand and ruffled the fine, blue-black fringes of hair that lapped at her neck. She drew back slightly, startled by his touch.

Undaunted, Led twirled his finger through a strand of her hair before withdrawing it casually. He almost seemed to enjoy her discomfort. "Where are you from?"

"The North," she said vaguely. "And you?"

"The road's my home." His eyes twinkled. "Did I hear you tell Bert that you're a mercenary?"

"That was his word. I said I'm a good fighter and hunter."

His smile was lazy, patronizing, his gaze over her slight, womanly form skeptical. "Really?"

Onyx's nervously fingered the choker at her neck. "What business is it of yours?"

Led threw his head back and laughed. "At last, the little snake shows her fangs!"

"Don't ever call me that again," Onyx growled.

"Sorry. It was just a pet name."

"I'm not your pet."

Led leaned back, grinning. "But are you a good fighter?"

Onyx drew back at this line of questioning, discomforted by the entire encounter. She took long breaths in the qhen way, struggling to contain—or even understand—the tangle of human emotions. For some reason, her human form responded strangely to this man. Perhaps it was because she'd been surprised, knocked off balance by finding him so unexpectedly. The only thing she knew for sure was that if she didn't gain control of her brain and tongue, she would lose what might be her only chance to discover Dela's whereabouts.

"I can fight," she said evenly.

"That's interesting." Led shuffled two coins between the fingers of one hand, watching her closely while he spoke. "You see, I'm something of a hunter myself. A bounty hunter. In fact, I was bringing a law-breaker here for the bounty some months back and, uh, lost two fighters in a freak accident. Struck by lightning, they were. I haven't found suitable replacements, and I need guards to help me deliver a valuable package to a prospective buyer in Kernen tomorrow." Led's admiring gaze swept over her. "Personally, I'm impressed by what I see"— he shrugged meaningfully —"but I'm going to have a hard time persuading the rest of my party that you're stronger than you look."

"You're offering me a job?" she asked, trying unsuccessfully to hide her surprise.

"Maybe." He was looking at her legs in the tight russet pants.

"If you're their leader, why do you have to persuade anyone?" she challenged.

Led's green eyes shot up. "I don't." They narrowed to slits. "But *I* can't afford to waste time settling arguments if *you* can't pull your own weight."

Onyx propped her elbows on the bar and placed her chin in her cupped hand. "You must know there's more to a good fighter than strength," she said softly. "Stealth and cunning are probably more important." She paused. "And magic doesn't hurt, either."

"You can do magic?" he whispered hoarsely. His eyes narrowed, and he looked around quickly. "Better drop your voice, making a claim like that. Nobody trusts magic or mages, not in this part of the world anyway."

"Until recently, humans thought dragons were but stories, too," she said, watching his reaction.

Led shuddered. "I've heard those rumors, too. But why should I believe you're a mage?"

She knew she was being tested on a number of levels. "Why should I care what you believe?"

Led took a long wooden pipe from his pocket and tamped tobacco into the bowl, considering her defiant reply with amusement. He was reaching for a candle on the bar when he felt something touch the pipe clamped between his lips. Led looked down his nose and saw Onyx's index finger in the pipe's bowl. A small flame leaped from her fingertip and ignited the tobacco. She withdrew her finger and blew away a thin trail of white smoke. "You're welcome," she purred.

Led was too stunned to speak, too impressed to care if anyone else saw the display.

"It's customary to respond with 'thank you,' I believe," she whispered.

Led chose, instead, to nod, but there was undisguised admiration in his emerald eyes. He pushed himself away from the bar. "The men'll be assembling here just after dawn—if you're interested."

"What's the job?"

"That's not your concern," he said, taking three coins from a small drawstring bag and stacking them on the bar. "I'm tired, so we'll have to discuss your pay tomorrow."

Onyx bit back a stinging retort. Like her, Led clearly would not brook insolence, and she was dangerously close to crossing the line between being intriguing and annoying. Besides, she would find out soon enough if the job involved Dela.

Just then, Led's rough hand touched her cheek, made rosy by the roaring fire, if not the exchange. "Are you going to show up, little Onyx?"

"You'll have to wait until tomorrow to find out," she said slyly. She slipped off the chair and sauntered up the stairs, followed all the way by the sound of Led's laughter.

Chapter 6

Onyx sat on the inn's long wooden front porch, her back to a square support post. The sky to the east was still dark purple, though approaching lavender. Few people were moving about yet, as first light began to creep between the buildings. A layer of winter ice and snow covered the whole town, giving the place a false sense of peace and stillness.

Despite Bert's advice to avoid the bounty hunter, whispered over a breakfast of fried bread and eggs, the raven-haired young woman was waiting for Led. If she was to free Dela, she had no choice but to join his band.

To Onyx's irritation, the sun was poking over the rooftops when she finally caught sight of Led striding through the street. He wore a glossy, polished leather breastplate and shoulder guards over a forest-green tunic. His muscle-hugging wool leggings were tucked inside the calves of laced boots that cuffed below the knees. Wet from bathing, his hair looked darker than it had last night, and his beard and mustache had been neatly groomed.

Behind him was a ragtag group of grubby ogres, snorting and scratching their thick green hides. Most wore uncured animal pelts decorated with feathers and small animal skulls and carried large clubs or crude spears. One had a copper cauldron strapped upside down on his melon head in lieu of a helmet. Strangely, Onyx found ogres much more repulsive now that she had spent time among humans.

"Dawn passed quite some time ago," she said stiffly.

Led gave a mock bow and laughed. "Good morning to you, too."

"These are the creatures you were concerned might not accept me?"

"You were expecting Knights of Solamnia?"

"No. I knew, uh—" Onyx stammered "—I expected they were ogres."

He looked at her strangely, then shrugged. "You take what you can get. Ogres are fairly good fighters, and they listen well enough, just so long as Toba clubs them now and then."

Led pointed to a hollow-cheeked man with an exotic slant to his eyes. He wore an overlarge coat with the fur collar turned up. Dwarfed by the ogres, the wiry little man snarled as he kicked one brute aside with a blade-tipped boot.

"That's Toba," Led offered. "My lieutenant. He keeps the ogres in fighting shape, one way or another. He lived in Salasia, near Taladas, which is crawling with ogres. That's where he learned how to handle them."

Searching her memory, Onyx vaguely recalled the homely man from the vision in the globe. Led's voice drew her into the present.

"I'm glad you decided to join me." His green eyes were fixed on hers, probing.

The black-haired young woman could not suppress a scowl. "I almost left. I'm not accustomed to waiting for anyone."

Led smirked ruefully and jerked a thumb over his

shoulder. "Blame them. They don't move very fast in the morning."

Onyx jumped from the porch to her feet and slammed her dark hands onto her hips. "Then don't tell someone dawn, when you mean midmorning."

It was Led's turn to scowl. "Let me tell you the three rules this party has," he said evenly, employing great effort to control his temper. His green eyes narrowed beneath thick, arched brows. "First, you do what I say, when I say it, with no questions. Second, if the cargo I'm paying you to guard is threatened, you will fight like a damned hellhound and won't stop until I say it's over. Third, if there is a battle, nobody searches bodies or gathers loot until the enemy is dead or run off."

Onyx hooked her thumbs under her rope belt nonchalantly. "So what's this precious cargo I'll be guarding?"

Led tensed. "You're violating rule number one."

Frowning, Khisanth decided on a new tactic. "What do I get in exchange for following your rules?"

"A share of the loot," Led replied.

"One share? And how many shares do you take?"

Led snorted. "More than one. Don't be obtuse."

Onyx lifted one eyebrow. "Do you really think one share is a fair split for a mage? The same share as one of those mindless ogres?" Onyx cast an artless, wide-eyed look at the throng milling in the slush behind Led.

The brown-haired man fidgeted imperceptibly. "No. More than that."

"How much more?"

"Whatever I decide." Led twirled one end of his red-brown mustache. "I'm the boss."

Onyx shrugged under her purple tunic. Turning on her heel, she took a step toward the inn's front door. "Not *my* boss. Find yourself another mage—if you can."

Led considered her as she stomped across the porch. She was more like a man than any woman he knew. She knew magic, too, and Led had never met a mage in all his travels, let alone one willing to do mercenary work. He let out his breath, sending tendrils of white fog into the chill air.

"Tell you what, Onyx."

The young woman stopped in her tracks, her back as straight as a pillar. She did not turn around.

"Give me a better demonstration of your, um, skills," he said softly. He eyed the villagers passing in the icy street. "Then I'll reconsider your pay level."

Onyx hesitated, considering how far she should take this tack. Her goal was to earn Led's trust, become a member of his party. Perhaps she should just agree to whatever he said.

Led took note of her hesitation. "Of course, if you *can't* cast spells, then you wouldn't be of much use to me. . . ." He spat casually and turned to leave.

Onyx's reptilian-slitted pupils flared inside yellow irises. "Now who's being ridiculous? I was merely scouting out a secluded spot for a demonstration." She looked at him archly. "Unless, of course, you'd like me to throw a fireball down the street?"

"Lower your voice and come with me, then." Leaving the ogres and Toba behind, Led took Onyx by the elbow and propelled her toward the mews between the inn and a wattle-and-daub house.

Onyx ducked through the door of the deserted building and jerked her arm away. Flexing the tension from her shoulders, she concentrated on controlling her breathing. She'd been bluffing about a fireball, which was still beyond her ability. She closed her eyes and focused on a simple spell, basic to the dark nature of a black dragon.

"Hey, what's going on?" cried Led, his voice cracking with surprise.

Onyx opened her eyes. She and Led stood in absolute blackness. Her dragon sight allowed her to see Led in the dark. He was groping about wildly, unable to determine up from down. Led wavered like a stalk of overripe corn in a summer wind, then crashed to the ground.

With a wave of her hand, Onyx dissipated the spell. As the darkness slipped away like mist, leaving sunlight, she extended a hand to Led. He slapped it away.

"I was talking about a demonstration of your fighting skills," he said. "Don't ever use your magic on me again." Flustered, he twisted his clothing back into place under his armor. "You'll get the same shares as Toba until you prove yourself in battle." He crossed his arms over his chest. "Take it or leave it."

"I'll take it," Onyx said, rocking back on her heels.

Led jerked his head to indicate she should lead the way back to Toba and the ogres. It was not just bruised pride that made the human wonder at the wisdom of taking into his party someone more powerful than he. Led was a man to whom power was everything. Still, he reasoned, stealing it was far less taxing than earning it.

* * * * *

A short time later, Onyx stood in flesh-pinching brigandine armor, waiting for a stable hand to bring in another horse for Led's approval.

Led had chosen this "lightweight" armor from his personal collection because, "It's the best quality suit the jackanapes who calls himself the village armorer can alter to your size without ruining it."

The armor was composed of a layer of small metal plates riveted to an undercoat of soft leather. Over that was a mantle of noise-muffling quilted cotton batting. If the armor had not been so uncomfortable, Onyx would have been amused by the irony of protecting her human flesh with a parody of her dragon form. At least it kept her warmer than her tunic and leather jacket had.

Following a few nips and tucks at the armorer's, Led selected a short sword from his weapons cache and buckled it around Onyx's waist. "Even if you never use it, just wearing it will make people think twice," he'd said.

Now Onyx stood girded as a warrior, watching as the stableboy led a black mare to her and held out the reins. Onyx took the lengths of leather awkwardly.

Nodding with satisfaction, Led patted the mare's shiny

flanks and said to the boy, "Tell your master we'll take her." Counting coin from his pouch, Led dropped ten into the boy's hand. "Not one piece more." The boy scampered off between piles of dirty yellow hay.

"I'll take her price out of your first pay," Led told Onyx. Adjusting a strap, he laced his fingers and held them out to boost her onto the back of the horse. "She's a nice piece of flesh. Her coloring suits you, too." Onyx placed her left foot in Led's hands and swung her right leg over the horse with great difficulty, unused to maneuvering in the cumbersome armor.

Led watched her clumsy handling of the beast with surprise. "Surely you haven't traveled entirely by foot all your life?"

"Not by foot, no," Onyx said. The mysterious glint in her eye suggested her magical abilities. Led looked properly impressed.

"I've got to check on a special order the cartwright's been promising me," he told Onyx after watching her first awkward attempts to ride the mare. Promising to return in short order, he left her to her own struggles in the paddock.

Onyx was relieved to see the backside of his long-legged stride so she could practice without his green eyes on her. Used to being a mount of a sort to the lightweight nyphids, she did not like the feeling of sitting on a horse one bit. The ride was jarring, not smooth like flying. More disturbing to Onyx, though, was the idea of turning control of herself over to an animal not half as intelligent as she.

Slowly, she learned to control the animal instead of allowing it to control her. Her shoulders ached from the effort to direct the animal, as well as the weight of the armor. The sun had risen past the midpoint, and the mare beneath her had churned the paddock to ankle-deep mud by the time a now-helmeted Led returned on horseback himself.

To her surprise, he was accompanied by his entire band of ogres and flanked by Toba, who sat upon the buckboard of a small, windowless box of a wagon, reins in hand. Khisanth sprang from the mare's back and led the creature by the leather bridle through the paddock gate.

"Yoshiki Toba, Onyx," Led said simply by way of introduction. "She's our new hand." Led's lieutenant eyed her willowy, muscular form skeptically, but said not a word. Obviously adding a woman warrior to their ranks was nothing new. Onyx wondered at Led's reasons for not telling Toba of her spellcasting abilities, but she knew she had already strained Led's tolerance for questions.

"You're doing better on the horse," Led observed. "Just in time, too."

"We're leaving now?" Onyx glanced from the last ranks of ogres up to the small wagon behind Toba.

Led pushed back the helmet he'd donned since she'd last seen him. "Any problem with that?"

"No!" she said quickly, her mind racing. How will I tell Kadagan and Joad I'm leaving? I don't even know where I'm going! "I was just surprised, is all."

"Me, too," said Led. "That fool cartwright has been stringing me along, taking a month to build this little wagon, if you can believe that."

"What kind of cargo requires a wagon specially made for it?" she asked artlessly.

"Something that's going to make me rich, once I get it to its new owner in Kernen," he said with a mysterious smile, then wagged his finger. "You've forgotten rule number one again, Onyx." Led dropped his helmet back over his face. "Take the right flank, and make certain you remember rules two and three." With that, he gave a shrill whistle and circled his arm once over his head.

The group set off for the southeastern gate. Onyx had to spur the horse to a trot to gain her place on the right of the wagon, opposite Led.

Once outside town the small train turned toward the mountains. Thin woods lined the road, thickening as the way led farther from town. Aside from an occasional sneeze or curse from one of the ogres, the group was silent. Onyx wondered whether Kadagan and Joad were watching from somewhere. If Dela was in the strange wagon Toba was driving, surely Joad would know. If she wasn't—I'll deal with that if it turns out to be true, thought Khisanth.

They established a steady pace, headed through the foothills, toward a place Led called Needle Pass, the only sizable gap through the Khalkist Mountains within a hundred miles. The gray clouds had been chased from sight by a strong, chill wind. Onyx swayed in her saddle with each of the mare's steps up the steep, rocky incline. She tried repeatedly to listen for any sound from the wagon, but her keen hearing revealed nothing.

After a short time on the trail, Onyx's entire body ached. She concentrated on the horse's mane, let the color and texture absorb all her thoughts. Slowly, the pain in her legs diminished. The weight of the armor no longer strained her back or curved her spine.

Hawks cried out as they circled above the lumbering party. The wagon's wheels creaked and rumbled over the frozen ground, occasionally crunching a rock or shattering a frozen puddle. Led's horse was perfectly abreast of the two that pulled the wagon under Toba's direction. The human's face was impassive, eyes always scanning ahead, his posture in the saddle ramrod straight.

Hours later, as the sun slipped over the western horizon, Led chose a campsite. The spot lay near a small pool that was constantly fed fresh water from a swiftly flowing mountain stream. Led gave a shrill whistle. The wagon rolled to a stop next to Onyx, the ogres behind it. Toba jumped from the buckboard and began firing off orders. The ogres established a makeshift camp in the narrow clearing, digging fire pits with their claws, while Led's lieutenant unhitched the wagon and posted himself as guard over the precious cargo. While Toba was about, there would be no examining the cart to see if Dela were inside.

Led sprang from his saddle and stepped around the wagon to help Onyx from hers. He settled the woman atop a large rock, then fished around in his leather pack. "Jerky?"

He held out a red-brown shriveled strip that looked like animal hide picked clean and left too long in the sun. She hesitated, not sure what to do with it.

"Better eat while you can," he said, holding it closer to her. Led tore off a piece of the jerky and chewed it vigorously. "It'll be a while before Toba gets a fire started and any food cooked."

He noticed then that the woman was watching the ogres, who towered over the shouting Toba. "You may not think they look like much, but you wouldn't believe where we started with them. No organization at all. None of them could even wield a club with any accuracy. They relied mostly on crushing opponents to death." He looked appreciatively at their ten-foot frames. "Not a bad technique, either, when you think about it."

"Why do they work for you?" Onyx asked. She watched the wiry Toba strike a violet-colored ogre with a club. The creature dug marginally faster, a vicious snarl erupting through its pointy green teeth.

"I killed their chieftain." Led took a long pull on a wineskin that hung from a frayed string on his right shoulder. "They hated him," he continued, wiping his mouth on the back of his fringed leather sleeve. "Blogrut was even greedier than most ogres, driving them hard, feeding them little, and giving them less than nothing of what meager booty they managed to find.

"We make sure that they're fed regularly, and that each of them gets some bit of treasure now and then, even if it's just a shiny button." He ducked his head through the wineskin string and handed the leather bag to Onyx. "They're as loyal as any human troops, so Toba and I sleep in shifts."

Within minutes the ogres had scraped out fire pits, gathered wood, and started several fires: large ones for warmth and a smaller one for cooking.

Led pulled some thick blankets from his saddle pack and tossed one to Onyx. "Unless you can sleep through an ogre's snoring, you'll want to bunk down here by my fire." He dropped his blanket and settled to the ground, leaning against the soft bundle. As Onyx did the same, Toba stepped up with three steaming platters of brown stew.

They ate the same way they traveled, in silence. Onyx smiled at the irony of sharing bread and meat with these people she might shortly have to kill.

"What's funny?" asked Led, mopping up the last of his plate with a lump of hard bread.

"Nothing," Onyx lied. "It's good to be out of town."

"You prefer the open spaces? Me, too," Led replied.

Onyx felt suddenly talkative, though she wasn't sure why. "It isn't the buildings I mind," she explained. "It's the people. I feel uncomfortable surrounded by strangers. I have to watch what I do and say too closely. I like more freedom."

Obviously bored with such prattle, Toba gathered up the platters and strode back to the cooking fire. Watching him go, Onyx wondered if the nyphids were also watching. She wished she knew enough about the maynus to use it to contact them. If nothing else, she suspected Joad could confirm whether Dela was in the wagon.

Led slid over next to Onyx, their elbows touching. She stole a glance at his profile; a brown weed was clamped between his white, even teeth. She had never been so close to another creature without killing it. Led exuded some unfamiliar, inviting scent that made her want to lean in and smell his skin. The impulse brought her nose halfway to his neck before her new human senses jerked her back. Led gave her a curious glance. Then, to her surprise, he reached up with a gloved hand and swept a strand of hair from her forehead.

Led pulled the weed from his lips. "What's that in your hands?" he asked, looking at the two stones she was shuffling between her fingers.

"These?" she looked down. "I found them along the trail and thought they looked interesting."

"Let me see." Taking them from her dark fingers, Led tipped the stones toward the firelight. One was pure black, with alternating bands of slightly lighter hues. "Hmm," he said. "This big egg-shaped one is onyx."

"Really?" She reached out eagerly to take the stone back.

Led yanked his hand away and smiled. "I think I'll keep it, if you don't mind. To remind me of you."

Onyx looked intently into his face. Behind his grin, the human was deadly serious. Her heart thrummed wildly. They fell into an awkward silence and stared into the fire, listening to the sounds of night.

"We haven't really discussed what I need from you," he mumbled without looking at her.

Onyx jumped. "What are you talking about?"

"I was asking what protection your spells could provide." His green eyes twinkled with amusement. "What did you think I was talking about?"

"I . . . didn't hear you," she muttered. Led saw her red face, and he smiled. "Is it your goal to be a bounty hunter all your life?" she asked, hoping to change the subject.

Led chuckled. "Actually, I'm a jack-of-all-trades. My first 'goal,' if you will, is to wake up every day with all my parts intact." He turned deadly serious. "My second is to be filthy rich. The package in the wagon is going to ensure that."

"It must be very valuable."

Led snorted. "You wouldn't believe what's in—" He looked anxiously over his shoulder to the other fire pit, where Toba watched the slumbering ogres. "Never mind."

He spit the weed from his teeth. "I've been thinking about what I'll do afterward. You mentioned dragons before." Led relit his pipe and squinted at her through the pungent haze. "Have you heard about the armies gathering in the south?"

Onyx leaned forward. "Armies?"

"I've heard, like you, that dragons have returned to the world. If they have, and nobody seems to know for sure, some people say there's going to be a war. A big war, with dragons on one side and who knows what on the other; probably the Knights of Solamnia, anyway. In a war like that, there's lots of opportunity for someone with brains. And if dragons are everything the stories say they are, I know which side I'd want to be on."

"So why haven't you joined them already?"

"I've been a grunt before, like them." He jerked a thumb at the ogres. "I'll never go back to it. Besides, everything's changed now that I've met you."

"I don't understand."

Led looked at her closely. "With my experience and know-how and your magic, we could lead such an army."

"Tell me more about dragons," she said, her back stiff despite her efforts to look indifferent.

"Rumor says that the core of this army and its greatest strength are the human generals who ride dragons into battle."

"Are you saying these dragons not only allow humans to sit on their backs, but they follow the directions of such obviously inferior creatures?"

Led gave a startled laugh. "That's an odd way of putting it. Dragons may be smart for animals, Onyx, but they're still just beasts. They're not civilized; they have no culture or society like humans; they live in the wild like animals."

"How do you know this? Have you ever seen a dragon?" she asked in a clipped tone.

Led fell back against the blanket roll with a snort. "I don't have to. If they were even half as smart as humans, why would they have agreed to go away for thousands of years?"

"Those dragons who were banished had no choice but to go underground—they were ordered by their goddess, Takhisis," she said a bit defensively.

"Some goddess," he laughed, then leaned forward again with interest. "That name sounds vaguely familiar. Wasn't she one of the old gods of evil that the Seekers talk about?"

"Seekers?"

"Boy, where have you been?" he cried. "Seekers are the clerics of the religion that's risen since the Cataclysm to take the place of the old, false gods who caused that catastrophe. Like this Takhisis."

It was Onyx's turn to give a bitter laugh. "Let me assure you, Takhisis is not a false god." Onyx locked her arms around her knees and considered how much she wanted to reveal to Led. "Do these 'Seeker clerics' possess magical skills, which only a god can grant?"

"I don't think so. . . ." he answered. "That's why no one believes in magic anymore. . . ." His voice trailed off. But Onyx could do magic. In the awkward silence, they both considered the implications of the odd conversation.

"So, are you interested?" Led asked at last. "In joining the army with me, that is?" he added quickly with a suggestion of a light-hearted smirk.

Onyx ignored it. "Only on my own terms. I'm not impressed with a system that subordinates a dragon to a human rider," she said firmly.

Both sat silently for a few moments. Something Led had said earlier puzzled Onyx. "What does this word 'evil' mean?"

He looked at her strangely, half smiling, waiting for her to grin back. "You're joking."

Her tawny eyes were wide with innocence.

Still not sure if she was baiting him, Led felt a bit foolish as he proceeded with a definition anyway. "It's a word cowards use to explain things that frighten them, like murder or theft. For myself, I don't believe evil exists."

Onyx mulled over those concepts. "So people think this evil is a bad thing?"

"The cowards do, yes. But I think it's very natural for the strong to eliminate the weak."

She shook her head vigorously. "It confounds me that humans control Krynn."

"I don't quite understand you, Onyx," Led said, his own dark head shaking in response to Onyx's. "First you make it sound like I'd be a fool not to join this army, yet you condemn its system, then defend the goddess who banished her own dragons. You're a bag of contradictions, Onyx." Led's green eyes sparkled as he reached out unexpectedly to stroke her dusky cheek. "I'm glad you're my ally, not my enemy."

Onyx realized distantly that he'd actually insulted her, but the thought was chased away by the sensations his touch evoked in her. Knocking his pipe against a rock to extinguish it, he leaned forward and brushed his lips in a warm trail where his fingers had just passed. His calloused hands took her by the shoulders. His fingers slid down her arms, lingering on her wrists. He continued downward and rubbed her slim fingers between his rough ones.

Onyx froze. For the first time in her life no instinct she

understood told her how to react. As a dragon, her thoughts ran almost exclusively to the basics: satisfying hunger, seeking shelter, acquiring treasure. These tasks were colored only by the indulgent joy she got from flying or swimming.

But she noticed a much greater range of sensations as a human. The texture of cloth or the feel of cold air on bare skin, the distinct flavors of cooked food, the way her pulse quickened from an admiring glance. The only looks she'd received as a dragon were fearful or envious, both of which pleased her greatly, but in a very different way. . . .

"You're a beautiful enigma, Onyx," Led said again softly, his whiskers tickling her cheek. His warm breath was a pleasant mingling of sweet wine and pungent pipe smoke. "I like solving a good mystery."

Onyx self-consciously took a pull on the wineskin, aware that the trees beyond their fire pit were already listing in her watery sight. She fought against the effects of the wine, even as she felt his fingertips dance down her spine through the thin cloth of her tunic. The young woman gave a shiver that had nothing to do with the cold.

Led pressed his lips ever gently down the bridge of her nose. "I'd kill any man who tried to harm you," he said in a husky voice, moving to sink his teeth into the lobe of her left ear in a manner even more disturbing than his unexpected possessiveness.

Some voice inside warned Onyx not to trust him. But dizzy from wine, she could not see how trust entered into these feelings he aroused. She trusted no one but herself anyway. She was in control and could stop this at any time. Besides, she told herself, if she was to learn in the qhen way what it was to be human, she must experience all that she could as a human. Live for the moment.

Onyx gave in to the wine, to Led, and dismissed her self-control. Instinct far different than she'd experienced as a dragon brought her dark, slim hand up to the back of Led's neck and pulled his bearded face down to hers.

Under a black, starless sky Onyx's senses spun away to the heights she had reached only in dragon flight.

Chapter 7

Onyx and Led rolled apart at last and fell into exhausted slumber as the night sky began to lighten. Curled under a fur blanket, Onyx did something she hadn't since waking from the Sleep as a dragon—she dreamed.

She was a dragon again, flying; Led rode upon her back, a sword in his hand. Together they commanded a vast army that cut down foe after faceless foe. Dragon and rider toppled towers, chased knights from their castles, and finally stood majestically before a conquered throng. The vision filled her unconscious mind with a great sense of satisfaction. Smiling in her sleep, Onyx hugged the covers closer and settled in for an agreeably vivid show.

The disguised dragon was almost surprised to awaken to the scent of damp ashes and the feel of a cold, hard boulder for a headrest. She was still a woman, still resting near the fire pit, now extinguished. It had all been just a dream. Not all of it, though, she thought smugly, flexing her stiff muscles at the memory of her night with Led. Still groggy, she kept her eyes tightly closed as if to recapture the fantasy. Neither sleep nor the dream returned.

Strange, Onyx thought, that this should be my first dream since waking from the magical Sleep. She began to wonder if the word "dream" was correct for what she'd experienced. Another thought came to mind, a possibility both frightening and fascinating.

Could it have been a vision of the future from Takhisis? Her *geetna* had predicted she would do great service for the queen. Perhaps it had been fate, not accident, that the nyphids awakened her and directed her toward Led. Was it Takhisis's wish that Onyx and Led fight as one for her glory? She paused. Where was Led, anyway?

Onyx rolled up onto her elbow, and her fur blanket slipped away. She felt her first twinge of modesty as she remembered she was unclothed. Cinching the fur up tightly under her armpits, the young woman discovered with dismay that she, alone, still lay close to the fire pit. She heard mingled sounds of activity and sat up to investigate.

Onyx's acute hearing detected splashing water. Following the noise through the snow-covered branches of the pine trees, Onyx saw Led in the distance, bobbing in the chill mountain stream, slapping water on his bare chest. The sight brought a blush to her cheeks and a smile to her lips.

Hearing orders being barked in the opposite direction, Onyx's gaze fell next on Yoshiki Toba. He was at the other end of the oblong clearing, running the ogres through a routine drill in hand-to-hand and weapons combat. They wore no armor, but many had round wooden bucklers strapped to their thick arms. Spiked clubs and crudely made spears appeared to be their weapons of choice.

If Led was bathing in the stream, and Toba was engaged in morning drill, then who was watching—

Onyx's gaze shot to the left. The wagon was parked out of the way, far back in the trees between the fire pit and the lanky lieutenant. There was no guard in sight.

Onyx sprang to her feet, yanked on her cotton batting, and tugged up her leather boots. Forcing herself to stroll, she circled the wagon. She had seen Toba leave the ogre's fire pit with a plate of food last night, headed for the rear of the wagon. Onyx hastened to the back and searched the flat wooden panel from top to bottom with her hands, but found no latch or crack to suggest an opening.

Onyx chewed her lip, thinking. There were only two sides she hadn't examined. The top of the wagon would be risky, since she would be in clear view up there. Dropping to her knees, she ducked under the frame. But the box hung so low to the ground that she had to turn onto her back and kick her feet into the dirt to push herself beneath it. The wagon was supported by thick metal straps and the two axles that stretched between the wheels.

Near the middle of the wagon was a small trapdoor, held shut by a dead bolt. Onyx carefully slid the bolt aside, then grabbed at the wooden door before it could swing down and bang into the metal strap.

Still on her back, Onyx gripped the edge of the wooden slot and pulled her head and shoulders toward the opening. It was so narrow that her face scraped the side when she managed at last to poke her head into the bottom of the wagon. Onyx peered around, calling on her dragon sight in the lightlessness. There, huddled in a corner, was a small heap covered by a dirty fur.

"Dela?" Onyx whispered.

The lump shifted slightly at the sound. The fur began to slip. Onyx caught a glimpse of disheveled blond hair. Her heart hammered in expectation.

Something grabbed Onyx by the feet. Her jawbone slammed into the rough opening as the hands around her boots labored to haul her from under the wagon. After three jarring tugs, her bruised face cleared the hole. The hands tugged again, and the back of Onyx's head dropped painfully onto the hard, frozen ground. She scrabbled and clawed to escape, but all she managed was to roll onto her front, so that she was pulled from beneath the wagon on her face. A blade-tipped boot kicked her in the side, rolling her onto her back again. Onyx looked up the legs that formed an inverted Y above her.

"Lose something, Onyx?" Yoshiki Toba's breath ringed his head as white steam. "If that's even your name." He snugged his feet closer to her sides, trapping her.

Onyx looked up at Toba's yellow-skinned face, speechless. Almost seeing Dela, Toba catching her spying—it had happened so fast she could scarcely think of what to say, how to explain away her presence under the wagon. She saw the anger in his eyes and knew there would be no fooling the watchful overlord.

"Got nothin' to say?" Toba chuckled. "I knew from the start there was something strange about you. Led's always had a soft spot in his melon for pretty women." He grabbed Onyx by the left arm and nearly tugged it from the socket. "Maybe you'll find your voice in time to explain to your *paramour* what you were doing under there."

Led! He'd throw her out of his band for sure. Then it would be impossible to free Dela in her human form. And what about her dream? She had to silence Toba before he told their leader. She had no weapons, nothing on but her batting and boots. She searched her mind for a spell that would kill him instantly, without a trace, but her magical skills simply weren't that developed yet. If she were a dragon, she could call on her breath weapon. . . .

Holding Onyx's arm tightly with one hand, Toba bent down and reached under the wagon. He fumbled until he found the trap door, then shut and bolted it. He straightened and glared at her with sinister eyes.

"Stand," he ordered. When she refused to plant her feet or lock her knees, he kicked her viciously in the legs.

Onyx felt herself start to panic. Then, quite suddenly, something burned the skin of her neck, and she cried aloud. The maynus. Pulling the choker by the vine with her free hand, she settled the tiny swords and globe atop her purple tunic. The maynus scorched her even through the cloth. It was the brilliant blue-white of the hottest fire. Onyx had never seen the source of Dela's magic do that before. The faces in the lightning bolts flashed through Onyx's mind. She heard Kadagan's voice from months ago: "We commanded it to lift thee."

She touched a hand to the scalding maynus. "Take him, and leave no trace," she whispered, not sure what to expect.

"Hey, what—?" Toba's muttered question was cut off when a white-hot bolt of lightning leaped from the globe. It snapped around his trunk like a lasso, pinning his arms to his sides. The wiry man's eyes went wide and fearful. He was too startled to scream at first. He wasn't given the chance later.

Toba's prominent cheekbones twisted and contorted, and his whole body seemed to melt into colorful, swirling vapor. Crackling, the branch of lightning pulled him toward its source, the globe at Onyx's collarbone. The churning mass that Toba had become withdrew into the maynus with a hollow sucking sound.

Stunned, Onyx peered down her chin to the globe. It had cooled to pale blue. Lightning bolts again danced and ricocheted within. To her further amazement, she thought she could see the vague outline of Toba's face pressing against the glass from the inside. Had she killed the human, Onyx wondered, or just trapped him in the magical globe? Either way, he couldn't talk to Led now. Onyx frowned. At least she didn't *think* he could communicate from inside the globe. She knew so little about the nyphids' artifact.

Rustling from inside the wagon brought Onyx's attention back to Dela. She could free the nyphid now. Dela would know what to do with Toba, too. Onyx dropped to her knees again and flipped onto her back to scoot beneath the wagon.

"Yoshiki Toba, you miserable scut, why have you left the ogres lumbering like aimless zombies in the clearing?" Led called from the stream, his voice bright with humor. "You'd better be making my breakfast. Onyx, are you awake yet?"

Half under the wagon, Onyx froze with indecision. She was so close to freeing Dela. Yet, if she didn't answer Led and he found her here, she'd be in the same spot she'd been with Toba. Only, strangely, she didn't want to kill Led, or even draw him into the globe. The dream was too insistent, its promise of glory too fresh in her mind.

Onyx clambered from under the wagon. Brushing vainly at her muddy clothing, she strode purposefully along the right side of the cart and back to the fire pit.

Led emerged from the trees on the beaten snowy path that came from the stream. Scrubbing his wet hair with a nubby cloth, he was still bare to the waist, his skin red with cold. Seeing Onyx, he smiled in warm greeting. "There you are." He let the cloth drop to his shoulders. "Good morning."

"And to you," she said, forcing a wan smile in return.

He peered at her curiously. "You're a mess. And your face is all scratched up. What have you been doing?"

Onyx hitched up her pants and managed a meaningful, blushing look over her shoulder to the woods behind the wagon. "I was . . . well, I unfortunately chose a very muddy patch. A branch snapped out, and, uh, you know. . . ."

Led nodded slowly. He frowned and looked about. "Where's Toba?"

Onyx shrugged, unconsciously tucking the silent, still-blue maynus back beneath the neckline of her tunic. If Toba was in there, he wasn't talking.

Led swore under his breath. "He knows we're in a hurry to get to Kernen."

"Maybe he's occupied as I was," Onyx suggested, looking to the woods.

"Could be," said Led a bit dubiously. He kicked the ashes to life in the fire pit, adding a handful of twigs to the smoldering pile. "If I have to fix my own grub because of it, he'll pay the price. Say, you're a woman. Don't you know how to cook?"

"Uh, no. I've never had to, actually."

"You probably just magic it up." Led sat on a boulder, pulled off his boots, and held his toes to the fire. "Nothing like a bath in a fresh mountain stream. Leaves you with cold feet, though."

Led shrugged on a tunic over his damp, curling hair. He glanced with disdain at the ogres across the clearing. "Wish I could get them to bathe once in a while. They think it'll make 'em sick."

The human's head snapped around toward the forest. "Toba! Where in the Abyss are you, man?"

After a few moments of awkward silence, Onyx sat on the boulder next to his and reached toward Led's own pack. "I'm starving. Do you have any more of that jerky?"

"Yeah, sure," Led said. He plunged his hand into the leather sack and retrieved a strip of the blackened meat, as well as a wineskin. He offered both to Onyx. "It's not breakfast, but it's better than nothing."

Onyx took the wineskin and drank greedily.

"That's it," snarled Led abruptly, slapping his knees. "I'm gonna take a look around for Toba's bony yellow hide." He pulled his leather armor from his horse and strapped it on, adding stiff leather cuisses to his thighs. Next, he gingerly slipped a chain mail coif over his head and adjusted it into position. Over that he placed a massive metal helm that dropped to his shoulders in the back, and came low over his brow and swept in from the sides to cover both cheeks. Last, he strapped his girdle around the chain mail at his waist and settled his sword so that the hilt was within easy reach.

Onyx gulped wine nervously as she watched him dress. She tried to slow her breathing to calm herself in the qhen way, but couldn't seem to focus as completely in her human form as she had as a dragon. Her breathing remained shallow, her pulse racing. Led walked the perimeter of the clearing, calling Toba's name into the trees. The human stopped and spoke to a green-skinned ogre who sat idly with the others where Toba had left them.

Onyx looked wide-eyed into Led's stormy face when he returned to the fire. "No luck?"

"It's just not like Toba to disappear for this long without telling me what he's up to. The ogres say they saw him heading this way. Didn't you see him?"

"No. I was probably still sleeping. Maybe he went out looking for food and wandered farther than he thought."

"Doubtful. He knows we have enough stores to last . . ."

Onyx idly traced a seam in her boot, unable to look Led in the eye. "Could he simply have run off?"

Led scratched his head. "I can't see it. He knew how much we stand to gain when we deliver the wagon. No, Toba's too greedy to just up and abandon his share."

Onyx took a long pull on the wineskin. "The fact remains that he's gone. How long are you willing to wait for him?"

"That depends." Led rubbed his chin. "Say, do you know some kind of spell that can find a missing person?"

Onyx stopped in midgulp, the crimson liquid splashing her lips. She handed him the skin and wiped her mouth on the cuff of her batting. "Yes," she lied. "I don't have all the things I need to cast the enchantment, though. But I can probably find the right kinds of roots and funguses in the woods. I'll go into the forest and give it a try."

Led watched her finger the odd choker. "Whatever. Just be careful. We don't know what happened to him, so keep your eyes open. In fact, maybe I should come along, too."

"No," snapped Onyx. "I can concentrate better if I'm alone. I can protect myself, if you're worried. I know magic, remember? Besides, someone needs to watch the ogres."

Led couldn't argue with that logic. He helped Onyx put on her brigandine armor. Pulling her horse around by the bit, Onyx put her left toe in the stirrup and swung her other leg over, then set the horse's head downhill.

Led tossed the wineskin to her. Sunlight streaked across his brilliant green eyes, and he snarled with annoyance. "With or without Toba, we've got to get back on the trail quickly. Come back as soon as you know anything."

Nodding, Onyx slipped the strap of the skin over her head and shoulder, then dug her heels into the black mare's ribs. They shot off down the rough-cut trail at a gallop. Onyx gave the horse its head. It stayed with the narrow trail that paralleled the same stream by the clearing.

Khisanth was grateful the lie had succeeded. She didn't use components to cast spells, but she was desperate to get away and think. She seemed unable to control her own actions as a human, particularly with Led's penetrating eyes on her. What had happened to her qhen training?

Though it was causing her no end of problems now, she

was not sorry she had—well, done whatever she'd done to Toba. It had been rash, definitely not qhen, but even Kadagan would have agreed that she'd had no choice.

The problem was what to tell Led that would make him abandon his lieutenant? Worse still, now that she was almost certain Dela was in the wagon, how was she going to free the captive nyphid? That *was* the point of this whole foray as a human, after all. She seemed to have lost sight of that goal recently, along with her qhen training.

Onyx closed her eyes for a moment and pressed her hands to her temples, as if the posture would silence the barrage of questions. If only she could reason now as clearly as she'd done as a dragon. Her eyes popped open. Why not? Onyx felt an overwhelming longing to assume her dragon form. *Then* she could think the problem through without the distractions of human emotions. It would calm her to feel like herself again, even for a moment. To not have to concentrate on every gesture or word. To be herself. The more she considered it, the better the idea sounded.

But did she dare?

Onyx cast a glance over her shoulder. She was some distance from the clearing where Led and the ogres waited. She concentrated to drown out the noise of the babbling stream. Beyond it, she heard only chirping birds and other forest sounds. No one had followed her.

Onyx looked up the trail, then back over her shoulder again. Nothing in either direction. Just to be safe, she prompted the mare to continue at a canter uphill for a short time, putting a little more distance between herself and possible discovery. Tugging the mare's head to the right just after a tall boulder, she quickly dismounted, looping the mare's reins through the branches of a young tree.

Onyx stepped away from the horse and into the protection of the enveloping pines. She pulled off her armor and clothing and stuffed them into the leather bag that had hung behind the saddle. Reluctantly she untied the thong holding the swords and the maynus; if she left it on during the transformation, the choker might well live up to its name before she could enlarge it with sorcery. Looking closely at the maynus once more, she was convinced anew that Toba, or at least some part of him, was trapped inside. Deciding she could do nothing about him right now, she added the whole necklace to the bag.

Onyx was joyful at the thought of doing something so reckless; every minute as a human was an exercise in self-containment. The woman's slanted, tawny eyes closed. When she opened them again, she was a black dragon.

Immediately she felt a stab of pain. Hunger. The little strip of jerky may have filled her tiny human belly, but it wasn't even a mouse to a dragon's enormous stomach. She hadn't feasted recently enough to satisfy her voracious appetite, and it was demanding something big.

Khisanth's dragon senses pricked up. Beyond her protective hedge of pines, she heard the mare wicker softly. Slaver rose in her mouth. Her heavy dragon body answered the call. She felt almost as if she watched herself lumber through the trees, crushing shrubs beneath her enormous feet. Blood pounded in her head, narrowing her field of vision until all she saw was the black mare ahead. The horse's eyes widened with terror when it spotted the dragon crashing through the underbrush. It leaped up and pawed at the air, straining at the reins that bound it to the tree.

The mare's wails were high-pitched and steady. Afraid of the attention the noise would surely draw, the black dragon swung her tail around in a vicious slap aimed at the mare's head. The strike snapped the horse's neck, silencing the beast in midscream. The creature dropped lifeless to the ground. Khisanth's jaws opened wide. She closed her sharp teeth around the mare and lifted it high, joyously shaking it.

Khisanth abruptly spat out the mangled corpse. Something about it tasted wrong, bitter. She espied the leather saddle and bridle. Snatching at them with a claw, she flung the offending morsels far into the woods. Then she returned her attention to the dripping horseflesh. Ravenous, exhilarated by the kill, the dragon sank her pointed teeth into the corpse. Tearing with abandon, she stopped only to gulp down whole chunks.

When the pounding in Khisanth's head began to slow, there

was little left of the mare except teeth and hooves. She'd crunched through the bones for the moist, delicately flavored marrow.

Swallowing the last knuckle joint, Khisanth fell into a sated languor, listening to her own mind. It was thankfully clear of the emotions that had confused her decisions as a human. She felt powerful again, in control. That was very good. But to her surprise, she also felt unpleasantly cumbersome. She missed the spriteliness, the freedom afforded her by her human form.

Heaviest of all, now, were her eyelids. The dragon wanted nothing so desperately as a nap. Into her drowsy brain came a vision of her last sleep, and Led. She was instantly alert. Sighing, she pressed herself to remember the purpose for changing back into her dragon form—to think clearly about a lie to disguise Toba's disappearance.

What would she tell him? Did it matter? Led was intriguing, but still merely a human. Yet she could not deny that she felt some sort of attraction for this man, that she had begun to appreciate aspects of her own facade of humanity because of him. Now, in her dragon form, she found it much easier to consider him objectively.

Once Khisanth reached her decision, she willed herself back into the form of Onyx, then located the saddlebag in the woods, retrieved her clothing, and dressed. The young woman envisioned the campsite near the pool and narrow clearing, and called upon her sorcerous abilities. Within the time it took to blink once, she was standing some ten feet from Led. Startled, the mercenary drew his sword. He relaxed only slightly when he recognized Onyx.

"Where's your horse?"

"She, uh, stumbled in a hole and threw me, then ran off. I couldn't stop her."

Led looked at her closely for a moment longer. Licking the end of his thumb, he dabbed at a crusted, brown spot in the corner of her mouth. "Found something to eat, did you?"

She pushed his hand away to wipe at the spot herself. "I couldn't find any sign of Toba."

A muscle jerked in the hollow under Led's left cheekbone.

"This just isn't like Toba. I checked the wagon, and there's no sign that he attended to, uh, its contents yet today."

Once again Led peered intently toward the tree line, speaking to himself. "I can't believe Toba would just up and leave. He's been with me for three years. There's something very odd about this." He ran his fingers through his hair in exasperation. "I can't waste any more time searching for him. I'll tell you this, though. If he does show up again, he'd better have a damned good story to tell or he'll never work for me again."

Led pulled the wagon back onto the trail and checked the traces. At his signal, an ogre stepped up onto the wagon. The vehicle's front end settled and groaned noticeably under the massive bulk. The ogre fumbled with the reins, and Led eyed the doltish soldier dubiously.

"There's nothing to be done about it, I suppose," he said stiffly. "Let's get a move on."

He blew shrilly between two fingers. Onyx took her place to the right of the wagon. The ogres collected up their weapons and filed to their usual positions behind. Without morning food except wine for himself, Led doled out traveling rations to the groggy, grumbling soldiers, climbed aboard his horse, and herded his troops onward toward Needle Pass.

* * * * *

Led's foul mood allowed for little conversation as they wound their way up the mountains. The rocky trail, if the narrow passage they followed through the trees could be called that, became slippery with snow the higher they rose.

By midday they came at last to Needle Pass. The horses pulling the wagon were showing signs of exhaustion, especially with the added weight of the ogre driver. Led called a halt, hoping to rest and eat at a point just beyond the gap in the mountains, a spot where the trail widened to a width of two wagons. The ogres spread out and pulled chunks of meat and coarse, molding bread from the depths of their packs. Led again offered Onyx a few strips of jerky. She wasn't hungry and gave her share back to him.

Except for the slurping and grunting of the ogres, the party ate in silence. Stone walls worn smooth by the wind rose to either side of the pass; Onyx considered the high, rocky cliffs curiously. If she were fighting as a dragon, those towering, stony ledges would be a perfect perch from which to swoop down onto an unsuspecting enemy.

Led suddenly cocked his head to the side. "Did you hear something?"

"You mean that tinkling, like bells, from back the way we came?" Onyx asked. "I've been hearing it for some time."

Led shot her an angry glance. "Why didn't you say something? Can you tell what it is?" he added, before Onyx could reply to the first question.

"It sounds like a group of horsemen coming this way, and they're making no effort to be quiet."

Led set down his food and moved back up the slope fifty or sixty yards, to where the trail crested the pass. He stayed close to the rock walls, taking pains not to silhouette himself against the sky. After several moments, he trotted back to where Onyx and the ogres waited.

"It's what I thought," he said, "a squad of Solamnic Knights in full panoply riding up the trail. They've got banners flapping and bells ringing. It's a wonder they don't send a herald on ahead to announce that they're coming." He shook his head, snickering. "That's the knights for you, all pomp and honor and stupidity masked as chivalry. I wish I could hide the wagon from them, but there isn't time. We'll have to make do."

Tapping three ogres, Led told them, "Stay with me. The rest of you, up into the rocks. You know the drill. Be ready for my signal, just in case. Be quick. There's one knight riding point— I don't want him to see anything unusual."

Twelve ogres clambered up the rocky cliffs on both sides of the trail. Onyx was surprised at how quickly and completely the bulky creatures blended into the cover. To her further surprise, Led calmly resumed his lunch. He patted the rock next to him.

"Are you going to attack them?" Onyx asked.

"If necessary. Now sit down." Remembering rule number two, Onyx complied wordlessly.

Led had managed to down four hearty swigs of wine and put on a mask of innocent surprise by the time the jingling rang clear. A snapping blue banner emblazoned with a red rose appeared on the western edge of the pass. Slowly it topped the crest, fluttering on the end of a lance, followed by a crested helmet and finally the rest of a knight riding a horse draped in yellow. Through his open visor, Onyx could see that he was very young, his wispy blond mustache almost invisible against his pale upper lip. The knight spied the couple, accompanied by three ogres, eating lunch on the rock. He rode straight toward them with no hesitation, but stopped the length of three horses short of them. The knight sat in stony silence and waited without looking at Onyx and Led.

The jingling of bells, clanking of weapons and armor, and clattering of hooves on frozen ground reverberated back and forth between the rock walls. Onyx spied eight more banners snapping in the chill wind. The knights on horseback beneath the banners topped the crest and proceeded down toward their point rider.

As the main group met up with the waiting knight, he jogged his horse backward to move behind the man at the fore of this larger procession. There could be no question about who led this group. The knight now in front wore a blue-and-red tunic over his armor. The visor of his helmet was also raised, revealing a deeply weathered face and a tremendous, drooping, snow-white mustache.

With a raised arm the commander of the knights brought them all to a halt. He sat still in his high saddle, surveying Led's party. With frank distaste, he stared at the ogres.

Led took the opportunity to lean close to Onyx and whisper, "Thankfully, Knights of Solamnia are completely predictable. Take your lead from me."

The commander spurred his horse several steps closer to Led. There was no welcome in his face. "I am Sir Harald Stippling. Part of my charge is safeguarding this road. Who are you? State your business."

Led calmly tore off a piece of jerky. "They call me Led—just Led. I'm a law-abiding trader carrying valuable cargo from Styx to Kernen." He appeared to be struck with an idea. "Say, I've heard rumors that there are bandits on the road. Perhaps we could travel together and you could protect my shipment. Isn't that your job?"

The knight's eyes narrowed with disbelief. "What law-abiding trader would hire such guards as these ogres?"

"Here in the wilds, I'm at the mercy of what is available for hire. Ogres are plentiful and easily replaced."

"What are you transporting that needs such protection?"

"The wagon contains merchandise of value to me."

"We shall see," muttered Sir Harald. He waved his arm again. "Hugo, Tammerly, inspect the wagon." As Stippling spoke, two knights spurred their horses forward amid a jingling of bells and approached the wagon.

In response, Led waved his arm as well. The three ogres on the trail sprang to their feet, interposing themselves between the knights and the wagon.

Led slid off the rock and stood, hand on sword hilt. "What's in that wagon is the business of the man who owns it, nobody else." Heart pumping with excitement, Onyx got to her feet and called an incantation to mind.

Leaning forward angrily in his saddle, Stippling sputtered, "This may be the frontier, but Knights of Solamnia are still the law. As the highest ranking knight here, I demand that you open the wagon." His expression stormy, Stippling drew his blade and waved it in a whistling circle above his head. The remaining six knights moved to surround the wagon, the ogres, Led, and Onyx. The two called Hugo and Tammerly drew their swords on the ogres in an obvious challenge.

The air in the narrow pass thrummed with a strained silence as both sides considered how far they would go to win the standoff.

Chapter 8

The cry of a hawk wheeling in the gray sky above cut the brittle silence. Heads tilted up, neither knights nor Led's party moved. Even the ogres seemed to sense the strain in the air. They stood as still as their large, hunch-shouldered bodies would allow.

Stippling broke the silence at last. "I'll warn you one last time. Open the wagon."

Led cleaned the dirt from under a fingernail with a small blade. "Or what?"

Led's indifference infuriated the haughty knight. For an answer Stippling snapped down the visor of his helm and clenched his fingers around the hilt of his sword. "Or face the consequences. I would have the woman withdraw, if I were you."

Led could feel Onyx stiffen with indignation. "Fortunately

for my troops and my cargo, you're not me," he cut in before she could fashion a fiery reply. "She stays."

Truth to tell, Onyx was eagerly anticipating a battle that was, at last, not of her own making. It would give her the opportunity to compare the full measure of a human's reflexes to a dragon's. The muscles of this body felt more tightly strung than those of her dragon form. The blood did not hammer deafeningly at her temples in the usual manner. There was no acid with which to scald the flesh from a foe, no tail to deliver a killing blow. Onyx felt the blade in her right boot, cold against her calf; it was a sorry replacement for a dragon's claws. She'd have to rely heavily on her spellcasting. Onyx readied her two best enchantments.

Stippling seemed to be spoiling for a fight as well. He obviously had no idea what he faced as he edged his horse forward. With swords and maces drawn, the knights followed his lead. Four knights rode past the wagon to the downhill side of the road, blocking escape. Four more, including the two Stippling had ordered to search the wagon, were still on the uphill side, spread out slightly ahead of their commander. Sensing what was to come, their horses pranced and tossed their heads in anticipation. Stippling leveled his sword at the chest of the bounty hunter.

Still Led had not drawn his own weapon. *Does he intend to let the knights open the wagon after all?* Onyx wondered. She'd never seen him fight, but his tactics were not what hers would have been. Then she remembered the ogres. Without moving her head, Onyx's eyes shifted to the rocky walls where they waited. Even she could scarcely make out the brutish heads peering around boulders above.

Of course Led had no intention of letting the knights see his prize. Calmly finishing his manicure, he put the blade away. "Do nothing and stay put," he whispered lightly to Onyx. Then, with incredible speed, he sprang forward and to the right, darting around the front of Stippling's horse. He snatched at the horse's bridle but missed. The horse lashed out its front hooves. One glanced off the greave on Led's left leg. The bounty hunter spun to the ground from the shock. He scrambled away before the rearing horse could trample him.

Led's maneuver, however little effect it had on Stippling, focused most of the knights' attention on him. They moved forward. Only three faced off with the ogres. The remainder closed in on the leather-armored man, still crouched defensively on his haunches near the horse's hooves.

An eerie wail broke over the scene. Hearing the strange sound from the rocks above, the knights looked up just in time to see several large boulders—propelled by Onyx's magic—hurtling toward them from the cliffs. It was too late to move. The rocks were slightly off target and just grazed the flanks of the stunned knights. One was bowled from his saddle. The rest raised their shields and hastily directed their shrieking mounts backward; they weren't retreating, merely trying to figure out whether the greater danger lay on the ground or in the cliffs.

The answer came when the hidden ogres rose up from their hiding places. They began pelting the road with skull-sized rocks. At first the stones hit their marks, crashing into heavy plate mail with loud clatters. The knights quickly recovered. Holding their rose-crested shields aloft, they easily deflected the stones.

"Lay on!" came a cry nearby. "Take no prisoners!"

The bounty hunter waved his forces forward. The three towering ogres charged into the milling, confused knights, whose gazes were still turned skyward. The ogres indiscriminately swung their clubs and thrust their rough spears at horses and knights alike.

But the trap had not been sprung in its entirety.

With the knights' attention turned to the action around them, the ogres above began to throw themselves from the cliff face like lemmings. Ogres rained down with greater force and accuracy than the boulders. Three more knights were sent sprawling from their saddles, and two of them were seriously hurt by the trampling hooves of their own horses. The horses were suffering as much from spear thrusts as their riders. Many of the steeds were down on their knees, their drapings covered in blood.

Everything was going according to Led's plan.

The knights had fallen more easily than even Led had hoped—so easy, in fact, that there had been no need for him to do anything but lean against a boulder and enjoy the spectacle. He'd held Onyx back from the skirmish with him, telling her with a wink that she was too valuable to sacrifice in a lopsided brawl. His tone was patronizing as he told her to be ready with her spells, in case the tide turned.

Onyx watched the ogres at their sport and felt cheated. She was reminded of Kadagan's parable of the sword: Onyx was like a mighty blade used only to pare apples. Soon the ogres will finish off the last knight, she reflected jealously, and I'll have had no fun at all.

Then the unthinkable happened.

A lone ogre hopped anxiously from one foot to the other on the cliff above, eager to join the fray. This exceptionally dim-witted creature grabbed its knees and flung its thirty-stone, olive-green body off the cliff without thought to where it was headed. The brute landed with the force and grace of an enormous gunstone, square on the roof of the small wagon. The monster's bulk smashed open the top and one side of the compartment. A second side splintered as he tumbled to the ground, landing in a heap of broken boards and splinters.

"No!" wailed Led. "My fortune!" He rushed forward, then stopped, paralyzed. An audible gasp rippled through the melee. All heads were turned toward the demolished wagon, and the creature huddled amid the wreckage.

Onyx knew the pathetic thing, shivering in a shabby, dirty tunic, had to be Dela. But the gray, wrinkled skin, sunken eyes, and swollen joints bore no semblance to the perfectly formed nyphid she'd seen in the maynus. Dela's tunic seemed to hold a bundle of sticks. Her hair, now dull yellow and matted and littered with straw, was barely recognizable.

Onyx silently screamed for the nyphid to run, but, surrounded by people, Dela was obviously too terrified or weak to move. Her mouth opened and closed with soundless screams. There was no place to hide in the ruined wagon. The nyphid threw her withered arms across her face and collapsed into the straw.

Do something! Onyx told herself. But what? She couldn't just grab the nyphid and run. Unless she intended to reveal her real reason for joining Led's group, she had to think of a way to make Dela help herself. A spell. She tried to think of one, but she'd concentrated for so long on enchantments that might aid in a battle, no new ones penetrated the fog of her confused thoughts.

Onyx felt the burning sensation around her neck again. Dela's maynus . . . The nyphid was surely too weak to use it herself. Onyx pulled the choker from under her tunic and let it rest on her armor. Placing her hand on the round maynus to screen it from view, she silently bade it to grant energy to Dela.

The maynus grew warmer still, and the glow that squeezed between Onyx's fingers turned from white to blue. A fine spray of light emanated between the cracks and bathed the sun-loving nyphid with warm energy. The light on Dela was so soft and diffuse that anyone looking at her would think her highlighted by a lone shaft of sun cutting through the cloud cover.

But instead of invigorating Dela, the light caused the shrunken creature to whimper and draw away, as if the ray were steaming-hot water. A thready sound rose in her throat. The more the light sought Dela out, the more acute her pain seemed to become. After only a few seconds, her agony was unbearable to hear.

Onyx commanded the maynus to stop, sensing that somehow, through her long deprivation, Dela had lost the ability to absorb or draw energy from the light. The nyphid's shrill screams thankfully ended as soon as the light disappeared.

Foes stood shoulder to shoulder among the fallen bodies of knights and horses. The battle was momentarily forgotten as the men stared, immobilized by the wretched form twitching in the debris of the wagon. Though half-dead, shriveled to little more than a skeleton, the nyphid still seemed able to ignite some desire to touch her. Stippling himself, his side streaked with blood, forced his steed forward. Leaning from his saddle, he tried to scoop her up in his arms. There was a flash of pale blue light and two screams. Stippling flew backward, his horse staggering to stay under him. The knight was dazed, his armor scorched, but he was still alive. Had the nyphid been healthy, the jolt would have killed him.

Dela's screams rang long and loud. The frightful sounds pierced the men's ears so that they clapped their hands to their heads. Her tiny body convulsed, but with almost no energy left, the defensive discharge had been too much for Dela. The wailing stopped. Her grotesquely sunken face abruptly softened into a faraway smile, as if the tortured nyphid alone was privy to some glorious sight. Her golden hair took on the brief, backlit glow it had once possessed. Then, just as suddenly, Dela's wizened body slumped forward, exposing the wings on her back. Like a drying forest leaf, her still body withered away until nothing remained but her tattered tunic.

Onyx stood staring for several seconds in disbelief. She had seen a race die.

After a time, something caught Onyx's eye, and she blinked. She thought she spotted a tiny lightning bug against the gray sky, fluttering above the remains of Led's wagon. A firefly in winter? She blinked again. Now there were two, twin yellow tails dimly blinking in daylight. A cold winter breeze rose swiftly, caught the tiny insects up, and carried them out of her sight.

"Well, there goes my fortune," Led muttered at Onyx, dismissing the dead nyphid from his accounts as if she were just another dice wager. Dusting off his hands, the bounty hunter turned to consider the distance to his horses; since there was no longer precious cargo to fight over, he might as well escape. Stippling's voice brought him up short and settled his course of action.

"As I suspected, you're the worst of scoundrels," the knight thundered. "I'll see you brought to justice for this poor creature's death, in addition to that of my fallen comrade. . . ."

Led drew his sword at last and whirled around. "Then I'll have to make it an even eight knights!" he cried. "Now's your chance," he told Onyx before charging into the throng.

The fight resumed with greater intensity. On foot and horseback, the seven remaining knights trampled and cut their way through the frenzied ogres in an effort to unite in a defensive formation. The knights had a small advantage while they kept to their horses, but Yoshiki Toba had trained the ogres well in brawling.

Toba had tirelessly drilled the warty monsters to approach horsemen from the right side. The mounted knights found it clumsy and difficult to bring their shields across their horses, and thus their right flanks were exposed. The ogres rushed forward with their crude spears extended or massive clubs spinning through the air. There came a subhuman growl and a tremendous crash. After the attack, an ogre stood over the crumpled body of a knight.

The ogres were viciously efficient, especially compared to those Onyx had fought as a dragon. As the battle wore on, two ogres doubled up against one knight. The soldier deftly knocked aside a club as a spear slammed into his chest. The tip shattered against the knight's heavy breastplate, and the force of the impact knocked him from his saddle. A third ogre crashed its club against the forehead of the furiously kicking and biting horse. The animal stumbled. A second blow sent it thudding to the frozen earth.

One ogre pinned the fallen knight to the ground and another struggled to wrench the helmet from his head. The man's left arm was useless, strapped to the heavy shield, but still he thrashed desperately with his sword arm, cutting several of the ogres who bore down on him. His helmet tore free. The human roared his defiance—before a spiked club crushed his skull.

Near the remains of the wagon, Led fought, bobbing and weaving to land a sword thrust at the still-mounted Stippling. Onyx spied another knight rushing at the bounty-hunter's back. Preoccupied with reaching his goal, the knight did not see her stride over a dead knight to hold her hands, burning like rag-soaked torches, to his tunic. The knight whirled about just short of landing a blow to Led. Onyx recognized his young face—he'd led the procession through the pass. He gazed at her in confusion at first. Then he felt the fire at the hem of his tunic, spreading rapidly under his armor. With a yelp, he took off running, as if that might allow him to escape the flames that threatened to engulf him.

Led paused for an instant to watch the knight, fanning the fires of his own death by his flight. Smiling, Led tipped his sword to Onyx, then resumed his attack on Stippling.

Suffering greatly, the ranking knight managed at last to break off from Led. He and the three remaining knights drew up across the top of the pass, facing downhill toward where the ogres continued clubbing and kicking the unconscious or dead bodies on the ground. Suddenly one man charged from the group, driving the startled ogres back along the trail. His long sword cut great whistling arcs through the air, and his horse kicked and pawed at the oafish monsters. Several ogres dived for cover as the knight rushed headlong into their backs. His sword chopped straight down through an ogre's shoulder, cleaving its ribs. The body tumbled away and wrenched the sword from the knight's hand. Without pause, he pulled up a heavy mace slung on his saddle and smashed it down on the head of a second ogre, which crashed to the trail, lifeless, just yards beyond its comrade.

Onyx summoned her magic. Instantly, the knight's helmet was engulfed in swirling lights and colors too thick to see through. An ogre jumped forward and poked him in the back with a broken spear shaft. The knight slashed backward blindly, but his blade found no target. Another ogre reached forward and grabbed the man's ankle, then gave a mighty yank. The knight toppled from the saddle, howling over his now-broken leg, then disappeared under a tumult of ogres.

Led motioned toward the three remaining knights, who were now advancing at a trot down the hill. Onyx could see in his eyes that Led didn't relish the thought of fighting these warriors; riding knee to knee, they were obviously better trained than their doomed fellows. The ogres were fearsome in a swirling melee, but they weren't equipped to face charging war-horses directed by skilled riders.

Onyx stooped to the ground and began scraping at it with her dagger. Fortunately, the Solamnics ignored her and concentrated on their more outwardly dangerous adversaries.

The knights thundered straight through the ogres, who scattered like pins in every direction. The knights wheeled and galloped back again, this time shifting to the right to ride down the smaller group of ogres. As they stormed into the brutes, Onyx stood with a handful of dust, spit into it, and rolled her hands together to form a clay spike. She hurled the spike into the air above the knights. Pulling a startled Led along behind her, she darted out of range, behind the boulder on which they'd eaten lunch.

The sky seemed to split open. Enormous icicles, sharp and glistening in the sun, materialized in midair and rained down, slashing at knights and ogres alike. Most of the Solamnics found shelter beneath their shields, but the ice pounded the horses mercilessly. Stunned and bleeding, the animals stumbled and finally fell. They lay on the ground, kicking feebly.

The ogres suffered as much as the horses, wailing and howling in panic. The ice storm sliced them into bloody ribbons before they could crawl away.

Crouching beneath their battered, dented shields, the knights inched their way downhill. Once out of the maelstrom, the warriors scrambled back to their feet. They shook their heads to clear the awful ringing in their ears and cut the straps from their now useless shields.

But Led was not about to let them regroup. With the few remaining ogres at his back, he led the charge. Without their horses or shields, beaten and dazed by the hail, the knights fell before the assault. Led took great pride in slicing Stippling's pompous head from his shoulders.

When the fight was over, the smashed and broken bodies of the knights and their horses were mingled together on the narrow road with the hulking carcasses of slain ogres. An unfortunate survivor of the hailstorm whimpered pitifully through its tusks, watching in horror as a tremendous pool of blood pumped unstoppably from its mutilated thigh. Led stepped up behind the doomed creature and cut its throat to end its suffering. The remaining ogres didn't object, merely clutched more tightly at their own bleeding sword cuts or licked their wounds like animals.

Watching from the fringe, Onyx caught a glimpse of movement out of the corner of her right eye. She swung her head about. A distance down the road, a knight was struggling to his knees. His armor was scorched black, helmet gone, hair singed nearly off. It was the young knight she'd set on fire. Assuming he would burn to death, she'd forgotten about him in the heat of battle. Blood ran freely down the dented plate mail at one shoulder. His awkwardly twisted leg also bore the signs of a clubbing. The young knight staggered with a clumsy gait down the hill, toward the thick woods on the east side of the pass.

"Hey!" she shouted. "One of them is getting away!" Onyx looked frantically back toward the scene of the fight. The ogres were stripping the corpses, dividing up the dead men's possessions. Led stared into the shattered wagon, shaking his head sadly. Onyx called again, but no one seemed to hear her.

Swearing under her breath, Onyx touched the knife in the top of her boot and set off at a dead run after the wounded knight. Rounding a boulder, she entered the forest and stalked through the brush, looking for signs of the man's passing. She stopped suddenly and held her breath, listening. In the distance she heard the clanking of his heavy plate armor.

Onyx spied a bloody trail in the leaves and snow and followed it toward the sound of the jangling armor. She could hear the knight's ragged, labored breathing as he struggled to run. Eyes ahead, she nearly tripped over the shield he had dumped along the way. At last she caught sight of him, half running, half crawling, dragging a leg.

He looked frantically over his shoulder, his brown eyes wide with alarm. Seeing how quickly the woman was closing the gap, the knight pulled himself up to run faster. In his haste, he lost control of his wounded leg. The foot twisted to the side and caught on a sapling. He fell to his face on the ground. Cursing, the knight rolled over and tried to struggle to his feet again. Onyx launched herself in a flying leap and knocked him back to the cold ground.

Straddling his stomach, Onyx looked into his face. The knight's eyes were the deepest brown she'd ever seen. His soot-streaked cheeks were ruddy with burns. His Solamnic mustache had been singed to stubble above smooth lips. To her annoyance he showed no fear, and was, in fact, similarly evaluating her.

"How'd you put out the fire?"

"I dropped and rolled. You forgot about me."

Scowling, Onyx reached back, raised the knife from the cuff of her boot, and swung it down in an arc toward his face. The knight wrenched his head to the side and batted at her arm. The blade bounced off the young man's mailed sleeve and recoiled out of Onyx's hand. The knife landed in the underbrush several yards away.

"You're going to die, you know," she said coldly, reaching out to squeeze his throat with her bare hands.

"Eventually." He tossed her easily from his stomach and onto the ground. Gritting his teeth against the pain in his leg, the knight rolled onto his knees and pivoted to face her. His own knife was now in his palm. He waved it before him threateningly.

"Please run away," the knight invited in a patronizing tone. "I've no wish to compound my transgressions by killing a woman today."

"Transgressions?" she repeated, though she knew from the little Led had told her about the Solamnics that the knights valued honor above all else. "You mean bolting from a battle and leaving your dead friends to be mutilated by ogres?" she asked archly.

His eyes narrowed in anger. "My comrades were all good men and true, but my dying won't help them now."

"That doesn't sound very chivalrous," she said. "Won't

you burn in the Abyss for your cowardice?"

The knight winced perceptibly at her choice of words. "I believe honor and chivalry must be tempered by wisdom and discretion. I'll be rewarded in the hereafter for the balance of my good deeds." The young man shrugged and gave a rueful smile that made him tense in pain. "But who really knows how one will be judged when the time of reckoning comes? Today I chose to put that day off, so that I may live to avenge my friends."

"Oh, will you?" Onyx lashed out with her nails and raked his face, drawing three thin lines of bright red blood on his left cheek.

Scowling, the knight lunged toward Onyx with the knife. The cold blade bit into her shoulder, bringing an involuntary yelp of pain to her lips. She looked up at his young face in angry disbelief.

The knight shook his head almost sadly. "You can't act like a ruffian and expect to be treated like a lady. Stick to your spells, witch. You aren't very good at hand-to-hand fighting."

Humiliation made Onyx's blood boil like molten metal in her veins. Her fingers came upon a fist-sized stone. Scarcely moving a muscle, like a cat creeping up on a field mouse, she closed her hand around the cool rock. Onyx swallowed an evil smile, smelling revenge.

Suddenly, the young knight raised his forearm and his fist shot forward in a quick, effortless, bone-snapping punch to the bridge of Onyx's nose. The rock dropped from Onyx's fingers.

"Not much good at all," she heard the knight say distantly. As daylight spun into darkness, her last vision was of the young man's face. She would never forget, nor forgive, the pity in his brown eyes.

Chapter 9

The cold air brought Onyx back to consciousness. There was no sound around her but the wind whispering through trees. Her arm and face throbbed. Even her eyes ached. She lifted her cheek off the wet leaves and wrenched her swollen lids open. What was she doing in the woods? Where was everyone? And what was the matter with her face?

Onyx touched a finger to her nose, then winced from her own touch. Her entire face was swollen and tender and caked with blood. The knight's final blow came to mind all too vividly. There was no sign of him now. She had no idea how long she'd been out cold. The light filtering through the trees was dimmer than she remembered. Led would be looking for her.

Dragging herself up, Onyx painfully followed the knight's bloody trail back to the pass. Earlier, she had sprinted through these woods like a deer; now it hurt just to walk slowly. Cresting the hill where the ambush occurred, she blinked in disbelief.

The bodies of the dead knights and their horses lay in the pass, plucked clean of their gear, some half-eaten by ogres. The smashed wagon remained in its place. The area where Onyx's magical hailstorm had pounded down was still covered in shards of ice. But Led, the ogres, and their two horses were gone.

Only a blind man could have missed the bloody trail left by the knight and Onyx's charge. Led could easily have followed it to her, if only he had looked.

Which could only mean that he hadn't bothered.

The human had abandoned her with less thought than he had his lieutenant, though Toba's mysterious disappearance coupled with her own might have spooked the man. Perhaps he thought there was something sinister prowling the woods, stalking his little group. That wasn't beyond the realm of possibility, especially since he was, or had been, transporting a kidnapped faerie creature.

Still, the thought that he had abandoned her so easily angered and humiliated Onyx at the same time. Her hands curled into fists. Before she could decide what to do about either emotion, she sensed more than saw a presence nearby and whirled about.

"Who's—Kadagan!" Like a feather, the nyphid drifted down from the cliff face. His brown hair had lost some of its glow; his eyes, too, were dull. New lines had formed around his mouth and eyes, turning his normally thoughtful features sour and sad. His two-foot frame was now so emaciated that beneath the furry vest, his green tunic hung like a dirty sack from his shoulders.

"Kadagan!" she cried, rushing up to him. She had never been so happy to see anyone. "I'd hoped you'd followed us." Onyx's smile fell. "You already know what happened . . . to Dela."

"Yes."

Onyx peered around him. "Where's Joad? I could use

some of his herbs right now. I ran into some trouble, as you can see. Is he nearby?"

"He is dead."

Onyx's heart jumped. "How?" she finally gulped. "Did some other humans catch him alone? Not Led!"

"No, it was nothing like that," Kadagan replied flatly. "Seeing Dela's death was simply too much for him."

Onyx put her swollen face in her hands and sighed. "I'm sorry, Kadagan. I did what I could to save her."

"Didst thou? It seems thou hast found thy human form less disagreeable than anticipated."

Both the question and the statement startled her, and instantly put her on the defensive. "I've learned to tolerate it, if that's what you mean. What's that got to do with anything?"

"Only thou knows the answer to that."

Onyx's eyes narrowed angrily at the nyphid's typically cryptic response. "How was I to know a stupid ogre would break open the wagon before I had a chance to rescue Dela? I commanded the maynus to give her energy, but it was already too late. If the maynus couldn't save her, what else could I do? What did you expect me to do?"

"I expected thee to rescue Dela." Kadagan closed his blue eyes wearily. "None of that matters anymore. The time of nyphids on Krynn is over. I came to say good-bye."

"What will you do now?" she asked softly.

"I will give back the energy I have gathered throughout my life, to enlighten others."

"Are you going to seek out more qhen students? Are you—hey, what are you doing?"

The nyphid stood with his eyes closed, swaying softly like a seedling in the breeze. His face grew even more gray. Onyx shook his shoulders and called his name, but he didn't answer.

Suddenly the corners of the nyphid's mouth pulled up in a mysterious smile. His paper-thin eyelids fluttered open and took on that same faraway look Dela's had before she died.

"Stop this, Kadagan!" Onyx snapped. "You can't leave—"

His birdlike shoulders withered like a leaf between Onyx's hands. "No!" she cried heavenward. Kadagan couldn't be gone! There was so much she wanted to learn, things that only he could teach.

Something landed on Onyx's upper lip. She brushed it away angrily. It was a firefly—the third one she'd seen on this cold winter day. Then Onyx remembered her trip with Joad to the beautiful, mossy grotto. It was the first time the elder nyphid had spoken to her. With a voice husky from silence, he'd told her that the grotto remained green and covered with fireflies the year round.

"Each spends its lifetime gathering energy. They give it back to us by illuminating the night. That is a life well spent."

Khisanth finally understood why Joad had broken his silence and taken her to the grotto. She understood, too, why a pair of fireflies had appeared above the wagon when Dela died. And she wondered whether Joad and Dela had known to wait for Kadagan, if they expected him to follow them so soon.

Khisanth slowly lowered herself onto a boulder. She felt light-headed from all that had happened, and she could barely breathe through her swollen, broken nose.

As she sat there, Onyx glimpsed something shiny and black, lying in the dirt. Slipping from the boulder, she stooped and retrieved the object. An angry knot formed in her stomach as her fingers closed around a large, egg-shaped onyx stone. The young woman clenched it tightly, as if she could still feel the warmth of Led's hand on it. In her dragon form, she would have crushed it to black dust.

Crouching on the cold ground of the pass, Onyx's mind ran through all that had happened on this very bad day. The more she thought about it, the madder she got. Everything had gone sour: she'd failed to rescue Dela; all the nyphids were dead; the knight had broken her nose and gotten away; Led had left her to die.

The more she brooded, the more her anger focused on Led. He'd abducted Dela, incited the fight with the knights. He had fanned her fascination with her human form and then seduced her.

Seduced her as a human, Onyx reminded herself. It was this body's fault that she'd fallen for all Led's talk. A blush rose to her cheeks when she realized just how completely she'd been taken in. Her body had betrayed her as surely as Led had. Khisanth could not set things right where the nyphids were concerned, but she could have her revenge.

In the time it took her to close her eyes, Khisanth felt her human form stretch painlessly, until her long arms became clawed, her wings sprouted, her tail took shape. Good riddance, she thought. Springing skyward with her hind legs, the black dragon spread her wings, caught a gust, and was airborne.

A party like Led's left very noticeable tracks. The trail west was easy to follow. Mostly it kept to the road.

Onyx spotted the group near dusk. Led sat with his back to a boulder. As on the night before, the ogres were gathered behind him, already asleep. Two fires burned low. In the form of an owl, Khisanth hovered just above the treetops to keep them in sight while forming her exact plan.

She soared up into the darkened sky beyond the reach of the firelight. At the apex of her climb, she willed herself back into her dragon form. Diving now toward the sleeping ogres, she summoned the acid up her long throat. Her breath blanketed the sleeping ogres in deadly acid fog. They awoke screaming in surprise and anguish, but their cries died as quickly as they did.

Led jumped to his feet and backed in horror from the grisly scene. He was totally at a loss to explain what had happened to the ogres, for Khisanth was already beyond the range of his limited human vision. He thought he saw a shadowy, winged form, but it was nothing he could identify. His mind raced through the possibilities. He knew of no bird that large, certainly none that was capable of slaying ogres by dissolving them. He stood with sword in hand, waving it back and forth nervously, looking skyward.

One ogre on the fringe of the group had been spared the full force of Khisanth's spray. Its left hand and much of its skin was burned away, but it was alive and nearly insane with panic. Foolishly it scrambled to its feet and started to run, a Solamnic long sword slapping uselessly at its side.

Eyeing the creature, Khisanth soared back to the camp, opened her jaws wide, and unleashed a thin stream of steaming acid that hit the fleeing ogre on the right leg. It dropped, shrieking and weeping, to its knees. Drawing the sword, the ogre pivoted on its knees and slashed the weapon skyward in a pathetic attempt at self-defense. Its yellow eyes turned on Led for help, but the human had disappeared.

A huge, shadowy form slowly dropped into the range of the firelight, then landed on a rock.

In the shelter of the trees, Led froze with horror. A dragon! The bounty hunter's breath stopped, and his hands turned instantly cold. He had heard of such creatures but never really believed in their existence. He felt terribly exposed, afraid to move. As stealthily as possible, he stepped farther back behind a tree trunk.

Khisanth hopped down and approached the injured ogre. Trembling with fear, the creature continued to wave its sword pathetically at her from its knees.

"I had a change of heart just after I let loose that acid," Khisanth purred.

The ogre's fear intensified at the sound of her voice. He dropped the sword.

"Acid is a painful but quick way to die. I'd rather your boss and I have time to savor your screams."

Khisanth sank her teeth into the ogre's right arm at the shoulder, severing bone and muscle with a great tearing sound. The creature's horrendous wails cut the air. Khisanth savored the sounds as she bit off the ogre's limbs one by one, then dropped the torso into a snowdrift. Unconscious at last, the ogre twitched once. His blood puddled on and melted the snow, and then petered out.

Khisanth turned her tawny gaze on Led, who stood partially hidden behind a tree. Ever so slowly she slithered to the edge of the clearing, coming face-to-face with the bounty hunter; he merely watched her come, fear holding him in place.

The dragon reached out a claw and lightly scratched Led's right cheek.

Trembling, he touched a hand to his cheek and saw blood on his fingers. "W-What are you going to do with me?" he managed to gasp.

"I haven't decided yet," she said laconically.

He looked up at her, nervous beads of sweat rolling down his brow. "I've heard dragons like treasure," he said. "Take anything of value you see."

The dragon gave a hoarse, raspy laugh. "Do you think, human, that I need your permission to do anything?"

"N-No," he stuttered.

"*I'm* in charge now." The dragon wagged a sharp claw at him. "Come into the light, where I can see your green eyes better. Did I ever tell you, Led, that I thought they looked like wet emeralds?"

Unable to refuse, Led stepped back into the camp. The dragon's question puzzled him. The beast knew his name, spoke as if they'd met before. There *was* something vaguely familiar about the dragon's voice, but . . . Surely a man would remember if he'd ever met a dragon.

"What a difference a day makes, Led." The dragon's tone was lazy. "Just yesterday you were saying that dragons aren't as smart as humans. And here you are today, at the mercy of one. . . . I guess that means you're a stupid human."

Led blinked. The dragon's words had a familiar ring; he closed his eyes and feverishly searched his memory for the meaning. When he looked up again, though, all thoughts of the mystery fled. Onyx stood before him, her arms crossed, unashamed of her nakedness. Her nose was broken, and dark bruises circled both eyes like a mask.

The woman looked into Led's green eyes and saw confusion turn slowly to comprehension. "You left me to die, Led."

Wide-eyed, he looked at her. "I couldn't find you."

Onyx's eyes were narrow slits. "You obviously didn't look very hard. There was a path to me a mile wide."

"I looked," Led said quickly, his tone pleading, "but I was afraid to hang around the scene of the battle for fear of discovery. I thought you'd disappeared just like Toba."

"I didn't," Onyx said coldly, then her voice became almost brittle. "Speaking of your lieutenant, would you like to see him?"

"You know where Toba is?"

The woman raised one brow and smiled maliciously. "I have an idea." Her fingers clutched the thong that held the maynus and swords. "Free him," she told the globe.

As if from thin air, the charred and bloody body of Yoshiki Toba tumbled to Led's feet. Jumping back, the mighty mercenary could not suppress a scream.

"Well, I guess that nearly makes us even—on that score, anyway. I killed your friend. You caused the death of mine." Onyx said. At Led's puzzled look, she added, "The creature in the wagon. The one you kidnapped, she was the last female of her kind. You killed her. You killed her father and betrothed, as well. My friends."

Led looked more confused still. Perhaps his fear is dulling his wits, the woman thought.

"My gods, you're dense." Onyx gave him a patronizing look of pity. "Is your ego so great you actually think you talked me into joining your little band?" She threw back her head and laughed. "It was my plan all along. I tricked *you*. I was going to rescue the nyphid you'd kidnapped. I would have stolen her from under your nose if you hadn't mishandled the situation with the knights."

Onyx tapped a finger to her chin. "Now that I think about it, we're not even at all. But then," she purred, "I'm just getting started."

She began to pace around the frightened human. "I suppose you think I enjoyed our little encounter last night, too. Don't flatter yourself. It was all part of my plan." Onyx couldn't keep from blushing at her own reminder of their union. She rubbed her temple as if it pained her.

Led suddenly seemed to regain use of his senses. The old, fearless smile came to his lips. He reached for her hand, his own trembling. "You spoke in riddles last night, with your talk of dragons and the gathering armies. I dismissed the idea because I didn't want to be an ordinary grunt. I didn't know about, well, you being a dragon. We'd rise to the top, you and I. Didn't I say we made a great team?"

Onyx let her cold hand rest in his as she considered his anxious words.

"You've got to believe me, Onyx. I thought you were the one who abandoned me." Led bent his head to hers, his lips brushing her cool ones. He pressed himself against her naked body. "We were so good together. I should have known better."

"Yes, you should have," the young woman mumbled in agreement against his lips. Onyx could feel Led relaxing against her, eyes closed. In a heartbeat, the dragon Khisanth replaced Onyx. She jerked him off the ground and held him up like a child examining a bug. Before the mercenary could cry out, his handsome face disappeared into the dragon's jaws. Then it was too late.

There was nothing left for him to scream with.

PART TWO

Chapter 10

Khisanth's neck muscles tensed into thick black cords. Her scales rose like hackles. There it was again, that malevolent, watchful presence. Someone was definitely following her. Or something. The dragon squinted skyward from the trail she'd beaten through the tamarack to her lair. Turning a full circle, Khisanth scanned the horizon. As before, she saw nothing to confirm her suspicion.

Ever since she'd started across the Miremier to the Great Moors in search of a lair, the dragon had not been able to shake the feeling that someone was watching her. That was many lunar cycles ago, when snow had still blanketed the tamarack and ice had covered the ponds—not long after she'd eaten her human lover. Led's death was a delicious memory for Khisanth, and she used it to reckon time—one season after the devouring of Led, four lunar cycles since, and so on.

She'd discovered the huge fen she now called home on a practice flight with Kadagan past the sandy desert on the western edge of the Endscape peninsula. Strong westerly winds had made flight difficult that day and pushed the heavy, pungent scent of stagnant water and rotting humus within reach of her sensitive nostrils. Kadagan had told her that the Great Moors were so vast that it took an entire day for the winds to push the clouds from west to east above them. Some instinct had told Khisanth that she belonged in such a bleak place, that a lair in the swamp would soothe her soul the way a cold meal sated her stomach.

After the events at Needle Pass, Khisanth couldn't bear the thought of living near there. She felt no kinship with mountains. Neither was she interested in returning to the tiny, unremarkable lair the nyphids had found for her in the grasslands of Endscape. The dragon had never liked it anyway.

Khisanth's soul had stirred with the memory of the moor. Taking whatever treasure she fancied from Led and the dead ogres, Khisanth had gathered up her maynus choker and headed straightaway for the swamp. She had not looked back.

Khisanth usually explored her pond, her territory, by foot as a dragon. To practice her qhen techniques she would occasionally take on the forms of smaller creatures indigenous to the area—such as field mice or mundane serpents—to view the swamp as they would. The dragon had been curious to see how her lair looked from a muskrat's reed-and-mud dam in the center of her pond. The furry, beaverlike creature had been delicious.

Now, as she approached the hollow tree lair she'd taken for her own, Khisanth's gaze fell happily on the area surrounding it. Large, looming willows and other water-loving trees fanned out to where the earth met the dark purple sky. Low-growing shrubs covered everything else, hiding slippery bogs. At odd intervals the dead gray stumps of stripped pine trees poked skyward through the greenery, giving the tamarack an invitingly bleak appearance.

Khisanth walked the perimeter of her small pond. The southern edge was flanked by graceful willows whose draping branches fanned the filmy surface of the pond. Their size attested to their ancient origins; most of them towered more than three times Khisanth's height. Best of all, their trunks were thick with knotted roots that formed tall, vaulted archways where the water lapped against them.

Khisanth stepped into the chill, murky pond and waded toward an enormous tree whose roots arched majestically some eight feet above the pool's green surface. She bent her head to the water and half ducked, half swam, through the archway into the tree.

Nature had hollowed the place as if it were intended as a dragon's lair. Bright, glowing lichen that looked almost magical clung to the moist, corklike walls. Pond water reached halfway through the chamber. Toward the back of the lair, the tree climbed onto the bank and provided solid ground for a bed.

Living so close to water, Khisanth had learned to glory in swimming, to revel in the feel of tepid water gliding over her scales and filling her nostrils. The feeling would never replace that of flying, but it was a close second.

She discovered a whole new world underwater, where fish and other aquatic creatures provided tasty tidbits so flavorful they surpassed even the most tender moose. Though she was the largest creature to swim in these waters, Khisanth had learned to glide beneath the surface so quietly that she could surprise beavers on their dams and gobble them whole, before panic could spoil the flavor of their meat.

Territorial skirmishes had given Khisanth the chance to taste creatures whose flavors, no matter how rewarding the kills, were unappealing. The lizard-bird cockatrice's ability to turn her to stone with its touch caused her to forego her favorite trick of biting off its head. Instead, she'd leveled it with her acid, leaving little to taste. Then there'd been that giant poisonous toad. Khisanth still shivered at the taste of its slimy, scaleless body filled with bitter—if not deadly—poison.

Still troubled by the thought of being followed, Khisanth curled up on the floor of her lair and fell into her favorite pastime: counting and sorting the treasures hung on her choker. Though the necklace had been conceived to transport her cache and leave her claws free, its constant presence around her neck had become a comfort, a talisman. She'd taken to stringing the skulls of her enemies between the shiny weapons as spacers, to keep the trinkets fanned out around her entire neck instead of sliding down to hang in a clump from her throat like a lead weight. She removed the choker only to add new valuables, or to count and stroke her baubles, or to stare into the most valuable of all her prizes, the maynus globe.

Khisanth's thoughts frequently turned to those who had given her the maynus and what they had taught her. The memories began warmly enough, of Kadagan's patient training and Joad's healing hands. But the remembrances always turned prickly when she would recall the younger nyphid's last words to her. They had planted seeds of doubt that easily germinated in the fertile, damp silence of the moors.

Khisanth knew now that she had not done everything she could to save Dela. If she'd not gotten so distracted by her human form, she would have killed the entire party the second she was certain Dela was in the wagon. Even before.

The dragon suffered no guilt at this failure, but she did feel regret. She deeply rued that she'd been so horribly wrong about Led. Yet, she was convinced that she wasn't responsible for that, either. She blamed her faulty thinking entirely on her human form.

As the dragon began to muse about the nyphids and the limitations of humankind, a familiar, unpleasant sensation dragged her attention back to her lair. Khisanth fell as still as stone, her musings banished. There it was again, that feeling. . . . Whoever it was had come close to her home this time—too close for Khisanth's peace of mind.

She was rising to her feet when a piercing series of shrieks rang out above her willow tree. Khisanth clapped her claws to her ear holes. Her head felt as if it would be split in two by the hideous noise, which seemed to come from the Abyss itself.

Khisanth knew of only one creature that made that sort of noise—a dragon. The spine-tingling, high-pitched screeches might have come from her own mouth. Khisanth dived through the archway to the pond and looked up just in time to confirm her suspicions. The body of an enormous black dragon, wings fully extended, sped away through the dusky sky. Its underbelly was well scarred.

Khisanth looked upon the first fellow dragon she'd seen since before the Sleep. The strange wyrm tucked its wings, turned sharply, and dived right for her lair. When it seemed the dragon would plunge straight into the tree, a slight twist of its wings sent it into a sharp bank. The wyrm—Khisanth could see he was a male now—leveled off just yards above the delicate willow branches, blasting leaves from their limbs. Still moving impossibly fast, the dragon curled his lips back from the yellowed knives of his teeth. The night exploded in a crackling billow of stinking green acid.

Bile engulfed the graceful, arching branches of Khisanth's beloved willow. The ancient tree split and splintered. Great holes opened as branches exploded and spun into the air. Raising a claw, the attacking dragon boldly swooped to within a tail's length of his astonished target. Retracting one talon, he raked two deep scratches into the living wood above Khisanth's head. Then, with a mighty pump of his wings and a last threatening screech, he rose above the sizzling willow and into the dark sky.

The shriek of challenge finally shook Khisanth from her daze. She gave a mighty slap of her tail that sent a wave of water crashing over the still-smoking husk of her willow tree, washing away whatever was left of the other dragon's acid. The corrosive bile sputtered wherever it touched the water. Khisanth's lair at the base of the tree was still largely intact, though hideously scarred.

Think twice, act once, Kadagan had always said. Khisanth called on her qhen training to still the fury and the urge to chase after the wyrm. She had learned the price of such foolishness the hard way—lost information from her first battle with ogres, pain and humiliation from the disastrous skirmish with the young Solamnic Knight at Needle Pass.

At least this unprovoked attack had solved one mystery. "He's obviously the one who's been watching me," Khisanth muttered aloud. But the intent of the assault still puzzled her. The dragon's acid could easily have destroyed her lair, if that was his goal. He was either a bungler or a rival for the same territory.

Her fury turned to puzzlement, then curiosity. Another dragon . . . It would be interesting to talk to another of her kind. Looking at her still-smoldering lair, she thought it unlikely he had conversation on his mind.

Khisanth sprang from the ground and into the air. She headed west, in the direction the other dragon had taken. From her one flight over the rest of the moors, when she had scouted for her lair, she knew the place was enormous. Even a simple flight from east to west would take many days, and the moor was twice as long from north to south as it was from east to west. A shrub-by-shrub examination could take a lifetime. Pushing herself hard, she hoped she would gain enough ground to catch sight of the dragon again, but she couldn't be sure of his flight trail.

After some time, when her wings began to ache and she had seen only Lunitari in the dark night sky, she landed. The dragon adopted the shape of the first creature she saw. Upon questioning, the blue-necked mallard admitted seeing another flying creature, much larger than itself. But it had never encountered the winged creature on the ground.

Khisanth traveled westward on foot in a variety of guises, from snout-nosed aardvark to zebra, questioning everything she met for some sign pointing to the other dragon's lair.

Her first useful clue came when, as a curly-tusked warthog, she learned of a place over which an enormous winged creature flew regularly. The other warthog had also heard loud rumblings just beyond a ridge of rocks to the north and west. Changing yet again into the sleek, weasel-like body of a meerkat, hoping to be overlooked as a rodent by a wary dragon in his lair, Khisanth scampered over a low ridge.

From the rise Khisanth surveyed the stretch of marsh ahead. With her magic, she detected dark emotions in the vicinity, too far away to read but too strong to come from even the largest bear, or even the deadly, many-headed hydra.

Khisanth knew better than to approach the other dragon's lair too closely, knowing from her own experience that his senses would warn him of intruders if they were too bold. Instead, she took to the sky as a dragon to scout at a distance.

A dragon's imprint on the area was unmistakable to another dragon's eye. The largest trees were withered and blackened, but left standing as signs of ownership. Where boulders jutted above the water or marshy ground, they were cut deeply with parallel claw marks.

At the center of this area was a knob of ground covered in reeds and rocks. The stones looked unnatural, as if deliberately placed there ages before. The pattern suggested a series of concentric rings, but most of the rocks were now tumbled and overgrown with rushes and swamp grass. Near the center of this knoll there was a blackness, clear indication of a lair.

Khisanth intended to leave a message not unlike his—the destruction of her tree. Blood once again pulsed pleasantly behind her eyes. Using the maynus, she banished the darkness from the night sky. A blinding beam of light shot forward from her claws to the entrance of the wyrm's lair, enveloping it in absolute brilliance.

As Khisanth had hoped, the other dragon crawled from the mouth of its lair and into the painfully bright light. Blinking against the light, the other dragon held up a claw arm to block it out. It kept the light from cutting at his eyes, but still he could see nothing but blinding whiteness around him.

Khisanth now had perfect opportunity to study her fellow black dragon, illuminated as he was. He had deep age lines around his eyes. His graying, spotted lips sagged on the sides like an old man's jowls, revealing more teeth missing than not. He was decked out in a necklace of sky-blue sapphires and forest-green emeralds with a matching anklet. Circling his massive head was a pearl diadem, a large pear-shaped ruby at its center.

Khisanth allowed herself a brief, smug smile at his pain and confusion. She chose her first words carefully. "Now, dragon, we meet on equal footing." She hadn't heard her voice in so long that its deep, even timbre pleased her.

The other dragon held as still as stone for a moment. His eyes, one orange, the other blue, shifted from side to side. "Is that you, Talon?" his old voice rumbled, curious and concerned. "Put out that light so that I can see you."

"No, I'm not Talon. And as for the light, answer my questions first, and I will consider dimming it." Khisanth watched for the other dragon to ready his breath weapon. His chest rose slowly, evenly. Still, her eyes never left him. "First, so that we may converse like civilized dragons, tell me your name."

"You say you're a dragon, but you don't sound like one. If you were a true wyrm, you'd know that dragons are not civilized. However, if you allow the absurdity of the term, 'civilized' dragons don't toy with each other this way. Either kill me," the older dragon challenged, "or douse the light so that I may see."

Khisanth's fury rose. "Civilized dragons don't attack each other without provocation," she countered.

"Of course they do. That's *all* they do. You really don't know a thing about dragons, do you?"

"So you admit you destroyed my lair!" Khisanth accused.

"Don't be ridiculous. I'm far too old for that sort of young-bull-marking-his-territory foolishness—haven't done anything but hunt small mammals and find new lairs in years."

The old dragon's confusion seemed too real to be dismissed. Besides, now that she could study him more closely, this old wyrm didn't look like the dragon she'd seen silhouetted against the sky above her lair. "Who are you, then?"

"The light, please."

"Oh, yes." Khisanth touched the maynus and silently bade it to go dark. The area sank abruptly into soothing dusk, and Khisanth landed before the cave.

"Much better," said the dragon. He blinked hard several times, opened his eyes and sighed. "Are you still there? It'll take some time for the spots to go away." He squinted into the darkness at Khisanth. "Ah, there you are. A young one—that explains a lot. Among humans I was known as Pitch, but dragons call me Pteros." He drew back suddenly. "You haven't come to slay me and take my treasure, have you?"

"No. I came to learn why you attacked my lair. But if it wasn't you, who was it—another dragon that lives nearby?"

Pteros looked thoughtful. "This dragon . . . was its belly covered with scars? Did it leave its mark on a tree—two straight talon tracks, with squiggles for tails?

"Yes and yes! How did you know?"

"That's Talon. I know because I've seen his marks outside lairs for nearly a decade, which is how long he's chased me around the moor."

"What does he want?"

"Treasure."

"Why hasn't he just slain you and been done with it? And why did he flee before fighting me?"

"You give me little credit," Pteros grumbled, then shrugged. "Talon hasn't managed it because I keep one step ahead of him, moving before he can corner me." His wrinkled lids squinted. "Frankly, I'm none too happy that you were able to find me."

"It wasn't too difficult," snorted Khisanth. "You left tell-tale claw marks on the boulders. "Why don't you go kill this Talon instead of running?"

"I told you, I'm too old for that fighting-over-territory sort of thing."

"Sounds like you're doing just that, whether you mean to or not," observed Khisanth. "If you don't wish to fight, why don't you just move from the moors?"

"Where would I move to? There isn't another swamp as lush and wide as this in all of Ansalon. Besides," Pteros continued without guile, "now that he's got you to focus on, he'll forget all about me. Nice knowing you." With that, the bejeweled old wyrm stretched his arthritic wings and swung his heavy tail around to reenter his lair.

"Wait a minute!" cried Khisanth, annoyed that he had so blithely dismissed her. "Why shouldn't *I* kill you and take your treasure?"

Pteros stopped, turned his orange eye on Khisanth, and tapped a sagging jowl, his expression thoughtful. "The last time a dragon asked me that was at a battle with Huma during the Third Dragon War." The dragon chuckled in fond memory. "Now *there* was a battle. Not this petty squabbling over swampland."

Khisanth's eyes grew wide. "You fought against Huma? *The* Huma? Huma Dragonbane?"

"Was there more than one?"

"Just how old *are* you?" she asked, studying his toothless jaw and wrinkled skin with new appreciation.

"What season is it? Summer?"

Khisanth nodded.

"Then that would make me one thousand three hundred seventy-eight human years, near as I can reckon." At Khisanth's gasp of awe, Pteros shrugged again, looking unimpressed. "I got a bit of extra time from the Sleep." He rolled his eyes. "Don't get me started on *that* subject."

Khisanth wanted to get him talking about everything that had to do with the dragons of old. Her mind reeled from the possibilities. She could learn from such a venerable dragon. A wyrm from the old days, when their kind had ruled by fear. One who had fought for their queen, Takhisis.

"I won't kill you if you agree to an arrangement."

Pteros used a sharp claw to scratch at a long, white scar on his belly. "And what arrangement would that be?"

"Take me on as an apprentice. Teach me everything you know. Tell me about the old days, when dragons were the rulers of all they saw."

"You've got that a little—"

"You look as if you've seen your share of battles," Khisanth cut in. With an admiring look she surveyed the other dragon's scars, though the flabby muscles beneath them gave her pause. "In exchange, I'll get you back in shape so that you can fight back against Talon."

"But I don't want to fight. I just want to be left alone in my old age to enjoy my hoard."

"Your old age will end prematurely if your luck runs out. You can't duck and run forever. Why should a dragon who fought Huma run at all?"

Pteros was strangely silent. "You're awfully sure of yourself for one so young. What help could you give me against Talon? You know nothing of dragon ways."

"I think you've seen an adequate display of my abilities. I managed to hold you at bay with a beam of light. Besides," she shot back with a smirk, "if you're any sort of teacher, I'll learn the ways of dragons so quickly I'll be the one concerned about *your* deficiencies when the time comes to face Talon."

Pteros answered her jibe with a toothless smirk. "There's one thing you must first do to persuade me you aren't simply after my treasure." The old dragon extended a talon and scratched his other, withered claw arm. Drawing blood, Pteros held the limb toward Khisanth. "We must blood-mingle in the tradition of those who came before."

Khisanth did not hesitate, thrilled to be participating in a ritual of her race. She tore open a scale viciously in her eagerness. Blood welled up; Khisanth's bright red droplets ran with Pteros's and mingled between their pressed arms. For long seconds, both creatures could see into the other's heart and mind. Recognizing purity of purpose in each other, they drew back from the ritual almost reluctantly.

"The arrangement is sealed," Pteros said with sudden sternness. "Never trust a dragon with whom you have not blood-mingled."

As steam rose from their blood on the chill night, the ancient dragon's words sounded almost prophetic.

Chapter 11

Pteros hauled his bulk from the pond and slithered onto the bank, the ground made warm and marshy by an unusually muggy late-autumn day. "Have you been practicing your spells, Khisanth?" Tiny green circles of algae clung to his scaly black body from snout to tail. "How about the fireball you begged me to show you?"

A smile of joy pulled up the corners of Khisanth's leathery mouth. "Of course. I have a few bugs to work out, but I can conjure a flame and toss it, though not very far. How about you? Have you been flying to strengthen your wings?"

"Of course. Don't I look trimmer?" Pteros stood on the bank and preened, admiring his newly tightened muscles.

The black dragons were cooling their scales in the tepid pond outside Khisanth's lair. It had taken all of her skill in persuasion to get the taciturn Pteros to partake of the pond's soothing waters. She had to talk him into doing anything more strenuous than sitting in his lair and counting his treasure. Pteros was proving to be fainthearted and rather joyless, as if he had already given up on his life.

Strangely, the old wyrm had opened up a whole new world for Khisanth. He knew, though seldom used, a wide range of difficult spells. The dragon shared his secrets willingly enough, but it was clear he could see little point in it. Khisanth was determined to learn everything he knew, and she hoped to renew the great old wyrm's zeal for life at the same time.

Pteros was reclining now in the webby shadows cast by the bare branches of a neighboring willow. The leaves of the tamaracks had turned color and tumbled from the trees since the dragons had blood-mingled. The landscape was the color of rust and mud. Brown cattails drifted apart in fuzzy white tufts. Plaintive, rhythmic honking above signaled the departure of the last of the gray-and-white geese that inhabited the summer moors.

"Your skill with magic is rather obvious," said Pteros from the shadows. "You're fortunate the skill comes so easily to you. Human spellcasters must spend years studying and memorizing words to perform even the simplest incantations."

"Yet another sign of their inferiority," sniffed Khisanth. The hot sun beat down on the dragon as she slithered onto the bank, settling onto her haunches. She let her hind legs dangle in the stagnant water. Her jaws snapped open to catch a large dragonfly.

"I'm curious about something," said Pteros after a time. "How did you learn to shapechange? It's a very advanced spell for one so young."

Khisanth saw no danger in telling the elder dragon about the nyphids—to a point. "It's not a spell, really. It's more a mental discipline." She tried to explain qhen as best she could, assiduously avoiding any mention of Led or the nyphids' deaths.

"I'm too old to learn it myself. Just show me how you do it," invited Pteros.

Khisanth spotted a red-winged blackbird springing from a withered cattail. The dragon unconsciously hooked an eyetooth over her lip as she concentrated. Her bones contracted painlessly, her wings shrank, and her leathery hide changed to feathers. Khisanth swooped around Pteros's head as a red-winged blackbird and settled her tiny, clawed feet onto the webbing of his folded left wing.

Pteros's face was filled with admiration. "I've heard of a few dragons who could change shape, but they could never become anything so small."

Khisanth hopped down from Pteros's wing and reassumed her dragon form. Situating herself in the shade, the dragon closed her eyes for a languorous moment and sighed with contentment. "Your turn, Pteros," she said, her voice lazy. "Tell me about the time before the Sleep. Were you at the battle where Takhisis struck down Huma?"

"You mean when she betrayed us?"

There was bitterness in his voice, which surprised Khisanth. Her eyes turned skyward anxiously. "Aren't you afraid of her retribution for such words?"

Pteros shrugged. "Thinking, speaking, it's all the same to a god." He pulled his wings tight to his body and dived into the pool headfirst, surfacing with a snort and a spray of water.

The ancient dragon slithered onto shore again. "No, I wasn't at the final battle with Huma. I was quite young. Even younger in experience than you now are."

"Yet you were good enough to fight in the Third Dragon War?"

"The *geetnas* pushed the young wrymlings more in my time, knowing that the queen was gearing up for war. They emphasized magical ability, as well as flight." Pteros settled himself into a ball. "It was a different time then, Khisanth. Dragons roamed freely, beloved children of the gods, and humans were but links in the food chain. But that was before we were betrayed."

The dragon's eyes took on a distant look. "Prior to the Sleep, one thousand thirty years before what the humans call the Cataclysm, the Great Moors were nothing but sea. I lived my young adulthood far away from here, in a small marsh to the west. My lair was at the mouth of what is still known as the Vingaard River.

"The seasons had passed perhaps ninety-six times in my life. I'd fought in fewer battles in the Third Dragon War than you could count on a claw hand"— Pteros softly touched a claw to a long-faded scar —"when the dragon elders announced our queen's defeat at the hands of the knight, Huma Dragonbane. In truth, it was the dragonlance that bested Takhisis. Huma was simply a warrior who had perhaps a bit more skill than most."

The old dragon's expression turned bitter. "The end result was the same, though. Takhisis exchanged our freedom for hers, ordering us to go underground and sleep. She was our goddess, and we had no choice but to obey, or die.

"Now I'm an old dragon," he continued bitterly. "Most of my prime years were spent in slumber." With an oddly equal measure of satisfaction and sadness, he gazed at his own reflection in the still water. "In the Sleep I did not age as I would have if awake, but those years are still lost to me."

"You have plenty of years ahead of you, if you'd only stop thinking of yourself as old and feeble," said Khisanth.

"I'm not certain I want to be useful in the world that exists today," muttered Pteros. "Nearly two hundred years ago I awoke underground without explanation, along with a handful of other dragons who had turned old while they slept. Each of us clawed our way to the surface, only to find Krynn a much different place than we had left it. Instead of soaring above men and striking proper terror in their hearts, dragons made pacts with ogres and their ilk," Pteros spat, a droplet of green acid escaping his jaws in his disgust.

"Pacts with ogres?"

Pteros nodded. "These agreements are part of Takhisis's newest plan to rule. She appeals to the corrupt natures of all creatures in an effort to recruit them. Once she attempted to dominate the world with dragons alone as her soldiers, and she lost. Now she thinks she needs more than her own children to defeat her foes."

"I've had no one to ask this before, but I have wondered. How is it that she's returned now?"

"Many human years ago, Takhisis found a way to Krynn from the Abyss. She walked the land as a human, awakening the elder dragons she'd known before the Sleep and telling them of her plan."

"That could explain why I didn't awaken until recently, and why you're so much older than I," mused Khisanth. "I'd been little more than a wyrmling at the time of the banishment. What happened to the other dragons who awoke with you?"

"We went our separate ways. I suspect most of them have joined Takhisis's armies."

"Why haven't you? Don't you want dragons to regain control and rebuild the world as you remember it?"

"Why haven't I?" repeated Pteros. "For the same reason I don't fight back against Talon—I'm too old."

Pteros snatched up a gopher that wandered too near in search of water, popping the silky creature into his mouth and chewing absently. "Frankly, I don't see victory for the Dark Queen this time either. She's casting her fate with humans and other rot, the very same creatures who engineered her last defeat." He spat gopher bones through the holes of his missing teeth.

"So Takhisis is personally gathering these forces? Is there somewhere I can go to see her?"

"Yes," chortled Pteros. "The Abyss, for the Dark Queen is trapped there again." At Khisanth's puzzled look, Pteros searched for words to untangle the rumors he'd heard over the years.

"After opening the portal to the Abyss, Takhisis was able to walk the face of Krynn, her avatar a dark-haired young woman, though in that construct her powers were minuscule compared to her five-headed chromatic dragon form. Then, suddenly, inexplicably after ten years, the path was barred. She's sought a new one since, which is really the crux of her newest plan. She seeks to recruit humans because she wishes to control them, and through them her armies from the Abyss. She intends to reopen the portal so she can return to

Krynn in her powerful dragon form."

Pteros gave Khisanth a conspiratorial look. "If I were Takhisis, I'd unite dragons of all colors and leanings, appealing to their racial heritage to persuade them to overpower humans."

Khisanth removed a stone from between the talons on her right hind leg, considering Pteros's words. "I've heard that the humans in her army rise to power by uniting with a dragon mount."

"Yes, I've heard that, too."

Khisanth squeezed her eyes shut. She'd hoped Pteros would be able to deny it. "Surely, once the superiority of a dragon's skills are demonstrated, the dragon and human in this arrangement have equal rank, if the dragon is not actually in command," she said.

Pteros simply shook his large, many-horned head.

"I would never willingly subordinate my skills to any human," said Khisanth firmly. "The rules would have to change if I joined the army."

"Ah, the arrogance of youth," muttered the old dragon.

Khisanth didn't consider it as arrogance; she simply couldn't see herself being ruled by a human. She believed there was always a way to turn a situation to her advantage. Like the situation with Talon. She knew it was just a matter of time before he struck again. She was preparing herself for it, learning new attack spells. Thoughts of the territorial dragon brought a question to mind. "Why hasn't Talon joined the army?"

"You'd have to ask him that. We haven't exactly chatted recently." Pteros touched the gems around his neck. "I suspect he's too busy coveting the treasures I've acquired in my long life to volunteer his services for free."

Khisanth admired the jewels around Pteros's neck. Her gaze clung to the pearl-and-ruby diadem around his dark head. Those two items alone were certainly worth fighting for. According to Pteros, they represented only a small portion of the treasure stored away in his lair. Khisanth had never been allowed in that hallowed place. If the gems he wore were any sampling, though, Pteros's treasure had to be beyond imagining in volume and value.

She caught the old wyrm admiring the maynus on her choker. "That's quite an interesting piece. I can't identify the glowing gem."

Khisanth hesitated. Her first instinct was to shield the globe and tell Pteros to mind his own treasure. She knew too little about the maynus to tell him much, anyway. Her gaze lingered on the worldly, magically advanced dragon. Struck with a thought, Khisanth made a quick decision. She told him all she knew about the maynus. Pteros's wrinkled snout pulled up into the first expression of interest Khisanth had seen.

"So it's an artifact, not a gem. You don't understand how it works?" he asked. Khisanth shook her head. Pteros reached out a claw arm. "May I see it?"

Khisanth hesitated again, then tugged the maynus from the choker vine and, between cupped claws, handed her most precious treasure to Pteros.

Pteros held the glowing globe reverently, turning it over and over. He peered inside. "Lightning . . ." He looked up at Khisanth. "Do you know where it's from? An artifact's origin can tell a lot about its function."

Khisanth did know. "Kadagan said something about its coming from the elemental plane of lightning. That fact meant nothing to me at the time."

Pteros was frowning. "It means nothing to me, either. I know of four elemental planes of existence—air, earth, fire, and water, but not lightning. Perhaps this Kadagan was confused." He continued looking into the globe closely.

"I don't know," said Khisanth. "He was very specific." She looked over his arm into the globe. "Do you think you can figure it out?"

"There's a fairly simple spell of identification that might tell us something," Pteros said as if to himself, "but it takes forever to cast. You say you've used it several times by just telling it what you wanted?" Khisanth nodded. Pteros clutched the globe. His eyes took on a greedy gleam. "Then let's give it a try."

"Wait!" cried Khisanth. "Do you think that's a good idea? I

mean, we don't know what it will do."

"And we never will unless we test its scope," said Pteros. He thumped his own chest. "If there's one thing I know, it's magic."

Khisanth felt strange playing the timid dragon to Pteros's brash one. She'd hoped, however, to see some spunk in the old dragon, so she nodded her head in approval.

"Let's see," said Pteros, his blue and orange eyes glittering with enthusiasm, "we'll try something relatively simple first." He closed his eyes and said, "Transport us to the meadow by the hedge of sumac."

Khisanth tensed involuntarily. In the beat of a heart, she and Pteros stood exactly where he'd directed.

"Not too impressive, since we both already know how to teleport," said Pteros. "I'll try something a little more difficult."

Khisanth looked about the wide meadow. "First, get us back home. I don't like standing out here in a field with a powerful artifact for Talon and everyone to see."

"Right you are," said Pteros. Holding the globe aloft, he intoned, "Maynus, take us home."

The sphere flashed. Fingers of light stretched out and pierced the two dragons, sawing through their bodies. There was no pain, only an intense tingling where the twitching light passed. Suddenly Khisanth felt much lighter. She didn't know what was happening and looked at Pteros for the answer. The older dragon tried to say something, but no sound reached Khisanth's ears. As more and more fingers of light wrapped around Pteros, Khisanth could see through him. The other dragon's black body dissolved into sparkling motes and was drawn, or rather flowed, into the maynus in his talons!

Khisanth's astounded mind drew up a vision of Yoshiki Toba similarly disappearing into the maynus, followed by the sight of his charred body tumbling to Led's feet. Frenzied, she raised herself on her hind legs and flapped her titanic wings to get away from the device, but no air beat against them. Her wings had no more substance than thistledown. Roaring furiously, Khisanth, too, swirled away into the globe.

Still roaring, the young dragon found herself immersed in a maelstrom of light and sound. Enormous bolts of blue-white lightning flashed all around her rematerialized body. Thunderclaps buffeted her so that it was difficult to inhale. The air smelled heavily, even tasted strongly, of chlorine. She could see Pteros next to her, his jaw moving in speech, but the thunder was so loud it was impossible to hear anything else. Green clouds boiled past in every direction—right, left, above, even below. There was no earth nor water beneath her, only air.

With that realization, Khisanth dropped like a rock. She instinctively clawed and scrambled and flapped her wings. Finally she rose, or at least was suspended. When she stopped the motion of her wings for a moment, she plunged again. Khisanth wasn't at all sure that it mattered, since there didn't appear to be any ground to crash into. Still, she strained her wings to keep from falling.

Nearby Pteros appeared to have caught on to the same notion and was fluttering his wings, too. She saw him working his jaw again. A shimmering cone shape radiated through the air from his snout. The wide end of the cone engulfed her, and she suddenly heard Pteros all too well.

"I've cast a shout spell!" he bellowed.

Khisanth clapped her claw hands to her ear holes, certain the drums would break. "Where are we?" No cone of sound spread from her mouth.

"Your voice isn't affected by my spell!" he hollered in explanation. Khisanth winced from the ear-splitting sound of his voice. "I presume you're wondering what happened, too! Frankly, I don't know—"

Pteros's deafening words were cut off by the sound of breaking glass. Khisanth could see before Pteros that the gems in his elaborate pearl-and-ruby diadem and sapphire necklace were shattering from the vibrations of his tremendously amplified voice. She thought of her maynus. Raising a talon to her choker, she remembered in a panic that she and Pteros were now inside the globe.

Before the riled young dragon could even put voice to the realization, an unearthly sound cut through the thunder. "The thing you call 'maynus' is here." The voice wasn't painfully loud like Pteros's.

Both dragons fluttered around to find the source of the sound. A round object, or perhaps a creature, floated about a dragon's length away, though distance was difficult to judge in the featureless ether. It was a sphere, about the size of a dragon's head, and pearly. It was lit from within by flashes of multicolored light. Spears of lightning shot and twisted outward from it as the object approached, seeming to draw itself along as if the crackling branches were legs.

The ball-like object passed near the dragons, where it spoke in an airy, reverberating tone, "Follow, Khisanth and Pteros."

Looking at each other in question, the two dragons found themselves drifting along behind the odd creature. Something about it seemed vaguely familiar to Khisanth. It led them to a blue, egg-shaped sphere and urged them to pass inside.

Instantly the booming thunder faded to a soft, distant thumping. The air was blue and clear; the odor of chlorine dissipated. Lightning continued to arc around the blue sphere, but never penetrated it.

"There's no need to flap your wings here," said the pearly globe. "You will simply float."

Khisanth let her wings drop to her sides and bobbed without effort. "Where are we?" she demanded. "How do you know our names? And where is my maynus?"

"In your Prime Material world, I was that which you called 'maynus.' "

"This is all gibberish," growled Khisanth. "Just tell me where on Krynn we are."

"I believe I know!" screamed Pteros. His voice blasted through the clear air, reminding him that it was still magically amplified. Blushing self-consciously, Pteros ended the spell's effect. "We're not on Krynn at all," he finished much more softly.

Khisanth scowled at Pteros, dismissing him by turning her scowl on the glowing creature. "Just tell me where I can pick up my maynus on the way out."

"I am what the nyphids called 'maynus,' but I am no longer yours."

"You don't seem to understand what it is I'm looking for, so I'll explain it to you," Khisanth offered with mock patience. "My maynus is a little inanimate globe that glows. You're a big, 'animate' thing that, well, glows." She tried to peer through the bubble. "A tiny luminous ball would be easy enough to overlook in all this lightning."

The creature throbbed slightly. "I will say this one more time. The thing you called 'maynus' is me. Here in my home world, you see my true appearance at last."

"—Or perhaps Pteros dropped it by the pond when he caused us to teleport to wherever we are," Khisanth suggested as if the creature hadn't spoken.

"We didn't teleport here at all, did we?" Pteros asked the creature. "The maynus 'gated' us to the plane of elemental air, didn't it?"

"Yes. . . ."

"I thought so," Pteros smirked.

"And no. I brought you to the plane of lightning. It's a plane of finite scope and tremendous energy, a 'quasi-plane' your wizards call it, which lies betwixt your world and that of elemental air. This haven where we can speak, and where you are safe from the lightning, is a pocket or bubble of elemental air."

Khisanth felt her patience run threadbare. "So what about my maynus?" she blurted.

Unperturbed, the creature continued. "I am an elemental being native to this plane. Millennia ago, I and others of my kind were taken against our will to your world on the Prime Material plane by the race known as nyphids."

Finally, something Khisanth could understand. "What do you know about the nyphids?"

"Everything. The very first of that species were the off-spring of a lightning elemental like myself and another elemental being from the neighboring quasi-plane of radiance. Being of two worlds, they belonged neither here, nor in the radiant world, and thus became our servants. Eventually they rebelled against their servitude and escaped to find a new home for themselves. They settled on the Prime Material plane. But they didn't leave alone. With the aid of the magic we had taught them, they captured many elemental beings and took us along as the source of their magic. I was one such victim.

"In your world, I was a slave, trapped inside my own form. Like a genie in a bottle, I could use my powers only to carry out another's orders. Unsuspecting of my true nature, you were also unaware of the many traditions and prohibitions regarding maynus use among the nyphids. Your carelessly worded request allowed me, after thousands of years, to finally return here, to my home.

"Unintentional though it was, you released me from bondage. As repayment I will return you to the Prime Material plane. Prepare yourselves."

Khisanth could hardly grasp all that the elemental creature had revealed about the nyphid's nature. What she did understand was that she'd lost her most valuable treasure. "If you truly are the maynus, your freedom has cost me a very valuable and powerful artifact. We need to settle on a purchase price for your liberty."

The maynus darkened. "On the contrary, I have offered you something of inestimable value—passage back to your home. Take the word of someone who knows the pain of exile. You cannot leave this place unaided."

"Now, look here—"

The elemental creature's attention became distracted to something outside their calm pocket. "There's Fraz, an old nemesis I haven't seen for an eon. . . ." The elemental globe began to slip through the edge of the bubble. "We have a score to settle." With that, the creature disappeared.

"Wait! Don't leave us here!" cried Pteros, starting to follow.

"Let it go. It's not going to help us," muttered Khisanth.

The old dragon whirled on her. "No thanks to you! We could have been home by now if your greed hadn't gotten in the way."

"*My* greed?" Blood pounded at Khisanth's temples. "Whose was it that brought us here in the first place? 'My, what a nice gem that is, Khisanth,' " she whined, mimicking Pteros. " 'If there's one thing I know it's magic.' "

Pteros looked more smug than chastised. "I believe I told you more than once that I'd rather you'd left me alone to polish my gems." He looked around sadly at the empty settings in his diadem and necklace. "Now I have nothing."

"So this is *my* fault?—Oh, never mind," Khisanth sighed at last. She was letting her temper and frustration control her. Khisanth closed her eyes and concentrated on her breathing, drawing in long, slow breaths to calm herself. When the blood slipped at last from her temples and freed her mind to think, she said, "We've got to figure a way out of here." She opened her eyes and looked at Pteros. The older dragon was just short of wringing his claws, his eyes wide with apprehension. Khisanth ventured, "What about teleporting?"

"Not powerful enough, I'm sure, to get us to a completely different plane of existence." Pteros scratched his wrinkled brow. "There is a gate spell, but I've never used it. I'm afraid I'm feeling a little too shaky to try it."

Khisanth knew it was hopeless to try to talk him into it. "We got in here, so there's got to be a way out. Didn't the elemental say the quasi-plane of lightning adjoins the plane of air? We'll just find that border and keep going until we find one that bumps into the Prime Material plane."

"I don't know. . . ." hedged Pteros.

"Have you got a better plan? We can't just sit in this bubble forever." She peered anxiously around.

"I'd be willing to consider it," muttered Pteros, settling himself as if for the long haul. "At least it's quiet in here, and we aren't likely to bump into Talon."

Khisanth's brow furrowed. She contemplated the ever-present lightning beyond the bubble. "What troubles me is that we're likely to bump into something far worse."

Chapter 12

Sir Tate Sekforde squeezed the shears. Snip! The last straggle of his pale mustache drifted to the rush-covered floor. Still peering closely into the polished brass plaque, the Knight of the Crown smoothed his whiskers against his upper lip. His mustache had grown back thicker, even a shade darker, in the year since the fire that had singed it from his face. He frowned at his yellow-tinged image in the plaque as three fingers traced the faint scars on his left cheek, white against his tanned skin. Tate hoped the nose of the woman who had forever marked him thus looked as bad. If she was even still alive . . .

It was Misham, the fifth day of the week, the one he had chosen for his holy day. It meant that as a candidate for the Order of the Sword, Tate could not do battle, earn profit, or speak harshly to anyone this day. He must also spend at least three hours in silent meditation and prayer to Kiri-Jolith, the patron god of the Order of the Sword. Lore said Kiri-Jolith was twin brother to Habbakuk, who was the patron of Tate's current Order of the Crown. When, as Tate hoped, he became a Knight of the Sword, the meditation to his new patron would grant him clerical spells. Until then, Tate secretly felt that it served primarily to slow down progress on his task of rebuilding Lamesh Castle. Four hundred fifty miles away in his tower in Solamnia, the High Clerist of the knights, who would decide whether Tate was fit to wear the sign of the sword, might never see him violate the rule, but the god Kiri-Jolith would know. And so every seven days, Tate complied.

As ranking knight of Lamesh Castle, Tate stood alone, the last to rise in the modest barracks he shared with his men. Not one to stand on formality, he nevertheless donned the off-duty attire of a man of his social standing—green- and yellow-checked tunic, green hose, and soft-soled, rawhide shoes. Last, he draped a black silk baldric, made by his lady mother, from right shoulder to left hip to carry the sword he never went without, holy day or not.

Thoughts of his family threatened to sour Tate's already somber mood, so he strode from the barracks and into the inner courtyard. The knight headed for the bake house located farther to the west along the north wall. Though the day was supposed to be spent in fasting, Tate believed that even the god Kiri-Jolith could not expect him to pray with any fervor on an empty stomach.

Abel, the baker Tate had brought with him from Solamnia, was a stout man who looked like he enjoyed his own pastries too well. He was doing his part to support the rebuilding of the castle into a Solamnic outpost. His ovens ran day and night, making a variety of baked goods that fed the workmen inside the castle, but were also sold to the people who were resettling the village beyond the castle walls.

The knight stepped into the man's domain just as Abel was using a long wooden paddle to retrieve a dark, round loaf from the stone oven. "What'll it be this morning, Sir Tate?" the baker asked, his chubby face flushed from the heat of the oven. "I've got a nice, big loaf of rye here."

"No thanks, Abel. Just a sticky bun, if you please." Tate winked conspiratorially. "I'm supposed to be fasting today, you know."

The baker retrieved a bun from a bowl on the table and handed it to Tate. "So it's Misham, again, eh?" Shaking his head, he poured water from a pitcher onto a mound of coarse-ground flour in a wooden bowl and began to stir so vigorously the meal spewed onto the table. "You work me so hard out here in the boondocks, I can scarcely keep track of the days."

Tate smiled, knowing the crusty baker would have it no other way. "And well I appreciate your sacrifice, Abel. Are you getting the flour as quickly as you need it?"

Abel snorted. "Barely. That fool in the granary—what's his name, Dol? short for Dolt, no doubt—he's as slow as molasses in the month of Newkolt."

"Now, Abel, he's doing the best he can. Especially when you consider he knew nothing about milling grain before we recruited him to operate the grindstone."

"Still doesn't, if you ask me." The baker let a handful of flour sift through his fingers. "Look at how coarse this is. Chunks as big as your head—"

Tate clapped the baker on the back to curb the man's favorite tirade. "I'll speak to him about it tomorrow, Abel," the knight promised. "Thanks for the bun," he added as he stepped back into the coolness of the courtyard, chuckling.

The knight chided himself; he should have known better than to ask the persnickety Abel such a question. In truth, Tate didn't mind dealing with complaints. He spent many a day resolving conflicts between the craftsmen who were working to repair and rebuild the ruined castle. The majority of the debates were sparked when a local craftsman questioned the opinion of one of the skilled artisans he'd brought from the more civilized region of Solamnia. He needed all of his diplomatic skills to solve those conflicts without obvious bias, which could cost him the craftsman. Tate needed every available hand to prepare the castle for the coming winter.

Before entering the temple to Kiri-Jolith for his three hours of prayer, Tate climbed the steps of the northeast tower and paced the walkway on the walls. The day was unusually warm for late autumn, the sky as blue as a sapphire. He wanted to enjoy a few moments of the last good weather they would have before winter turned the landscape bleak.

How far we have come in eight-odd months, he thought, surveying with pride the scene in the courtyard below. When Tate's party of thirty or more had arrived to reestablish the abandoned stronghold south of Kern for the forces of Good, the castle had been in ruins, looted and laid to waste by centuries of roving monsters and mercenaries.

Tate had stumbled upon the architect's original renderings of the castle, stuffed behind a loose stone in a wall of the great room. He was using the faded and torn plans to restore as much of Lamesh as possible to its original condition, though he was forced to use more wood and less stone, due to availability. The entire western cliff face had been in advanced decay and needed immediate shoring. The only significant alteration to the design was the conversion of a portion of the original lord knight's personal apartments into a temple to Kiri-Jolith.

Within the castle walls, work was moving according to schedule. Tate's master architect, a man named Raymond of Winterholm, who had accompanied Tate from Solamnia, was an excellent planner. Normally, temporary structures would have been erected to house workers and key personnel while construction occurred. In laying out the castle, Winterholm wisely positioned the main wooden buildings near the walls that needed the least work, so they were permanent structures from the beginning. Most of the key workmen currently lived inside the castle. Once it was finished, they would either return to Solamnia or build houses of their own in the adjoining village. Ultimately, only those folk crucial to the castle's defense would live within.

Turning, Tate looked down upon the town, which was quickly growing beyond the walls on the eastern side of Lamesh Castle. Crumbling sections of the old town wall cast a wide circle, suggesting that Lamesh had been a sizable village in its heyday before the Cataclysm. People were returning to the village more quickly than even Tate had expected. The simple presence of the knights in this wild territory promised order and authority. Since ogres and other creatures inhabited the mountains in greater numbers these days, many people chose to relocate within the protective shadow of the castle.

As the village awakened that morning, boys carted water with buckets on yokes, girls hunted eggs in corners where range hens had laid them, mothers issued orders to all. The support beams of new houses were a common sight these days. The first tavern had already sprung up to meet the needs of the many craftsmen who'd come from all corners to find work. Behind old, rebuilt homes, women gathered honey and tended herb gardens, drying their produce for winter use. Goats bleated; roosters crowed; dogs barked; cows lowed to be milked. The plaintive wail of bagpipes floated up from unseen lips. Tate felt something akin to a father's pride for this village.

Beyond the ruined walls of the town, a man led a horse and plow through a field where corn had just been harvested. More than half of the crops were already in, filling the granary and storehouses. Hayricks and corn shocks dotted the rolling landscape. Sheep grazed on a nearby hillside, their dirty white coats grown out since spring shearing. Lina the weaver had already turned it to fabric, enough so that they wouldn't have to buy more during the cold months. Tate's plan for a self-sufficient community was becoming a reality even more quickly than he'd hoped. Still, there was much to be done before the first snowfall.

The Knight of the Crown dreaded the approaching winter, and not only from the standpoint of preparations; Sir Tate Sekforde hated the cold. It seemed to bury itself in his bones on the first frigid day and stay until buds returned to the trees. Winter would undoubtedly seem even colder without the centuries-old conveniences of the family castle back in Solamnia. Tate could just see his stuffy younger brother

Rupport, feet propped on a hassock before a roaring fire in the family's private apartments, thick tapestries covering the old stone walls of Castle DeHodge.

You have no business envying Rupport, Tate scolded himself. You gave up your claim as eldest son of your own accord. Truly, envy was not what Tate felt for the brother who'd been so ashamed of their father's common heritage that he'd taken their mother's maiden surname, DeHodge. Sir Rupport DeHodge. Even his name sounded pompous.

It was Tate's opinion that knights like Rupport had caused the decline of the order. Rupport had inherited his supercilious nature from their mother, whose noble family's history with the knighthood could be traced all the way back to Vinas Solamnus. Thirty years ago, the DeHodge family's fortunes had declined beyond their ability to deny it. The Cataclysm had caused less physical damage to their castle near the High Clerist's Tower than the social aftershocks to their finances. An only child, Cilla DeHodge had reluctantly agreed to an arranged marriage to a wealthy merchant from downriver at Jansburg, for whom she felt nothing but contempt.

Gedeon Sekforde was a kindly, street-smart man who loved his wife despite her many faults, not the least of which was the disdain for him she never bothered to hide. In exchange for restoring her family's lands with his merchant money, Cilla bore him two sons. While Cilla DeHodge Sekforde pushed her sons toward the knighthood, Gedeon Sekforde gave them the freedom to choose whatever occupation they wished. Though both embraced the knighthood, their reasons were very, very different. Rupport read his own intolerance and bigotry into the writings of the Measure and espoused them as his knightly goals.

Tate read the voluminous set of laws that defined the term *honor* and saw obedience to the *spirit* of the laws as the chief goal of the knighthood. It was Gedeon Sekforde who encouraged Tate to read between the lines of the Measure when his elder son would question the accuracy of the younger's interpretations. When Gedeon died, Cilla and Rupport's unfeeling snobbishness, not an uncommon trait among members of the knighthood, became unbearable to Tate. To escape the prevailing attitudes in Solamnia and in hopes that the frontier would allow for freethinking, Tate formally renounced his claim to the family estates and signed on with Stippling's expedition.

Not a month out of Solamnia, however, the venerable Knight of the Rose's party had been ambushed by ogres and mercenaries in a pass through the northern Khalkists. Tate alone had survived. Burned, his leg injured, he had stumbled and crawled his way to the village of Styx. Giving himself just one day to rest, he bought a horse and headed straight-away for the High Clerist's Tower back in Solamnia to report the deaths. And to apply for entry into the next level of knighthood, the Order of the Sword. He knew just what quest he would be assigned: to complete Stippling's mission of establishing a Solamnic outpost at Lamesh.

On the return trip, the Knight of the Crown had had a lot of time to think. The clerical spells that only Knights of the Sword received through prayer would certainly be useful, especially if ever Tate were in a situation like the ambush again. What was more, his reasons for joining Stippling's troop had not changed; he had no wish to settle in Solamnia. The High Clerist and the Knightly Council had not been keen at first to agree to such a monumental quest by so young a knight. A number of particularly arrogant knights, mentors of Rupport's no doubt, had even questioned Tate's bravery, since he'd had the audacity to survive. Tate had wondered more than once if the staid old Council of Knights hadn't ultimately agreed to his request simply to brush him off, presuming that he would fail. In a land so remote that it didn't even bear a regional name, news of a Crown Knight's defeat would not tarnish the knighthood in Solamnia. . . . Tate shook away the aggravating reflection. Unkind thoughts were not allowed on holy days either.

He remembered his sticky bun. Tate's mouth was open wide around the sugared tidbit when Sir Wolter Heding's voice boomed behind him.

"Ah, ah, ahhh!" the old knight scolded in singsong. "You weren't about to eat that, were you, lad?"

"I was thinking about it, yes."

Sir Wolter came to stand before him. He was a large man by anyone's standards, slightly corpulent, with a hooked nose and a strong jaw that was usually covered with stubble. "A candidate for Sword Knight eating on his holy day? Tsk, tsk, lad."

"That's 'Sir Lad,' to you." Tate's mouth was scowling, but his brown eyes were smiling as he handed over the sticky bun. To Tate's annoyance, his sponsor in the knighthood popped the bun into his own mouth.

"Ha! That'll be the day!" chortled Sir Wolter over the bun. "You may be lord knight of the castle because of your quest, but I still outrank you by—"

"Centuries," filled in Tate. "Yes, I know, you knew Vinas Solamnus."

"And don't you forget it," laughed Wolter, poking his young friend in the chest.

"Not for a moment, Wolter." Neither would Tate forget that Sir Wolter Heding was likely the reason the Knightly Council had finally agreed to let him undertake Stippling's assignment as his quest.

Sir Wolter had sponsored Tate as a squire. Since Tate's own father had not been a knight and Wolter had no children of his own, they formed an unusually tight bond. The elder knight had taught Tate everything he knew about knightly behavior and endeavor: horsemanship, weapons, archery, wrestling, hunting, fieldcraft, even teamwork. When Tate signed on with Stippling, Sir Wolter alone had understood his reasons for leaving Solamnia. When Tate returned after the ambush, Wolter had spoken up for the young man. The elder knight recounted an endless list of Tate's acts of courage, feats of strength, and skill.

In the end, the council had been swayed only when Wolter volunteered to accompany young Sekforde and act as witness. The elder Knight of the Rose had long ago earned the right to sit hearthside and recount tales of bravery to children. He was the kind of knight Tate aspired to be, embracing the intent, not the letter, of the Oath and the Measure. Sir Wolter's advice was infrequent but insightful, and always relayed in private, in respect to Tate's authority.

"Speaking of forgetting," Wolter said with bushy eyebrows raised, "I didn't see you at morning worship." Wolter eyed Tate's attire. "Hadn't you better get your dandified self down there and pay Kiri-Jolith his due?"

Tate colored, looking properly chastised. "I stopped for a brief moment to enjoy the good weather and lost track of time."

Wolter pushed him toward the steps. "I'll come and tell you when three hours have passed." He winked. "Just in case you get equally absorbed by your prayers." The old knight knew how difficult Tate found it to meditate for an entire day, especially with the castle in so much need of attention.

"Get you gone," Wolter said more kindly. "The meditation is as important to your quest as anything else. I'll keep an eye on things, don't you worry."

Tate clambered down the circular tower steps. He passed by the blacksmith's shop, forge always glowing to meet the constant demands of the craftsmen. He saluted the two sentries at the gate house, though he didn't know their names, or those of many of the younger knights.

The temple to Kiri-Jolith was defined more by function than decor. In reality it was a walled-off section of the first lord knight's once-sumptuous apartments. Long ago stripped of its riches, it now contained just six rows of hard wooden benches and a small altar, decorated only with the god's bison head symbol. The room was always cold and dark, lit by a single candle, which was meant to aid concentration.

The temple was empty now as well. Tate slipped inside and onto the wooden bench nearest the altar. He was glad for the privacy, since it allowed him to pray aloud and thus remain focused. Tate cleared his throat awkwardly.

"Kiri-Jolith, Sword of Justice, hear my call. Guide this humble knight in his quest for honor and justice. Help him to see grievous wrongs and right them. Let him never stray from the path of obedience. Keep his will and his sword arm strong in your service."

Tate chanted the lines over and over. He envied those knights who could simply meditate, free-form, for hours on end. He was not gifted with profound words or thoughts. Tate fancied himself a man of action.

The knight was reciting the prayer for the one hundred thirty-seventh time when shouts in the courtyard sliced through his already fragile concentration. One word alone was enough to draw his attention.

"Fire!"

Tate's heart skipped a beat. Fire in a castle could mean disaster. Certain Kiri-Jolith would understand the distraction, the knight jumped to his feet and was on his way to the door when a young squire, his thin face glowing from sweat, burst through it. He nearly knocked Tate down.

"Sir Tate!" cried the squire, his voice thin and reedy from inhaling smoke. "There's fire, sir! Sir Wolter sent me to get you." The youth collapsed on a bench, unable to draw a breath.

"Where is it?" The youth couldn't get enough air to speak. Tate shook him impatiently. "Damn it, tell me!"

"Bake house," the squire managed to rasp.

The bake house . . . It was next to the granary. They'd had to rebuild a lot of it with wood. He thought of Abel—everything had looked fine just a few short hours ago. Tate bolted through the door and headed for the opposite corner of the courtyard, where black smoke choked the sun. The normal bustle of the castle had been replaced by near panic. As Tate approached the bake house, it came to him that he'd broken another of the laws of the holy day. He'd spoken harshly to the squire.

A good morning was suddenly turning very bad.

Abel, covered in flour and soot, ran to and fro in front of the small building, clutching at everyone who came near enough, begging them to fetch water. A few ran to the well, others with more level heads went to nearby shops or to the stables to find buckets. The stonemasons, working above the kitchen and very near the burning bakery, scrambled down from their scaffolding and joined the force; the blacksmith bolted from his forge; the sentries left their posts to help. Even a small fire could rage out of control and consume an entire building in the time it took to organize a fire brigade.

The well was more than a hundred paces away, too far to form a continuous water supply line to the fire. Dozens of workers ran back and forth, sloshing water from heavy wooden buckets all the way, to splash a few gallons onto the rapidly growing blaze.

Wolter dashed out of the knights' barracks, weaving and dodging his way through the sprinting water carriers. He had barely reached the scene before Tate grabbed him by the shoulders. "I thought you were keeping an eye on things!"

Sir Wolter's eyes already appeared red from smoke. "I couldn't be everywhere there was flame," the old knight said sadly, "and neither could you."

"Send word out to the village," Tate told him. "We need every man, woman, and child who can carry water, and every container that will hold it."

Wolter immediately collared half a dozen boys and dispatched them with Tate's message, along with a warning to "run their hearts out, and pound down people's doors if necessary."

Meanwhile, Tate had captured the distraught baker and removed him a few score paces from the tumult. "Is anyone still inside?"

The baker shook his head vigorously. "No, sir, I don't think so. But all my implements are there, everything I need to do my job. It's all being destroyed." Abel's wide eyes turned back toward the smoking, half-timbered building, and he started to pull away.

Tate grabbed the man's arm and commanded his attention. "How did it start?"

"It was Kaye, sir, the apprentice." Abel wrung his flour-covered hands uncontrollably. "The boy's apron must have caught an ember when he crouched down to feed the fire. Suddenly it was burning and Kaye, why, sir, he nearly expired of a fit right there. Lucky for him young Idwoir was nearby, waiting for a biscuit. Idwoir ripped the apron off the boy and tried to get rid of it, but it fell to the floor.

"The reeds on the floor caught up next. Idwoir tried to douse them, but I guess he was too excited because he missed the flames. Before we could fetch more water, the whole place was filled with smoke so bad it choked a man just to be near it. Oh, I'm awfully sorry, Sir Tate. This is a catastrophe, that's what it is."

Tate was in no mood to soothe the man's nerves. "See if you can help by passing a bucket," he ordered, then turned back to the fire.

The blaze was intensifying rapidly. Tall flames were visible through the windows, gyrating in the black billows. Yellow smoke, so thick that it looked like raw wool, streamed upward through the thatched roof.

By now, villagers were arriving with leather and wooden buckets, cooking pots, ancient helmets with chin-strap handles, even crockery mugs and tin cups. Wolter and the other knights directed them into two long lines from the bakery to the well.

"Every able-bodied person available, and some not so able, is here," Wolter reported. "We've got to make sure we keep rotating the men at the front. It's hot as wizard fire, and no one can stand it long when they're up close enough to throw on water."

One line of people, containing mainly men and matrons, passed the heavy, sloshing buckets from the well to the fire. Empty containers traveled back to be refilled along the other line, passing through the hands of grandparents, children, young women, even some ailing residents who, Tate realized, must have left their sickbeds to take a place in line.

With the bucket brigade operating at full speed, the fire seemed to be held in check. Tate marched up and down the lines, yelling encouragement. The roar of the flames mingling with the grunts and shouts of the fire fighters was nearly deafening.

On returning again to the front of the bakery, Tate found

Raymond of Winterholm, the master architect. The man's
forehead was furrowed with anxiety, his face filmed with
perspiration. The heat here was nearly unbearable.

"What's your opinion, Master Raymond?" Tate shouted
over the din. "Are we beating it back?" The knight's heart
hammered in his chest from the excitement and exertion.

"That's hard to say, Sir Tate," the architect bellowed back.
"There's so much smoke we can't get a good look at the
extent and direction of the fire. At the very least, we've
slowed it down. And a good thing, too. Those support beams
to the left of the bakery are reinforcing the new upper portions of the east wall, where the mortar isn't completely set. If
we lose those beams, the battlements could crumble."
Wincing, he ran a hand through his hair. "I don't want to
think about how much more damage that would cause."

Tate clapped the man on the shoulder, trying to be reassuring though his own doubts were great.

A torrent of flame suddenly burst through the thick roof of
the building. The column of yellow smoke that had been
pouring upward ignited into a writhing pillar. And then, a
vast portion of the roof broke away and tumbled downward.
Spitting fire and smoke, the roof section broke off and
crashed into the midst of the people below, who had charged
forward with buckets of water.

Men, women, and children scattered from the sudden
onslaught, dropping buckets as they ran; all but two, who
were pinned beneath the searing mass. Their screams seemed
to have no effect on those who scrambled for their lives, but
in moments, knights converged on the scene.

One of them, armed with a long-handled military hook,
plunged the weapon into a bundle of thatch. As he pulled
aside the burning mass, Tate and another knight grabbed the
two victims and dragged them out into the central courtyard,
away from the heat and danger.

Both men appeared horribly burned. Their clothes were
scorched, their faces blackened, much of their hair fried
away. Remembering his own painful, narrow escape from
burning death, the young knight thanked Habbakuk tha

both were unconscious.

Momentarily the barber, a dwarf with long braided locks, rushed up and began gingerly peeling the smoking clothes from the victims. Tate watched helplessly for several moments until Sir Wolter jolted him, saying "You'd best come back to the fire. We've a new problem."

The hole in the roof was acting like a chimney; the sudden rush of heat and flame through the opening drew a blasting draft into the house. The building had become a furnace.

"That's not the worst of it," the older knight added. "We can't possibly put it out, but we must keep it from spreading. There's new construction to the left of it and the granary to the right."

Once again Master Raymond was at Tate's elbow. "Sir, that new construction must be protected. If the supports burn away, anything could happen."

"But if we lose the grain," Tate responded, "we can't sustain the castle and village in the coming winter." Though he already knew and now feared the answer, Tate asked Sir Wolter, "How full is the granary?"

"Dol tells me it's about half full," Wolter replied.

"Damnation!" Tate slammed his fist into his hand. "That's not just our food for the winter, it's next year's seed. Take whomever can be spared from the bucket lines and start emptying the granary. I don't care where you put the grain—dump it on the ground if you have to, but get it out of there."

Turning to Raymond, Tate barked, "Find the head groom and have him get all the horses out of the stables. We can't chance losing them, too."

"Of course," Raymond replied. "If the granary goes up, the stables will be next."

Tate cut him off. "I don't intend to lose either of them. Get some people on top of the granary and tear off its roof. Don't leave any kindling up there for a stray spark to ignite. Then use chains or ropes or whatever else you can find and hitch some plow horses to the granary. If it catches fire, pull it down and scatter the pieces so there's nothing for the flames to climb."

"What about the new wall?" the architect asked.

Tate peered through the smoke at the scaffolding behind the kitchen. "We'll just have to hold the fire off as best we can." After Raymond ran off into the smoke, Tate rubbed his face in his hands. Great Huma's ghost, he didn't have all the answers, even if they expected him to.

Tense minutes later, Wolter and Raymond were again back at Tate's side. "We're ready to topple the granary, but I hope we don't have to," the knight reported. "What with the heat and the smoke, getting the grain out is next to impossible. It's going awfully slow because the men have to work in short shifts to keep from searing their lungs."

"And the wall supports?"

Raymond's soot-streaked face looked worried. "The beams are scorching, and the ropes are smoking like a dwarf's pipe. If the bakery collapses soon, and I expect it will, we'll be a lot safer."

Strangely relieved by the news that the bakery was about to fall, Tate relaxed slightly. But cries of "Water! Water!" from the fire fighters cut short his brief respite.

Tate's heart nearly choked him when he saw bucket passers and fire fighters standing idle, shuffling their feet and looking quizzically back toward the well. A few empty buckets were still moving down the line, but no newly filled ones came forward.

At the well, the blacksmith and the farrier both dripped sweat. They stood panting, their hands on the rope that disappeared down the dark shaft. Tate stopped his headlong rush by crashing into the side of the well, clutching the rough stones to keep his balance. Before he could blurt out the obvious question, the farrier answered it.

"We've drained it to the bottom, Sir Tate. It's just filling at a trickle now, not nearly as fast as we've been taking it out. And we've already drained the cisterns, too."

"How much water can we get?" Tate asked softly, almost a whisper. Everyone's eyes were on him.

The blacksmith arched his eyebrows momentarily as if to apologize. "We can get one bucket in the time it took us to get ten or fifteen before."

Tate stood straight as a pike and glared at the sky, darkened with smoke and soot. "Gods' teeth!" he screamed. "Am I to be opposed by fate at every step?" He stared into the roaring sky, then turned to the men waiting by the horses. The words to command the destruction of all their hard work choked in his throat. Tate waved his arm.

"Pull down the granary," Wolter bellowed, correctly interpreting the gesture.

Grooms tugged on bridles, chains lifted off the ground, then grew tight and strained. Slowly a chorus of "hiyaa" and "g'yon there" gave way to groaning timber and splintering lath. The granary building leaned at the top, then buckled at the bottom, and collapsed into a dust-obscured heap of rubble. Flames shot up and danced across its surface. As the horses continued dragging the massive timbers, they scattered the burning matter across the inner courtyard. Women and children swarmed around it to beat out the flames with brooms and blankets.

Unchecked, the fire now raced along the wall support beams above the kitchen. With no water to hold back the flames, the kitchen would soon be engulfed the same way the bakery had been.

The throng of people who had worked so hard to slay the wicked fire now watched it rage out of control. As a group, they backed across the courtyard toward the temple and the main gate, then stood and watched, eyes streaming with tears, as the kitchen was consumed. Above the kitchen, workers' scaffolding swayed in the heat. Ropes smoldered before snapping loose. Support beams, already charred, began to glow from within.

As the blaze in the kitchen reached its height, the first of the wall supports collapsed. The sound was like nothing Tate had ever heard before—like a whip crack, only as loud as an avalanche.

Uncured mortar, weakened further by the heat of the fire, could not hold up the massive stones. One stone slid out and crashed through the kitchen, casting up a shower of sparks to more than twice the height of the curtain wall. Several more stones followed, then the entire upper section of the wall poured down.

The castle shook under the blows, and people claimed later they were actually knocked off their feet by the shock. When the dust cleared, Tate didn't know whether to laugh or cry. A gaping hole forty feet wide and twenty feet deep made the wall look worse than it had four months ago, when the restoration had just started. But in collapsing, the stones had buried the kitchen, extinguishing the fire that had caused them to fall.

Wolter came to stand by his slack-jawed friend. The old knight's face was streaked with soot and sweat, gray hair hanging in his eyes. "We'll rebuild, Tate. We did it once, we can do it again."

Tate nodded numbly. In spite of his misery, Tate recalled a legend his father had told him often. It was about two ancestral enemies who fought for hours only to ultimately kill each other with simultaneous deathblows. As a child, Tate had thought the story epitomized the ideals of honor and passion. Now, it just seemed a waste.

Chapter 13

Fed up with inactivity and Pteros's indecision, Khisanth slipped out of the elemental air pocket. Outside was the same turbulent world as before, featureless, constantly changing, lit by lightning and pounded by thunder. Khisanth pushed herself away from the bubble and drifted slowly, trying to focus her thoughts on escape.

Suddenly a flash of lightning ripped into her flank, convulsing the muscles there and forcing a bellow of surprise and pain from the dragon. Looking back in anger, Khisanth saw her hind leg kicking uselessly in spasms caused by the lightning. The randomness of the attack infuriated her; she couldn't even "think" like lightning to anticipate the next bolt. As though answering her thoughts, several more bolts of lightning shot past dangerously close. She flapped back into the airy haven.

Pteros was just as she'd left him. He eyed her scorched scales and asked apprehensively what happened. Frustrated and impatient, Khisanth refused to answer.

"Did you see some other creature? Or has the elemental come back?" No answer came from Khisanth. "Why would the elemental attack you? Do you think it was the enemy the elemental had mentioned? Fraz, was that its name?"

"It was just a bolt of lightning."

Pteros was silent for a while. His head slumped on his forepaws. He stared forlornly at the shimmering blue wall.

"You've got to try that gate spell, Pteros."

Hearing the uncompromising tone in Khisanth's voice, the ancient beast answered without raising his head. "That spell is something I learned from an elf captive long, long ago, near the end of the war. I've forgotten most of what the elf told me about its use. I seem to recall it wasn't something we could use to go elsewhere, but rather a portal to bring something to us." Pteros looked worried. "It would be most imprudent to try it."

The ancient dragon's timidity in the face of emergency brought Khisanth's anger back full force. "Does that mean you won't try anything, for fear of making things worse? How much worse can they get?"

Khisanth's words only made Pteros look more miserable.

"Your friend is right. Creating a magical gate here is most unwise. In fact, even the discussion of it might attract the attention of creatures more powerful than yourselves, plentiful indeed on a quasi-elemental plane."

Khisanth and Pteros whirled in the bubble to find the source of the unnaturally deep voice. They both lurched back at the sight of a bestial, yet beautiful face pressed through the side of the air bubble. The face resembled a gorilla's, but with large, fan-shaped ears and a bald, pointed pate. The fur was white, almost a blindingly pure white, and the lips and mouth bright crimson. But most startling were the eyes, which promised incredible yet sinister intelligence.

Khisanth eyed the beast warily at a distance. "You speak as if you've met such a creature."

"I am one." The creature stepped fully into the bubble. His

body, half the height of a dragon's, was thick and muscular and covered with sleek, pale fur. Like the face, the rest of the creature was vaguely simian, except for an unnaturally long tail that ended in bony barbs. The creature moved through the lightning environment with an easy grace that told Khisanth he was no stranger to this realm. "How is it you were foolish enough to come to my little plane without the means to leave?"

"If you're as powerful as you say, you already know the answer to that," Khisanth said boldly.

Pteros gasped at her reply. "Actually, a lightning elemental brought us here against our will," the old dragon explained hastily. "Perhaps you've seen it, a globe-shaped creature filled with white bolts of lightning?"

"I *knew* the elemental to which you refer, yes." The creature's meaning was unmistakable. "That one won't bring unwanted creatures here anymore." He raised one brow. "You would both be wise to choose your words carefully, lest you give the impression you don't like the realm of Fraz."

With no apparent physical effort at all, the creature whirled across the bubble at tremendous speed. He stopped a short distance behind the two dragons.

"Very well, Fraz, now that you've killed our elemental, can you return us to the Prime Material plane?" Though her tone was bold, Khisanth was wary of this creature who had disposed of the elemental, something Khisanth was not at all sure she could have done in this place.

"It's within my power to send you anywhere you want to go, and some places you'd rather avoid, too. Because I find you and your lost friend so amusing in a helpless, pathetic kind of way, I'm willing to help you. You must do something for me first."

Fraz allowed that to hang in the air for a few moments before continuing. "While I have many friends, I have even more enemies. In that regard, I am truly wealthy. I'd like you to engage one of them in a true contest of fighting skills. You needn't slay it."

Pteros summoned the nerve to ask, "Why must we fight

someone you don't even want us to kill?"

The creature drifted close to Pteros and stared into the dragon's eyes. "Because I am the most powerful creature in my realm, and it would amuse me."

"What if we refuse your challenge?" asked Khisanth.

"Call it a command, call it an order, call it a request you can't refuse." The creature's tail flicked like a cat's, motionless except at the tip. The bony spikes clicked against each other as they flexed. Then Fraz shifted so he appeared to stand on all four limbs, like a gorilla, and walked through the air on his knuckles. He circled around the dragons twice, never looking away.

Abruptly Fraz tapped his chin with a razor-sharp nail. "There was another creature here recently from the Prime Material. He tried to refuse. Perhaps you met him, a slight fellow with slanted eyes and charred flesh?" Though the reference to Yoshiki Toba had meaning for Khisanth alone, she was suitably impressed.

The creature's sinister eyes shifted from side to side as if he were concentrating. Fraz pointed a fingernail at Pteros. "Charred flesh would be your fate." He turned his gaze on Khisanth. "You, on the other hand, would be forever trapped in my cozy realm, which would be the greatest punishment for you, if I'm reading your mind correctly."

The dragons were silent. "Good, I see you've agreed to my contest. You will be fighting a storm giant. He's a crafty old fellow named Comenus who has been a thorn in my side for too many centuries. Seeing how two mighty black dragons pitted against a lone giant isn't much of a contest, I've decided you'll fight not as dragons but as serpents. Feathery serpents, I think, for variety."

As he spoke, the beast traced a glowing symbol in the air with a yellowed fingernail. The completed symbol hung before them, and Fraz positioned his talon beneath it as if balancing the glyph. A puff of breath started the device spinning and spitting tiny sparks. Suddenly, with a flick of Fraz's finger, the sigil split in two and flashed across the bubble to burn into Khisanth and Pteros. Color swam before Khisanth's eyes.

When her vision cleared, she saw, where Pteros had been, a snake with wings. His body was all black, with two large wings that had red spots at the base. He resembled a monstrous, serpentine blackbird, like those Khisanth had seen so many times in the swamp. Glancing down, Khisanth saw that she looked the same.

The dragon despised being compared to a snake. She squeezed her eyes shut and willed patience, but it alluded her. The infuriated dragon tried to belch murderous acid from her stomach to blanket and obliterate Fraz, but all that came forth was a weak growl. Instead of being angry, Fraz seemed tremendously amused, laughing out loud at Khisanth's feeble effort to attack. "No! No! Please don't burp on me, oh mighty dragon," he mocked. In a blink, he turned deadly serious. "That is all your acid is to me."

Fraz abruptly opened his mouth, far wider than it should have been able to go, wider than his jaws could allow, and then wider still, until his maw was twice the size of his head. He exhaled, filling the elemental bubble with heat and stench.

But a swirling cloud appeared before Fraz. His mouth returned to normal and closed. "Move forward to see what I am showing you," he commanded. The dragon-snakes moved up reluctantly as the mixing colors formed shapes and pictures. A huge man, with light green skin and dark green hair, dressed in a flowing tunic, sat in a titanic chair. A massive sword rested across his knees. "This is your foe, Comenus. Concentrate on this place you are seeing, and whichever direction you travel, you will arrive there. Remember this place. Proceed straightaway to Comenus. He's expecting you." The image, as well as Fraz, dissolved into a swirling cone of colors, but the undulating laughter echoed in the bubble for moments afterward.

Khisanth searched her mind for some qhen advice of Kadagan's. What she fixed on was not qhen at all, but the reason Kadagan had given her for choosing her as the instrument of Dela's rescue:

"Dragons and humans have long been enemies, and the enemy of my enemy is my friend."

"We need to find Comenus."

"You, a snake, are planning to fight a storm giant?"

"I'm not staying here forever." Khisanth didn't care whether Pteros followed her or stayed behind. All his tales of heroism aside, he was proving to be nothing more than a tired, timid old creature.

"How will you find him?"

"By concentrating on him, as Fraz said."

"Wait for me!" she heard Pteros call, more afraid to be left alone than to follow.

Khisanth darted through the bubble and into the seething tumult beyond. Once removed from the protection of the pocket of elemental air, the two snakes were buffeted like leaves in the wind. Moving in a continuous direction took tremendous effort. Khisanth had no idea where she was going, but she concentrated on the image of Comenus. After much fluttering, she spotted something approaching through the seething clouds and flashing lightning. She slowed down to get a good look. Pteros winged up alongside.

The approaching object was becoming more distinct through the turbulence. Comenus. The storm giant was enormous, far larger than Fraz's image had made him look. The giant would have been much taller than Khisanth, and nearly as massive, even in her natural form. His skin was pale green, his beard and hair a darker shade of the same color. A narrow jeweled crown circled his brow. Across his shoulders was draped a tunic of silk and spun gold, while torcs of gold and electrum circled his biceps.

Comenus sat on a throne that appeared to be made of dark clouds shot through with lightning. Lying across his lap was a sword half as long as Khisanth's body. Propped against the back of the throne was a bow as thick as a tree, with arrows like lances. The throne was propelled through the air by some invisible means, like everything else in this realm. As the chair approached the two snakes, it, too, slowed then stopped, a mere fifty or so paces away.

Khisanth had hoped to find Comenus in another elemental sphere so she could talk to him. Out here, in the deafening thunder, she could not hope to communicate with the giant. As if in response to her thought, the thunder died away, the lightning stopped flashing. Even the wind dropped. It made sense, Khisanth guessed, that a storm giant would have control over the elements.

After he had silenced the storm, Khisanth expected Comenus to address her, but he sat impassively. So Khisanth broke the silence. "You must be the storm giant, Comenus."

Instantly the giant was on his feet, shouting in a voice that outdid the thunder, "Fraz has sent you to slay me!" The sword floated at his side within easy reach while he snatched the bow from its rest. An arrow disappeared from the quiver and reappeared nocked on the bow. When the giant drew the enormous bow, it sounded like a tree crashing in the forest. Khisanth was shocked that a creature so large could move so quickly. She and Pteros scrambled away from the enraged titan, but not fast enough.

The shot cracked like thunder. The arrow rushed past Pteros, its steel tip missing him by a hand's breadth, but its immense feather fletchings grazed his wing. The impact spun the snake-dragon around in a spray of blood from the lacerated wing. Pteros flew back, nursing his wound.

The giant touched the bowstring a second time, and another arrow jumped from the quiver to the bow. As he drew it to his shoulder, Khisanth called, "We don't want to kill you. What could two tiny snakes hope to do to a storm giant? We only want to talk!"

The giant's bow was still poised and ready to fire at Khisanth. Even though she was minuscule next to the giant, Khisanth doubted Comenus would miss at such short range.

"You're right, Comenus. Fraz sent us to fight you. But we are not his allies. First, Fraz slew the elemental that could send us back to our home plane. Then he changed us from dragons into these ridiculous snake things. The last thing we want is to see his wish fulfilled."

The giant's expression was blank. "It would be faster for me to simply kill you." He loosed his arrow. It streaked straight toward Khisanth. There was no time to think, but her reflexes were still those of a black dragon in her prime. The snake body twisted aside, stretching to get out of the huge arrow's path. The iron tip, razor sharp and spinning through the blue air, sliced through Khisanth's tiny right wing at the first joint. She watched in mixed horror and fury as two-thirds of her wing tumbled away. In spasmodic flight, she barely managed to land on the storm-giant's cloud.

Comenus set aside his bow and grasped his sword. As he extended the weapon, there was a burst of smoke. Abruptly Fraz appeared in front of the giant, facing Khisanth. The giant froze in place, as if time had stopped.

"You've lost," the ape-creature said, then wagged a hideous finger. "Tsk, tsk. You tried to betray me. Still, you did come." Fraz looked suddenly sorrowful. "I know what. I'll send just one of you back to the Prime Material. But which one?"

Pteros rushed forward from where he'd been cowering, favoring his injured wing. "Send me, Fraz. Her injury is worse than mine. She won't be able to fly anyway."

The old dragon's pleas hardly surprised Khisanth. The whole scene seemed unreal, even less tangible than her dreams of flying with Led. Why had the storm giant just stopped moving? The more she thought about that, the more she thought there was something odd about all of this.

Then Khisanth remembered another of her discussions with Kadagan. The nyphid had been explaining the difference between illusion and reality. Khisanth's ability to change shape, he said, was reality. And because of that, it was more powerful than any illusion; in fact, it was more powerful than magic of most types. With that thought foremost in her mind, Khisanth closed her eyes and projected herself back into her own body.

She felt immediately, and knew even before opening her eyes again, that Fraz's spell was shattered. When she did look, the dragon saw her body returned to normal, her wing whole and unharmed. The same happened to Pteros. Comenus and his throne and his weapons were gone.

Only Fraz remained. "Ah," he exclaimed, "so you've penetrated my little game at last."

In amazement, Pteros stared at his restored body and health. When he looked up, his eyes were dull and pitiful.

Khisanth wanted to rip Fraz's smug, sneering face right off his head. But by anyone's reckoning the creature had displayed an impressive amount of power. "All right, Fraz," she said as calmly as she could, "we passed your little test. Now send us home."

Suddenly, Fraz's head cocked to the side, and his expression changed from smug superiority to alarm. He spoke, seemingly to someone, but the dragons heard only Fraz's voice. "Yes, mistress . . . I understand . . . It was a harmless game, mistress, no disrespect was intended . . . Of course, as you wish."

Giving both dragons a malicious grin, he said. "You owe your return to the Prime Material plane to that which we all serve." Fraz's eyes seemed to penetrate Pteros for a moment. His voice was full of rancor when at last he said, "I just hope you like the destination I've chosen for you."

* * * * *

Before the Cataclysm, the area of the Great Moors had been a sea. Mem Citadel was an island stronghold, a fortified base for the sleek ships that plied those waters. But the Cataclysm made islands sink and the sea bottom rise. The citadel now stood on a slight rise in an otherwise bleak and featureless expanse of bog.

In its heyday, Mem Citadel had been an impressive castle. Following the Cataclysm and centuries of disuse, its inner walls were crumbled, but the outer battlements were still largely intact.

On this steamy morning, it rose out of the swampland like a foggy apparition. The eastern length of the crumbling, limestone wall had sunk a noticeable depth into the marsh. As a result, the northern and southern edges sloped sharply downhill. The eastern wall's crenels and merlons, the low and high segments of its battlements, were in the greatest state of decay, likely the result of the stress caused by the citadel's sinking foundation. The gate in the center of what must have been the front wall had crumbled away, and only two towers remained, on the southwest and northwest corners. Much of the rubble from the inner wall had fallen outward, making passage difficult between the walls. The lower stories of the main keep still stood, tilted slightly and surrounded by the tumbled stones of its upper floors. All of the wooden buildings were long gone.

Inside the four thick walls were the same low shrubs and scrub pines that dotted the Great Moors, only these were trampled down from some great weight.

The croaking and chirping of frogs filled the air, punctuated by the buzzing of insects. But these natural denizens of the bog were very sensitive to intrusion. On this morning, when the glaring light and crackling noise erupted in the center of the bog, the insect sounds dropped away to silence. A shimmering circle appeared in the air. Its outlines were vague and shifting, and filled with flashing lightning. A jagged bolt of electricity shot out of the form to scorch the ground. Smaller lines of current danced between the ring and the ground, twitching in a constant dance.

With a crack that echoed off the fortress walls, a portal opened in the shimmering field, and two enormous shapes tumbled out of it to sprawl on the soft ground. Before they could disentangle themselves, the portal and its swirling frame disappeared. In moments a pair of black dragons stood shaking their wings and surveying the area.

When his eyes fell on the decaying fortress, Pteros froze. Khisanth noticed the other dragon's alarm, and her eyes followed his to trace out the castle. She had never seen it before.

"This is Talon's lair," Pteros whispered. "He lives here, in a tunnel beneath the courtyard, in what remains of the citadel's dungeon. It's no accident that we're here. Fraz must have read in my mind where I'd least like to be. After the elemental lightning place, of course."

Khisanth was surprised at how well Pteros seemed to know the other dragon's lair. "Thanks to Fraz," she said, "you'll have to confront Talon whether you want to or not." She rubbed her claws in eager resignation. "He must surely detect our presence in his lair."

Khisanth could see the fear on Pteros's lined face. "I've a plan. Quickly, fly around behind the citadel, with good altitude. When Talon emerges to sniff me out, he'll spot me. Right then, you dive into his back and hit him before he knows what's going on. Even if he hears your dive, he'll be staring into the sun when he turns toward you. That moment of confusion is all you'll need to split him open."

Pteros was scared. "Do it," Khisanth hissed. "You've wallowed in your fear long enough. Be a worthy member of your race again, Pteros. Write new tales of valor for yourself." Pteros nodded once at her call-to-arms and flew off shakily. She watched until he disappeared from sight.

Many minutes passed before Khisanth detected the sound of movement inside the fortress. The noise grew steadily louder until suddenly, two dragons in flight burst over the top of the fortress wall.

Where had the second dragon come from? Pteros never mentioned any other besides Talon. The dragons swooped low past Khisanth, taking care not to get too close. They were obviously hoping to intimidate her, so she stood her ground resolutely. Soon they landed between her and the castle, just as Khisanth had hoped they would, where they stood momentarily eyeing her.

Khisanth took the opportunity to study them, as well. The larger of the two appeared also to be the older. His scales were sleek and shiny except over his left eye, where a nasty scar made the eyelid droop. The second dragon, who seemed nervous, bore no visible scars, but her claws looked particularly long and sharp to Khisanth. From Pteros's descriptions and her own brief encounter, she knew the older to be Talon, but who was the younger? A sibling, or even offspring, perhaps?

Talon approached Khisanth slowly, cautiously looking behind her. "Who are you, and why have you disturbed our sleep?" he asked. The second dragon glanced nervously around the sky.

"Don't you recognize me?" Khisanth snorted. "Of course, you did strike my tree and flee like a coward without facing me." Where was Pteros? Khisanth screamed inwardly, glancing to the skies yet again. The best moment to strike was fleeting away.

The bigger dragon's eyes narrowed suspiciously as memory dawned. His comrade, who had been watching the area behind Khisanth, stepped back toward the ruins without a word and suddenly stiffened. She tapped Talon's shoulder and pointed somewhere beyond Khisanth.

Khisanth twisted her neck and was angered to see Pteros circling high above, clearly visible. Already the younger dragon was working her way around to the left of Khisanth. The smooth tone of Talon's voice was soothing and appealing to Khisanth, but she remembered Pteros once mentioning the dragon's magic, and she steeled herself against the voice.

What was Pteros doing? Why had he shown himself, and why wasn't he attacking?

Khisanth had no time left for wondering. The young dragon was nearly behind her, and Talon continued talking in those flat, steady tones that probed into Khisanth's mind, dulling her wits. He was weaving a spell of some sort.

I must get above them, Khisanth realized dimly. Focusing her strength into one mighty leap, she took to the sky. Her head was clouded as if filled with fog, but the sheer physical effort of the standing take off and steady climb rapidly cleared her judgment.

As soon as Khisanth was airborne, both dragons were after her. She had a small advantage from being the first into the air, but she would lose altitude if she turned to fight. She continued climbing, pushing her wings as hard as possible, but Talon and his partner were keeping pace.

Khisanth glanced skyward. Pteros was still circling! "Is he insane?" she growled. Then she heard a deafening roar from below, and a blast of hot bile splashed against her hind legs and tail. The pain was unbelievable. It burned like nothing she had ever felt before. Khisanth thought she knew what an acid burn felt like from those few times when she had contacted some of her own spew. But those experiences were nothing compared to this. She felt as if her lower half was being scraped away by hot needles.

Anger consumed her, at these two dragons for attacking her, but also at Pteros for what she could only consider betrayal. Was he planning to watch her die, or was he simply too scared to intervene?

Desperate now, reeling from the pain and hardly able to continue flying, Khisanth wheeled in the air and pointed herself at Talon. She did not just dive, but drove herself earthward with all the force of her wings. She could see the green spittle still dripping from Talon's pulled-back lips. The dragon's eyes were filled with hateful glee, but the look turned to shock at the sight of Khisanth's sudden plunge.

Talon tried to swerve away, but Khisanth was moving too fast. The two massive dragons smashed together, and Khisanth locked her limbs around her foe. Her claws raked across Talon's back and belly. Her jaws closed on the twisting, serpentine neck, fangs stabbing through leathery scales and veins and threatening to crush her foe's windpipe.

Both dragons plummeted, locked in their death embrace. They flailed and flayed each other with enormous claws. Black scales and gobs of blood and gore sprayed behind them like a grisly wake as they rushed ever faster toward the ground.

With her jaws securely clamped around Talon's throat, Khisanth disgorged a blast of acid. The other dragon shrieked and exploded into a fury of writhing and twisting limbs. The acid streamed into the wounds in Talon's neck, flooding his throat, drawing into his lungs. He was drowning in thick, oozing heat that devoured him from the inside. A grating bellow blasted a cloud of greenish steam from Talon's maw. The acid sprayed frantically in every direction, but still the dragon writhed and convulsed in Khisanth's iron grip.

Unable to feel her own hindquarters through the searing pain, Khisanth was about to pump another blast into Talon. They smashed into the ground, Khisanth atop Talon. Khisanth was stunned for several moments, but reflexively maintained her bite on her enemy's throat. As she regained her senses, her front claws pinned the beast's neck, and she tore upward, nearly ripping Talon's head free of his body.

The black dragon was already dead, suffocated, consumed

by the ravenous acid. Clouds of steam billowed upward from the hissing, bubbling wound. Acid from Talon's stomach seeped out through the horrid slashes and punctures in his abdomen and sputtered on the ground.

Khisanth raised her head in a thunderous bellow of victory. Her head swam and her body throbbed. She tasted Talon's bitter blood on her fangs, and her own blood raced.

Then she saw Pteros and the other dragon circling and swooping high overhead. Both dragons bled from numerous wounds. Pteros's wings were tattered. Still he managed to stay in the air. For all his fear and worry, Pteros's age and experience still showed in the contest with the much younger beast. Everything Pteros lacked in speed and reflexes he made up in cunning.

Time after time they raced past each other, claws raking and acid erupting. On their eighth or ninth pass—Khisanth had lost count—Pteros suddenly rolled, exposing his belly but also bringing his powerful rear claws into the attack. One of the enormous, hooked talons sliced through the other dragon's hide and snagged a rib. The younger beast snapped as if a leash had been pulled, then spun out of control through the sky. Khisanth could see that her flank was torn apart, the rib pulled outward. From the flailing of the body she guessed she was still alive, but barely.

For many long seconds the body plunged, finally crashing into the stones of the ruined castle. The impact shook apart a nearby portion of wall, and its collapse added to the din and debris. Khisanth could see the body as the dust cleared, bent unnaturally around its broken spine.

Khisanth struggled to her feet. The fire in her back legs and tail was gone, replaced by a throbbing ache. She could see that many of her scales were gone, revealing raw patches of burned flesh. But though these wounds hurt, she could walk and believed she could fly.

With her anger once again building, she watched Pteros's descent. She was tempted to take wing and attack him in the air, but something in his manner held her back. He was still high above the ground and dropping fast when he suddenly crumpled, then crashed into the mossy bog like a stone.

Khisanth approached him, ready to exhale a deadly cloud at the first sign of attack. Pteros lay on his side, watching through heavy eyes as she approached. When she neared, he raised his head, struggling to get to his feet. He couldn't.

Pteros's left wing was broken and nearly amputated; Khisanth marveled that he had flown at all. But the real wound was in his abdomen. In turning to attack the young dragon, he had exposed his belly, and the monster had slit Pteros open. The claws of his right rear foot were embedded in his own flesh, trying to keep the wound from opening. Even so, Khisanth could see his organs pressing out as Pteros's own bulk sought to burst him open.

"You meant to abandon me to your enemies. Did our blood-mingling mean nothing?"

"I didn't mean to betray you." The strength of his voice surprised Khisanth, who expected to hear a dying rasp. "I was just so frightened. Long ago, Talon drove me from my lair in this stronghold and stole my hoard."

"You must have known there were two. Why did you never tell me about the other dragon?" she demanded.

Pteros gulped stiffly as a spasm rocked his body. "I didn't know, I swear it. That's why I was so scared."

Khisanth felt nothing but pity for the dragon she'd once revered for his venerable age. He was now as terrified of dying as he had been of living. Half in anger, have in mercy, Khisanth stepped forward and placed her left foot on Pteros's neck, pressing it to the ground. The ancient dragon looked up at her helplessly as the talons of her right claw sliced across his throat.

"The Dark Queen calls you, Pteros. Go to her bravely in death as you would not in life." She knew the dying dragon heard her, but could not reply. Slowly, the life disappeared from his eyes. Pteros's wrinkled lids closed one last time.

Once again, Khisanth stood alone in her realm.

PART THREE

Chapter 14

Highlord Maldeev's admiration for his black dragons was undisguised as he studied his two best wyrms engaged in mock battle above Shalimsha Tower's drill field. Directly behind him to the north were the makeshift tents of the bulk of his troops. Past the encampment was the tower itself.

The highlord's appearance on the reviewing stand this day was as much ceremonial as official. As a consequence, he was wearing his battle regalia of crimson enameled plate armor with the dragon highlord helmet that completely enclosed his head and face. The mask was a simple affair, smooth at the sides and top, save for the two horns, with generous eye, nose, and mouth holes. The suit was well-insulated for comfort at flying altitude, which made it quite warm for sitting on a reviewing stand.

The dragon highlord was reminded of a sunny, late

autumn day several years before. It was the day the dragon who called herself Khisanth flew brazenly into the stronghold of the Black Wing and made clear her intent to join their ranks. Maldeev had a keen eye for dragon flesh and had instantly recognized that this one dragon was worth three or four others and would be a tremendous addition to his newly formed branch of the Dark Queen's army. It pleased him to recall that he'd been so very right about Khisanth those years ago.

In a roundabout way, the ruined state of Shalimsha Tower had helped to bring Khisanth to the wing. Maldeev had found the tower in total ruin, a tower the higher-ups in Neraka had directed him to occupy. More roots and weeds stood than walls. Most had obviously tumbled centuries before during the Cataclysm. Maldeev had ordered his humans and ogres to repair first those places that affected his personal comfort.

The workmen had not yet completed the renovations to his apartment when Maldeev heard Khisanth's ear-splitting screech in the courtyard. The highlord bade the workmen silence their chisels and mallets. He poked his head out to find a strange and beautiful dragon in the courtyard below, preening for the benefit of the gathering throng. Without stopping to dress, Maldeev stepped out onto a balcony over the courtyard in his dressing gown.

No one could call a dragon slim, but the one in the courtyard was unusually well-muscled and lithe, with nary a trace of fat beneath her glistening scales. She wore an odd chain of swords splayed around her neck. Head held proudly, the female dragon had only to tilt her massive head slightly to level her fiery eyes with Maldeev's, even though he stood on the second level of the tower. Highlord and dragon locked gazes, sizing each other up. Neither spoke. The dragon did not look away in deference to the highlord's authority.

There could be only one reason the dragon had come to Shalimsha Tower. "Fly," Maldeev said, his tone more suggestion than command.

Without benefit of a ledge, the dragon leaped into the air.

She gave a short demonstration of her skills, including aerial somersaults, wing-overs, and especially impressive midair stops and starts. The dragon seemed to all who watched her to defy the laws of nature.

"How does a rider affect your dexterity?" Highlord Maldeev asked when she again landed gracefully, soundlessly, in the hushed courtyard.

"Not at all, since I'll take no rider," the newcomer responded in the highlord's own Common tongue. Though a female, her voice was moderately deep.

"Then what use are you to me? To the forces of the Dark Queen?" Maldeev asked, eyes narrowed, calloused hands on his silk-covered hips.

Prancing only slightly to cool herself after her demonstration, the dragon said, "Try me for a span of time at your discretion and find out."

The highlord hesitated, considering how to handle such a spirited dragon. There was no question he wanted her in his army, but he couldn't let her think she had the upper hand.

"Can you afford to turn away anyone who would serve the Dark Queen?" the dragon pressed while he pondered.

At that, Maldeev made his decision. Clasping his arms behind him, the highlord turned on his heels and strode out of sight without another word to the dragon. Moments later, a lesser commander emerged into the courtyard and instructed some soldiers milling about to secure a spot for the new dragon next to Jahet's, temporarily quartered in the northern length of the tower's open-air outer ward.

Two years had passed since. The carving of dragon stables in the nearby mountains was almost complete. The number of dragons had risen to five since Khisanth had joined. Maldeev had not spoken to Khisanth once in that time. He couldn't address her directly—for a highlord to speak with any dragon but his own was unseemly, even insulting to his own mount, and an implied elevation of rank.

Maldeev monitored Khisanth's progress by watching the drills and asking for reports from Jahet, his dragon soul mate. Maldeev had begun to notice of late that Khisanth made all the other dragons—even Jahet, the highlord confessed with a measure of disloyalty—look a bit sluggish.

Seeing Khisanth and his lead dragon flying together, it was difficult to believe that Jahet's reaction to Khisanth had been lukewarm at first. The two seemed inseparable now. Maldeev frowned at Jahet's obvious lack of judgment—it was most unwise for the number one dragon to so obviously prefer the number five dragon over all the others.

Therein was the problem. Maldeev could not promote Khisanth to the level of her ability, because she was still unwilling to take a rider. She'd lost none of her arrogance. Khisanth's resistance bordered on insubordination. That made Maldeev look bad. Word would spread to the other wings that the highlord of the Black Wing couldn't control his dragons. Thinking of the recent problems he'd had with Neraka, Highlord Maldeev wondered if it hadn't already. . . .

Damn, but sometimes these dragons were more trouble than they were worth, thought the old cavalryman. Horses did as they were directed, or were killed on the spot.

Maldeev resolved to deliver an ultimatum at his afternoon meeting with Jahet.

* * * * *

Khisanth's horned hind feet touched down on the dusty plain that served as the Black Wing's drill field. Her massive sides heaved, ribs rising and falling beneath her black scales, glistening with sweat. Khisanth leaned heavily against a lone oak in the otherwise barren field as she struggled to draw huge gulps of air into her aching lungs.

Jahet landed heartbeats after Khisanth. The other black dragon's joyous laughter sent the froth of exertion spraying from her maw. Kicking up dust, Jahet pranced about to keep her legs from cramping. Sunlight glinted off the uncut, apple-sized diamond that she wore like an earring through her left nostril.

"You won again, Khisanth," she conceded through her panting, "but only because you decided, midway to the goal, to turn the flight into a race!"

Khisanth drew long, deep breaths to slow her breathing enough to speak without panting. "I'll wager the enemy won't give us advance warning, either," she managed at last, making a show of licking a sore muscle so that she could avert her gaze.

Jahet had the grace to smirk at Khisanth's impertinent, though accurate, observation. She gave the other dragon a glance of unabashed awe. "By the queen's ten eyes, you're fast, Khisanth."

Khisanth stifled the urge to gloat. Instead, the dragon said, "Your performance was impressive as well, Jahet."

The Black Wing's ranking dragon gave an ironic snort of laughter. "Highlord Maldeev's mount had better be!" She swung her heavy head around to glance at the Black Wing's highlord and commander, who stood some distance away, watching the drills from the reviewing stand. "If I were a more suspicious dragon, I might think you were angling for my job," Jahet concluded, a mischievous gleam in her eyes.

Khisanth's own tawny eyes widened in genuine alarm. "You know I would never—"

"Never take a rider, is what you mean," concluded Jahet for her. Her expression turned serious. Jahet thought about starting in on a familiar lecture, then changed her mind. "I have something important to tell you, Khisanth," she confided, "but not here. We've risked too much, speaking in the open, already."

Jahet looked at the three mounted dragons still in flight formation in the cloudless blue sky above. Her gaze abruptly shifted to the long, northern leg of the drill field, to the troop tents and Shalimsha Tower directly behind it. Between them and the tower stood Maldeev in his reviewing box, arms clasped behind his back. The highlord liked to come to the field at least once a week and personally monitor the progress of his generals and their troops. As an old horse cavalry commander, he derived a special thrill from watching the dragons' flight drills.

Jahet looked back to the younger dragon at her side. "Meet

me in my antechamber as soon as possible" —she looked to the dragons in flight again— "and let no one see you." Jahet's left eye shifted away to look to the sun for the hour. "I need to feed, and I haven't much time before a strategy session with Maldeev."

With that, Jahet turned toward the dragon barracks. She'd intended to walk, but decided to step up the pace toward the newly mined dragon lairs in the deforested foothills to the west. Taking a short two-step hop, she extended her wings and glided just above the grassy slope, dropping to the ground again when the land leveled into the glade before her lair.

Alone on the dry, barren field, Khisanth watched with a sigh from her soul as Jahet went. The fatigued black dragon was in no mood for the lectures Jahet delivered with greater frequency these days, but Khisanth didn't wish to offend the ranking dragon by ignoring a summons to her antechamber. Khisanth couldn't remember Jahet's asking any of the higher ranking dragons to her lair. Perhaps Khisanth was headed for a dressing down. She thought it more likely that Jahet had invited her because, unlike the other dragons, she and Jahet were friends. More than friends, for they had secretly bloodmingled in the way of those who had come before.

Strangely, she and Jahet had become friendly despite Khisanth's determination not to. Trust no one but yourself— Led's betrayal had taught her that. Pteros had so much as told her. Even before she'd made the decision to join the army forming in the south, she'd resolved to keep her own counsel among humans and dragons because of them. Her ego would never allow her to tell anyone about Led or Pteros.

First Led, whom she'd briefly but utterly trusted, had considered her sole value a night's pleasure. Khisanth had difficulty deciding who was the greater fool in that fiasco, though she ultimately concluded it was Led, since he was not alive to learn from his folly.

Then Pteros. He'd disappointed her as much as betrayed her. All she'd asked for was a small part of his vast knowledge and experience. She couldn't forgive him his weak spirit. In her reflective estimation, worse than leaving her to die was the fact that he left behind none of the treasure of which he had bragged, except the gemless diadem she'd removed from his broad, bloodied forehead.

There was much Khisanth respected about Jahet. She was more concerned with advancing her own considerable skills than comparing herself to the other dragons. Jahet had every black dragon's exceptional greed. While Khisanth admired that, it prevented her from telling Jahet some things, including the range of her magical skills. She was especially careful to conceal her shapechanging ability, thinking the other dragons would feel threatened by the unusual power.

Jahet had disappeared beyond the trees now, and Khisanth realized she would have to hurry if she was to meet with Jahet before the other dragon began her feed. Covering the distance quickly on foot, she plowed through the thick row of ponderosa pines left standing to disguise the entrances to the dragon warrens. Khisanth unconsciously ducked her head as she stepped into the tall cavern that served as the central meeting hall. She needn't have, since the cavern had been carved to twice her own height to accommodate even the tallest of dragons who might eventually join the wing. It was pleasantly dark inside after the annoyingly bright sunshine she had never grown to like. Water dripped steadily in the far recesses of the cavern.

Jahet's rank demanded the privilege of quarters separate from the other four dragons. To the right and left of the meeting hall, like the legs of an enormous spider, three large dens, or lairs, had been carved, each at half the height of the central hall. That made six chambers, with room to excavate more if necessary, though two were currently empty and awaiting dragons.

Lairs that fed into the main chamber were assigned in descending order of rank from the first lair on the left. Khisanth's was the last one, located at the right rear of the meeting chamber. As a result, and to the great irritation of the others, her lair was the most secluded and private.

Her long tail softly brushing the dirt floor, Khisanth walked clockwise around the chamber to steal a quick glance into the other dragons' lairs. It was forbidden to physically wall off the entrance to one's lair, for "security reasons." The rule was Dimitras's, adjutant to Brigade Commander Wakar. He was the human officer responsible for maintaining the dragon wing's morale, which Khisanth always interpreted to mean keeping them under control. He enforced the no-walls rule as strictly as any human among dragons could, preventing physical impediments, such as rocks or vines.

Dimitras had no control over the dragons' magical defenses, however. Like most humans, he was terrified by what he didn't understand, a long list topped off by dragon magic. All of the dragons had devised some sort of magical screen that limited or altered the view into their lairs.

The second-ranked dragon's defenses were the most impressive and long-lasting. Khoal was a well-scarred, battle-hardened, ancient male with tremendous greed and an extensive knowledge of magic. He was like Pteros with too much conceit, thought Khisanth. For his own amusement, the confusion of others, or simply to prove his superior magical skills, Khoal varied his spells daily. Some favorites included a wall of force, which created an invisible barrier that allowed others to see into but not enter his lair, and an illusionary door that couldn't be moved even by touch or disbelieving the illusion.

The most impressive and offensive of Khoal's protective spells was discovered by the fourth-ranked dragon. Neetra, young and even more rash than most black dragons, had refused to attend flight drills one day, alleging that he had a stiff wing. Khisanth had raised an eyebrow at that, since Neetra prided himself on his strength over Khoal's bulk or Khisanth's agility. It was also widely known that Neetra felt the competition between Khoal and himself more keenly, since Khoal was the only other male in the stable. No one above or below Neetra in rank chose to order him to the field, since his absence would only make the others look better. Dimitras knew better than to try to force a dragon to do anything. So

Neetra stayed in his warren, while the others filed out and onto the drill field.

Khisanth remembered thinking as she passed it that morning that the opening to Khoal's lair didn't show its usual signs of a protective spell, as if he'd left and forgotten to cast one. Engrossed in drilling, everyone in the camp heard shrill howls and saw flashes of ghostly blue light cut through the row of trees that hid the entrance to the lairs. Rushing inside, they'd found Neetra in his cave, missing a fang, his eyes red orbs in his soot-covered face. He nursed a claw that was blistered and cracked open. The cave wall opposite Khoal's den was blackened except for a vague outline at the center. Khisanth and the others could only speculate on the exact nature of the spell Neetra suffered that morning. Neetra's hate-filled look and Khoal's smug expression left no question that they shared some bitter secret.

Hurrying now past the other lairs, Khisanth removed the protective wards from the archway that led to her own lair. She was momentarily annoyed that Dimitras had not yet delivered the live, large mammals for the dragons' usual feeding after the day's drill. Highlord Maldeev forbade the dragons to hunt for themselves, saying it drew too much attention to them. Even so, Khisanth had slipped away several times as a vulture. Flying far from Shalimsha, she'd changed back into a dragon and fed heartily, just for the sheer pleasure of it. Khisanth would have liked to gulp something to tide herself over now, but her gnawing hunger would have to wait until after her secret meeting with Jahet.

Khisanth had many secrets. In addition to her ability to shapechange, she knew of a shortcut to Jahet's secluded lair that ensured absolute secrecy—even from Jahet. At the back of Khisanth's chamber a fresh mountain stream cascaded in a steady, three-foot-wide waterfall through a vertical crevasse. Desiring to swim one day, but too large to fit into the flow as a dragon, Khisanth used the opportunity to keep her qhen skills honed. Shapechanging into the form of an alligator she'd once seen in the moors, she stepped into the falls and discovered a small, dry crevasse in the stone wall behind it.

Curious, she'd followed the narrow crack for some distance. To her great surprise, it led to a similar crack in the back of Jahet's lair. The other dragon seemed unaware of the crevasse, likely because it was concealed on her side by a curved rocky outcropping that ran from floor to ceiling; her size prevented her from seeing beyond it.

In a blink, Khisanth shapechanged into a small brown field mouse, darted behind the curtain of cold, falling water, and slipped through the crevasse. In this form, the distance to the back of Jahet's lair seemed miles, but soon her little mouse nose smelled fresh blood. Poking her pink nose and black eyes just beyond the stone curtain into Jahet's lair, the dragon-turned-mouse could see her friend feasting on a cow, its side torn and bloody, eyes open wide in death. The smell of fresh blood tickled Khisanth's hungry stomach. The ranking dragon had many privileges, concluded Khisanth, not the least of which was that Jahet got her meals delivered first.

Suddenly the dragon looked up. Her frenzied gaze fell upon the unexpected mouse at the back of her lair. Khisanth was glad that Jahet had already eaten, or she might have been a snack, and not allowed to skitter around the perimeter of Jahet's cave. Khisanth ran as fast as her mouse legs would carry her to the antechamber and reverted to dragon form beyond Jahet's vision.

The antechamber to Jahet's lair was large, with a very high ceiling that curved slightly away from the entrance. The stone walls were rough and glistened with moisture; the high humidity of summer made these quarters reasonably comfortable for the swamp-loving dragons.

Displaying proper dragon etiquette, Khisanth waited until she heard Jahet finishing her meal before announcing her presence. "I'm at your disposal, Jahet."

Jahet's head swung around to face the opening between her lair and the antechamber. She pulled stringy pieces of raw meat from between two razor-sharp fangs before speaking.

"That's strange, I didn't sense your approach," said Jahet, looking a bit puzzled as she shuffled forward to enter the chamber. The dragon's meal had made her slightly sleepy, so she circled slowly around and finally lowered her form to recline on the cool stone floor.

"I asked you here because you and I both know your skills are being wasted. You'll never rise beyond the fifth rank if you continue to refuse a union. It's a credit to the highlord's belief in your abilities that you've maintained your position without a rider."

"There you have it!" cut in Khisanth quickly. "Many thought Maldeev would send me away after the first month for declining to take a rider. But he hasn't. I've maintained my current position for nearly two years without a rider." Jahet's was a familiar lecture, as were Khisanth's answers.

"You used to be the third-ranked dragon, before two others joined." Jahet's eyes narrowed. "You and I both know you've maintained the fifth ranking simply because no other dragons have stepped forward in the last year. One inevitably will."

"I'll deal with that problem when it arises," Khisanth said a trifle defensively.

"But why should you have to, Khisanth? Think how far you could climb in status if you took a rider! I'm certain you'd overtake Khoal and be ranked second in no time."

Khisanth's thick-boned wings rose in a semblance of a human shrug. "I've learned the value of patience—a dragon's life is long. Someday I'll rise to the second rank without the hindrance of a human."

Jahet's brows raised, and she looked askance. "Do you think I bend more than my knees to Highlord Maldeev?"

Khisanth lowered her guard momentarily, one eye blinking rapidly at her own unintended slight. "I wouldn't presume to interpret your relationship. I only know that I've yet to meet the human who's proven himself the equal of a dragon." To her annoyance, she remembered one who'd managed to break her nose, but she'd been a human then, too. That didn't count. "Perhaps you've found the only one in Maldeev," Khisanth suggested as a conciliatory afterthought.

"Flattery doesn't become you, Khisanth," Jahet said sourly. "I haven't summoned you to argue, but to warn you. I risk much telling you this," she continued, dropping her voice to a whisper, though there was no one around to hear them. "That which you both want and fear may happen sooner than you think." Khisanth looked puzzled.

Jahet pressed on. "Maldeev has been watching your progress, and I sense his pleasure. The nature of his questions tell me that he's anxious to move you up in the ranks, but feels he can't unless you take a rider."

Khisanth shrugged noncommittally, but inwardly she felt a jolt of delight at the news. "Maldeev is highlord. He'll find a way to raise my rank if he truly believes it to be in the best interest of the wing to do so."

Jahet smirked at her. "Ah, but you're forgetting the other dragons. . . ."

"I try to," Khisanth cut in wryly.

"You have made enemies among them," acknowledged Jahet, "partly because of your superior skills. They also feel you receive favored treatment."

"Don't I?" Khisanth asked with brutal honesty.

Jahet nodded. "It's true. Our friendship has not helped them accept you." It was impossible not to notice the other dragons' animosity for Khisanth, despite the fact that Jahet didn't interact with them off the drill field, since her lair did not adjoin theirs.

"Neither has your refusal to take a rider, nor Maldeev's tolerance of it."

"You've put your talon on it—they're jealous," said Khisanth.

Jahet wagged a digit at her defensive friend. "Don't underestimate the power of their envy." She locked eyes with Khisanth. "Make no mistake, Maldeev and I allow you privileges for our own purposes, but neither he nor I can protect you from their spitefulness. Any blatant intervention on our parts would simply make matters worse."

"I'm not asking for any help. I can handle the other dragons," Khisanth said stonily.

"Yes, I suppose you could," agreed Jahet, "*if* we were trying to defeat them. But, lest you forget, they're on our side."

Khisanth laughed humorlessly and spoke her mind before she could stop herself. "Frankly, I can't see that those dragons are on anyone's side but their own." Khisanth's feelings about Khoal, Dnestr, and Neetra's disloyalty was just that—a feeling. She believed that even combined, they weren't smart enough to cause the wing any real damage with their spiteful little tricks. What was more, they didn't appear to relish each other any more than they did her; Neetra and Dnestr toadied to Khoal's face, but sniggered behind his back.

"You know as do I that it's unusual—even unnatural—for black dragons to work together," said Jahet. "I'm sure you've felt a conflict yourself." She blinked slowly, considering her words. "I believe the others are as loyal to the wing as can be expected." The ranking dragon's tone became clipped. "At any rate, I didn't ask you here to discuss the behavior of the other dragons. I'm addressing yours."

Khisanth looked up in surprise. She'd never heard that rancorous tone of Jahet's directed at her. "Are you suggesting that the others are more useful than I?"

Jahet inclined her head slightly. "They're of more use to the wing with riders on their backs, yes."

Khisanth tried unsuccessfully to mask her shock and outrage. "Is that a directive to take a rider? Or are you ordering me to feign friendly relations with the others? We both know they're petty and scheming, that they would rather devote years to my downfall than expend energy elevating themselves or sharpening their skills."

"As long as you don't slay each other," Jahet responded coldly, "your relations with the other dragons mean little to me or the wing." Seeing Khisanth's stubborn expression, Jahet softened her words. "What I am telling you, as your friend, is that both you and the entire wing would benefit from your taking a rider."

Khisanth's willful expression still did not change. Looking pointedly at her stubborn friend, Jahet took a deep breath and decided to disclose the full extent of the news. "The fact is, Khisanth, I'm not sure that you'll have a choice on this subject for much longer. Maldeev doesn't know that I read his mind with a spell, but he's considering several of his commanders for an arranged union with you."

Khisanth could not hide her shock. "It's gone that far?"

Jahet nodded coolly. "You would be allowed to choose between them, I believe."

If Jahet had been any other creature on Krynn, Khisanth would have slashed her to death in sheer rage. It took every ounce of her accumulated wisdom to persuade her that her friend was simply the messenger of this vile news. Talons curled into painful fists, Khisanth shook visibly when she managed to bitterly croak, "Isn't that democratic?"

"This is not a democracy."

Khisanth's eyes flashed. "You of all dragons should know that I can't be forced to cooperate with this plot. I could leave the wing as freely as I arrived."

"Could you?" Jahet asked archly. "Technically, we dragons are free to leave whenever we wish—who but the queen could stop us?" she said, her words ripe with meaning. Khisanth looked away, her nose held high.

Jahet's patience with her recalcitrant friend was running threadbare. She was, after all, a black dragon. "Maldeev awaits," she said. Tucking her long tail to skirt around Khisanth, the dragon headed for the exit to her lair. "Ponder what I've said, Khisanth," she muttered with a dismissive toss of a claw. "My advice is to do what's best for you—and our queen's army. They are one and the same." With that, Jahet waddled through the opening and was gone.

Frowning, Khisanth watched with mixed feelings as the ranking dragon departed. She couldn't be angry with Jahet. The other black dragon had gone out on a limb to warn her. Khisanth suspected that Jahet was dangerously close to violating the spirit of her union with Maldeev. No matter how friendly she was with Khisanth, she was bonded to Maldeev by the Dark Queen herself.

Khisanth knew only that she didn't want to leave the Black Wing—that had been an angry threat. It was her goal, and she believed it to be Takhisis's, that she rise through the ranks on her merits alone. Khisanth had managed to dodge the question for a number of human years, because her superior skills could not be denied. She had hoped—no, worked, hard—to prove that she needed no rider. The dragon couldn't see what had changed, what had prompted Maldeev to force a choice. But something definitely had.

"Flow with whatever happens, stay focused by accepting whatever is," Kadagan would tell her whenever she grew frustrated. Qhen had taught her that denying the existence of a truth would not change it; refusing to acknowledge the presence of a rock in the path would not negate it.

Khisanth was faced with the emotional whims of humans who had built the evil army on protocol they weren't eager to disregard. If Khisanth wanted to fight for her queen, she might have no choice but to trust a human on her back.

* * * * *

At that moment, one very highly placed human in the Dark Queen's army waited impatiently for his dragon. Highlord Maldeev stood in Shalimsha Tower's great hall, checking the time on his water clock. The massive machine was built and maintained by gnome slaves. Maldeev despised their flighty, constant gibbering. He kept them alive only because their mechanical artistry was unequalled. If they could build a device such as this clock, he expected he could find other uses for them in the upcoming campaign. Suddenly Maldeev was struck with the obvious solution to the gnomes' chatter. He made a mental note to have the barber remove their tongues.

The bulky water clock was one of only two items of furniture in the long, rectangular hall, the other being an ornate, claw-foot chair for Maldeev's use only. The highlord's second renovation to the tower, after his apartments, was to remove the entire length of wall that divided the courtyard from the great hall. This allowed his dragon to enter the cavernous hall for private meetings, without Jahet resorting to spells whose use made the human highlord uncomfortable. The tower's original banquet hall was the only protected place in the castle large enough to accommodate Jahet's bulk.

Thick, irregular timber trusses stained dark with pitch arched overhead from one long length of wall to the opposite side, supporting the roof of the great hall. Maldeev had ordered the restoration of tapestries that had originally lined the plaster-covered stone walls, but had been used as blankets by previous occupants of the tower. The walls were pale, bare, and cool even in summer while workmen hastened to complete the refurbishment of the tapestries.

At the shorter eastern length of wall, adjoining the kitchen, was a deeply recessed fireplace, tall enough for a human to walk into. It burned constantly, even in summer. Maldeev's elaborate chair, twice his height, was set before it. Jahet's large entrance allowed light in the room by day. The fire, aided by beeswax tapers on rock corbels, lit it by night.

Maldeev considered the waning sunlight through narrowed eyes. Jahet was dangerously close to breaking for the first time a central element of their oath to each other. "Never keep your soul mate waiting." They'd made the vow during their union ceremony some five years earlier, agreeing that such a tenant showed respect for the value of each other's time. And now Jahet was wasting his.

Still, Maldeev had to conclude that his union with Jahet had proven satisfactory beyond even his lofty expectations. They had performed the ceremony just after he'd returned from the city of Neraka far across the mountains to the west, where the Dark Queen had raised her temple—the Temple of Istar reborn.

The idea to raise his own branch of the army rallying under the banner of Takhisis had not been Maldeev's. In fact, Takhisis herself, through a minion, had issued him the mandate to recruit evil black dragons and form what would henceforth be know as the Black Wing. As usual, the memory of his time in the dark temple brought both a cold trickle of fear and a rush of pride to Maldeev.

At the time of the mandate, Maldeev had been distinguishing himself as an excellent tactician in one of the first branches of Takhisis's army, the blue dragons under Highlord Bakaris himself. Maldeev was widely known to remain calm under fire; he was also a peerless horseman. He had risen quickly to the level of brigade commander of mercenary cavalry in the Blue Wing, headquartered in Sanction, the city made famous by its constantly erupting volcanoes.

Maldeev had been in the tent-city of Neraka, near Sanction, on a clandestine intelligence mission to the combined evil forces. Neraka had sprung up at the base of Takhisis's Temple of Darkness. A discussion of troop numbers was heating up among some midlevel commanders of the White Dragon Wing when a messenger stepped into the unadorned tent and informed Maldeev that he was hereby summoned to the temple. Maldeev was stunned. Who but the very lowest of commanders knew he was in Neraka, let alone this tent?

Thinking he might very well be walking to his death, Maldeev had little choice but to follow the messenger into the city. The young brigade commander had seen the twisted temple from the distance—who could miss it? He'd once read that "it clawed its way into the sky like a bird of prey, overshadowing the city below into perpetual night." That was certainly true, he'd thought as he walked behind the messenger through the northwest gate and into the crowded market square. Maldeev bumped elbows with black-robed mages, as well as the dark clerics who were numerous among the Dark Queen's personal troops.

He distrusted mages. They reminded Maldeev how easily his location could be known by anyone in authority. What he couldn't understand was why anyone important cared. Had he somehow been set up by soldiers in the Blue Wing whom he'd deliberately stepped on or otherwise betrayed to achieve his current rank?

Maldeev could well remember walking the twisting and tilting halls of the black tower. Though a skilled tracker, he quickly became confused by the route through countless anterooms and seemingly pointless chambers. Maldeev followed the messenger up a narrow, endlessly spiraling staircase that eventually led to a door. The door opened onto a large, spoon-shaped platform of cold red marble. The messenger pushed him through the door and disappeared.

Maldeev stumbled forward into the darkness. There was no light at all. It took long seconds for Maldeev's eyes to adjust. Still he could see nothing beyond the slightly glowing marble at his feet. The air didn't move, as if Maldeev stood in the eye of a storm. The still atmosphere was oppressive.

"Step forward, Maldeev," a dark, muffled voice hissed suddenly, as if from behind a mask.

Maldeev shuffled toward the voice mechanically, seeing nothing beyond the vision of his feet at the ends of his legs.

"Stop."

Maldeev did as he was told, desperately squinting into the absolute darkness. He thought he spotted a shadowy hint of a horned mask, but then the image was gone.

"Why have I been summoned?" he managed to ask.

"Silence, or I will reconsider the choice!"

Maldeev could feel eyes studying him for many long minutes. Finally, the muted voice said, "We have an empty platform in this hall, waiting for the highlord of her majesty's black dragons. You have been chosen to assemble that new wing in the name of Takhisis."

"Who are you to have chosen me?" Maldeev hadn't meant to sound impertinent. He simply wished to know the identity of the speaker.

A cold hush suddenly descended over the area, which was already unnaturally still. Maldeev felt as if the breath were being choked from his body by an unseen force. Then the surrounding air seemed sucked away. Maldeev's knees failed him. He tumbled to the cold marble, gasping for breath.

Just as suddenly, cool, sweet air rushed almost too quickly into his lungs. Maldeev stood again, coughing. He now knew who had chosen him. This was the Queen of Darkness's temple, after all.

Maldeev asked no more questions after that, content to receive detailed directions from the disembodied voice. They included the location of Shalimsha Tower as the headquarters for the Black Wing. He was also advised to tax the locals to amass a war chest and to recruit ogres and other mercenary troops. There was a final command to immediately perform the union ceremony with a worthy dragon under Takhisis's watchful eye, for no one could be highlord without a dragon.

Maldeev was offered two black dragons, who had already traveled to Neraka and volunteered their services to form the core of the wing. One was Khoal, an ancient male with great power. But he was also excessively vain and independent. The other was Jahet, a younger female. While she could not match Khoal for sheer power, her intelligence appealed to Maldeev. They worked well together from the start. Maldeev had never regretted his choice.

The way Maldeev had been recruited to start the wing also heavily influenced the way he ran it. Secretive, doling out information on a need-to-know basis, he sometimes called soldiers in just to keep fear of him uppermost in their minds. He had a mercurial temperament that caused even his most trusted advisors to tiptoe around him at all times. All but Jahet, that is.

Maldeev's infamous temper was in full bloom by the time Jahet's horned hind feet touched down beyond the enormous doorway. The highlord didn't greet her. Sullenly slumped in his oversized chair, Maldeev craned his neck back to stare her in the eyes. The human raised an eyebrow and directed her gaze to his softly humming water clock.

In retort, Jahet looked calmly to the sun behind her and back to his stormy face. "My timepiece is not as accurate as yours," she said with a disdainful glance at the cumbersome water clock. "We dragons aren't obsessed with time as are you short-lived humans. I've broken no vow to you, Maldeev. Besides," she added, her look almost coquettish as she shuffled forward, heavy tail dragging the loose rushes noisily behind her. "I was on a mission for you."

The sound of rustling made Maldeev wonder if he hadn't been imprudent to order new reeds and herbs for the floor today. Jahet detested any pleasant odor and would do whatever she could to soil and mark the room with her own scent.

Maldeev knew better than to consider breaking the enormous dragon of such an odious compulsion.

"I was delivering your message to Khisanth."

Maldeev nodded, remembering the request. Spinning the claw-footed chair away from the fire to show Jahet his profile, he slowly lowered his bulk into it again. His arms settled lazily on the rests, and he asked, "She doesn't see it as an ultimatum yet, does she? You let her think you were giving her a piece of friendly advice, yes?"

"Isn't that what we agreed I should do?"

"Yes." Maldeev knew Jahet well enough to sense when she was hedging. "And?"

Jahet could see no valid reason for not telling Maldeev that the conversation hadn't gone exactly as scripted. "It was necessary to tell Khisanth you were considering soul mates for her."

"What?" exploded Maldeev, leaping from the chair. "That will drive her away! Why didn't you just suggest in the strongest terms that she take a rider?"

"You think like a human, Maldeev," said Jahet. "I've made that suggestion for years, with no result. Khisanth would continue riderless as long as we allowed it because she believes it's in her best interest to do so. Always remember, Maldeev, self-interest is a black dragon's *only* motivation." Jahet looked pointedly into the highlord's steel-colored eyes. "No matter what they may claim."

Jahet flicked her long red tongue unconsciously. "Also remember, no one but Takhisis can truly force a black dragon to do anything. Khisanth will do our bidding *only* when she realizes that the best course for her future—her only future, considering the upcoming war—is with the Black Wing. She wants nothing more than to stay, but she's got to believe that the only way she can is to take a rider."

The black dragon blinked slowly in the face of the flush-cheeked highlord and lowered herself to rest comfortably on the floor. An irritating, cloying, fresh scent wafted to her large nostrils, threatening to make her sneeze. She would have to do something about that smell before leaving.

"I know Khisanth," continued Jahet, ignoring her itchy nostrils for the moment. "If I were her, I'd be furiously tearing apart my lair in rage, making Dimitras's pitiful life even more unbearable." Jahet let her tongue dart between two talons to retrieve an overlooked shred of raw meat. "Khisanth doesn't indulge in shows of rage like other black dragons, but I know her passions run as hot. She has an obsession for the wing. I'm confident that her decision will be to our liking."

Maldeev seemed somewhat mollified, the flush having left his cheeks. Still he paced, slapping a fist to his hand. "She *must* take a rider! We will not be allowed the luxury of reducing our forces by even one cavalryman, sending a barebacked dragon into battle in the upcoming war!" He glowered up at Jahet. "Why does she refuse to see that?"

Jahet drew up her wings in an odd shrug. "She sees only that her solo performance during drills far exceeds that of the other dragons who bear riders. She's right"— Jahet nodded her head slightly to the side —"with the obvious exception of me." She waited for the highlord's inevitable compliment to her superior skills.

"I don't ride you during daily drills," muttered the highlord. Jahet's glower went unnoticed by Maldeev. "Just think how Khisanth would be with a rider between her wings," he said almost wistfully.

His mood abruptly turned dark again. "I don't need this frustration now, Jahet," Maldeev said. He was already made painfully aware of his low ranking among wing commanders. The commander of the Black Wing was still awaiting his first shipment of draconians. Highlord Ariakas had begun to fill his ranks at least three years before with the creatures, who were reputedly so evil and indestructible they made ogres seem weak. Maldeev knew he was the last of the highlords to be issued the vicious creatures, the result of corrupted good dragon eggs.

Even behind Toede, that contemptible hobgoblin excuse for a highlord. . . .

And then there were the rumors new recruits brought of

knights amassing numbers in a stronghold not far to the north. Maldeev's dragons ran routine scouting flights. They reported seeing a refurbished castle near the town of Lamesh, but Khoal, Dnestr, and Neetra had said the troop numbers were too small to consider a threat. Still, the very presence of stiff-necked knights in the region was yet another burr in Maldeev's side.

The highlord's eyes narrowed to slits as he angrily spun the chair back to face the fire and plopped into it sulkily. "Tell Khisanth—" he spat over his shoulder, then amended in a sarcastic tone, remembering Jahet's advice about dragons "—suggest to her highness that she's got one day to decide that taking a rider is 'in her best interests.' "

"Or what?"

Maldeev's voice took on a razor-sharp edge as he stared into the fire. "I'm relying on you to see that it doesn't come to that, because that would be in *your* best interests. See that you don't disappoint either of us, dear Jahet."

Nodding calmly at the implied threat in the highlord's dismissal, Jahet said nothing. She stood and waddled toward the open wall. Though silent, the dragon would have the last word before departing for her lair.

Turning to stare right into Maldeev's eyes, Jahet relieved herself on the highlord's beloved fresh rushes.

Chapter 15

Khisanth popped through her side of the crevasse and reverted to dragon form just in time to see the other dragons returning from the drill field. Khoal, Dnestr, and Neetra all stopped first at the livestock pens to fill their bellies.

Khisanth sighed. Another chance to snoop and pry was gone.

"We're gathering in the conference chamber shortly to discuss important business, Khisanth," Khoal called over his wing. Though he couldn't see inside her lair because of the spell she had placed on the archway, Khoal's dragon senses obviously told him she was present.

"But we aren't scheduled for—"

"Be there!" he barked. Never patient, and now famished, the ancient dragon didn't allow further conversation. Swinging his tail around, Khoal snatched several bawling calves from the holding pen, dragged them into his lair, and magically darkened his doorway.

Khisanth's talk with Jahet had left her in no mood for confrontation with the other dragons, but the lowest ranking dragon could ill afford to be openly insubordinate now. At least until she decided whether she would comply with the highlord's ultimatum or leave the wing.

Khisanth hated everything about these pointless meetings of Khoal's. She corrected her thought inwardly; the point was to give the ancient dragon the opportunity to lord his rank, since Jahet did not attend. Ostensibly Khoal called them to make plans for the improvement of the wing, which would then be submitted to the lead dragon for her review and approval. However, the sessions always dissolved into petty squabbles over perceived slights during drill, violations of protocol, or complaints about the quality of livestock Dimitras brought them. In Khisanth's memory, nothing constructive had ever evolved from one of Khoal's power sessions. Jahet had never received one suggestion.

Khisanth had ways of making the meetings more tolerable. According to protocol established by Khoal, the dragons were to enter the chamber for a meeting in reverse order of rank, to signify each dragon's value to the wing. As lowest ranking dragon, Khisanth's time was not considered as valuable as the others, thus she could be kept waiting. However, Khisanth always made it a point to linger in her lair until the assigned time passed. Unable to enter until she did, either Neetra or Dnestr, impatient young toadies both, would inevitably lose control and shriek for Khisanth to hurry up, shattering the air of pomp and circumstance Khoal strove to impart on his tedious meetings.

Neetra had the honors this day. "Damn your wings, Khisanth, for holding up the meeting again!" the young male snarled from the archway into his lair. "I wager you'll be late for the war."

Khisanth stepped at last into the enormous central chamber. "I'm sorry if I kept you waiting, Neetra," she said in a sugared voice. "I was feasting and must have lost track of time." The black dragon settled her bulk into a lazy circle at her assigned place, opposite from where Khoal would sit. "And I've so been looking forward to today's meeting." Hastily filing into the room, Neetra and Dnestr could detect no expression of sarcasm in Khisanth's placid face. Deliberately ignoring her, they took their places in the circle, each on a side of Khoal. They sat as straight as eager dogs, watching for their second-in-command to arrive.

As usual, Khoal did not disappoint. Head held regally, his gaze directed to some mystical point above theirs, the ancient dragon took long, exaggerated strides into the chamber. He wore his usual embroidered ceremonial cape, which softly scraped the floor. In his claw he carried a gem-encrusted staff from his own personal hoard. Reaching his appointed spot, Khoal tossed the cape back over his wings and settled onto a large, straw-stuffed mat reserved for his use. He set the staff on the floor before him, careful to ensure that the largest gem, a ruby with no less than thirty distinct facets, faced up to catch the light.

Using a simple cantrip, Khoal produced a flame from his pointer talon and held it to an incense burner that had been placed by his mat before the meeting. Smoke rose from the brazier and quickly filled the room with the musty scent of stagnant water, an odor favored by black dragons.

"The one hundred twenty-seventh meeting of the dragons of the Black Wing will now commence," he intoned. "In the interest of time," continued Khoal in his best formal voice, "we will proceed straight to the day's business: scouting assignments."

Khisanth was happy to hear him shorten the meeting, but more than a little surprised that they were skipping the usual prayer to Takhisis. "Why the emergency meeting, Khoal?"

"Silence, Khisanth!" he barked. "You have spoken out of turn."

Khisanth could hardly keep from rolling her eyes. She settled for slumped posture and an indolent expression. According to Khoal's rigid protocol, dragons had to wait until those ranked above them had spoken at least once, unless directed with a question.

Khoal took note of her sloppy pose with a disapproving eye. "To answer your insolent question, this isn't an emergency meeting, just an unscheduled one. It's my opinion, as second-in-command, that we must reevaluate tonight's reconnaissance schedule. There'll be a full moon that will aid anyone observing us from the ground." The ancient dragon's eyes took on a more than usually malicious glint. "You'd know all of that, if you hadn't left drill early."

Khisanth suffered Khoal's jab in silence, mainly because she knew her indifference would infuriate him. She also knew that his bad temper had started long before she'd joined the wing. Like Pteros, Khoal had fought very briefly as a young dragon in the Third Dragon War before the Sleep. To hear Khoal talk about his role in the war, which he did constantly, the ancient dragon had once single-handedly fought Huma to a standstill for days until reinforcements arrived. Jahet had told her that, from the moment Maldeev had selected the young female as his soul mate over Khoal, the elder male made it no secret that he felt the position was rightly his due to age and experience.

Before Khisanth had arrived, when Jahet and Khoal had been the only two dragons in the wing, Highlord Maldeev had suggested that Khoal spend his time in the search for a rider worthy of his talents. Otherwise, Maldeev had implied, the riderless Khoal would find the number two position similarly filled. Khoal had secretly sneered at the suggestion, and particularly at the threat. Though he was never overtly contentious to Jahet, he'd subtly continued his campaign to outshine and ultimately oust the other dragon.

Until the sunny day Khisanth landed in the courtyard.

The young female dragon with the strange necklace, an impressive number of battle scars, and an impenetrable aura had been undeniably threatening to Khoal from the start. Khoal had always considered his enormous bulk a significant advantage. In addition to intimidating opponents, even other dragons, his size allowed him to crush foes quickly. But from the first time Khoal saw Khisanth's dexterity, on ground and in flight, the elder dragon knew his cumbersome weight might actually be a disadvantage against her.

That very night, Khisanth's first in the wing, Khoal had made major steps toward a union with a rider to secure his position. Conventional wisdom said that the best dragon and rider union existed between opposing sexes, but there were no female officers to choose from in the Black Wing. Khoal knew that he could not wait, or hope to influence Maldeev to dispense with Jahet. He chose Maldeev's second-in-command, the human general named Wakar, as much in need of a mount to maintain his ranking as Khoal needed a rider. Theirs became a merger of convenience more than complementing skills, as was Maldeev's and Jahet's. Khoal felt to this day that his union with Wakar was the best he could hope for, as long as Jahet was alive.

"The new flight schedule is as follows," Khoal said now, his tone imperious. "I will fly north and personally monitor the Solamnic outpost that interests our highlord. Dnestr will fly west, in a sweep from Alek-Khan to Ak-Baral. Neetra will cover the east by air, from Ogreshield to Sprawl." He looked at the fifth-ranked dragon under knobby brow bones. "Khisanth, you will fly south, to Delphon."

"Why south?" Khisanth demanded. "I usually fly east by northeast—I know the route by heart."

"Perhaps you know it too well," remarked Khoal with raised brows. Khisanth compressed her lips tightly. "However, that isn't the reason I want you to fly south. It has come to my ears that the forces of Good are gathering in or near Delphon. Even you must realize that's far too close to Shalimsha for the security of the wing."

"Besides," Neetra cut in eagerly, "your eyes are—"

Khoal waved a claw, and Neetra's words were cut off by a silence spell. Khisanth was stunned by the display. The dragons protected their belongings magically, but they refrained from casting spells on each other, since the potential for disaster was profound.

"I'll suffer no more lapses in protocol!" snapped Khoal, his red eyes boring into the obviously embarrassed young male.

"You'll endure the same, Khisanth, if you speak out of turn again."

Khoal clenched and unclenched his claws. "I'm sure what Neetra was trying to say is that your eyes are keener than all of ours and would be able to determine the nature of the activity from a greater, safer distance." Khisanth was struggling to believe Khoal had complimented her, when his veined eyelids raised and he spitefully added, "Unless you don't think you're capable of completing such an important mission."

Dnestr and Neetra snickered. They always did whenever Khoal put Khisanth in her place. She gave the obsequious pair a glare that wiped the sneers from their scaly black faces.

Khisanth's evaluating eye settled on the other female. Dnestr was ranked third because she was slightly smarter and more even tempered than Neetra. Her greed certainly rivaled his, frequently overriding her common sense, particularly when it came to Khoal. Dnestr seemed genuinely to look up to the elder dragon, which confounded Khisanth.

"You should be glad for the assignment, Khisanth," purred the third-ranked dragon now. "Delphon is so near, you'll be asleep in your lair before midnight."

"That will be all, Dnestr!" the ancient black snapped. Returning his haughty gaze to the dragon across from him, Khoal said, "Well?"

Caught in the midst of a yawn, Khisanth touched a claw to her chest and feigned an innocent look. "Oh, is it my turn to speak? I can never keep the rules straight—that's your strength, isn't it Khoal? Since mine is flying faster than any other dragon, I'm sure that, as Neetra so graciously suggested, I'll have no trouble completing the assignment to Delphon."

The angry bile Khisanth saw catch in Khoal's throat made suffering the dragon's insults worthwhile. Eyes narrowed to furious red slits, Khoal extinguished the brazier and snatched up his ruby staff. Stomping into his lair, he sealed off the archway with a spell. Awarding Khisanth petty glares of their own, Dnestr, then Neetra, scurried after.

Khisanth's eyes followed their departure, but her mind was elsewhere. There was something very odd about this meeting. First, no prayer to their patron god; that had never happened before. Khisanth was also at a loss to explain Khoal's wordless retreat. It was very unlike him to miss the opportunity to put her in her place. In a strange sort of way, her comeuppance was conspicuous by its absence.

Did Khoal know that Maldeev was trying to force her into a union that would jeopardize his own ranking? Was he being nice to her, in his own backhanded manner, as insurance against the time when she would outrank him? Suspicion grew in Khisanth's gut, but she had no real clue to the motive behind Khoal's behavior.

Khisanth was only further confused after she returned to the lair late in the night from her flight to Delphon. She'd seen few signs of life in the ruins of the fortress there. In fact, there had been so little to see that she'd spent more time devising ways to dodge Maldeev's ultimatum than actually spying. The dragon intended to report her lack of findings directly to Khoal, but he didn't appear to have returned from his own recon flight to the north. Dnestr and Neetra's lairs were similarly dark. A negative report could certainly wait until the morning. With a shrug of her shoulders, the black dragon retired early for the night.

* * * * *

A river? The young, freckle-faced sentry peered closely at the dark ribbon snaking toward him from the north. Unlike a river, this thing had two distinct ends and was a bit spotty in the middle. It was no river of cold mountain water. This was a stream of humanity. An army on the march. The flashes of silver he'd thought were moonlight on rushing water came from polished weapons of steel.

The sentry's pulse quickened. Perhaps it was a newly raised company of mercenaries coming to join the Black Wing. But that made little sense—why would they march at night? Could they be the draconians everyone knew the highlord was expecting? They would be coming on foot from Neraka to the north. So why hadn't he been told to look for them? The boy scowled. With no instructions, Sergeant Bild had thrown him up into the north guard tower tonight for the first time. How could he be expected to do his job if no one told him anything?

The young sentry glanced over his shoulder at the alarm bell suspended from a wooden tower in the courtyard. That bell was to alert the garrison in the event of an emergency. Was this an emergency? How could he be sure? The sentry looked back out onto the plain. That black, snaky shape sure looked like an army.

The whole garrison was asleep. Waking everyone now, if his sergeant had simply forgotten to tell him to expect an army, could be the worst mistake of the young soldier's life. It could be the last one, too, he realized. It would be his word against Bild's. Fat chance of anyone believing him. The boy rubbed his face. Sounding the alarm seemed more and more like a very bad idea.

What if it was an attacking army? The Black Wing wasn't at war yet. No one had told him to expect an attack. He could ask the soldier in the south guard tower to take a look, but they would both have left their posts; there was a stiff penalty for that. After a moment's reflection, the soldier decided to alert his sergeant and let the more experienced man have a look. Then the mistake, whosesoever it was, would be kept between them. Yes, that's it, he thought as he scrambled down the lashed ladder from the guard tower, clutching his spear.

It was a short jog to Bild's quarters. Facing the heavy wooden door, the sentry paused to decide just what he would say. In the silence, he heard sounds from inside.

Having heard nothing for hours but the quiet of the night, the soldier was surprised that someone else in the fortress was awake. There was no mistaking Bild's gravelly laughter. The young sentry was even more surprised to hear it echoed by a woman's high-pitched titter.

He close his eyes and rubbed his freckled face again.

Waking the sergeant would be bad enough, but interrupting him while he . . . . No, that was definitely a bad idea.

The soldier turned away from the door and stood forlornly in the open-roofed yard, wondering what to do next. There were other sergeants, though he didn't know their names. He'd just have to find one, and fast.

Dashing past the row of doors under the colonnade, trying to decide which one to knock on, the soldier was surprised again to see light filtering out through a shuttered window. What luck! He would be saved the awkwardness of having to wake someone.

The sentry scurried down the steps cut into the ground that led to the basement of the tower. He stepped up to the door and rapped tentatively. Immediately he heard movement inside. Footsteps approached the door. "Who's there?"

"My name is Caithford. I'm on sentry duty."

"No, you aren't," the voice responded. "You're knocking on my door when you should be on the ramparts. What do you want?"

Rattled, the soldier stammered back, "Uh, I've seen something. Down on the plain to the north. It looks like it might be, um, an army."

Feet scuffed on the floor inside the room. A heavy bolt clanked and the door swung inward, revealing one of Maldeev's dark clerics. This one was the dark-skinned elf, Andor. Behind him, the walls of the candlelit chamber were lined with stoppered bottles containing powders, tiny creatures suspended in oil, and other things so gruesome and odd he couldn't assign them names.

"Yes? Well?" The cleric shifted to obscure the human's view.

The shocked sentry jolted upright to attention, slapping his spear against his shoulder. The mysterious, hooded clerics were feared by the soldiers, but young Caithford did his best to hide his apprehension. "I apologize, your reverence, I saw the light and thought one of the sergeants had these quarters."

"Never mind," Andor muttered. He pulled the hood of his

cloak up over his dark head to cover his ears and slipped the deep cowl up around his neck. "If you think it's an army, why didn't you ring the alarm bell?"

The boy's face reddened. "It's pretty dark, and I couldn't see much more than a black trail. Maybe it's nothing, maybe draconians. . . ."

The young soldier's inexperience was clear to see. "Hurry now," the renegade dark-elf mage said, pushing the boy up the steps. "Take me to your post and show me this legion of soldiers."

Minutes later, both men stood atop the guard tower staring down toward the plain below the stronghold.

The elf's heightened sense of sight confirmed the sentry's fear. "That does indeed look like an army." Andor glanced toward the horizon, still dark, though lightening. "We have some time yet before dawn. Wait for me here—don't sound the alarm until I return."

Glad to have the weight of responsibility lifted, the sentry stepped aside, making room for the cleric to approach the ladder. But instead of leaving the tower, the dark elf reached below his cloak into a pouch at his belt. He removed a vial and held it up with the crescent moon behind it. The crystal shone faintly in the eery light, refracting bars of light onto the cleric's face and robes.

Wide-eyed, the sentry watched the cleric unstop the vial while muttering prayers and incantations beneath his breath. In one swift motion he tossed the contents of the cruet down his throat, then swiftly replaced the stopper and vial in his pouch.

Nothing seemed to happen for several moments. But then the dark blue cloak sagged and collapsed to the floor. A shadow flowed out of the pile of clothing and slipped over the brink of the guard tower. The sentry peered over the edge and saw the inky black cloud racing across the rocks toward the plain. The human moved in a wide path around the robes on the floor to stand as far from them as possible.

Andor sped across the broken ground. He was in a four-way race, pitting his cunning against the coming dawn, which would reveal him clearly; the advancing army, which would shortly reach the Black Wing's citadel; and the limited duration of his potion. But this was an opportunity for advancement Andor was not going to waste.

It was possible, he thought, that the youth was right; perhaps this was the troop of draconian reinforcements Maldeev expected. That possibility faded completely when Andor saw the banners waving atop the army's sharp-tipped pikes, when he saw the well-groomed, skirted, and barded horses. Atop the mounts were grim-faced humans in luminously polished plate mail.

These were Knights of Solamnia.

The human at the front of the parade of knights was obviously their general. His plate mail armor was polished to rival a looking glass; pressed into the metal on his left breast was an oval the size of a human hand, inside which was an elaborately detailed crown.

The visor of the general's closed-face helmet was pushed back for greater visibility and comfort while he rode; blond curls escaped its confines above dark brown eyes. His face was surprisingly young, by human standards, the double Solamnic mustache so lightly colored and sparse that it was difficult to see. His cheeks were covered with a light stubble, presumedly to mask three razor-thin, parallel scars on one cheek, though it did little toward that end.

The fresh-faced general was flanked by two knights, one younger still, the other much older, thick with gray hair. They, too, wore polished chain mail, with crossbows slung on their backs and swords girded. Behind them on horseback were at least one hundred well-armed knights, possibly more. Following the knights, Andor estimated, were fifty or sixty sergeants mounted on horses and armed with lances and swords; another one hundred fifty men-at-arms carrying spears, bills, shields, and halberds; another eighty or so archers; and pulling up the rear, a general assortment of motley humans, no doubt short-term levies and down-and-out sell-swords.

The cleric knew he needed to get specific information if he

was to impress Maldeev with his courage and cunning. He picked the knight who rode at the general's left shoulder and surged forward to merge with the human's moonlight shadow.

"Where are you going?" the living shadow asked the knight's shade.

"Marsssh souuthh. . . ." it responded in the slow, lazy, dark-toned drawl of most shadows.

"I can see that!" snapped the cleric impatiently. "Where to, and what for? Answer quickly, or you'll be making tracks for a gully dwarf!"

"Taahhhwer . . . fight eeeevil draaagguns. . . ." it said immediately, heeding Andor's threat.

"That would be Shalimsha, all right," the shadow mumbled worriedly. At their current rate of travel, Andor estimated they would reach the stronghold of the Black Wing within the hour, for a surprise attack at dawn. He would have to fly like the wind to have any chance of warning the wing in time to mount a defense. The cleric's thoughts turned from personal glory to self-preservation. Andor whipped his shadow around to the south and began to race for the alarm bell as if his life depended on it.

Chapter 16

Khisanth's sensitive hearing woke her with the first strike of clapper to bell. The dragon sat bolt upright on the dirt floor of her lair. Irritated at the intrusion to her sleep, she listened for confirmation that the ringing of the claxon had been a prank. But the tolling continued—frantically—and Khisanth knew that this was no trick, not even a surprise drill. Something was definitely wrong at the tower. She sniffed the air almost delicately but detected no odor of fire, which so frequently plagued towers like Shalimsha. What else could have caused such commotion? Determined to learn the cause of the ringing claxons, Khisanth removed the magical wards on her archway and stomped off, headed for the meeting chamber and the exit beyond.

Khisanth came to the archway. Suddenly her snout met with a wall, both clear and hard, where there should have been only air. The dragon was too big to suffer injury from the unexpected blow at such a slow speed, but it did put her back a step. A wave of aggravation replaced her first moment of confusion. Khisanth impulsively, stubbornly, dipped her left wing shoulder and prepared to ram her way through the archway. Her whole body crashed flat against an invisible barrier that sent her leathery flesh quivering in recoil. The black dragon tried again and again to smash through, but her attempts proved futile.

Dragon rage boiled her blood. She remembered Kadagan's teaching. *"The angry dragon will defeat itself."* Think clearly, she told herself. Answers came in moments.

Someone had erected a magical wall of force to trap her in her lair. The black dragon knew in a flash that somehow, the barrier and the claxons were linked. She could see through the invisible wall that the other dragons were not about. Khoal was the only one of them powerful enough to create something like this—he used it frequently to seal off his own lair. Even the vindictive ancient dragon would not have trapped her here simply to make her look bad for missing a surprise drill. Those claxons were ringing for the first time to signal an attack.

A terrible sense of foreboding blossomed in Khisanth, fanning the fires of suspicion kindled in Khoal's meeting the day before. Who would attack the wing, and how were the other dragons involved? Khoal had sent her on a wild-goose chase to the south while he went north. The stronghold of the Knights of Solamnia was to the north. Khoal had been reporting for months that the number of knights in residence at Lamesh was pathetically low. "It appears to be nothing more than a renewed farming community, with a few knights around to keep the monsters at bay."

Khisanth thought about that, but there were still too many pieces missing to complete the puzzle. She had to get out of here and learn the whole truth. The dragon closed her eyes and summoned a mental picture of herself standing on the drill field. Nothing happened. She could still feel the cool, musty air of the cave against her scales. Khisanth's eyes popped open. The teleport spell hadn't worked. Suspicious, she hastily tried her flaming talon cantrip, but wasn't able to summon even a spark. Khoal had dampened her magic, too.

Out of desperation, not expecting it to work, Khisanth closed her eyes and concentrated all her energy into changing her shape. To her surprise and relief, Khisanth felt her enormous weight fall away. She'd found a loophole in Khoal's spell. He and the other dragons thought they'd trapped her here, but they didn't know of the mental discipline that allowed her to shapechange, or of the narrow crevice that linked her lair with Jahet's.

The dragon had changed into her favorite diminutive form, a brown field mouse. Wasting not another moment, she scurried the long distance through the crevice and darted around the rocky curtain on Jahet's side.

At first glance, Jahet didn't appear to be in her lair either. Khisanth skittered past piles of her superior's gems, which looked like unscaleable mountains to a mere mouse. Jahet had very likely left for the tower with the first sound of the claxons. For a brief moment, Khisanth wondered if her friend could be in league with the other dragons. She discounted the thought almost before it was finished.

Khisanth abruptly heard noise in the antechamber. She scampered on mouse feet toward the sound and stopped cold in her tracks. Looming more than twenty-five feet above the field mouse was the ranking dragon, throwing herself again and again, to no avail, against an invisible barrier on the archway that led outside. Jahet's red eyes were wide and frantic, like a trapped cow's. Slather sprayed in thick ropes from her maw. Her breathing was ragged.

Khisanth felt a flash of relief that Jahet wasn't part of the conspiracy. They had pinned her in as well. But it also meant her emergency escape route had been cut off.

Perhaps she could squeeze through some small crack between wall and floor on the side that faced the ponderosa pines. Once outside, she'd revert to dragon form and get the answers to her questions. The more she thought about it, the more certain Khisanth was that it could work, even if it meant she had to change into a shape even smaller than a mouse . . . like a spider.

The field mouse was forced to dance to the side suddenly to avoid a nasty but accidental tail slap from Jahet. The ranking dragon was giving in to her temper, still thrashing about in fury and frustration. Khisanth then realized the flaw in her newest plan for escape.

It left Jahet still trapped in her lair.

Her concern for Jahet's escape had nothing to do with friendly feelings. If Khoal, Dnestr, and Neetra had betrayed the wing, Khisanth would need Jahet in the ensuing battle. To free Jahet, Khisanth would have to reveal herself.

"Hey, Jahet, down here!" the dragon-turned-mouse bellowed as loudly as her tiny vocal chords would allow. "Look down here, it's me!" she hollered in Dragon.

Jahet stopped her thrashing to locate the source of the faint sounds that rose up from the darkness below her. Squinting, craning back awkwardly, the ranking dragon could barely make out the minuscule shape of a mouse at her left hind foot. "You've certainly picked a foolish time to squeak a challenge at me," Jahet growled. With that, she turned her attention back to the invisible barrier.

Khisanth stomped in frustration. She cupped paws around her soft muzzle. "Hey, Jahet! It's me, Khisanth!"

Jahet's jaws locked tight. The mouse was undeniably speaking in the Dragon tongue. If that weren't odd enough, the creature had the temerity—and bad timing—of calling itself Khisanth! Jahet decided to silence the pesky little creature once and for all. She bent low and swung out with her claw to snatch up the rodent.

Abruptly Jahet was snout to snout with the black dragon Khisanth. "Khisanth! What the—"

"I can shapechange," Khisanth supplied quickly, stepping back to give them both more space.

"Why didn't you tell me before? I nearly crushed you!"

Khisanth looked mildly indignant at the reproach. "My position in the wing requires that I fly and fight," she said stiffly, "*not* that I cast magic. I have personal reasons for concealing the skill. I don't know the extent of your spell abilities, either," she said accusingly.

"We are not equals," said Jahet with similar starch. "We shouldn't be fighting with each other now." Her expression turned from displeasure to frustration as she regarded the invisible wall. "This must be the work of those worthless clerics Maldeev was forced to accept from Neraka."

Khisanth measured her words carefully. "I don't think they're the magic-wielding culprits here, Jahet."

Jahet squeezed her red eyes shut. "Don't start your old 'the-other-dragons-aren't-loyal' story. I'm not in the mood."

"How else can you explain why we're the only two dragons trapped in our lairs?" Khisanth challenged. "I looked—Khoal, Dnestr, and Neetra are gone."

Khisanth saw confusion in the ranking dragon's eyes as she digested the news. Khisanth could understand her puzzlement—trapped as they were, the situation suggested more questions than answers. Jahet didn't even know as much as Khisanth did about the others. It would take too long now to fill her in—time better spent getting free.

Khisanth held up her claws in surrender. "Never mind them now. We've got to think of a way out of here. Then we'll be able to see for ourselves what's happening outside."

"Let's teleport," suggested Jahet.

Khisanth shook her head. "I doubt it'll work here. I tried it in my lair—magic seems suppressed."

"Then how were you able to shapechange?

Khisanth struggled for the words to explain qhen. "The only thing I can figure is that shapechanging is more a mental than a magical discipline. The distinction must be a loophole in the spell that negates our magic." Khisanth snapped her talons. "You've given me another idea." She rubbed her claws together in preparation. "Stand back."

At a loss for any other solution and growing more desperate, the highest ranked dragon did as the lowest bade.

Khisanth concentrated, trying to sharpen the edges on an old memory. On the first seasonable day one spring back in the Great Moors, the ice on her pond had nearly all melted, and she'd gone to ground in search of fresh, warm prey. But the selection had been strangely slim, considering mammals' penchant for warm weather—a few young, foolish ground squirrels and an elderly, nearly blind ferret. Khisanth had an excellent long-term memory for meals.

She had been about to close on the ferret when the ground began to tremble, then shake violently. Suddenly—unexplainably—a twenty-foot-tall, budding maple tree shot out of the ground and fell over. Sharp talons emerged in the tree's wake, digging a tunnel to the surface at a rate that had impressed even Khisanth. A hideous, snout-nosed creature emerged, tangled in the dirt clods that dangled from the tree's torn roots. Snarling and slathering wildly like a rabid dog, the gigantic creature thrashed itself free. It had an elliptical, bluish-green body covered with thick plates and scales. The creature snatched up the fear-frozen ferret and choked it down in a gulp.

The dragon had watched the creature solely out of curiosity; her taste was more particular than to consume something so hideous and tough. That's why she'd been so surprised when its milky-yellow eyes and sky-blue pupils locked onto the largest meal it had ever seen. It sprang into the air like a jackrabbit, launching directly at Khisanth, four clawed feet raking and scratching. It seemed not even to notice that Khisanth was twice its size.

The surprise move had left time only for instinct. Hot green acid spewed from Khisanth's jaws and splashed across the creature's exposed underbelly. In moments, the thing was digested. She'd killed her first bulette, a rare and widely feared carnivore. Now she was about to become one herself.

"You'd better step into your lair," Khisanth advised. Standing in the archway between her two chambers, Jahet looked mildly annoyed at what she considered Khisanth's theatrics, but again did as the other dragon suggested.

Painfully aware of the claxons still pealing outside, Khisanth hastily envisioned her own powerful dragon body transforming into her memory of the bulette's. She felt herself grow shorter, stiffer under the plates and scales; her vision was not as keen. But the most significant change was one she'd never before encountered in a shapechange; her mood shifted abruptly. She felt jumpy and agitated, with an overriding impulse to burrow frenetically. It took all of her dragon sensibilities to make herself dig in a logical place.

The bulette Khisanth sank her squared, pawlike claws into the packed dirt floor of Jahet's antechamber and sent it flying on either side of her armored flanks in two steady, thick black streams. Digging under the outside wall, her claws tore through layers of hard clay and rock, until a hole large enough for a bulette to pass through was carved. Her claws bit into the base of the supporting wall itself to make room for a dragon's escape. When she finished, Khisanth was not the least bit tired.

Khisanth was anxious to doff the bulette form and quickly did so before calling to Jahet. The other dragon had watched the bulette with amazement from between the growing mounds of dirt and rock in the antechamber.

In deference to her rank, Khisanth waved Jahet through the underground trench first. Hurrying after, she heard Jahet's angry gasp from the other side of the ponderosas. Khisanth stepped through the hedge of trees and stopped next to her friend to view the fortress in the early light.

An army at least six hundred strong, colorful banners waving, was launching an all-out assault on the Black Wing of the Dark Queen's army.

* * * * *

Maldeev stepped onto a parapet above the courtyard, hands in their usual position on his breech-covered hips. The yellow light of the torches made his rippling chest look as if it were carved of the palest marble. Under his highlord helm, Maldeev's expression was beyond anger as he tried to make sense of the chaos around him.

The early morning atmosphere had changed from the softly glowing calm of a sleeping encampment to a torchlit frenzy of activity; half-dressed, droopy-eyed men hopping about, pulling on clothing, barking orders without true understanding or purpose. This was not how he'd trained his troops! Why weren't his commanders restoring order? Where was that dandy, Wakar, his second-in-command?

What was the meaning of this unexpected call-to-arms? It was still dark, several hours before the scheduled drill. The wing was not yet at war. Someone had intentionally disrupted the order of the compound. Maldeev scowled in the direction of the bell tower, where the claxons still rang, looking for the culprit. He blinked, then looked again. The rope jerked up and down, but he saw no one pulling it.

Magic. Maldeev's eyes narrowed to tiny black slits. Andor and the other two dark clerics . . . He'd reluctantly accepted their presence at Neraka's insistence, distrusting magic as he did. If they were in any way responsible for initiating this prank, Maldeev would see their heads roasted slowly until their skulls exploded!

Where in the Abyss were the blasted clerics, anyway? Maldeev spun around and stormed back into his chambers. He began dressing in his armor as quickly as he could; he had to do it alone since no amount of bellowing brought a servant to his aid. Maldeev had pulled on just one boot when he heard a cry outside that cut through all the din, a cry that made his blood run cold.

"Army of knights approaching from the north!"

Maldeev's mind dashed frantically through denial, past the expected questions, and settled on acceptance. Obviously, the pathetically small company of knights from Lamesh had decided to launch an attack on Shalimsha. It would be a swift and easy slaughter, especially with the aerial support from his dragons.

Speaking of dragons, he recalled abruptly, he'd seen neither hide nor tooth of Jahet, nor any of the dragons. Maldeev angrily jammed his foot into his other boot. Where in the name of Takhisis were those greedy and undependable black beasts who were supposed to win the war for the Queen of Darkness?

Maldeev could scarcely believe how wrong things had gone in one short night. If he had any hope of righting them, he'd first have to reorganize his ragged troops. Then he'd find those dragons and kick their lazy hides from here to Neraka! With that pleasant thought propelling him, Maldeev charged from his apartments, headed for the stairway that led down to the courtyard. And the chaos.

Chapter 17

Studying the crumbling north wall of Shalimsha Tower, Sir Tate Sekforde felt a momentary twinge of regret that it hadn't been
possible to drag a catapult from Lamesh. Two or three well-
placed boulders would have tumbled the remaining links in
the wall like a child's set of wooden blocks. As it was, the
fortress would be so ridiculously easy to breach, Tate never
considered trying to batter down the central gate. The knight
couldn't conceive of raising an army without repairing the
outer curtain. He could only conclude that the man inside
who called himself a highlord must be very arrogant to
assume no one would attack him.

Tate's legion of soldiers, along with their baggage wagons,
pack animals, and all the train of war, had marched over the
parched land for four and a half days—thirty-three leagues
in choking dust. At least it wasn't hot, thought Tate, just

damnably dry. The knight was grateful enough for the relative coolness. He was wearing his heavy plate mail, the only heirloom he'd taken from Castle DeHodge. Still, the constant clouds of dust didn't help the sore throat he'd woken with on the morning they were to set out. But he couldn't delay the march if they were to take advantage of the waxing moon. Tate was glad they hadn't. They'd marched the last three miles tonight in moonlight so bright it looked as if daylight's wick had simply been turned down. Now the sky was lightening toward dawn; the time for attack had come.

"Sir Wolter," Tate called to his sponsor, who was talking to some men-at-arms a short distance away. The stout, gray-haired knight nudged his horse next to Tate's. "Take fifty knights, our best swordsmen, and get them into position near that big breach." He pointed at the largest section of crumbled wall, to the right of the north wall's arched wooden gate. "Tell them to wait until Regist's archers have flanked them and picked off the few bowmen on the ramparts. Then send the knights in, led by a handful of crossbowmen who can shoot into the breach just before the charge. The crossbows can fall back after firing. Obviously, the attack will have to be made on foot. Find a place to shelter and tether the horses."

"What about the dragons?" Wolter's bushy gray eyebrows were raised.

"What about them?" snapped Tate. "They're supposed to stay out of it, if that's what you're asking. Khoal said he'd be able to delay the other two evil dragons from joining the fight, if not keep them out of it entirely."

"Let's hope we can trust the word of a traitor."

Tate heaved a sigh. "Look, I know what you think of my arrangement with the black dragons. Let me assure you, it's not a situation that I would have initiated. The dragon came to me, not I to him. How could I reject an opportunity to disable the Black Wing, the center of evil in this region? Isn't that why we came to the frontier?"

Wolter extended his hand as if to deflect an angry response. "How do you know it's not a trap?"

"I consulted Wallens," said Tate. The lord knight beckoned

to a soldier with bookish eyes and a solemn face. "Tell Sir Wolter what you've read in the ancient annals, what the order knows about the nature of black dragons."

Sir Geoffrey Wallens lowered the hand from his brow to his saddle pommel, pausing briefly on the way to stroke his thin brown mustache. "Black dragons are driven by greed, self-aggrandizement, and self-preservation, mostly in that order. They are evil, unpredictable, and unreliable. Unfortunately, sir, they are quite capable of breaking their bond to us, as they have to their own kind."

Scowling, Tate waved the too-honest knight away. He gave the grim-faced elder knight an earnest look and directed his gaze to the crumbling walls. "Come on, Wolter. If this is a trap, it's not a very good one. Why didn't they repair the walls? The dragon spoke truthfully about Shalimsha's layout—mountains with dragon lairs to the west, the north wall easily stormed. The chaos inside the compound looks genuine to me, too." His brown eyes scanned the mauve, early-morning sky. "I see no signs of dragons perched for attack, either."

Sighing, Wolter peered about to make sure that only Tate could hear him. "Look, lad," he whispered, "I understand you think you're doing what you must." He shook his helmeted head. "Call me old-fashioned, but it just feels wrong to make a pact with creatures renowned for evil. I'm certain the Council of Knights wouldn't approve."

Tate laughed without humor. "They scarcely approve of me!" He grew suddenly serious. "I truly believe there's no dishonor for the knighthood in this. I've prayed for months to Kiri-Jolith, and I have sensed no displeasure for the plan."

Tugging up his gauntlets, Wolter managed a rueful smile. "If you've spoken to your god, you shouldn't have to answer to a crotchety old knight like me." He clapped his young friend on the shoulder. "Now, if you don't mind, I've got some knights to assemble." Wolter's well-worn plate armor disappeared in the throng of soldiers.

Tate's eyes followed him fondly, then slipped past to evaluate the inside of the fortress. With any luck, they would soon be fighting there. He was surprised at how similar the layout of Shalimsha Tower was to Lamesh. There was no central keep here, either. Instead, the few buildings that had been repaired lined the inside walls, with a courtyard in the center. Must be a regional thing, Tate thought, since keeps were very common in Solamnia. He could see why the open courtyard would be an advantage for an army with dragons; a keep in the center of the courtyard would make it difficult for dragons to land.

Two years had passed since the fire had damaged Lamesh and destroyed part of the garrison's stockpiled grain. Tate had vowed by the end of that lean, hard winter to never eat another potato. He and his men had worked tirelessly to rebuild the burned sections so that they were better than before. News of their progress had spread to Solamnia; in the spring, fifty-two more young knights, eager for the chance for quick advancement, made their way to the frontier at Lamesh, further speeding up the reconstruction. That reinforcement also strengthened Tate's troops to the point where he could field an army and still leave behind thirty men-at-arms with a handful of knights to defend Lamesh Castle. That was a small garrison, but the castle was strong and well situated.

Tate had been stunned, impressed despite himself, when he met his first dragon, the one who called himself Khoal. He'd been poring over some account ledgers on an early spring day, a tedious task he despised, when his adjutant ushered in a glassy-eyed farmer. Expecting to hear some complaint about the taxes, the lord knight was taken aback, to put it mildly, when the man calmly told him that he'd just met a black dragon.

"He was as nice as any creature you'd like to meet, and pretty. He wants you to meet him in the hills at sundown."

Back in Solamnia, Tate had first heard the rumors of dragons returning. At Lamesh, he'd even spoken to several eyewitnesses who claimed to have seen black dragons flying in the area, and others who had encountered physical evidence on the ground. Obviously, the creatures were not allies of Good. The farmer showed definite signs of having been magically charmed, for no one would call the first dragon he met, particularly a black one, 'nice.' Aside from being surprised, Tate was certainly intrigued. "Why does this dragon wish to meet with me?"

"He said he has a business proposition."

Tate had plied the farmer for more information; the man had favorable, but not particularly informative things to say about the creature who had bewitched him. Though Wolter strongly disapproved, Tate rode into the mountains at the appointed time with two other knights. They dressed in the full ceremonial armor and regalia of their order, as they would on any other diplomatic mission. His primary motivation had been curiosity.

With the farmer as a guide, they had no difficulty getting to the rendezvous point. The spot was a shallow valley at the foot of the mountains. The farmer indicated that only Tate was to approach closer than a hundred paces, and that he should leave his horse behind. Tate agreed as a practical matter, since he suspected the horse wouldn't react well in the presence of a dragon.

The enormous beast was perched on its belly on a slab of rock that was slightly higher than Tate, forcing the knight to look up at it. Its foreclaws curved around the edge of the rock shelf, talons like sickles. Leathery wings were folded intricately along its flanks. Tate was mildly surprised to note that while the creature was covered in flat, leathery scales, like a reptile, it also had smooth patches of hide. The dragon's coloring was astounding. Never had Tate seen such black. It was liquid and luminous like ink, polished and impenetrable like onyx.

Its most arresting feature, though, were its eyes, set in a head nearly as long as Tate was tall. Dozens of paces away, Tate could hear its breathing and feel the rush of hot air from its lungs. But the eyes were quick and bright, despite being as big as a man's head.

Tate had expected to face a monster that was dull and horrid. He had found instead a beast with majestic, if unsettling, beauty. To the knight's surprise he felt more awe than fear in the presence of the magnificent animal.

Human and dragon studied each other at a distance. Finally the dragon spoke. "So this is what a Knight of Solamnia looks like up close."

"I should say the same about dragons," admired Tate, eyes on the dragon's supple scales, gleaming like polished marble in the last rays of daylight.

"I was not admiring, only remarking," said the dragon stiffly. "You look much like any other human—puny and pale. Though your armor is better than most."

The haughty demeanor was no surprise. Such a slur coming from a human would have started a fight. Tate ignored it. "You speak the Common tongue."

"I speak twelve languages."

Tate blushed, feeling foolish. He spoke only one other, his native Solamnic.

"I haven't much time before my delay will be noticed," growled the dragon. "On behalf of myself and two comrades, I propose a deal. In exchange for three pieces of land at Warden Swamp in your Solamnia," the dragon had said, "my comrades and I will help you disable the Black Wing."

Under darkening skies, the dragon laid out the entire plan that night. Tate had been too stunned to respond. The dragon left him to think it over, promising to return within three days for Tate's answer. The lord knight of Lamesh had thought long and hard, prayed on bent knees to Kiri-Jolith as though all three days were holy ones. In the end the young knight had agreed, for the very reasons he'd told Wolter. Though he never saw the dragon's comrades, Tate met with Khoal twice after that, to determine the timing of the attack the dragon proposed against the Black Wing's stronghold.

What Tate hadn't told anyone was what he'd promised the dragons in return; Warden Swamp was not his to give away. Tate had no doubt the Council of Knights would never approve the residence of three black dragons in the middle of Solamnia. They barely wanted Tate there. He had resolved early on to find an answer to that problem when the need arose—if it ever did. Though Tate still stood by his decision, he wasn't without trepidation. There were countless ways the magic-wielding dragons could yet betray the deal. Tate tried not to dwell on such thoughts. He had cast his lot with them; there was no turning back now.

"Sir Wolter has assembled the knights, as ordered, sir." The messenger, a junior Solamnic Knight, sat his charger uncomfortably at speaking to the lord knight, switching the reins from hand to hand. After several initial volleys of flaming arrows to create smoke and confusion in the compound, Tate's archers had begun to address arrows at the enemy bowmen on the battlements. "The knights await your signal, sir."

Tate hesitated. He'd never sent men into battle before. Remembering his prayers to Kiri-Jolith, the Knight of the Crown gave a brisk nod over the throng of armed men to Sir Wolter. The Knight of the Rose ordered the charge. The tense atmosphere suddenly exploded with the whoops and war cries of the attacking knights. They followed on the heels of the brave crossbowmen without armor or shields, chosen to blaze their trail to the breach. Two of seven bowmen fell within seconds to enemy arrows from above. The knights, slashing and stabbing with swords, axes, and halberds, pressed on across the rubble and through the wall.

When the knights were fully engaged with defenders inside the breach, Tate waved Wolter back and instructed him to create a similar, secondary line of attack on the other side of the gate, using slightly less than two-thirds the number of knights. The battle-hardened elder knight nodded his approval of the plan and set off to implement it.

Before Tate the battle raged with the roaring cries of attackers and the defiant shouts of defenders. Clanging metal and thudding arrows competed to be heard above the squeals and groans of dying men and the whinnies of spooked horses. Many a gay tunic and shield crest was besmirched with the blood of the first men to die, their abandoned weapons smeared and tacky from the dust that rolled like brown fog across the battlefield.

Tate stayed behind, monitoring progress, waiting for the moment the storming of the breach was complete. His gaze continually swept the sky, looking for signs of the dragons.

So far, so good. Still, Tate was tense, anxious for this to be over. He cleared his throat impatiently and spat vehemently on the ground. "Sir Albrecht," he snapped to a young knight he'd held in reserve, "what is your view of things? Speak quickly."

Albrecht spurred his horse forward to ride up even with Tate. "Lord," he fairly shouted, "the men are hotly engaged, and pushing the enemy back into the fortress in waves! See for yourself!"

"I wish I could." Tate wiped his dry mouth with the back of his leather gauntlet. "Damn this dust! I can tell where my troops are only by the clouds they raise. It appears we're pressing them back now, but they were surprised," he said, speaking his thoughts aloud. "Soon they'll regroup and the fight will get much hotter. With any luck and Kiri-Jolith's blessing, the dragons will stay clear of the battle. I'd hate to fight them and this army, too."

Just then, as if the gods had heard his words and mocked him, Tate saw a number of enormous, swiftly moving shadows darken the dusty air about the fighting knights. Almost afraid to look up, the knight saw the pale underbellies of three black dragons circling not far above the castle, armed riders on their backs. They didn't appear to be attacking yet. In fact, looking above the clouds of dust, Tate thought he could see their irate highlords prodding them in vain to swoop on the attackers.

Tate wasn't about to wait for them to turn on his men, if that was their plan. Sir Tate Sekforde brandished his sword and waved the remainder of his troops onward toward the primary breach, to draw this battle he alone had started to a quick close.

* * * * *

"Who are they?" demanded Jahet. "Where did they come from?"

"My guess would be they're Knights of Solamnia from Lamesh."

Stunned, Jahet looked away from Khisanth's impassive face. The lead dragon quickly scanned their ranks of archers, cavalry, and infantry. "But they have no dragons. How can they possibly hope to win against our aerial attacks?"

"I believe they have three dragons on their side," said Khisanth tersely.

Jahet's thick lips ruffled. "Look," she said, pointing to Khoal, Dnestr, and Neetra, soaring low over the fortress. "They're with their riders—our commanders."

"Then why haven't they attacked the enemy yet?"

"Because I haven't been able to give the order!" snapped Jahet. "I've been trapped in my lair!"

Khisanth took note of Jahet's frustration and adopted a tone meant to persuade. "Jahet," she said, her voice sanguine, "how do you explain the unexpected size, let alone arrival, of this army of knights? Who's been flying recon to the north? Not me, not you—but Khoal." Khisanth paused, letting Jahet absorb that truth. The anger lines around Jahet's snout and eyes eased a bit.

Khisanth pressed on. "They've obviously been lying about troop numbers at Lamesh. Khoal rearranged the schedule yesterday so there was no chance I'd go north and spot their approach. And so I'd return early enough to be sealed in last night." She could see Jahet reluctantly absorbing the truth of it. "Why is it so hard for you to admit their treachery?"

Even before she'd finished the question, Khisanth knew the answer from the look on Jahet's face. Their betrayal was a black spot against the ranking dragon. Khisanth actually felt an unfamiliar twinge of pity for the other dragon. Jahet's allegiance to Maldeev, if not the Dark Queen, was so great, she obviously felt great shame at the disloyalty of dragons under her command.

"No one but Takhisis could have made them suppress their own greed, Jahet." The ranking dragon said nothing, her gaze focused below.

From their vantage point on the piney ridge to the west, Khisanth and Jahet could see into the courtyard. It was a scrambling tumble of disorganized humanity that was pushing south toward the tents and drill field. Fires burned unchecked inside the compound. Smoke mingled with dust to form a haze over the courtyard. Chickens squawked and skittered around; dogs barked. They watched as Khoal, Dnestr, and Neetra dropped from the air and landed on the drill field amidst the confusion.

"I can't figure out why those three haven't attacked the wing yet," mused Khisanth, "but we've got to get them out of the battle before they do."

"I'll bite their heads off myself!" spat Jahet, preparing to take flight toward the drill field.

Khisanth reached out a claw to stop her. "Think, Jahet. If we show up late and strike at our own dragons, we'll look like the traitors."

Jahet scowled. "I hadn't thought of that."

Khisanth put in quickly, "I have another idea that will remove them from the fight without engaging them for the whole wing to witness."

Jahet leaned in eagerly. "Tell me, quickly!"

Khisanth grimaced. "I don't think I want to tell you the details," she said uneasily. Before Jahet could voice her protest, Khisanth cut in with, "Let me explain. Someone has to restore order to our ranks, or the knights will burn the tower to the ground without Khoal and the others having to lift a wing against us." She regarded the disorganized masses of soldiers still scrambling aimlessly in the tower below.

"Maldeev must surely be wondering where you are. You must go to him, tell him what we know of the dragons. Together you need to fly against the knights—eliminate their archers. The troops will rally behind you at once. There's one problem, though."

Khisanth paused, snaring her lower lip between razor-sharp teeth as she considered the three dragons, who were gathered on the southwest corner of the drill field. "It's essential that the other dragons think we're still trapped, at least until I can implement my plan for sending them away. Can you manage to stay hidden for that long?"

Jahet winced, realizing that the entrapment in her lair had caused her to break her vow to never keep Maldeev waiting.

She glanced at the knights, still launching flaming arrows and charging the walls. "I must join the highlord immediately, but I could try teleporting directly into the great hall, then send someone into the courtyard to find him."

She winced slightly again. "I'm a little rusty at teleporting, though—haven't used much magic since my union—Maldeev doesn't trust it around him. If I make it to the hall and find Maldeev, it'll take us a few moments to formulate a solid plan to reorganize the troops."

"That'll have to do," said Khisanth.

The lead dragon closed her eyes promptly, preparing to cast the dimly remembered spell, then opened them again to ask, "I could—I should—order you to tell me your plan."

Khisanth shook her head and gently nudged the other dragon with her snout. "You're better off not knowing. Highlord Maldeev's dragon must be above such skulduggery. If I succeed, their threat will be eliminated without tarnishing either of our names.

"If I fail," Khisanth shrugged philosophically, "I'll be beyond such mortal concerns. You'll be safe, too, because they won't even suspect you know their true colors, until it's too late for them."

"I'm trusting you to not fail, Khisanth." Jahet squeezed her large eyes shut tightly and was gone, leaving only a wispy trail of jet-black smoke drifting in the golden glow of dawn.

The ranking dragon had no way of knowing that Khisanth was about to break a vow of her own, made over the dead body of her lover one cold winter day.

* * * * *

The tall, raven-haired young woman purposefully pushed her way through the teeming throng of harried soldiers who were trying to assemble on the drill field to stop the flow from the courtyard. Her tawny gold eyes were focused on her intended destination.

Like many of the mercenaries around her, including the dead one she'd looted, the woman's torso was covered to the top of her hips by a hardened leather cuirass. Leather tassets suspended from the cuirass protected her thighs. Wool pants were stuffed into the tops of her soft leather boots. Though her clothing was ordinary enough, her exotic good looks would never have allowed her to blend into the crowd. Neither would the fact that she was the only female soldier within the ranks. Fortunately for Onyx, the men and ogres around her were too busy fearing for their own survival to give her more than a curious glance.

Knowing that success depended almost solely on her ability to project confidence, Onyx marched straight toward the dragons at the southeastern corner of the drill field, then stopped at a distance to observe. She knew in an instant how they had remained grounded. She could hear their riders, including second-in-command Wakar, trying in vain to get them airborne.

"We are forbidden to attack unless the ranking dragon or her highlord gives us the order to do so," Khoal was saying stubbornly. Wakar and the others threw up their hands and marched off to join the fray in the courtyard.

Onyx watched them depart, then looked over her shoulders for eavesdroppers. No humans but riders would willingly get within earshot of three dragons, which is why they were so surprised to see the young woman below them.

"I come from Lamesh."

At first they seemed not to hear her. Khoal fixed his hot-orange eyes on her suspiciously. "Human, you're either very foolish or very brave to get so close to dragons for curiosity's sake."

"I am no curious onlooker," said Onyx fearlessly. Looking about again, she lowered her voice. "I am a messenger from the Knights of Solamnia."

All three dragons dropped their jaws and afforded her glances ranging from disbelief to distrust.

"Then you are both brave *and* foolish," Khoal said cautiously, "walking into the enemy camp and announcing your position. What makes you think we won't slay you on the spot?"

"Because we all know that we are on the same side in this battle," said Onyx evenly. "My commander sent me to reward you for your services. Keeping Maldeev ignorant of our numbers and impending attack has been most helpful." Onyx kept her words deliberately vague, since she was only guessing about the alliance between the knights and the dragons.

"I don't know what you're talking about," said Khoal quickly, his voice low and threatening. "I think I will kill you now." Onyx could see him summoning the acid from his stomach.

"My commander will surely interpret an unprovoked attack as a sign of bad faith," she cut in. "You don't want to risk losing the reward for which you've worked so hard."

"I certainly don't," said Neetra quickly. "I didn't fly all those long reconnaissance missions to keep Jahet and Khisanth from the north for nothing! If I can get out of this without risking my hide, I say all the better."

Onyx felt her blood boil at the mention of her dragon name. She was forming a response when Dnestr, the smarter of the two intermediate dragons, frowned and said, "It seems odd that the knights would send you in the midst of the battle to give us our land."

Onyx took note of the last remark. She thought quickly, while Khoal watched her closely. "My commander thinks your uninvolved presence here adds to the general confusion—you know, dragons on the field frightening his knights. Besides, the battle is nearly finished, thanks to your entrapment of the other two dragons in their lairs. What's more," Onyx continued, managing an almost embarrassed look, "it would be best for the image of the Knights of Solamnia if they could avoid open confirmation of an alliance, however brief, with black dragons. You understand."

Neetra and Dnestr had only confirmed the alliance, and were obviously convinced by Onyx's explanation. Khoal, however, still looked skeptical. He said nothing as yet, neither denying nor confirming his involvement, watching the interaction between the human and the younger dragons.

"How do we get our land?" Neetra demanded greedily.

Onyx's eyes widened against her will. "Obviously, no one can lead you there this moment. My commander has ordered me to direct you to fly into the Khalkists, near Ak-Baral—do you know where that is?" Dnestr and Neetra nodded eagerly. "Wait there. Another agent will find you after we have won the battle, as we inevitably will, and lead you to the reward you so richly deserve."

The two dragons considered the crowd of evil soldiers milling at a distance, and they hesitated.

"Fly!" Onyx prompted. "Tell your riders you're evaluating the enemy's strength, if you must. Before they realize the truth, you'll be gone. Besides, what human would dare try to stop a dragon?"

The argument was enough for Neetra and Dnestr. Giving the silent Khoal the pitying look they would grant a fool, the two dragons leaped into the air and took wing to the west, headed for the mountains.

"You're not joining them?" asked Onyx.

Ignoring the question, Khoal looked down his nose at the young woman far below at his feet. "Funny you should mention the wing's other two dragons." The dragon's voice trailed off meaningfully. "When Jahet and Khisanth failed to appear after the claxons rang, I began to wonder if they were not betraying the wing." Khoal circled once around the ram-rod still woman.

"Then Neetra and Dnestr, those foolish young dragons, confessed to me that they'd made a pact with the Knights of Solamnia and arranged a pre-dawn attack. What's more, they'd had the last-minute inspiration to trap Jahet and Khisanth in their lairs"— Khoal locked his gaze onto Onyx's tawny eyes —"without telling a soul." His brows raised. "Strange that you would know about it."

Khisanth did not for a minute believe in Khoal's innocence. Still, she couldn't prevent her face from falling at the realization of the trap into which she'd stumbled.

The dragon bent low and hissed into her ear with hot, meat-scented breath, "Why don't you tell me your commander's name?"

Khoal had been a liar his whole long life. Not even his natural greed prevented him from recognizing one on sight. As the ancient dragon pressed in, evaluating the best way to slay the foolish young woman, he was only mildly interested in her motives for trying to trick him. He was certain he never met her, and yet there was something vaguely familiar about her voice, her cocky attitude. As his eyes focused on her shiny black hair and he prepared to claw her face from her skull, Khoal was about to receive the first true surprise of his long life.

The old dragon blinked. His face seemed to turn ashen beneath his scales. Where the young woman had stood was his most hated foe, that ambitious sycophant, Khisanth. Before his mind could make sense of it, the other dragon's mighty tail raised, delivering a vicious, air-snapping blow that sent him staggering. Khoal sailed some thirty feet, crashing into vacant tents and a small gathering of soldiers who'd wandered too close. Rolling himself from his side and back to his hind feet, Khoal sounded his rage in a bellow that sent all human and ogre soldiers within a hundred yards diving for cover.

"So, Khisanth, you can shapechange," snarled Khoal, circling slowly around his opponent. "I should have guessed. You tried changing yourself into Jahet often enough, with all your showing off to Maldeev. Unfortunately for you, you can't change into a better fighter than me." Khoal's chest rose with pride. "I learned my skills before you were even a wyrmling," he gloated. "I fought in the great war against Huma."

Khisanth threw back her head and laughed aloud, a hateful, braying sound. "And we all know how *that* turned out!" She circled around in tempo with Khoal, keeping her eyes on his wrinkled, hoary face at all times. "Perhaps if our queen had more able fighters then, the history of dragons on Krynn would be much different, and we would not be answering to lowly humans. . . ."

The taunt hit home. Roaring wildly, Khoal lashed out with his right claw. Khisanth darted to her right. Anticipating the dodge, the ancient dragon swung his tail and delivered a slap that hit squarely. With nothing to break her tumble, the younger dragon rolled over and over, wings snapping against the dirt of the drill field. Finally she skidded to a thundering stop. Propping herself up with her claw arms, Khisanth regarded her foe with bitter and true hatred. She tried to think like her opponent to gauge his next move. She could see the light flicker away in his eyes, as if his thoughts were elsewhere briefly. Khisanth knew that look. Khoal was casting a spell.

Not sure what to expect, Khisanth quickly cast a general defensive spell. Instantly, her enormous black body was engulfed in a faintly shimmering sphere that looked vaguely like a bubble. Khisanth hoped Khoal wasn't going to cast anything too powerful, or her protective globe would prove useless.

If Khoal had not been concentrating on his own incantation, he might have noticed her shield in time to alter his spell. The six bolts of lightning that flashed from the tips of Khoal's long, pearly talons bounced off her shield, zagged around wildly, then fizzled out. Khisanth's globe twinkled and winked away.

"Tell me, Khoal, when you awoke this day, did you sense it would be your last?"

The taunt, in addition to his thwarted spell, only served to further enrage Khoal. The ancient dragon charged like a bull directly at Khisanth, the ground shaking in his wake. He turned, preparing for a wing buffet. Reacting quickly, Khisanth focused her thoughts on the first image that came to mind; the female dragon abruptly became a seven-foot-tall owlbear. Aiming his buffet to connect with Khisanth's head at dragon height, Khoal's wing swept harmlessly over the owl-headed bear. While the ancient dragon's back was turned, Khisanth reverted to dragon form. Springing high into the air, she delivered a stunning, one-footed kick to Khoal's right flank, a blow that sent him reeling, snout-first, into the dusty field.

Khoal scrambled onto all fours and spun around. Humiliation had turned the dragon's yellow eyes fiery and streaked them with blood. "I'll pull your entrails out and eat them while you still live!" Khoal snarled, rabid slather spraying from his jaws.

"Shouldn't you be winning, to make such a vow?" Khisanth asked artlessly, stepping backward to contemplate her next move. The dragon knew she wouldn't be able to shape-change indefinitely; her energy was already flagging. Khoal's rage was making him careless. That's good, she thought, let his own anger defeat him.

Squealing in panic and pain, an ogre whose rags and fur had caught fire ran at full speed into Khisanth's flank. The hysterical brute flailed at her scales, trying to climb across the obstacle, too blinded by fear to turn aside. Glancing back, the dragon swept her wing outward, shoving the doomed creature away.

Khisanth's head jerked up in time to see that Khoal had closed the gap between them. The black dragon's neck shot forward, and sagging old lips pulled back to expose his long, jagged teeth. He was heartbeats from severing Khisanth's head from her neck.

Again, the spry young dragon did the first thing that came to mind—she changed into the familiar form of the brown field mouse, far, far below the slathering jaws of the enraged dragon. She hadn't time to be smug about the close call, because Khoal was thinking fast as well. He raised his hind foot and, creating a cage of sorts with his spread wings, prepared to stomp the little mouse.

Khisanth knew she was trapped. She couldn't revert to dragon form easily in the small area; even if she could, Khoal's foot would crash into her skull before she could topple him. Or would it?

Taking a chance, Khisanth summoned her dragon form. The instant she felt the change begin, the dragon reached out, snagged Khoal's hind foot, and struggled to tip him off balance before he could squash her. Khoal was a much heavier dragon than Khisanth, thick-muscled and dense. Just as Khisanth was beginning to despair of toppling the ancient dragon, her form expanded beneath him. She felt the crush of his incredible weight for only a moment, before the stunned dragon tumbled from her back and crashed unceremoniously to the ground from a height of at least twenty feet. The impact knocked the wind from his lungs. Khoal lay in a heap, gasping raggedly for air.

Khisanth launched herself at the other dragon. Before he could raise a claw to defend himself, Khisanth sank her teeth into Khoal's fleshy chest, tearing away large, bloody bites, scratched at his eyes and face with her claws until Khoal couldn't see through his own gore. But the killing blow came when Khisanth simply leaned in, clamped her jaws around his neck, and twisted until she heard a loud snap. What was left of his eyes rolled back into his enormous skull. Khisanth unclenched her claws and let Khoal's head drop to the dirt with a loud, flat thud that raised an enormous cloud of dust.

Khoal's death gave Khisanth great satisfaction. The black dragon turned her sights to the knights who'd penetrated Shalimsha's north wall and were engaged in battle with the wing inside the courtyard. Khisanth would need to hear the death cries of a great many humans to still the hatred throbbing at her temples.

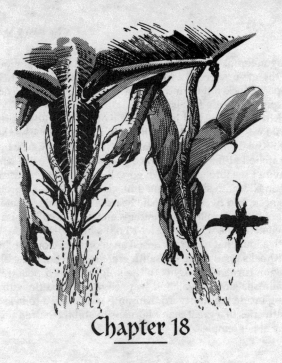

Chapter 18

"Look, sir, they're fleeing." Tate followed the finger of the young knight who pointed skyward. There he saw two black shapes, winging upward like monstrous bats. A general cry of amazement burst from the knights as they watched the creatures take flight and streak straight away over the mountains.

A hint of hope crept into Tate's heart. Two dragons . . . That left three unaccounted for. Still, three was better than five. Tate studied the shapes a few moments longer, until they dropped from view behind the distant range. Satisfied that they wouldn't return, he intended to plunge into the melee seething just inside the breach. A battle still raged beyond the walls, though Tate believed the odds of victory had increased tremendously with the dragons' departure.

But again Tate was stopped when Sir Albrecht emerged from the rolling dust at a gallop and reined up before him.

He was covered in brown filth so thick that his sweated horse looked as if it had rolled in mud. When the knight flipped open his visor, even his eyes were circled with grime where it had filtered through the eye slits.

Tate gripped Albrecht's arm to steady the panting knight in his saddle. "What is it, Albrecht?" Tate shouted. "What have you seen?"

"I bring an ill report, I fear." Albrecht drew a long breath and licked his lips with a dry tongue. "The battle was well in hand. Then the dragons appeared."

Tate's grip tightened on the knight's arm. "We saw two leave. Are others attacking us? Or them?"

"Neither, at first," panted Albrecht. "Two took wing, then two others battled between themselves. Both fought like creatures possessed. Finally, one managed to knock the other down, then nearly devoured it." Albrecht shuddered. "It was incredible—and gruesome."

Tate pulled a heavy glove from his left hand and slapped it angrily against his tunic where it draped across his thigh, raising puffs of dust.

By now the din from the courtyard was impossible to ignore, dramatically shifting from the sounds of active battle to the chaos of a rout. Vague clumps of shapes could be seen through the obscuring dust, running through the breach toward Tate. Men-at-arms, he concluded. No Knight of Solamnia would run in so cowardly a fashion.

"Follow me," the lord knight commanded, spurring his horse toward the commotion.

Soon the knights were surrounded by men-at-arms falling back to higher ground. Tate noted that at least they still carried their weapons, so the position had not crumbled completely. He and his retinue immediately set about driving the reluctant soldiers back toward the breach and the courtyard beyond. First they tried bold words of encouragement. When that failed, they turned in their desperation to leveling threats of punishment if the soldiers didn't resume their fighting. Tate had never seen men so fearful in his life. He managed to collar a sergeant who was himself dragging a trooper forward.

"Sergeant, these men have fought battles before. Tell me what's happened to cause such panic?"

The sergeant sent his charge reeling forward with a kick in the seat. "There's a dragon loose amongst the men, sir. It's only this damnable dust concealing the creature from general view that prevents every last one of our soldiers inside from scattering like mice."

Tate scanned toward the line, but saw only outlines and shadows. "Where is it?"

"Damned if I know," replied the sergeant. Pointing forward, he added, "Somewhere in there."

"Is there only one? Can you account for a second one, still alive?"

"No, and I hope I never do," shouted the sergeant. Then he turned and plunged forward again into the throng, shoving men ahead of him and yanking those who stumbled to their feet. Soon he disappeared from Tate's view.

The commander turned to Albrecht. "I've got to ride forward and see what the situation is for myself."

"You can't," objected Albrecht. "It's too dangerous."

"The real danger is in not doing it," Tate shouted back. "Ride down the line and assemble as many knights as you can, then bring them back. Go and be swift."

Albrecht wheeled without a sign and rode away. Tate guided his horse forward, threading into the mass of armed men who seemed to be milling but fighting no one. His horse scrambled through the tumbled rocks and bodies piled in the breach and emerged into the din and dust of the inner courtyard.

Even through his dust-caked nostrils Tate detected the stench of blood and burned flesh. He expected the first and had smelled it many times before on battlefields, but the second surprised him.

Through the noise of the battle, Tate heard Wolter's booming voice shouting encouragement to his soldiers across the yard, at the second breach. With the knights inside the walls at two places, Tate knew the defenders couldn't hold in the open for long. If they could be cut off from retreating to the inner buildings, the battle would be won. Except for the dragons . . .

An inhuman bellow shook the air. Tate's horse was spooked and reared up, nearly throwing the knight to the ground. Only with great urging could he get it to move forward again. The terrified horse's nostrils flared, its eyes bulged white. Suddenly an enormous dark shape loomed before them. The awful stench of blood and burned flesh mixed with something even more monstrous, and it made Tate gag. His horse reared again and backed away in terror.

The ground was littered with bodies and weapons. Bubbling pools of some atrocious, noxious liquid seeped into the darkened soil, surrounded like the spokes of a ghastly wagon wheel by the scorched limbs and other portions of bodies that the acid had not devoured.

At the center of the devastation was the towering shape, growing ever more distinct as Tate approached over the dead bodies. It was clearly a dragon, spattered with gore and devouring a path through the remains of Tate's slain men. His stomach nearly turned again when he heard the sickening crunch of metal and bone being ground together.

Twenty paces from the beast, Tate's horse would go no farther. Reluctantly, Tate dismounted. No sooner had he touched the ground than a huge black claw crashed down next to him, ripping open the horse. The noble animal screamed for less than a heartbeat, then was silent. Tate could hardly believe how quickly the dragon had lunged. He found himself staring into its glowing orange eyes.

Brandishing his sword, Sir Tate Sekforde welcomed his fate as he imagined Huma might have.

* * * * *

Khisanth felt the warmth of the horse squeezing between her talons. It was another death, only one of so many that day. Each one brought the sense of power and satisfaction that only came with killing. The veneer of civility and reason that surrounded her at most times was easily stripped away by violence, replaced by bestial instinct and fury. Sensation devoid of thought. Khisanth saw only life and wanted to make it death. She wanted to feel life flowing out from her victims, to squeeze it or burn it or tear it out until only something repulsive remained.

Now this man stood before her, holding a long sword and a shield thrust bravely toward her. She had seen others with this courage today, and killed many. For some, the courage failed. They were especially delicious; Khisanth could actually taste the fear and panic let loose in their bodies by her presence.

Khisanth peered more closely at this knight. There was something curious about him, his stance perhaps. She couldn't see his face behind the visor of his helmet, but the dust-caked emblem on his tunic tugged at her memory. The dragon ground her claws into the corpse of the horse to feel the satisfying crunch of its bones. The sensation sparked a recollection. There were horses nearby the last time Khisanth had seen this man. She had eaten a horse not long before. He was a knight, a man of Solamnia. Her eyes widened in understanding.

The ambush. The event from years ago leaped into her mind. Once again she saw the knights crashing to the ground from their horses and the murderous ogres swarming over them. She saw the young knight who, on fire, had fled, rising from the ground and tearing on foot into the woods. She felt the pain of her broken human nose, the humiliation of having let him slip away. The anger at Led's betrayal. Her claw unconsciously squeezed the horse into unrecognizable pulp.

As the light of recognition flashed in her eyes, the knight recoiled visibly, almost as if he shared Khisanth's memory. Could he recognize her as a dragon, having only seen her as a human? She doubted it. Led had not. All of these thoughts raced through Khisanth's mind in the span of moments. She wanted badly to kill this man, to have revenge. Suddenly the rest of the battle didn't matter, the other humans and knights and horses barely registered on her senses. This Knight of Solamnia grew large in her vision, and his taunts from years before rang in her ears.

* * * * *

The dragon's claw slashed the air and raked Tate's shield. The Knight of the Crown reeled backward and stumbled in the litter. His hand splashed into a pool of acid. The knight rolled away from the cursed spittle and uttered a strangled cry as he clawed at the glove with his right hand. It came off in tatters, revealing patches of smoking skin underneath.

The dragon aimed another blow at Tate. The knight ducked aside and snatched up his dropped sword. Having missed with the first swipe, Khisanth swept her claw back again.

The knight was learning quickly and expected the attack. Instead of slamming into his body, the dragon's claw collided with a slashing sword. Steel bit into dragon scales and cut the flesh underneath—not deeply, but enough to cause the dragon to bellow with rage. Tate stepped backward, crouching, as if making himself smaller would lessen the thundering in his ears.

The dragon didn't react to pain like a human. She neither withdrew to examine her wound nor debated whether she was fit to continue the fight. The enormous black creature lunged forward with the unbelievable speed of her kind, striking again with the injured claw.

This time the blow caught Tate's shield on the edge. One talon pierced the thick wooden target just above his forearm. The knight was jerked off his feet as the shield was wrenched from his arm. He felt as if his arm would be pulled from his shoulder, but the shield's leather straps snapped like bullwhips cracking.

Tate tumbled to the ground yards from where he had been standing. Miraculously, he still held his sword, but he knew his shield arm was dislocated at the shoulder and broken at the wrist. Already his hand was turning black and blue around the burns. More splattered acid seeped through the armor on his legs, devouring leather straps and cotton padding and eating into the flesh of his calf.

The dragon loomed over him, leering with orange eyes that bespoke evil beyond the human's understanding. Yet they were hauntingly familiar. An unusually barbaric neck-lace, made of swords and animal skulls, hung around her thickly muscled neck. The rancid mouth opened to reveal teeth like spear points fouled with human flesh. Tate waved his sword feebly at the dragon.

Instead of the painful oblivion he expected, the knight heard the dragon's inhuman bellow and felt the ground shudder as the beast thrashed away. Tate opened his eyes and saw the monster scraping its injured claw down its flank, snapping off more than a dozen arrow shafts that protruded there.

Tate felt hands slipping under his shoulders and lifting him up. He gazed into a human face again, the face of a sol-dier whose name he didn't know. Then he heard the strong voice of Wolter shouting commands to archers, followed by the solid twang of bowstrings and thunk of arrows hitting their target.

Tate stood with the help of the archer. "Bring my sword," he breathed.

Before anyone could comply, Wolter loomed above Tate, his fatherly eyes shining out from a grimy face. Blood and dirt darkened his tattered tunic and caked his charger. Tate reached up to the knight. "We've got to kill the dragon. Give me your sword, Wolter."

Wolter gripped the extended hand instead. "I know that, lad. You've fought valiantly, but you haven't the strength. Lead the surviving men back through the breach and to a safe distance, where we can regroup. I'll join you there." Wolter turned and muttered to Albrecht, "Get him safely away."

Tate didn't like the tone of voice, or the look in the tired old knight's eyes. "Wolter," he called, "don't risk it," but his voice was so weak Wolter seemed not to hear him.

The elder Knight of the Rose swung down from his skittish horse and addressed the archers. "Loose one last volley on my command and then retire—now!"

Dozens of bowstrings thunked as one. The dragon screeched at every impact, more in anger than pain. The missiles were little more than pinpricks against the thick hide and scales on her flanks, but she had been robbed of her prize knight.

Sword raised above his helm, Wolter plunged forward toward the waiting monster.

Once again she forced the acid up her throat and blew it in a steaming haze toward the rushing knight with the gleaming long sword, and toward the line of men with bows. Many fell screaming as it burned or seeped through the openings in their light armor. Those who were able fled in pain and panic.

Stumbling and swearing, Wolter ripped away the acid-drenched tunic and pulled off his pitted, hissing great helm. Melted holes showed in the chain mail beneath. His face was burned and blackened. He shook the rapidly dissolving shield from his left arm. Clutching the long sword in both hands now, and with the name of Kiri-Jolith on his lips, he charged ahead.

The sweeping claw of the dragon met the knight's stabbing blade. The sword pierced the bony scales and impaled itself completely through the flesh. Bloodied talons ripped through layers of metal. Wolter's body tumbled across the ground to land in a sprawl. Feebly he reached for the dagger at his belt, but the dragon pounced with her jaws open. Dust surged up around them, obscuring the scene but not the sound.

"Wolter!" cried Tate, helplessly watching his friend's fatal fall. Bending down in his stirrups, Albrecht grabbed his horrified superior by the belt and dragged Tate's struggling weight across his saddle. Albrecht spurred his horse into a gallop and waved the survivors from Lamesh to follow him through the breech. Leaving the horrid scene of monsters and destruction, the two Knights of the Crown, one unconscious, the other in shock, sped off toward the foothills.

* * * * *

In the Black Wing's camp, Khisanth licked at the lacerated claw. Around her, ogres and mercenaries gleefully set about the business of killing the injured and looting the dead. Minutes later, Jahet swooped overhead and then landed nearby, Maldeev on her back, holding a bloody mace.

"We've survived, if not emerged victorious," Jahet said, trying to raise spirits. "Your brilliance in battle will be legend," she added to the other dragon, casting a glance at the destruction surrounding them.

Khisanth eyed both Maldeev and Jahet sardonically. She made no reply to Jahet's comments. Instead, she asked, "You have dealt with Dnestr and Neetra?"

The other dragon nodded. "It is done." She could see the anger in Khisanth's eyes. "What's wrong? We were losing, but look around us now. Hundreds lie dead. Solamnic knights litter the field."

"We made the best of a bad situation brought on by treachery. Three of our own kind turned against us. What hope is there for the Dark Queen's cause if her agents so readily turn on each other?"

Khisanth rose to her feet. "I've spoken many times of my amazement that humans rule the world while dragons live in the shadows. I couldn't understand how such a thing was possible. After today, I begin to comprehend."

Anger squeezed Khisanth in its enormous grip. She tipped her head back, raised a bloodied claw to the skies, and howled, "Takhisis, I've called you my queen! Can treachery be your plan?" The black dragon blasted her fury and frustration into the sky, exhaling a cloud of acid that rocketed upward. Spraying out, it rained back down in sizzling droplets and gobs. Ogres, men, even Jahet and Maldeev, scrambled out of the burning mist.

Only Khisanth did not emerge, for she was no longer on the Prime Material plane.

Chapter 19

Khisanth stood among the burned and broken bodies. Her raised and clenched claw was extended toward the smoke-filled sky. Suddenly the dragon felt her bones contract and expand simultaneously, as if she were being squashed and stretched. The pain was excruciating. Khisanth wondered briefly if she hadn't suffered more grievously in the fighting than she'd thought. Craning her neck, the dragon looked down the length of her spine, but saw nothing that should cause such torment.

Is this how it feels to die? Must your soul be torn to incomprehensible bits or compressed into nothing, to leave no trace behind?

Khisanth didn't take a step, or even twitch a muscle, but the world around her shifted, wavered, like summer's heat on pond water. As she peered through the haze, the landscape around her altered dramatically. Battlements, even the mountains, were gone, and the land stretched on forever, empty and flat against an eerily glowing red sky. The sky itself seemed to merge with the sandy ground, leaving no horizon, showing no stars nor moons nor sun. And yet, for all the radiant red, the area seemed as black as shadow.

At least, unlike in the plane of lightning, there was ground here. Khisanth dropped to all fours and stepped warily, half suspecting the ground to drop away beneath her like quicksand. Movement was slow, but there was nothing to walk to, no landmark for which to head. Khisanth scanned the entire area, but still saw nothing.

Until she looked forward again. Misty vapors were slipping upward from the sand before her and coalescing into vaguely human forms. Blobby, molten flesh ran more than rested on their amorphous frames. They looked like anguished, twisted, mobile, melted candle wax. Only the occasional suggestion of a face separated one from another.

"What—who are you? Where am I?" she demanded.

Silence.

Suddenly, like an unstoppable, soundless tidal wave, a row of the hideous creatures surged forward. They raised molten claws from the depths of their blobby forms and raked the air before the black dragon.

Khisanth darted backward—into an equally dense row of the silent and bizarre creatures behind her. She saw more than felt claws sinking into her scales from before and behind. Each did little enough damage, but together the growing legions of nameless creatures were beginning to draw blood, and pain.

Like a sickle through tall grass, she swished her tail from side to side, sending the creatures tumbling across the sandy landscape. Some snapped in half like cold and brittle wax, then lay still, but more quickly rose from the sand behind her to replace them. The ones in front of her tore relentlessly at her chest, forelegs, anything they could sink a claw into. Khisanth kicked and lashed out and bucked around wildly like a horse, trying to throw them off. Then she noticed that the ones that had snapped in half had, like worms, formed into two new, tenacious creatures.

Desperate, she summoned the bile that waited in her stomach. It surged up her throat and shot out between her jaws in a hot green stream. Khisanth pivoted, aiming her acid downward, shaking gruesome creatures from her and into the corrosive acid. The creatures' faces twisted into even greater anguish as they dissolved. Hope flickered in Khisanth's breast. She shook and spewed with a fury, until every last creature was reduced to smoldering gray patches.

To Khisanth's utter shock, the pieces not eaten by acid had begun to reform into many, many more creatures. They seemed angered, even in their silence.

The grotesque beings suddenly darted back from her, though she had made no move, nor spoken a word. Then Khisanth saw the reason.

Rising up behind the last row of creatures, silhouetted against the glowing red sky, were much taller, winged beings. Perhaps half Khisanth's height, they were thin with wiry muscles. They stepped closer, kicking the trembling blobs from their path. These new creatures looked reptilian, with long, prehensile tails—though eight feet tall, they reminded Khisanth strongly of the much smaller stone gargoyles that were poised on the corners and turrets of Shalimsha Tower, meant by its builders to chase away evil spirits. These were not made of stone, but leathery flesh, like her own underbelly. Six of them were black as night, and two were vivid green.

"Who are you?" Khisanth demanded, repeating her last words to the newcomers. She pointed at the quivering creatures who had worked so hard to tear her flesh from her bones. "And what are they?"

Lemures—mindless spirits. They can't answer.

Khisanth looked around, startled. The voice had spoken inside her head. She spotted a red reptilian creature staring closely at her and decided it was the one that had answered her telepathically.

"We're abishai, sentries on the Abyssal plane," it said, its

251

tone very low-pitched and slow, like stone would sound if it could talk.

"The Abyss?" Khisanth squealed, a sound she'd never heard from her own throat.

Without answering, the creatures snapped into formation, boxing Khisanth in with two abishai on each side of the dragon, save for the front. She began to walk forward, feeling a strange tug at her thoughts. Dimly she realized she must be under a spell, to respond without complaint or contest. Only after the spell faded was she able to resist.

Khisanth dug in her heels. The black and green creatures stopped in their tracks. Even eight creatures, large by any other standards, could not hope to budge a dragon who did not wish to move.

The red abishai extended its tail toward her and revealed the small stinger at its tip. "Poison," it said. The creature looked around anxiously, as if something would emerge and slay it for communicating with the dragon. Nothing did.

The warning was enough for Khisanth. For now. They started forward again.

The sentries stopped marching abruptly, though their destination looked not a whit different from their departure point—dark red, glowing sky, like a fire the size of the world burned in the distance. The shifting sand made it difficult to tell up from down. "Wait."

The small battalion of abishai disappeared into the dark red sky as mysteriously as they had arrived.

Khisanth detested mystery of any sort. Where did they go? Did their absence mean the lemures would return? The thought of those brainless creatures clawing at her relentlessly made her feel more trapped than the escort of abishai had. Every nerve tingled at the tips of her scales.

But the lemures did not return. Nor did anyone—or anything—else. She waited. And waited. Khisanth thought it nearly possible that an entire cycle of seasons could have passed while she waited, for what, she didn't know.

Then, to Khisanth's utter amazement, a wall of fire shot up out of the sand like a geyser. Through it stepped a creature she would have mistaken for another abishai, if it hadn't corrected her thoughts.

"Cornugons are the Abyss's greater baatezu," it said in a sepulchral tone. "The distinctions between them and lesser baatezu like abishai are obvious."

Looking more closely, Khisanth began to notice subtle differences—the flesh-covered horns, the slightly more human-looking face, deeply slanted eyes, and protruding tusks instead of rows of equally jagged teeth, like the abishai. And this one gripped a large barbed whip in its talons; the abishai were armed only with claws.

"I am instructed to take you to your meeting." The cornugon nodded its horned head once toward the wall of flame.

"Meeting? With whom? Why was I brought to the Abyss?"

The cornugon simply stood, looking toward the blazing wall.

Khisanth felt something pulling at the corners of her confidence, until she noticed the beginnings of a most unfamiliar sensation—fear. Most oddly, she was developing an irrational fear of staying where she was. Not that a trip to the Abyss shouldn't inspire terror, she told herself. Still, fear was totally alien to Khisanth's nature. There was no new reason for it to rise at that moment.

Except if it were magically inspired. Dragons were naturally resistant to magic. The cornugon's magic must be powerful indeed for a fear spell to affect her so. The dragon felt another unfamiliar twinge of fear.

Before Khisanth could step toward it, the fire wall came to her. She felt its flames tickle and lick at her hide, but the fire didn't burn, wasn't even very warm. The white-orange flame slipped down her back and over her tail and left her standing in a place that looked exactly the same. The sky and sand glowed red as before.

Yet, it *felt* very different. The cornugon was gone, but Khisanth had the distinct and unshakable impression that she wasn't alone. Cutting through the strange dimness of the barren landscape was the long, spiny back of a dragon. Huge, and very close, but very dim.

"Who are you?" Khisanth began, but the momentary relief she felt at the sight of something familiar was knocked away, along with her breath. The area seemed to grow darker, though it was more a darkness of the mind, since the sky's faint redness didn't change. Struggling to breathe, Khisanth could see the dragon's long, unusually thick neck start to swing around to the left.

Like a tightly coiled spring, the neck unwound, and five heads completed the turn, snaking and writhing and hissing softly. Khisanth dropped to her knees in reverence and awe. She cringed before one of the three creators of the world.

In the Dark Queen's present form, the name She of Many Faces seemed most appropriate. Each head represented a type of evil dragon: white, black, green, blue, and red. The colors ran the length of each neck and into the forepart of the dragon's body. They blended into three strips of gray, blue-green, and purple over her back and hindquarters, and merged into a muddy brown tail.

Takhisis's black head slithered closer to the trembling black dragon, hissing softly. *You have displeased me greatly, Khisanth.*

Takhisis's lips didn't move, but Khisanth heard the queen's even, almost sensuous voice directly in her head.

"Then I *am* dead," said the black dragon.

Not yet. Five sets of dragon eyes all bore into Khisanth's, their message unmistakable.

It is my belief that you are yet useful to me, especially now that you have slain three of the only five black dragons worthy of being in my service.

"Worthy!" cried Khisanth. "But you don't under—"

Silence! the Dark Queen's voice cut in sharply. *You are clever enough to know that everything happens with my knowledge, if not consent.*

Khisanth, for once, was struck speechless.

Of course I knew of their betrayal with the knights. Black dragons are the greediest and most solitary of the evil dragons and must be watched accordingly. The tongue of Takhisis's black head darted out, as if to acknowledge and accept the evaluation of its brethren.

"They betrayed you and exposed your entire Black Wing to decimation. Why didn't you strike them dead?"

They were much more useful to me alive. I would have appealed to their greed, offered them more than the knights—their very lives—and turned their betrayal to my advantage. They would have feared my eternal wrath forever after.

Takhisis paused. Her blue head hissed wordlessly. *As it was, you helped them destroy the wing.*

Khisanth found her voice. "I saved the wing!"

Only vanity would make you view the devastation at Shalimsha as a victory, the same vanity that has made you refuse to take a rider. . . .

"But you don't—" Khisanth stopped the thought.

I know of the betrayals that have forged your personality—and your pride. You have gleaned less from them than you should.

The five heads swayed to an unheard cadence. *You need consider only this one example: If you had taken a rider after your arrival at the wing, you would have secured the rightful position of second dragon. You gave inferior dragons like Khoal power over you. Had you been their superior, they could not have betrayed me.*

"Maldeev could have made me second dragon without a rider!"

It was not his rule to break, the voice cut in sternly. *I determined the policy regarding riders. Maldeev is simply an agent whose function is to enforce my edicts. Again, only vanity would make you think yourself worthy of his risking a god's retribution.*

You are right about one thing, though, the voice said in a slightly conciliatory tone. *Humans are an inferior race. That is the crux of the whole, upcoming war. They currently control all of Krynn. Until I can return in physical form—which I am using them to help me accomplish—they are necessary annoyances. Like lemures.*

That last comment, spoken with a hint of amusement, reassured Khisanth that she was not beyond redemption. "I thought I was honoring my queen. Must I take a rider?"

Only if you do not wish to repeat your mistakes and risk my wrath a second time.

"Humans are so easily swayed by emotion. How will I find one who is both worthy and true?"

You will live to do much greatness in my name, Khisanth, but trust no one. What you seek is a human worthy of your talents. Look in unexpected places. You will know him when the time comes.

The Dark Queen's five heads began to turn away. *There is much work and little time to rebuild the Black Wing. Commit my words to memory, Khisanth, for I fear a second meeting would not go as well for you.*

"Thank—" was all the humbled black dragon could squeeze out before the majesty of the Queen of Darkness faded into the barren landscape.

Just as abruptly and with scarcely a puff of smoke, Khisanth left the Abyss. She landed squarely in a scene nearly as bleak as the Infernal Realms. Around her, in the scant light of dusk, soldiers with battle-blackened faces picked through the charred wreckage of Shalimsha Tower.

Chapter 20

Though the late summer day was gray and rainy outside the great hall, only one candle was lit inside. The shadows it cast mirrored Maldeev's mood. The dragon highlord sat, slumped in his ornate, claw-footed chair, hands curled tightly around the miniature dragon heads at the ends of the armrests. He heard his water clock whirring behind him. Maldeev didn't care to look at it. He wanted no joy to intrude on his dark humor.

"We've got to rebuild, and quickly," Jahet was saying, her words drumming an annoying rhythm in his brain.

"What do you think I've been doing since those damned knights attacked me? The remaining troops are in the process of rebuilding the tower—*again*. Salah Khan has spent time recruiting humans to the north to replace those lost in the slaughter. Any minute now I'm expecting two regiments of these new draconians Neraka keeps yammering about. If they're any good, I'll call in the promise of more soon after."

"But we need more dragons now," said Jahet.

"That's *your* job," snarled Maldeev, folding his arms. He sank deeper into his big chair. "I've done mine."

Jahet closed her eyes to silence an equally angry retort.

The tension between Jahet and Maldeev had become palpable since the battle, almost a living, breathing thing. But, out of respect, they had stopped just short of accusations, not asked the obvious questions that burned in both their throats.

"How do you propose I go about that?" Jahet asked, her tone snide. "Shall I put up posters in pubs, like Khan is doing to recruit human mercenaries?"

"How would I know? You're so fond of pointing out that I don't understand black dragons," said Maldeev. "How did the others come to join the wing?"

"Word of mouth," said Jahet. "The news will get out to the surrounding swamps that we're looking for recruits."

"We can't wait for that."

Jahet sighed in agreement. "I'll think of something."

"You'd better," the highlord spat, jumping to his feet to pace around on the reed-covered floor. "The decimation of the Black Wing—by our own forces!—was the last thing my reputation needed now." He snorted angrily. "I'll wager all the other highlords are laughing at me even as we speak!"

Jahet tried to think of something comforting to tell her soul mate, but nothing came to mind. The betrayal of his own forces—before the war had even started—*was* an enormous black mark on Maldeev's record. On hers as well. All Jahet could manage was a weak, "We'll restore order and come back even stronger."

Maldeev was forming a response when they both became aware that the dim natural light inside the hall had been abruptly cut off. Looking toward the courtyard, they saw, to their utter amazement, the dragon Khisanth. She looked to be seeking an audience. Maldeev's first thought was to grab his highlord mask, since it was rare, if ever, that a highlord's troops should see his face. Something stayed his hand from the mask that hung from a knob on the back of the ornate chair.

Curiosity made Maldeev wave the other black dragon into the vast chamber. Now doubly surprised, Jahet spoke first.

"This is a grave violation of protocol, Khisanth."

Like a dog, Khisanth shook the rain water from her scales before stepping inside and answering, "True enough. But what I have to say affects the entire wing, more specifically its highlord and most trusted dragon. I thought it efficient to address you both at once."

Khisanth glanced up at last and saw their skeptical, annoyed looks. "If you're more concerned with protocol than rebuilding this wing as swiftly as possible, then perhaps I've overestimated you both." The dragon turned to leave.

"Give me cause to listen," Maldeev challenged. "Quickly."

Khisanth turned back halfway and laughed ironically. "I'd say it was already worth your while, since I'm one of the only two dragons you still have on your side."

"Thanks to you, that's true enough." Maldeev blinked in disbelief at the dragon's gall.

Khisanth didn't flinch from his reproach. "Once I learned of the betrayal, I did what I thought best to minimize the damage." Her eyes narrowed as she added, "If their human riders had been the least bit perceptive or intelligent, the dragons couldn't have plotted without their knowledge."

It was Jahet's turn to flinch. Khisanth had unwittingly laid bare the unspoken crux of the tension between Jahet and Maldeev. Why hadn't his commanders known? Why hadn't she known, as the leader of the dragons? It didn't help that Khisanth had obviously avoided implying the latter about her friend. The question was obvious.

The conversation's turn made Maldeev uncomfortable as well. "Clearly, their human commanders were inferior. As you well know, they've paid the price."

Khisanth did know. She and Jahet had been given the honor, for the amusement of the remaining troops, of tearing apart second-in-command Wakar and the other two officers, including Dimitras, in a dragon tug-of-war on the drill field.

Maldeev arched one brow at Khisanth. "Surely, you don't risk my wrath—twice—simply to point out my faults." Jahet knew his calm tone of voice meant Maldeev was far angrier than if he'd shouted.

"No," Khisanth agreed, nodding once. "I've come to tell you both that I've decided to comply with your request to take a rider."

The announcement hung in the air between all three of them for several moments. Finally, Maldeev turned away and busied himself stirring the fire. "Fine," he said. "I've selected several for you to choose from. I'll arrange for you to interview them immediately."

"I will not."

Maldeev looked up.

"My compliance with your ultimatum has two conditions. First, I will choose my rider entirely on my own, and in my own time. Second, you'll guarantee my position as second-in-command to Jahet from this moment on."

"That's extortion," fumed Maldeev.

Khisanth's expression was mild. "That's a narrow way of viewing it. As I see it, my proposal allows each of us to get what he wants."

"What would prevent you from delaying the decision forever, once you're handed the position you've long coveted?" Maldeev demanded.

"It is not in my interest to do so," was Khisanth's unnervingly calm response.

Maldeev was about to argue further when Jahet leaned down to whisper in his ear. "I've said before that self-interest is a black dragon's only motivation. Go ahead and agree. Once we replace the other dragons, we can always renege if we need to."

Maldeev clenched and unclenched his fists. He didn't like being squeezed into making any decision. Yet he was intelligent enough to see the value in this—and even to add wit and pluck to Khisanth's long list of attributes.

"All right," the highlord growled at last. "You shall have this your way." He squinted up at her. "See that I'm not disappointed."

Just then, Maldeev's new second-in-command cleared his

throat loudly just outside the door. "Sir," he called, without stepping in to intrude, "the wall sentries have spotted the draconians approaching from the northwest."

"Excellent, Salah Khan." Maldeev nearly smiled, but managed only a joyous scowl. Initially, the highlord had dreaded the arrival of these odd and grotesque mutations of Good dragon eggs. He was of the old military school. They'd had no magic, dragons, or any of the other oddities of modern warfare. Combat then was between men on foot or horseback, with swords and clubs. But now, with his troop numbers so low, he welcomed the injection of strength. Draconians were rumored to be exceptionally strong.

The highlord snatched up his trademark mask from the back of the enormous throne and pulled it down low over his face, to end at his collar. Rubbing his hands together, Maldeev strode eagerly toward the courtyard, his hobnailed boots pounding across the floorboards. Without turning his head, he called back to the dragons, as if he'd just remembered them, "Come along and review my new troops."

The two dragons looked at each other before following at some distance. "You've certainly had a change of heart," said Jahet. Her conversational tone sounded tight, forced. "Did your mysterious disappearance from the battlefield have anything to do with this metamorphosis?"

Khisanth well knew that rumors and speculation were rampant on the subject. She had no interest in or concern with quelling them. There was something mystical—prophetic, even—about her journey to the Abyss and the Queen of Darkness, something that made Khisanth want to hug the details to herself.

"I've had an awakening, yes," said the newly appointed second-in-command. "You could even take a measure of credit for talking me into it," she added. "Make no mistake, though. My goals have not changed, simply my route to them. I intend to play an important role in returning the dragons to rule."

"Does that important role require you to step on me?"

Khisanth heard her friend's thinly disguised suspicions. "I

think there'll be enough positions for all dragons worthy of serving our queen."

They caught up with Maldeev then at the far southern edge of the drill field, and both fell into an unusually strained silence. At least the rain had stopped.

"There they are," breathed Maldeev with near reverence, pointing to the endless stream of creatures marching against the gray sky. Their formation was tight, a narrow ribbon in the grassy northwestern foothills, made greener by the day's rain. The beleaguered highlord could scarcely contain his excitement at the sight of the approaching dragon men.

Maldeev had never before seen a draconian, let alone met one. His awed tones were based solely on the draconians' reputation as the meanest, most fearless and indestructible fighting creatures ever known. They were also known to be fond of ale and spirits, which made them especially sadistic. Heeding the advice of the Red Wing commander with whom he'd arranged delivery of the draconians, Maldeev had removed all spirits from the reach of the troops. The human rank and file had grumbled in protest, but Maldeev suspected they'd all agree once they encountered a drunken draconian, as would inevitably happen, despite his best efforts.

The sounds of shuffling troops on the move got louder as the dragon men approached. Now Maldeev could clearly see the face of Horak, the human with whom Maldeev had exchanged missives. The Red Wing commander would join the Black Wing to lead the draconian forces in the upcoming war. Horak's back was ramrod straight in his bright plate mail. Poking through the narrow openings in his imposing great helm were wayward tendrils of copper-colored hair. Horak had a quill-thin, carrot-colored mustache and slight beard that was likely the result of many days on the trail.

Raising high a banner on his pike, which still held the symbol of Ariakas's Red Wing, Horak signaled his troops to halt some two hundred yards from where Maldeev and his imposing black dragons waited. The armored horseman spurred his black gelding in the ribs and galloped swiftly up to Maldeev, kicking clouds of choking dust up from the field.

Horak pivoted to stop as if on a steel piece. He pushed his helm back so that its face rested atop his red head.

"Field Commander Horak," he said crisply. His gelding pranced fitfully after the long trek. "I'm pleased to report that we lost only eleven of five hundred twenty-three draconians in two hundred miles, due mainly to infighting. The rigors of trail life seem to bring out the worst in them."

"Excellent!" crowed Maldeev. No introduction of himself was needed or expected.

"We will review the troops momentarily. But first, we must replace that." Maldeev pointed with near disdain at the banner on the tip of Horak's pike. The highlord snapped his fingers. Maldeev's head adjutant stepped forward anxiously, in his hands a folded piece of black-bordered cloth. Maldeev revealed a glorious rendition of the Black Wing's own banner, designed by Maldeev himself. On three sides of the rectangle—two long, and one short side that would be attached to the pike—was a three-inch border of darkest black. Inside that was a white rectangle, a contrasting background for the black dragon depicted in impressive detail, down to scales made from overlapping ovals of black silk. Most striking of all, though, was the dragon's red, forked tongue, lashing out from bared teeth to form the banner's outer, short edge.

Horak restrained any signs of flinching. It was an abrupt but necessary symbolic shift of allegiance from the Red to the Black Wing. The human forced a look of eager pride to his freckle-flecked face. Slipping the banner's loops over the tip of his pike, he waved it over his head. The humans and ogres who had gathered behind Maldeev whooped joyously.

Behind Horak, the draconians seemed unmoved, which momentarily surprised the highlord. Catching his expression, Horak said, "Don't be concerned, Highlord. They are loyal servants of the Dark Queen. Draconians are devoid of emotion, except for hate . . . and love of ale."

Maldeev shook away his dismayed look, annoyed at himself for showing his lack of knowledge before this new commander. The dragon highlord squinted at the troops, evaluating them. "Which are the baaz, and which are kapak? Tell me, how do you make such creatures without magic?"

"The brass-tinged ones in the front with the hooded capes and short wings are the baaz. They were the first made. A hardening liquid is injected into the eggs of Good brass dragons, which remains in their adult bodies. The liquid hardens to stone if they're killed, which also traps any weapons inside them."

Horak pointed directly at a baaz near the front of the legion. "You may notice that some of them look vaguely human, like Gorbel. With a minor mask over his snout and a long, bulky cape, he makes a fairly convincing man—I frequently use Gorbel in particular as a spy."

Maldeev nodded his appreciation.

"All in all, baaz are small but exceedingly powerful, nearly two-thirds of the assembled troops."

Horak removed a gauntlet and pointed a finger. "Behind them are the kapaks, made from copper dragons." He shook his head wistfully. "Unfortunately, they're neither as smart nor even as tolerable to look at as the baaz, with that strange hank of mane dangling from their jaws. They also refuse to wear clothing of any sort. Those large, leathery wings make them fair gliders, though they would be considered pathetic compared to dragons." The red-haired commander gave an appreciative look to Jahet and Khisanth, who were listening and watching with silent but scarcely concealed disdain.

"Fortunately," continued Horak, "kapak respond well to orders from humans. They'll even listen to the more intelligent of the baaz. Their hand-to-hand skills are matchless in combination with the venom of their saliva."

Maldeev rocked back on his heels, arms crossed tightly before him. "Very impressive," he breathed.

"You should see the newest draconians," Horak said abruptly, his tone conversational. "The gold auraks have magical abilities that rival a dragon's. They can't fly, but their intelligence more than makes up for that.

"And the sivaks . . ." He whistled. "Their skills are boundless! Their silver wings spread in flight are a sight to behold! As strong as giants, perhaps, they can shapechange at will. In fact, when someone does manage to slay them, they automatically change into the form of their slayer for three days, then burst into flames and destroy all around them. Wonderful effect!"

Horak sighed wistfully. "Dragon Highlord Ariakas just received five hundred of each. What I wouldn't do to earn command of some of them one day. . . ."

The tips of Maldeev's ears burned red. He was receiving Ariakas's rejects! His moment of triumph had dissolved into degradation. "When can I expect my allotment of auraks and sivaks to replace these wretched abominations?" he asked through gritted teeth.

Horak seemed at last to sense his error. "Sir, baaz and kapaks are still far superior to humans in sheer physical strength and fighting ability. They have served Highlord Ariakas well. With their help, the Black Wing will surely rise in status and—"

"Ariakas has arranged it so that he still has the greatest fighting force, while the rest of us struggle along, looking like pathetic imitations of highlords in his shadow!" Maldeev slammed one gloved fist into the other. "Well, I will not accept his charity, or his rejects!"

Jahet stooped slightly to squeeze her highlord's shoulder in a possessive gesture that suggested caution. The very last thing Maldeev needed now was to appear unhinged before a newly reassigned commander. The dragon closed her eyes and breathed a sigh of relief when she saw Maldeev struggle to regain his composure and shake off any outward signs of rage.

"You're right, Horak," said Maldeev smoothly. "We'll use these draconians to fight for the Queen of Darkness. With them, the Black Wing will surpass even Ariakas's performance in the upcoming war!"

"Yes, sir." Horak was knocked a bit off balance by Maldeev's extremes of behavior, but recovered quickly. "My troops and I are fatigued from the march from Neraka. Where will we be quartered?"

Maldeev hastily gave directions to his adjutant to place the commander's and his human officers' belongings in quarters within the inner curtain, near his own high-ranking soldiers.

"As for the draconians," said Maldeev, "we've made preparations for the construction of tents." The highlord drew an arc in the air with his finger to indicate the area where Horak's troops now stood. "They'd better start building, if they wish to rest anytime soon."

Horak gave a brief salute. "Very well, sir," he said. The commander pulled on his gelding's bit and headed off on foot to establish a camp for his troops.

Jahet dismissed Khisanth, who was not unhappy to take wing for the warrens.

Watching the other dragon in flight, Jahet herself turned to leave. "I'd better get started on my recruitment of dragons," she said to Maldeev.

"I am very pleased about Khisanth's turnaround," Maldeev said, almost to stop Jahet from leaving.

"It's good news, but I predicted it would happen."

"You don't sound as pleased as I would expect," observed Maldeev. "Don't you trust her motives?"

High above Maldeev's head, Jahet's wings shrugged, but her eyes were contemplative. "No more or less than ever. She's a black dragon." Jahet's eyes narrowed slightly. "But she *is* different. Something—the battle, perhaps—has changed her."

It didn't settle Jahet's concerns to see the look of undisguised admiration in her highlord's eyes as they both watched Khisanth's dark form in flight against the backdrop of deep green pines.

Chapter 21

Fighting the overwhelming urge to nap, Khisanth absently picked with a sharpened talon at a shred of carrion lodged between a knifelike incisor and her black-spotted gums. The newly promoted second-in-command dragon of the Black Wing was squeezed into the meager late-afternoon shade of a lone oak tree on the crest of a bluff in the mountains southwest of their destination: Lamesh Castle. Even during years of endless drill and preparation for battle, Khisanth had not realized how truly tedious war could be.

It isn't a war, yet, Khisanth reminded herself. The Black Wing was preparing to launch an isolated offensive against the Knights of Solamnia who had, just months before, brought the fledgling wing to its knees. For nearly four days, the dragon had been flying as an advance scout for the north-bound army.

The assignment had proven to be a tedious exercise: fly north for a half hour, wait for a half day for the plodding draconians to bring up the rear, fly north for another half hour. It frustrated Khisanth that, unfettered by the army, she could have flown the distance from Shalimsha to Lamesh in less than three hours.

The second-ranked dragon of the Black Wing knew exactly how far it was to Lamesh, because she'd been flying reconnaissance there every other day since Khoal's death. Her shapechanging ability was no longer a secret after her battle with the ancient dragon, so Khisanth used it freely on her missions for the wing. Her form of choice was a big black raven, which allowed her to fly directly into the Solamnic compound and closely monitor the rebuilding of its forces.

The decision to retaliate against the knights at Lamesh had been made months before, when Khisanth was able to consistently report that the knights had not regrouped to any significant extent. They appeared to have replaced very few of the patrician warriors, and acquired, at best, seventy-five mercenaries. That low number was consistent with the Black Wing's own difficulties in recruiting many new sell-swords in the sparsely populated, isolated region.

All of this was fine with Khisanth. It meant there would be fewer bodies to wade through when the time came for her revenge. The knight who had broken her nose at Needle Pass and then slipped from her clutches at Shalimsha would not escape again. The dragon looked forward to the day when his sword and skull jangled on her necklace with the rest of her trophies.

Looking to the south with heavy-lidded eyes, Khisanth realized that the wing had made more progress in the last hours than she'd expected. They'd picked up the pace significantly after rounding the Hand of Chaos, a sharp southern leg of this isolated section of the Khalkist Mountains. The procession was perhaps a quarter league away, down the southern slope of the bluff upon which Khisanth was perched. Jahet hovered just above the ground at the head of the impressive file of troops. Airborne behind her, prodding troops along, were two newly recruited black dragons.

There were three dragons under the ranking black dragon's command now, due to Jahet's active recruitment in the Great Moors. Khisanth had suggested that any uncommitted black dragons would gravitate to that swamp upon awaking from the Sleep, as Khisanth herself had. The two very young, "green" dragons, a male who called himself Lhode, and a female known as Shadow, were a refreshing change from their predecessors. Lhode and Shadow looked up to the older, seasoned dragons; the relationship came as near to kinship as black dragons could. Unfortunately, they simply weren't as adept at flying and fighting as those they had replaced. That would come with time and experience.

The battle against the Knights of Solamnia had brought another important change: the dragons were no longer an autonomous division. The reorganization made good sense. Everyone knew Maldeev had divided the dragons to prevent the concentration of power that had made the betrayal of Khoal, Dnestr, and Neetra so possible and so devastating.

Each dragon was now assigned to a specific fighting unit, to provide the ground troops with focused air protection. Not coincidentally, the leader of each unit was also the dragon's soul mate. As Dragon Highlord Maldeev's mount, Jahet was to oversee the entire army. Lhode would control the ogres with his ogre rider, Volg. Shadow and her rider and soul mate, Horak, were in command of the draconians.

As for Khisanth, her promotion had come at a price. She had all but promised Maldeev to take his lieutenant as her rider, in exchange for allowing her to fight this one battle unfettered. If she had not yet grown used to the idea of the very logical union between equal counterparts, she had accepted its inevitability. Once her scouting assignment was completed, Khisanth was to coordinate her efforts with Salah Khan and the ranks of humans.

The front ranks of the wing were now close enough for Khisanth to clearly see Maldeev in gleaming plate mail, his horse, as well as those of his officers, decked out in dress black-and-white skirts. Khisanth could see only flashes of the highlord behind the waving folds of the Black Wing's banner, which he insisted on bearing on the tip of his own pike. The commander's joy at being in the field again was evident in his eyes through the holes in his horned helm. The wing's first offensive was obviously a moment Highlord Maldeev had long awaited.

Riding closely on his left flank was the black-masked Salah Khan, newly promoted to dragon highmaster and second-in-command to Maldeev himself. He had been Wakar's adjutant, having risen to his post after the former second-in-command's death. A coldly efficient tactician, Khan was notorious for a temper easily ignited by underlings. Most everyone was already intimidated by Khan's ever-present black head wrapping; it was rumored that the cloth covered a featureless face, destroyed long ago in a duel with a wizard. Salah Khan was an introspective human whose long, pensive silences frequently appeared to unnerve even Dragon Highlord Maldeev.

Behind the leaders, the black dragon could see the small number of horse-mounted calvary, to be used in the event of a rout. Maldeev had made it clear he would take no prisoners. Behind them strode the remainder of the human mercenaries, archers, and swordsmen. Next in line, Volg prodded his ogre troops from behind, Lhode coaxing them along by air. Bringing up the rear were Horak's charges. He led his draconian troops by horseback, using the Black Wing banner Maldeev had given him as a focusing point for the dull-witted creatures, with Shadow hovering overhead.

The exact date for the attack had been set after the arrival of the draconian forces. The monstrous reinforcements had visibly boosted the morale of the wing, at least those who were not asked to live with the abominations.

While they were an annoyance and an insult to the dragons, it was the ogre troops who suffered the most from the nearly mindless draconian killing machines. Certainly, no one had any love or sympathy for the brutish ogres. Ironically, the draconians had replaced ogres as the most distasteful forms of life in the army of the Dark Queen. Volg, the ogre's field commander, complained frequently in his halting ogre accent to Horak, the draconian field commander, but Horak seemed to encourage competition between the units; neither did Volg receive help from their immediate superior, army commander Salah Khan.

Drills for the entire army had become more frequent, specific, and intense. Humans, ogres, and draconians all scaled ladders in preparation for a siege; arrows were made, and weapons polished. The ogres protested loudly on the latter score, seeing no value in expending energy on something that didn't make them fight any better.

Waiting now for the front rank of officers to close the gap, Khisanth nibbled a blade of grass, much greener here than the drought-parched region around Lamesh. Angry-looking, black-limned clouds were beginning to form in the western sky, suggesting rain. The hot afternoon had already turned muggy.

Out of the corner of her eye, Khisanth saw Jahet flying toward her. Pulling back her wings, the highlord's dragon dropped gracefully to her hind feet with nary a hop.

"Maldeev is considering launching an immediate attack."

Khisanth looked to the darkening sky and arched a brow. "Is that wise?"

"Salah Khan and Volg are trying to talk him out of it." With a sigh, Jahet settled herself into the shade next to Khisanth. "It's quite comfortable here. While Lhode and Shadow and I have been securing Shalimsha with just a handful of useless soldiers, you've had it pretty easy these past days," she said with mock jealousy.

"Easy? You mean boring," growled Khisanth, struggling to her feet. "Let's go."

Standing almost reluctantly, Jahet took wing mere heartbeats after Khisanth. The two of them made an impressive sight, gliding effortlessly, enormous shadows skimming the land beneath. The highlord had stopped the procession in a small gully on the spine of a neighboring bluff. They dropped within a length of Maldeev.

"We attack immediately, while there's still a chance for

surprise," the dragon highlord was saying.

"There is that school of thought, Highlord," Salah Khan said diplomatically. His voice was muffled by the black wrapping around his head. "There are also those who believe that surprising the enemy *at any cost* is unwise, particularly in a battle of this size, when we so outnumber the enemy. If this were a small ambush, then, perhaps . . ."

"Ogres bushed," Volg cut in rudely. He'd stomped his way to the front ranks after the procession halted.

Horak, too, had ridden up from his position back with the draconians. Beads of sweat glistened on the brow of the newest of Maldeev's officers, curling his copper hair into tight ringlets. He'd heard Volg's comment and was twisting his red mustache confidently when he said, "My draconians are ready to follow you instantly, Highlord. Unlike the other, uh, soldiers," he stumbled with a pointed look at Volg, "they need little sleep or food."

Volg scowled. "Darkness come!" He pointed a warty finger to the east before adding slyly, "Ogres see fine, but humans not."

"There's another very real problem, Sir," interrupted Khan, getting his first good look down the slope toward the citadel known as Lamesh. "No one mentioned a moat." His eyes, the only things visible in his face wrap, suddenly narrowed with surprise and concern. "It would appear that the moat feeds a waterfall over a cliff, as well. It'll be much more difficult to breach than our plans have allowed."

Maldeev looked with irritation at his number two dragon, the only one among them to have seen Lamesh. "Well, Khisanth? Didn't you notice these things?"

"Yes," she said without guilt. "I reported that they were digging a *trench* at least two fortnights ago. In itself a trench would not change the method of attack. However, the water is a new development." She gave Maldeev a wry look. "Perhaps they've been expecting us."

"We'll wait until morning!" snapped the dragon highlord. Spurring his horse, Maldeev cantered off and stopped a short distance away to gather his thoughts alone.

Maldeev's advisors would all have been surprised to learn that their highlord had actually made the decision to delay the attack after Horak's pandering. Not that the highlord was immune to bootlicking. Actually, it was one of his favorite benefits of rank.

The problem was Horak. The very capable human commander didn't know he was the least trusted of Maldeev's officers, even placing behind the vulgar ogre, Volg, solely because he'd been under Ariakas's command.

Nourished by Horak himself on his first day at Lamesh, Maldeev's hatred of the Red Wing commander had swelled, running so deep and silent, like the roots of a fast-growing willow, that even Jahet could not guess its full measure. Maldeev would take Ariakas's leavings and turn them to gold for the greater glory of himself.

He was Takhisis's chosen.

Maldeev would seize every opportunity, take any chance, to align himself more closely with the Queen of Darkness.

"Orders, Highlord?" Khan cut into his thoughts.

Maldeev shook away his preoccupation and whistled for Jahet. "Tell your dragons to refrain from flying and move on foot into the forest to the west. The rest of the wing will follow." Jahet nodded and backed away to do her highlord's bidding, pulling Khisanth along with a glance toward Lhode and Shadow at the back of the ranks.

Turning to the other commanders, Maldeev continued. "In this battle, my greatest concern is to prevent any of the knights, their men, or their people from escaping. We will certainly have lost all chance for surprise by tomorrow morning. To stop escapes tonight, I want detachments to set up overlooking the fortress and the town. Humans will watch while it's light, to be replaced by ogres and draconians during darkness."

That settled, Maldeev lifted his pike and directed his horse to pick its way down the bluff to the west, following after the dragons.

* * * * *

Tate lowered the spyglass from his eye. He knew the Black Wing would come to Lamesh Castle. The knight hadn't been surprised by the news from the sentry. He'd just hoped it wouldn't be so soon. It was too soon. . . . The reinforcements Tate was expecting from Solamnia hadn't arrived yet. Soon they might not need to, Tate thought grimly, feeling an unusual defeatism. The rain wouldn't help matters, either.

Standing on the southern battlements, the Knight of the Crown snapped the glass back up to his right eye. He wiped a raindrop from the cloudy lens. The view through it was not much closer than seeing with the naked eye. Tate used the glass because it had been Wolter's.

He saw no dragons. He should be able to see the enormous black creatures, even without the spyglass. Yet, Tate could identify only officers, a vast number of humans and ogres, and then some other strange creatures for which Tate had no name. An attack didn't appear to be imminent, since the black army was bivouacking.

Still, he would have little time to mount a defense. Tate slipped the brass cylinder into a loop on his belt and then turned to leave. He stopped short, not quite sure where to go first. Sir Wolter would have known. Tate rubbed his face wearily, glad his men were too preoccupied assembling arms and equipment to notice his indecision.

Nothing had been the same for Tate since Sir Wolter Heding, his sponsor and friend—his father, for all purposes— was slain in the ill-fated attack on Shalimsha. Lamesh Castle's lord knight seemed to have only two moods these past months: anger and shame. Tate had been so sure Kiri-Jolith approved of the plan. Wolter had advised against it. It was the only time Tate had ignored Sir Wolter's advice.

That was the greatest part of his shame, which Tate would have admitted only to Wolter. Tate knew men died in battle. He'd witnessed the gruesome deaths of Sir Stippling's party. The knight had just never given thought to its happening specifically because of him. Not to Wolter, anyway. By virtue of his wisdom Wolter always seemed to rise above such earthly concerns. Wolter would have been telling stories at hearthside in Solamnia, if not for Tate.

The young knight's anger always focused on the black dragon whose last strike at Tate had ended Wolter's life. Something about her had been hauntingly familiar. Her odd necklace had struck an uneasy chord in his memory that the knight was still unable to identify.

Shaking away the unsettling reflection, the lord knight looked upon the new moat with a glimmer of satisfaction. Anticipating a counterattack, he'd had the foresight to dig the trench and fill it, despite the muttered protests of the workers. Tate had devoted a great percentage of his manpower to accomplishing it so quickly, but too soon it would prove its worth in a land-based attack. Unfortunately, it would do nothing to stop the dragons he was certain must be lying in wait somewhere. That he couldn't see them only made him more apprehensive about what they were planning. He was only slightly mollified to remember that when the dragons entered the battle, he was at least prepared now to fight them on their own level. The knight made a mental note to feed his own winged creatures, which he'd been careful to keep out of sight of spies the Black Wing might have sent north.

Tate leaned over the inner wall and yelled into the courtyard, "Albrecht, sound the alarm in the village. Take a handful of men to gather the people into the safety of the castle. We have little enough room in the inner ward, so instruct them to bring only their children, the clothes on their backs, and perhaps weapons, if they're of use. Tell the gate guards to keep watch for smugglers." He gave a small motion with his head. "Quickly now." Nodding up at his superior, Albrecht hastened off toward the east gate, gathering a small trail of knights in his wake.

Tate considered calling Albrecht back to order the torching of the village so its stores wouldn't benefit the enemy, but he decided against it. They would need every hand in the battle; burning their village, no matter how tactically sound, would earn the lord knight no supporters among the villagers. Better to let the enemy do that dirty work.

Next, Tate jogged to each of the bastions, starting with those on the southeastern and southwestern corners, which faced the encamped army of the Black Wing. Tate instructed the sentries there to watch closely, first and foremost for signs of impending attack, secondly for dragons, and then for any parties departing from the enemy's main body. He told their counterparts in the northeast and northwest towers to alert him immediately if they sighted either dragons or the appearance of wooden mantelets near the eastern or northern gates to prevent escape.

That reminded Tate he needed to get his own spies out quickly, before the enemy could seal them into the castle. Spotting Wallens coordinating the stockpiling of rocks and arrows on the south battlements, he put the knight in charge of selecting and dispersing agents to more accurately assess the enemy's strength and intent.

Tate saw Abel the baker scurrying about, the flour on his apron turned to paste by the lightly falling rain. The stout man was bossing knights and youths alike in the filling of pots and jugs of water. The containers were then placed on the battlements to be dumped on enemy soldiers as they scaled the walls. The light rain was making it difficult to start fires to boil the pots of water. The blacksmith lent his bellows to the task, and before long flames stirred and stayed. Long, forked poles were distributed along the walls for toppling ladders. Bundles of arrows wrapped in oilskins to protect them against the rain were deposited behind the battlements. Archers checked their bowstrings, carefully packed inside their doublets or padded armor, to be sure they were dry. Crossbowmen shook beaded water off their heavily oiled weapons.

Before long, the frightened villagers, grumbling about the rain, began to pile through the eastern gate, crowding the courtyard. Albrecht set them to work immediately preparing bandages, fetching and carrying supplies for the soldiers, and rounding up the livestock running loose in the compound.

After everyone was fed a thin stew from the enormous pots that would too soon hold boiling water for the defense, Tate called an emergency meeting of his four-man council of knights. Since the great room was filled with displaced villagers, Albrecht, Wallens, and Auston met with him in the light of a single taper in their barracks. Tate's batting felt wet and clammy against his skin.

"You've all seen, or at least heard about, the mobile barricades beyond the gates," Tate began. "We are now sealed in, unless we choose to try fighting our way out.

"It appears, however, that we are badly outnumbered. The enemy has a sizable army of humans, ogres, and some sort of creatures no one here can identify. Prudence demands we assume they have dragons, as well, although no one has seen them." Heads nodded quiet agreement around the table.

"Considering the seriousness of the situation, I want to send an emissary out to talk to their commander."

Agreement was replaced by surprise. "Surely you don't mean to discuss surrender?" asked Albrecht.

"No," replied Tate. "But we have a huge number of women, children, and old men here in the fortress. We must at least try to arrange safe conduct for them away from the battle."

Auston cleared his throat. "Sir, I would be honored to serve as message bearer. I've had some diplomatic experience, settling ethnic disputes with the barbarians in the Estwilde region of Solamnia."

Tate clapped the eager young knight on the shoulder. "You're just the man for the job, then, Auston."

A short time later the knights were reassembled inside the south gate. Lanterns, spitting softly in the light rain, cast their dim light across the scene. Auston sat proudly, if somewhat nervously, on his horse. Tate shook the young knight's hand. "Come back swiftly and safely."

Nodding, Auston touched his helmet in salute to Tate as he rode out the gate. Two guards hastily closed and barred it behind him.

Rather than wait anxiously back in the barracks, the knights separated to double-check the castle's defenses. Tate went to the stables below the barracks and fed the griffons. The horses had been moved above ground to accommodate the five horseflesh-loving winged creatures he'd purchased at great expense from a trader.

An hour later, there came a shout from the rampart. A nervous guard peered out and saw a white horse, returning alone in the pale moonlight. Tate ran from the stables up onto the wall to see what caused the commotion. He watched with the sentries and knights gathered there as the horse cantered back to the south gate. Guards flung back the heavy wooden doors and hustled the horse inside. Snorting, eyes wide and fearful, the white creature circled through the courtyard and the thronged people there, stopping before Tate, who'd hastened down from the battlement. The courtyard grew strangely still, as if everyone inside was holding his breath.

The apprehensive lord knight began to search the creature for a note or message of some kind concerning Auston's fate. The horse itself provided the answer. Its hairy lips ruffled, and a voice very like Tate's own said through the horse's mouth, "You can't act like ruffians and expect to be treated like ladies." Tate visibly paled.

"What does it mean, Sir Tate?" Albrecht asked, noting the expression of understanding growing on his superior's face. "And what have they done with Auston?"

"It means no deal," Tate said numbly. "Auston's dead."

"The unprincipled bastards!" snarled the usually contained Wallens. "What'll we do now, Sir?"

Tate tried to rub the weariness from his eyes. "See to your stations one last time tonight, then get some rest while you can," the lord knight said. "Tomorrow promises to be a long, hard day."

Tate was already walking away from the dazed Albrecht and Wallens, his thoughts on a distant time. Three fingers traced the scars beneath the whiskers on his cheek. Now he knew why the dragon at Shalimsha had seemed so familiar. The witch-woman from the ambush . . . Tate didn't understand magic well enough to explain how it could be done, but he was certain the human fighter was now a vengeful, black dragon. It was obvious from the message that she hadn't forgotten their encounter, either.

A muscle twitched in Tate's wet cheek. The dragon's quest was nothing compared to the knight's: to avenge his friend, Wolter. She was a worthy adversary as a dragon, he mused, recalling the battle at Shalimsha.

He found it all very curious how their paths had crossed and recrossed. He wasn't a man to believe in omens, but if ever he did . . .

The Knight of the Crown felt a sudden, overwhelming desire to pray to his patron, Kiri-Jolith. He'd spent little time in temple since the battle at Shalimsha. Tate told himself he was too busy reorganizing troops and bolstering morale to devote one of every seven days to inactive prayer.

The truth was, without the old knight to steel his resolve, Sir Tate's interest in rising to the Order of the Rose had waned. In a secret corner of his soul, Tate had even dared to wonder if Kiri-Jolith hadn't abandoned him first.

As the lord knight picked his way through the sleeping bodies in the courtyard, he couldn't help thinking that many were taking their last mortal rest. The thought propelled Tate faster toward a long overdue talk with his god.

Chapter 22

Maldeev was feeling confident. The highlord sat apart from his four black dragons, who waited restlessly for daybreak on a rocky cliff west of Lamesh. He knew that when the sun crested the horizon to the east, Salah Khan would issue the order for the ground troops to advance on Lamesh's south wall. The second he saw the knights' attention devoted there, Maldeev would lead the dragons in an attack on the west wall. It was a plan the highlord was certain couldn't fail.

The pace of the assault had gone from boring to breakneck in one long night. The draconians, under Horak's watchful eye, had chopped down trees that the ogres turned into makeshift bridges for fording the moat and ladders for climbing crenelated walls.

Maldeev had flown to this vantage point with the dragons late in the night. Though the steady downpour was an uncomfortable nuisance for the highlord, it seemed to act like a mental balm for the black dragons. They'd dropped into sleep after foraging for food in the mountains farther west.

Wound as tight as a spring, the highlord had been the first to awaken, though he wasted no time in rousing the others to draw a crude battle diagram in the dirt. The plan had changed little from the one drawn up at a war council of officers and dragons the day before the march north. Truly, the only alteration was to the role of the dragons, and that was as obvious and simple as the dirt in which Maldeev had drawn it.

"Whoever built Lamesh obviously did not consider aerial attacks," the highlord said. "It must have been built during the time your kind was banished from Krynn."

"Technically, we still are," Khisanth interjected mildly. "The Dark Queen's return to Krynn is the point of the war, isn't it?"

"Yes, I guess so." Maldeev's eyebrows raised unpleasantly at being openly addressed by a dragon other than Jahet. Perhaps Khisanth had presumed too much from the highlord's willingness to let her respond to the knight's emissary the previous evening. Maldeev had had the messenger slain instantly by Jahet. The highlord had intended the riderless horse to be his answer to the request to let women, children, and old men go free. But Khisanth had insisted that she'd fought the leader of the knights and knew just what response would shake him. Maldeev had allowed it, seeing no harm.

He stood, stretched, and looked again to the sky, which was starting to show signs of dawn between the swollen rain clouds overhead. "Prepare yourselves. It's nearly time."

Atop Jahet, Maldeev was to lead the dragons. Volg and Horak would direct their ogre and draconian troops forward in the initial southern charge, so Lhode and Shadow would pick them up on the battlefield after the dragons joined the fray.

Since Khisanth had no rider, she stood by, almost idly watching Maldeev pull on the last of his war attire, a pair of tight leather gauntlets that flared at the wrists. He pulled something from a small bag tied to his waist and held it to the light. It was a plain gold ring topped by a smooth, flat circle of onyx. At length, Maldeev placed it over the gloved index finger of his right hand.

"New ring, Maldeev?" Jahet asked idly as the dragon shrugged to adjust the ornate saddle he'd tossed up between her wing blades.

"Yes," the dragon highlord said quickly, withdrawing the band almost self-consciously. "Andor insisted I take along a protective ring." He saw Jahet's interest stir. "He *is* my dark cleric, after all—it's his job to think of such things. I only took it to humor him. You know how I hate magic—didn't even want Andor near this battle." With a shrug, Maldeev wiggled the ring from his gloved finger.

Jahet shook her head slowly. "You already know what a mistake I think his absence is. Wear the bloody thing, Maldeev," she prompted. "What will it hurt? It just may come in handy." Maldeev jammed the black-and-gold ring over the gloved index finger. Jahet looked satisfied, though she wondered at this new, acquiescent side of her soul mate.

"Jahet," Maldeev called to his dragon, tipping his head to indicate that she should turn her ear to him. The highlord whispered briefly, and Jahet's face lit up.

"I'll ask her," she said to the highlord. The ranking dragon turned to Khisanth. "Maldeev has suggested, and I concur, that you ride as our wing dragon." She looked intently at her friend. "This is offered to honor your solo value, Khisanth. It's not an order."

The younger black dragon felt pride swell in her breast. "It would be *my* honor," she said. Maldeev nodded once and strode away to mentally prepare himself for battle.

"Stay close to us, Khisanth," Jahet whispered to her suddenly, with the highlord out of earshot. "I sense a recklessness in Maldeev I've never seen before, as if he believes he can't lose. . . ."

Khisanth nodded. She heard a distant noise and cocked a sensitive ear to the west. A trumpet . . . the knights had sounded the alarm.

"Fly!" cried Maldeev. Jahet dropped her left shoulder to

the ground. Using it as a step, the highlord bounded into the saddle and swung his broadsword over his head thrice. Jahet sprang from the ledge, covered the short distance to the ravine below the cliff, and arched into a dive, Khisanth in sync at her left side. Pulling up short just above the gurgling, waterfall-fed reservoir at the bottom of the ravine, Jahet prepared for ascent.

Not even a feeding frenzy would have stirred Khisanth's senses as much as the thought of what they were about to do. She felt that old, familiar bloodlust in her veins. The dragon drew on that energy for speed, summoned every drop from the farthest reaches of her body to propel her skyward in stunning opposition to the waterfall pounding earthward.

Khisanth crested the cliff face beside Jahet. One hundred knights stood on the walkways between the double crenelated walls, bows in their hands. They were poised in profile to the dragons as they fired arrows down upon the attackers to the south. Khisanth opened her jaws to loose a primal scream that split the humid morning air. The knights spun around in unison at the nerve-shattering shrieks of four bloodthirsty dragons. Most froze, bows dropping uselessly from many a hand at the sight. How she loved the look of panic she caused in the eyes of men! She smirked at the sight of the humans in their knightly finery, trembling in her shadow.

Khisanth kept Jahet locked in the corner of her right eye. The ranking dragon banked left slightly to address the limited forces on the cliff wall, compelling Khisanth to hook as well. While Maldeev sliced heads from shoulders and Jahet breathed acid, Khisanth angled herself to the southwest corner. Lowering her shoulder just slightly, she swept a fifty-foot stretch of wall clean of fear-struck knights with the edge of her wing. As she swerved away, she grasped the last man in the line with her claws and flung him screaming over the cliff to the ravine below. At a nod from Jahet, they climbed quickly in unison to prevent attacks against their bellies,. They dived again into the frenzied throng, scattering men like chickens.

On the opposite wall, Lhode and Shadow were carrying out a similar maneuver. Neither dragon had ever fought in a battle before, but they had practiced this sort of coordinated attack many times on the drill fields and walls of Shalimsha. But those drills had been against dummies, never against a determined enemy. And Tate's knights, while not as prepared for this battle as they might have been, had spent months licking their wounds after the defeat at Shalimsha and devising ways to fight dragons.

Neither of the two inexperienced dragons expected anything like what awaited them on the northern wall. After flying straight up the cliff wall and blasting acid down the length of the northern rampart, they looped and formed a line, Lhode ahead of Shadow. They raced down the wall picking off the dazed and injured survivors with their claws, wings, and tails. At the end of the wall was a bastion, which they had to swerve to avoid.

Lhode approached the bastion and turned away. Shadow followed, keeping her eyes on Lhode. But as she passed the stone tower, eight men with thick iron grappling hooks ran from the doorway and flung them at the beast. Most of them missed, but two snagged the front edge of the dragon's left wing while a third cut into her leg. Heavy chains anchored the hooks to the walls of the castle. Almost instantly Shadow hit the end of the chains and was flipped tail over head. The chains snapped under the terrible impact, but the dragon tumbled over the wall and fell outside, crashing into a throng of Maldeev's men who were crossing the moat at the base of the east wall.

Immediately archers who had fled the walls at the dragons' appearance rushed back out and poured arrows into the thrashing monster below them. Rocks pelted down and thumped off the dragon's scaly hide. In her frenzy to regain use of her wings, Shadow crushed dozens of panicking men of the Black Wing, toppled their ladders from the wall and destroyed the makeshift bridges they had thrown across the moat.

Seizing the opportunity, a group of knights and men-at-arms threw open a sally port on the eastern wall and charged out. The attackers there were already in disarray, and this sudden counterattack scattered them back into the town. Twenty knights and sergeants armed with twelve- to sixteen-foot spears rushed toward the thrashing dragon while others held off the enemy soldiers.

Even with these long weapons, the attackers had to get well inside the dragon's wingspan to be effective. A dozen or more were crushed or dismembered by Shadow's flailing wings and tail. But the dragon was impeded by the moat and driven to near panic by the shower of stones and arrows from above.

Slipping inside the reach of her thrashing wing, one knight drove his spear into the dragon's neck. Shadow screeched and belched acid to dissolve the weapon's shaft. But before she could win free, two more men rushed forward and plunged their pikes into the great beast's heart.

A tremendous cheer rose from soldiers on the wall as Shadow's body fell slack. Her slayers simply let go of their weapons and rejoined the rest of the sortie party as they fell back inside the castle.

Jahet and Khisanth were circling away from the castle when Shadow was snared by the defenders. Their first inkling that something was wrong came when Khisanth spotted Lhode flying by himself, trying frantically to catch up with the two other dragons and the highlord.

"Take us over the eastern wall to see how Salah Khan fares," ordered Maldeev, oblivious of events there.

The dragons climbed briefly to get above the archers in the castle and to better survey the battlefield. Maldeev flew into a rage on seeing the mauled body of Shadow lying in the moat along the eastern wall, amid the wreckage of that attack.

In the wake of Shadow's death, the castle's defenders were solidly in control of the battlements. Pointing with his mace, Maldeev indicated one section of wall for each dragon to attack: Lhode to the north, Khisanth to the east, and Maldeev and Jahet to the south.

Wheeling in unison, the dragons circled the castle once

before diving again into the heartened defenders. It seemed that wherever their shadows passed, men felt the fear of burning death. When the dragons' screams reverberated from the walls, those warriors with faint hearts dropped their weapons and ran for shelter. The ones who stood their ground were swept away, others who sheltered behind the battlements were burned and suffocated by acid.

Broken ladders and piles of dead ogres and stone-hard draconians beneath the southern wall testified to the bitterness of the escalade. Khan had voiced concern about the draconians being the ones to lead the charge—if they made it to the top and were killed, the baaz would turn to stone and crush anything beneath them on a ladder; a dead kapak would similarly shrivel his fellow troops with acid.

But now that the dragons had cleared the ramparts, ogre and draconian forces clambered freely up and over the walls. Flaming arrows arced overhead and into the courtyard, not discriminating friend from foe, though they did little to the brutish ogres or machinelike draconians.

A lone, anguished cry suddenly cut through the din of battle raging in the inner ward. Khisanth looked up. Her eyes narrowed upon spotting the knight she'd been waiting for. The visor of his helmet was open, showing his face clearly.

Tate showed no signs of fear, only rage. The knight shook his fist skyward, then turned unexpectedly and darted into the arched doorway to the citadel's main keep.

Startled, Khisanth's first instinct was to chase him down and obliterate him from the face of Krynn, once and for all. But something felt wrong, and she realized what it was— she'd lost sight of Jahet. Almost too late, she spotted the dragon and her highlord nearby, locked in close combat with a handful of sword-wielding knights who had put their backs to the southeast tower wall and were now fighting desperately. Jahet was in no real danger, but she couldn't close with one knight without others attacking her.

Neither dragon nor highlord appeared to notice the three archers crouched in Jahet's shadow, barbed tips aimed purposefully at her underbelly.

Khisanth knew she could neither get around Jahet nor accurately use her breath weapon in time to stop the shots. The dragon did the only thing she could think of—she slammed into Jahet. The ranking dragon was knocked off balance and out of harm's way, nearly dumping Maldeev from the saddle. The highlord grabbed the saddle horn and righted himself. Then he cast a stormy glance at Khisanth, in time to see her take an arrow in the lower abdomen, an arrow meant for Jahet.

Khisanth touched down on the battlement briefly and looked below at the small, feather-tipped stick protruding from her belly. Reaching down with almost clinical detachment, she snapped the arrow at the base and flung it away. Her eyes turned on the wide-eyed archers who still crouched beneath her. One jumped up and began to run. Jahet's hind claw reached out and snatched him up; flapping her wings rapidly, she flew straight up about fifty feet and uncurled her claws, dropping him into the courtyard. The archer's comrades had only seconds to contemplate his demise. Khisanth unleashed a stream of green acid that reduced them all to shrieking, then silent puddles of half-eaten flesh and bone.

The three remaining dragons were now together on the top of the east wall. Maldeev was formulating a plan for them when his mount murmured, "Griffons!" Khisanth's head snapped up from the sizzling remains of a knight.

Two wooden doors twice the height of a man had been thrown wide open, and several of the lion-bodied creatures with the wings, heads, and forelegs of eagles were poised for flight. On the back of the lead griffon was Tate.

Khisanth had never before seen these creatures, notorious for their obsession with horseflesh. Though shorter at the shoulder than the average human, the creatures' furry yellow thighs looked dense and well muscled. Golden feathers adorned their front halves, from wingtips to razor-sharp beaks. Tate's griffon stepped from the confines of the threshold and spread its wings to an incredible span of twenty-five feet, the length of a dragon. Emitting the shrill cry of its eagle cousin, Tate's mount sprang into the air, followed closely by four other griffons bearing knights.

"They can't hope to survive a battle in the air against us," scoffed Maldeev.

"They won't have to," observed Khisanth, nodding toward the griffons, who had begun knocking lumbering draconians and ogres from Lamesh's battlements, "if they keep that up."

Maldeev snarled, then dug his heels into his dragon. Jahet and Khisanth tore fiercely after the griffons. To the dragons' amazement and annoyance, the smaller griffons darted away from the cumbersome dragons like startled flies.

"Get them!" Maldeev cried, while Jahet tried desperately to comply.

Laughing aloud at their frustration, Tate tugged his griffon to tuck a wing and bank abruptly to the left. His heels dug in and drove his griffon to sprint away from Lamesh, headed southwest between tree line and cloud. The other four griffons had scattered to every corner of the compass as well. Lhode looked about to pursue, when Maldeev barked, "Lhode, return to Volg and protect your unit. Cover Shadow's unit as well. Jahet, Khisanth, and I will chase down their leader."

Khisanth felt oddly clumsy and ponderous watching the griffon's agile movements ahead of them. The more powerful dragons quickly closed the distance to less than ten feet. Tate watched them approach over his shoulders. Khisanth could see through the holes in his helmet to the fearless look in his dark brown eyes. His hand was on the grip of his sword. Tate's griffon shrieked and wheeled abruptly to face the pursuers.

"Stand and fight, *brave* knight," jeered Maldeev, maneuvering Jahet into face-off position.

Tate appeared not to have heard the dragon highlord's insult, or even noticed the human. In fact, he was looking around Maldeev at Khisanth with obvious interest. "I didn't piece it all together," he said to her, "until I got it from the horse's mouth."

"We'll not meet again, you and I," Khisanth said. "I wonder, will your brand of knighthood hold you in good stead at the door to your god's domain?"

Tate's eyes narrowed at the presumption of his death.

"The principals of Good are the only things worth living—or dying—for."

"Damn you, Khisanth," Maldeev snarled suddenly, "do your job and kill the bastard!"

Rattled, Khisanth called forth her acid and sent it spraying from her maw at the same time Jahet stretched her right wing forward for a wing slap. Neither connected, as the griffon bearing Tate shot up into a thick cloud. Khisanth could see and hear her acid sizzling uselessly through the branches of a tree beneath her; Jahet and Maldeev tumbled slightly before recovering from the missed slap.

"Follow him!" bellowed Maldeev, nudging Jahet's flanks with his heels.

"We can't chase him through the clouds," snorted Jahet. "We're likely to bump into him and get wounded ourselves. You're letting your rage control you, Maldeev." She looked behind her at the battle at Lamesh. "Isn't it obvious he's just trying to keep us away from the battle?"

"If you'd been doing your job," said Maldeev, "he'd be dead by now, and we'd be back in the fray. Now, think of some way to find him in these damned clouds!" His tone of voice assured that he would not be swayed.

"I've an idea for drawing them out," interjected Khisanth. She spoke quickly to Jahet.

The ranking dragon nodded. "You'd better cast it. My spells aren't what they used to be." Jahet could feel Maldeev shifting in the saddle, growing more impatient. "Do it!"

Khisanth got the idea from a favorite trick of Pteros's; the old dragon used it to entice meals to come to him. She quickly summoned the scent of raw horseflesh from her memory of eating her own mount. Focusing intently, Khisanth envisioned the strong, meaty aroma slipping through the confines of her skull and being swept up by the winds.

"What's that awful stench?" demanded Maldeev, shuddering.

Neither dragon, whose salivary glands were furiously working, could respond. Answering the illusionary scent of its obsession—horse meat—the griffon shrieked like an eagle and flew out of the protection of the cloud, headed right for the waiting dragons. Tate tugged furiously at its rope bit but couldn't compete with the griffon's driving hunger.

Maldeev caught on to the nature of the spell Khisanth had cast. "Brilliant!" he crowed to the dragon.

With wings fully extended, the griffon rushed mindlessly toward the scent, bringing Tate within striking distance.

Struggling to control his mount, the knight pulled a morning star from his saddle and swung it around his head. The spiked ball at the end of its chain circled ever closer to the highlord's head. Jahet angled slightly and took the blow herself. The morning star bounced harmlessly off her scales.

Maldeev gave Jahet a two-tap signal and pressed his legs tightly to the dragon's sides. Jahet abruptly rolled over to throw off their opponent. She completed the rotation and squared off again, stunned to see that it had neither unnerved Tate nor increased the distance between them. In fact, the knight had pressed in closer and switched to his sword, waving it at the dragon and highlord as if daring them to strike. She couldn't even unleash acid at such close range because the inevitable splash would strike Maldeev. She decided to pivot and hit the knight with her tail.

Khisanth couldn't see how close they were. The roll-over maneuver had put Jahet between Khisanth and Tate. The wing dragon moved to dart around Jahet's head when the sun sliced through the cloud cover. Khisanth was nearly blinded by a flash of brilliant light glinting off something in Maldeev's hands.

Jahet's left wing lifted for a backhand strike at Tate, but she abruptly reared and choked uncontrollably, her red eyes wide. The gagging sounds stopped within heartbeats. Jahet began inexplicably to drop like a rock from the sky, with Maldeev clinging to her back.

The knight and griffon were forgotten as the wing dragon was struck dumb, witless. What had happened to Jahet?

"Khisanth!" she heard the highlord cry.

The sound brought the dragon from her stupor. She blinked and saw that the lifeless dragon and thrashing human separately spiraled earthward.

Khisanth forced herself into a nosedive. Gauging Maldeev's speed, she focused her sights on a location between his falling form and the treetops, swooping underneath him and into position. The highlord sprawled awkwardly with a jarring thump upon her spine. Maldeev clawed his way to where a saddle would have been.

Maldeev was speaking into Khisanth's ear, but she could scarcely hear him as she watched the body of her friend crash unceremoniously through the canopy of trees below.

"He must have killed her!" Khisanth heard Maldeev at last. He clung to the scales on her neck. "It's an incredible bit of luck that you were riding as wing dragon, or I would have dropped to my death as well."

On the ground, the broken branches settled around Jahet's still, twisted body.

Khisanth's eyes shot skyward to where she'd last seen Tate. The knight was gone. Then her fevered eyes spotted the knight's bright silver armor against the dull sky. He was relentlessly spurring his griffon toward Lamesh.

She engaged all the speed Jahet had envied in her and quickly closed the distance between them. Khisanth was angling herself for a mighty tail slap when Maldeev's voice, high-pitched with agitation, penetrated her pounding head.

"What do you think you're doing? I'm without a saddle back here. Disengage immediately!"

"Then you'd better hang on," she said coldly, and Maldeev clutched her scales. Like a whip, Khisanth's tail snapped against the griffon's lionlike hindquarters. The creature shot forward, its feathered head jerked back hard. Knight and griffon began tumbling earthward. Khisanth shot forward to bat them back and forth between her wings like a cat with a mouse in its paws. The disoriented griffon, its wings broken in many places, began to spiral out of control.

Khisanth snatched the knight from its back and let the creature plummet. She did not even follow its descent, concentrating instead on her own landing. She scarcely felt Maldeev scramble from her back.

Khisanth squeezed the talons of her right claw tightly around Tate, pinning his arms and compressing the metal of his armor. She held him up before her eyes, pushed back his visor, and inspected him as a child would a bug. Almost tenderly the dragon traced a talon along the scars she'd scratched into his flesh. "What a waste. You were in the wrong army," she said.

Though he gasped for breath against the pressure of her claw, Tate's heartbeat was slow and steady. Looking into the dragon's tawny eyes, Tate did not appear afraid. Instead, the knight calmly turned to consider the gray sky. "The barbarians say it is better to die on a good day than live through a thousand bad ones. I think, perhaps, they are right."

"You'll find out sooner than I." Khisanth flicked one long talon and pierced Sir Tate Sekforde's brain. The Knight of the Crown didn't scream. Retracting her talon, Khisanth watched the light fade from the knight's brown eyes as his lifeblood spurted onto the claw that held him.

"Now we are even," she said at last. But when the final flicker of life left Tate, the dragon was surprised to discover she didn't feel the great satisfaction she'd anticipated. Instead, she felt strangely hollow.

Khisanth let Tate's body drop to the ground. It rolled to a stop at the feet of the highlord. The dragon looked from the dead knight to Maldeev and back, more than a little disquieted by the fleeting thought that she'd slain the wrong human.

Chapter 23

"After the ceremony, there'll be no more incidents of disobedience like the one at Lamesh," Maldeev was saying, pacing before the highly stoked fireplace in the great hall. "When I tell my mount to disengage, you will do so without question. You might have killed me!"

Khisanth looked up with one lazy eye from her reclined position on the reed-covered plank floor. "As I recall, I saved your life. What's more, my disobedience"— she shivered at the patronizing word —"led to the demoralization of the remaining knights. The battle was over within minutes."

Maldeev scowled. "You're being amply rewarded for that." He stopped his pacing to look squarely at the dragon. "I'm getting the distinct feeling you don't realize the honor I've bestowed upon you."

Khisanth sighed. She knew her attitude did not reflect

recent events. "It's just that I always envisioned Jahet in the position. I keep waiting for her to return." That was partly true, Khisanth reminded herself. While she had been moody since the events at Lamesh, the highlord seemed to be adjusting to his soul mate's death with the stoic detachment necessary for a truly effective highlord.

The other part of Khisanth's unease, the part she couldn't tell her soul-mate-to-be, was that she couldn't forget her comparison of Maldeev and Tate.

"Did it really never occur to you under what circumstances you would assume the number one rank?"

Khisanth's eyes focused; Maldeev was looking at her incredulously. "I never thought that far ahead."

"I don't believe that." Maldeev returned to the fire to stir the coals pensively. "I think we are fated to be together."

Khisanth propped herself up on one elbow. "What?"

"I can tell you this, now that we are to be soul mates," he said through the mask he would continue to wear in her presence until after their union ceremony. Rocking back on his heels, the human appeared to choose his words carefully.

"I didn't seek my position as dragon highlord. Takhisis herself selected me, from all the officers in her service, to raise the Black Wing."

Khisanth looked suitably impressed.

"I know that you, too, have been god-touched."

Khisanth looked startled. She had told no one, not even Jahet.

"Were the rumors incorrect?" Maldeev asked, though he already knew the answer. Andor, his dark cleric, had long since confirmed that a black dragon had had audience with the queen in her domain and had been sent away alive. The dragon could only have been Khisanth.

"I spoke with our queen, yes."

"What did she look like?" Maldeev pressed, his voice eager. "What did she say?"

"Hideous . . . and breathtakingly beautiful," remembered Khisanth dreamily, giving voice for the first time to the odd contrast. "She told me—warned me, really—to pursue our common goals more intelligently." She paused, wondering if she should share the next memory with Maldeev, then plunged ahead. "She told me to take a rider, said I would know the right one when I met him, and that I would do great things in her name."

"There you have it! She was telling you your destiny!" Maldeev had begun pacing again, working himself into a lather. "How else can you account for the foresight that brought me to suggest you ride as wing dragon? What greater thing could you do in her name than unite with a dragon highlord selected by the very god who bestowed the prophecy?"

Khisanth was beginning to see the logic in his argument. She could hardly reject the wing highlord to join with Salah Khan now anyway. She felt mildly reassured. Any reservations she felt likely resulted from her former resolve to remain riderless.

Still, something else plagued her, something she could not share with anyone, something she needed to do before she could move into her new role. When Salah Khan stepped into the great hall and nodded curtly to his once-intended before addressing Maldeev, Khisanth took the opportunity to slip from the room.

* * * * *

Three hours later, Khisanth was in the guise of an eagle. Her sharp eyes scoured the hilly landscape south of Lamesh Castle. She was looking for Jahet's body. The heat of battle distorted her memory of the location; still she thought she had to be close.

As she flew, Khisanth told herself the intense desire to lay her friend's body to rest was simply a last gesture of respect for Jahet. They had, after all, blood-mingled. Jahet was the only dragon who had not betrayed her. Jahet had served the forces of the Dark Queen admirably, died with honor, and deserved better than to rot in the sun or provide food for timid, pointless creatures who would not have dared approached her while she lived.

Khisanth would have liked to sink her friend into a swampy grave, a fitting tribute for a black dragon. Unfortunately, she knew of no marshes nearby, and felt it would be even more disrespectful to magically carry Jahet's body around the countryside looking for one. Jahet's soul would have to be content with a covering of rocks.

The black eagle was nearly blinded by a sudden, powerful flash of reflected sunlight from the ground. She waited for the spots of brightness to fade from her vision before shifting her position and squinting cautiously below again. There, covered in large part by broken branches, was the oddly twisted neck and head of Highlord Maldeev's soul mate.

Khisanth quickly descended. She could see only flashes of Jahet's black body through all the branches that covered her. After landing, Khisanth returned to dragon form and began to clear the brush away with her claw arms. She took great care not to further desecrate Jahet's mortal form with scratches from her talons.

Now that her view was clear, Khisanth could see that looters had taken the saddle and Jahet's diamond nose stud. Despite that, it appeared that no creatures had ventured forward to taste their first dragon. Except for the odd twist to her neck, Jahet's body was intact, as if she were asleep.

"Well, Jahet, you were right and I was wrong. Maldeev is still pushing me to take a rider. Unfortunately, we were both wrong about who it would be."

Khisanth leaned in closer to whisper conspiratorially, "I think I may have to break my original vow to never take a human rider." She grimaced slightly and shook her head. "I can't shake the feeling that Maldeev is right, that this is the sign from Takhisis for which I've been waiting."

"That's right, I never told you about my meeting with our queen, did I?" The black dragon laughed without humor. "I could tell you what the Abyss is like, but you probably know more about it now than I do.

"Takhisis told me that when I met the human worthy of my talents, I would know it," said Khisanth. "How else could I interpret the fates that placed me near you and Maldeev when you were struck down? Maldeev would have been disgraced to lose his dragon, not to mention dead if I hadn't plucked him from the sky. Even I'm forced to agree that a highlord is worthy of me. This is my fate."

Her problems seemed trivial compared to Jahet's. "You're beyond such earthly concerns now, aren't you? What's it like to die?" Khisanth recalled the physical torment she'd suffered traveling to the Abyss while alive.

Almost without meaning to, Khisanth began to look for the killing wound. She ran her eyes over Jahet's length. The dragon could find only minor nicks and dents in the scales. There was no obvious wound here. Khisanth paused to remember her position to Jahet at the time of the dragon's death. She was certain that the side now turned skyward had been away from Khisanth, facing the knight Tate. Could Jahet have died from an earlier wound to her other side?

Before undertaking the immense task of turning the hefty dragon over, Khisanth had another idea. She retracted her talons and lay a gentle claw onto the body to examine the vulnerable skin between scales. Startled, she pulled her claw back. Jahet felt as smooth and cold as black glass, and equally as hard. Khisanth had touched enough dead creatures to know that they did, in fact, turn ice cold—but they were soft and bloated and squishy. Stiff after many days, yes, but never hard like glass.

The dragon's puzzlement deepened. She reached out with the intention of rolling Jahet over. Her claw again touched Jahet's glassy spine, but when she exerted the first trace of pressure, Khisanth heard a noise like the crackling, snapping sound of ice settling in winter. Without even conscious thought, she snatched back her claw, but it was too late. She had started a chain reaction that she was powerless to stop.

Before her stunned eyes, Khisanth watched a crack appear where she had touched Jahet. The crack raced forward and fractured into thousands of tiny lines, like the thin, silvery strands of a spiderweb. Within mere heartbeats, the entire length of Jahet's body, from snout to tail, had shattered like an impossibly large pane of glass. The fractured corpse caved in on itself and crumbled into a heap, sending the stunned dragon reeling back.

The deafening sound of breaking glass rang in Khisanth's ears for many moments as she tried to make sense of what had transpired. Almost absently, she noticed slivers of pink-veined rock just beneath the layer of black glass that had been Jahet. It looked like quartz. Blood.

Khisanth's mind turned to the obvious. Only magic could explain the odd and swift transformation of the dragon's body. Khisanth was certain she would have known before Jahet's death if there had been something inherently different about the dragon's magical abilities.

Impulsively, Khisanth cast a spell to tell if the glass were magical. She waited impatiently for the expected answer, and was surprised to detect only a negligible amount of magical energy, which would be the last vestiges of Jahet's nature or traces of Krynn's own elemental magic.

Poison? It was possible, considering Jahet's symptoms before death; she'd choked, then grew stiff and soundless. Khisanth knew little about poisons, but she doubted any mundane poison was potent enough to instantly kill a dragon.

Out of the corner of her eye, Khisanth saw something floating above the shards, and she looked up slowly. A misty form was coalescing. It stretched and rose like thick white smoke to hover high above the splintered glass, reminding Khisanth of the tormented creatures she had encountered in the Abyss. The twisting, gyrating cloud was vaguely dragon shaped, if only from the suggestion of a tail and snout. There were two large black gaps in the white mist above the nose and one below—eyes and a mouth—which seemed to melt and sag in steady and unrelenting anguish.

Khisanth had seen enough in her life that she felt neither threatened nor surprised. Perhaps she had reached her capacity for amazement. "Were you Jahet?" she asked calmly.

For an answer, the misty, swirling thing flared up high, a sharp contrast to the azure blue sky, then dropped back down to nearly Khisanth's height.

"Your death was unnatural, and because of it, you're in torment, aren't you?" The apparition flared again.

Khisanth closed her eyes and thought of Dela those years ago in the wagon. There would be no rocky grave for Jahet. With a cold, hard certainty forged in the fires of experience, Khisanth knew what she must do to end the suffering of Jahet's spirit. Bolts of white-hot fire surged from each of her six talons and bore into the pile of shards, with a hundred times the intensity of a glassmaker's torch.

Khisanth held the flames to the glass beneath the apparition until the shards began to melt. The faceted splinters turned shiny, like wet, polished stones. The dragon directed her flaming talons to the liquefying glass until her claw arms ached and the flames petered out, as if determination could inspire heat enough to fire up glass. When she could hold her arms aloft no longer, Khisanth sat back on her haunches and watched the red-hot glow of molten glass slowly recede, sinking into the earth from which creatures of magic first received their powers at the beginning of time.

As the slag dwindled, so did the ghostly apparition of Jahet's soul above it. Upon later refection, Khisanth was never quite sure if she had actually witnessed its vague expressions of torment turn to ecstasy, or if she had simply projected her own hopes onto the mists.

The dragon flew from the small glowing pile at dusk, long after the misty phantom had dissipated. Flight was painful, for the efforts of her claw arms had affected her wing muscles. She pressed on, anxious to put distance between herself and the memory of the strange abomination Jahet had briefly become.

Khisanth could not resist the temptation to look back at the softly glowing mound of hot glass. For one brief and explosive moment, a thin pillar of flame shot high into the twilight sky, as if trying to touch the constellations themselves. Then the flame was gone.

Chapter 24

The dark cleric's room in the basement of Shalimsha tower was small, cramped, and dark, just the way Andor liked it. As personal cleric to Dragon Highlord Maldeev himself, he rated a much larger space, even a room in the airy upper floors of the tower. But that would not have suited Andor's tastes, developed as a youngster in a home carved into the base of an enormous vallenwood tree. Andor was a Qualinesti elf.

Dark elf now, Andor reminded himself bitterly. Cast out by his own people after his study of magic had taken an evil turn, Andor had been pronounced a dark elf and forbidden to call himself a Qualinesti until his actions again reflected the good natures of his people. Unfortunately, bitterness over his banishment had only cemented Andor's affiliation with evil. The cleric always hid his delicately pointed ears beneath a dark, coarse-spun hood that also kept his hairless elven face in perpetual shadow. He preferred that people feared him for his skills, instead of scorned him, or worse still, pitied him for his outcast status.

Andor was kneeling at the altar to Takhisis in Shalimsha's temple, preparing for the union ceremony he was to perform later in the day between Maldeev and Khisanth. His role was to serve as the channel between the queen and her mortal servants, thus his mind would link with the Dragon Queen's during the ceremony. The thought brought fear to the cleric's heart.

She will see my guilt, Andor thought with certainty. She will know the reason for the shame I have borne since the attack. He had to explain himself first. Andor began his fervent prayers.

"Dragon Queen," the dark cleric began, using the name by which Takhisis was known among elves, "I must humbly beg your forgiveness. I did not intend that my skills be used against one who served you. I didn't know, didn't ask the purpose. It was not my place to question . . ." The dark elf's voice trailed off, knowing he sounded weak willed, and very guilty. Andor had a sudden thought.

"I know you can read my thoughts if you've a mind to, but you must realize the depth of my regret for my unwitting part in the betrayal. To prove that my allegiance to you is as steadfast as ever, I'll reveal the name of the one who has betrayed us both."

The dark elf leaned in needlessly and whispered, "His name is—"

Andor's voice was abruptly silenced.

* * * * *

Carrying a torch in one hand, Khisanth, as the black-haired woman Onyx, rushed down the narrow, twisting staircase. Not that she liked the human form, but it had its uses. She could never have gotten to the basement of the tower in her enormous dragon form.

The dark cleric Andor would know, if anyone in

Shalimsha would, what sort of spell could have caused the hideous transformation of Jahet. Khisanth could not erase from her memory the sight of the glass dragon shattering.

The young woman had to hurry now. The union ceremony with Maldeev was to take place at sundown, and much needed to be done beforehand. Khisanth took the last two steps as one and hastened down the corridor, which was narrow as two humans side by side, though very tall. A young soldier had told her that the dark cleric's door was the second one on the right. Passing the first, she stopped before a small, solid oak door, light in color from lack of exposure to sunlight, with a half-oval top. To her surprise, the door was ajar; she could see dim candlelight flickering through the crack.

Onyx knocked loudly. She heard nothing. Peering inside, she slowly pushed the heavy door open. "Andor?" The young woman stepped in tentatively and looked around. Maldeev's dark cleric was in shadow, on his knees at his shrine to Takhisis. "It's Khis—I mean Onyx." She held up her torch as she approached. "I've come to ask your counsel about a magical spell." Onyx's voice caught in her human throat.

Andor, the dark cleric of Dragon Highlord Maldeev, was facedown on the altar, blood trailing from his mouth. A diamond-encrusted knife protruded from his back.

* * * * *

"Murder within the high ranks of the wing, and on the day of our union," Maldeev muttered darkly. "I hope it's not an ill omen. . . . What this is is damned inconvenient, since Andor was to perform the ceremony." The highlord pushed back the sleeves of his robe and threw a log on the fire, sending sparks flying.

"I'm sorry I had to be the bearer of such news on this day," said Khisanth.

"What *were* you doing in the basement, anyway?" the highlord asked without turning.

"I . . . wanted to ask Andor some questions about the

ceremony," Khisanth lied, remembering Jahet's words about Maldeev's distrust of magic.

"You could have asked me," said Maldeev.

"I didn't wish to bother you with minor details," she said quickly. "We'll have to launch an investigation into Andor's death—"

"Yes, of course. Tomorrow," Maldeev said. "Right now I have to arrange for that other little cleric—what's his name, Wiib?—to perform the ceremony. Wait here for me, I have something to discuss with you when I'm finished," he ordered, then strode out the door that led to the interior of the tower.

Khisanth lay her head on her claws, her lips pulled back in a grimace of annoyance. Did he think she had nothing to do today but wait for him? She hoped to get in a quick feast and nap before the festivities. The dragon could make no sense of Maldeev's water clock, but the sunlight coming in from the courtyard told her that there was less than a quarter day left before sundown.

She could take care of one of those tasks here, she realized. Settling in for a nap, Khisanth's head jerked up when a knock sounded at the small door through which Maldeev had just left.

"Come," she said.

Salah Khan's black head wrapping poked through the opening. He saw that Khisanth was alone before the fire. "Excuse me, Number One. I was told the highlord was here," he explained. "There is a problem between the baaz and kapak draconians that requires his immediate attention, and . . ." The human's muffled voice trailed off awkwardly.

Khisanth had noticed a decided chill in the air during all encounters with Salah Khan since the battle at Lamesh. They both knew that if not for Jahet's death, Khisanth would be exchanging vows with Maldeev's second-in-command today, not the highlord.

"Highlord Maldeev said he would be returning momentarily. Enter and wait," she invited, nodding toward a spot near the hearth.

The human commander paused, considering. "Thank you," he said at last, then stepped around the door. He moved in to stand before the fire with his arms clasped stiffly behind his back.

Dragon and human waited together in uncomfortable silence. Khisanth feigned sleep; Salah Khan stared straight ahead. Finally the human broke the stillness.

"I wish you well in your impending union, Khisanth," he said. "The wing will benefit from the combination of your's and Maldeev's impressive skills."

"Thank you, Khan," said Khisanth.

The human seemed to relax a bit and even turned to look at the dragon. "Highlord Maldeev must be favored by the gods to have merited union with two such impressive dragons in one lifetime."

Khisanth only nodded, feeling her spine tingle slightly at the reminder of Maldeev's own assessment of their union.

Salah Khan clasped his hands together and turned his masked face toward the ceiling. "I only thank Takhisis that our brave highlord had the foresight to wear a magical ring into the battle that killed the mighty, faithful Jahet." He was watching Khisanth closely out of the corners of his eyes. "Just think, if he had not overcome his distrust of magic simply to appease Andor and Jahet, why, he might be dead himself!" The human shuddered.

Khan shook his wrapped head. "We shouldn't dwell today on such grim thoughts of what might have been. This day is a monumental one for the entire Black Wing," he finished brightly.

Khisanth could hardly hear the human over the thoughts Kahn's artless words had sent tumbling through her brain.

"Do you think Highlord Maldeev will be much longer?" Salah Khan was asking, looking anxiously toward the door. "I really must be getting back to deal with the problem between the draconians. . . ."

Khisanth struggled to her feet. "Tell the highlord I couldn't wait any longer," she instructed, her tone brusque and distant. "Tell him I had something to attend to, that I'll see him in the temple at sundown." With that, the black dragon stormed out of the large doorway and into the courtyard.

Watching her hasty departure, Salah Khan smiled beneath his mask.

* * * * *

Why hadn't she thought of it herself? Khisanth stormed inwardly. The dragon-turned-rodent scurried through the corridors of the tower, pressed into the shadowy corners where wall met floor.

There were only three magical things in proximity to Jahet in the battle that had killed her. Jahet herself, Khisanth, and Maldeev's ring.

Wear the bloody thing, Maldeev. What will it hurt? It just may come in handy.

Jahet herself had talked Maldeev into wearing Andor's creation.

Andor and his ring were the key to the puzzle. The dark cleric was central in, if not the instigator of, a conspiracy against Jahet. His mysterious murder supported the idea that he didn't act alone. Khisanth could think of no reason the cleric would want Jahet dead. Now he was dead, too. Someone had silenced him.

That left only the ring as evidence. Khisanth couldn't suggest to Maldeev, today of all days, that he might have unwittingly played some part in Jahet's death. The highlord would be furious and refuse to allow her to inspect the ring. She would simply have to find and examine the ring without his knowing it.

Which was why Khisanth was scurrying toward Maldeev's chambers as a mouse. She hadn't much time before he would return to change for the ceremony. As if to confirm the thought, a young serving girl in muslin cap and apron passed by the mouse, sloshing boiling water from two heavy, gray pine buckets. Setting the pails down before the highlord's door, the girl knocked perfunctorily, knowing the highlord was not yet present. She turned the knob and kicked the door open. The girl didn't see the brown mouse that skittered in behind her before she kicked the door closed with her heel.

Khisanth's first look at Maldeev's chambers surprised her. The decor was austere for a man of his rank. The main room was spacious enough to hold a dragon, if one could only get inside. The far wall consisted almost entirely of walk-out windows that led to a southern parapet overlooking the courtyard. Maldeev had spoken his first words to her from there, she remembered.

The windows were divided by a ten-foot-wide section of wall that provided the backdrop for Maldeev's bed. Khisanth's eyes widened at the sight of the only luxurious item in the room; three steps led up to the enormous, canopied thing draped with netting and covered with mounds of soft pillows.

Khisanth looked around for anything that might house a ring and spotted a wooden clothing press on the short, eastern wall. At this distance and angle, she could just make out a chest on top. Looking to the serving wench who was pouring the water into a copper bath, Khisanth hugged the wall and made her way to the press.

Now what? she asked herself. How was she going to get to the top of the towering wooden cabinet? Then she spied the tapestry hanging behind it and had her answer. Extending her delicate ivory nails, Khisanth sprang from her hind feet and hooked her little claws into the weave, pulling, pushing her way up the wall tapestry. Coming just past the top of the press, Khisanth launched herself at its smooth, polished surface, and nearly skidded off the far side. She stopped the skid by latching onto an embroidered cloth beneath the chest, which was twice her height and three times her length.

Khisanth's little heart hammered against her ribs at the near accident. Pausing only a moment to slow her breathing, she fiddled with the simple clasp on the chest until it snapped up with a soft "ping." She raised up on her hind feet, pushed the lid of the velvet-lined chest over her head, and peered within.

Khisanth pushed aside several ribboned, wax-sealed scrolls and an elaborate silver circlet she had never seen the highlord wear. Spotting a number of rings in the dim recesses of the box, Khisanth slipped her hind quarters over the edge to get a closer look. For someone who never wore rings, Maldeev sure seems to have a lot of them, she grumbled inwardly, trying to recall the brief memory of the ring he had worn at Lamesh. It had been smooth and black, like smoky glass, she remembered, with a gold band. Her eyes fell on it, and her pulse jumped with excitement. Running her paws over the flat, smooth stone, then over the edges, her right claw met with a catch.

"Highlord!" she heard the serving wench cry suddenly.

Khisanth's mouse head shot up from the box. Maldeev was marching into his chambers, whistling a tune softly. He patted the serving girl on the bottom in an obviously familiar gesture.

"I wish we had time now, my dear," he said wistfully, as he began stripping off his clothing. "It'll have to wait until after tonight's festivities." Bare-chested, Maldeev headed across the room for the press. Khisanth dived into the box.

"I was delayed by some unpleasantness, and I'm not even sure I'll have time for a bath now."

Maldeev would surely see that the lid of his chest was open, and then he would look inside and find her! How on Krynn could she explain this? She was so close! Khisanth looked at the ring next to her in the box. What had the knight Tate said? "Live to fight another day," or some such thing. It made more sense to her now in her much smaller mouse form.

Khisanth sprang from the box, scrambled across the press, tiny nails clicking against the wood. Maldeev was mere steps away, head bent to the task of fastening his cuffs. Heart hammering, Khisanth launched herself at the tapestry and sank her claws in. She paused one frantic heartbeat to catch her breath, then slid paw over paw down the wall hanging, and dropped soundlessly to the floor. Hugging the floorboards, she made for the door.

"Someone has been in my chest," she heard Maldeev say angrily when he reached the press. "What do you know about it, girl?"

The young serving girl's voice trembled. "I know nothing, sir. I came in just moments ago with water. There was no one here. I swear I have walked only between the door and the tub, sir."

"Where is the ring?" he screeched, shuffling frantically through the items in the box. He sighed in relief. "Ah, good, here it is. Nothing seems to be missing."

Khisanth didn't need to see Maldeev's hands to know which ring he'd been so frantic to find. She was not surprised to see him step back and hold a gold-banded black gem up to catch the light of the lanterns. In the yellow light, the high-lord's face was aglow with a smile of malicious contentment.

* * * * *

As the sun sank behind the mountains in the west, trumpeters in two crisp lines on the temple steps announced Khisanth's arrival. The black dragon touched a claw to her sword-and-skull choker to make certain it was properly centered around her neck before stepping through the archway.

Khisanth felt a bit light-headed, and only partially because she had not had time to feast. She had the same disorienting feeling she did when shapechanging, as if she were standing outside herself, watching her stiff-legged approach. Would she have the strength to do what she must?

Khisanth was vaguely aware that the crowds of human soldiers gathered in the temple for the union ceremony were cheering her name. She blinked away the smoke from the many burning braziers and stepped forward. Maldeev stood waiting at the front of the temple, before the altar to Takhisis.

The temple had been one of the first structures Maldeev had designed in the renovation of Lamesh, and it reflected his tastes. Cold, clean lines, smooth edges, open spaces, all arching toward the front of the temple, to end at the simple altar. The shrine to Takhisis was really just a smooth black marble slab held aloft by two uncharacteristically ornate columns. The pillars were each a carved image of a chromatic dragon with five intertwined dragon heads.

Two silver chalices waited for Khisanth and Maldeev on the black marble slab.

The trumpets blared again, reminding Khisanth that she was supposed to join the highlord at the altar. The dragon stepped forward mechanically, past the cheering men, past Maldeev's second-in-command in the front row. Salah Khan's expression was as unreadable as ever through his black head wrap. He stood without cheering, though he looked up and nodded once as the black dragon passed him.

Khisanth moved to stand next to the dragon highlord of the Black Wing, resplendent in a red-velvet, fur-lined cape, horned highlord mask, ceremonial dagger . . . and black ring.

Wiib, the short, bald cleric who was taking Andor's place, stepped from the shadows behind the altar, swinging a smoking brazier on a chain. He set the brazier on the stone floor, took a scroll from the depths of his coarse robe, and unfurled it. Wiib cleared his throat.

"Maldeev and Khisanth. To blood you are committed, by blood you shall unite your bonds to the almighty Queen of Darkness. Together you shall fight for her glory and in her cause." The little man lifted a chalice in each hand and extended it toward the man and the dragon. Khisanth had to stoop down to receive it. "Drink the essence of Takhisis."

It isn't, really, Khisanth reminded herself, but having met the Dragon Queen, she could not stifle an involuntary shudder. The dragon took the small chalice of red wine in her right claw and tossed it down her throat. Next to her Maldeev did the same.

Khisanth set the chalice on the altar and turned abruptly to face the throng, clearing her throat. "We have completed the highlord's portion of the ceremony. Now I propose a traditional dragon ritual to signify and secure undying trust."

Maldeev looked up at her, clearly surprised, even with his mask to cover his expression.

"We will mingle blood." Khisanth held her left claw-arm

out and raked a talon from her right claw over the tough hide, bringing a fine bead of red blood welling to the surface. She nodded toward Maldeev to do the same.

The highlord hesitated for a moment, eyes shifting. When he could find no reason or way to decline, Maldeev pulled his cape back from his left arm and slipped his dagger from its sheath. Khisanth's eyes lingered on the diamonds twinkling around the hilt, then blinked to bring herself back to the task at hand. Biting his lower lip, the highlord nicked his forearm just enough to raise a thin line of blood to his white skin.

Her pulse pounded at Khisanth's temples as she held her enormous forearm to Maldeev's small white one. Their blood collided. The dragon was almost physically knocked back by the brutal assault to her senses brought on by the revelation of Maldeev's true feelings, true mind.

She saw hatred for all creatures, a desire to kill anything more powerful than he, revenge, betrayal, greed, naked ambition, and not one ounce of kinship with anything. . . .

There was now no doubt in Khisanth's mind who had killed Jahet. Murdered Andor. She yanked her claw arm back to end the excruciating mingling.

The dragon's first reaction was to rip Maldeev apart and devour him before his men. Somehow, Kadagan's teachings penetrated her numb brain, bade her be calm, to think. The dragon despised the highlord, had not one whit of respect left for the human. She'd had more regard for the knight Tate than for this pitiful human who stood next to her, and she'd impaled Tate. Funny how she had so carefully kept herself from taking a rider. Now she was uniting with the most despicable human she had ever met.

The words of the Dark Queen came, unbidden, to mind. *Trust no one. What you seek is a human worthy of your talents. Look in unexpected places. You will know him when the time comes.*

Khisanth closed her eyes. She'd misread the signs, selected her rider in the most obvious of places. She thought of Tate, remembered her own comparison between him and Maldeev after she'd slain the knight. The dragon would not be so foolish as to misinterpret the queen's words again.

Khisanth became suddenly aware that Maldeev was staring at her with a strange, expectant look. The dragon made her decision.

"Maldeev and Khisanth shall not betray," she mumbled the traditional words, knowing as she did that Jahet had spoken them before her. The difference was that Khisanth knew what Jahet had not; the vow was a lie. The knowledge gave her immense power over Highlord Maldeev.

Khisanth allowed the ceremony to come to a close around her. All of this pomp and circumstance was symbolism for the enjoyment of humans, anyway.

After all, she was Khisanth, touched by the Dark Queen herself. Astinus would record the great deeds done by the magnificent black dragon in the name of Takhisis.

She had only to wait, and to watch her back.

Epilogue

Khisanth had been ever-vigilant as the Black Wing's ranking dragon. For over two years, she watched for Maldeev's betrayal. So intently, in fact, that she didn't see the frontal attack coming from Maldeev's second-in-command.

Salah Khan's campaign of whispered lies eventually earned him the position of highlord of the Black Wing. The masked human had been like a viper in both dragon and highlord's ears. In many subtle ways, Khan had reminded Khisanth to be watchful. In not so subtle ways he had told Maldeev that Khisanth was too greedy to be trusted. The tension between Khisanth and Maldeev had become palpable.

Then one day, as the queen's war machine neared completion, Maldeev had decided to participate in an otherwise routine drill, claiming he needed the practice with his dragon. Without warning or consulting Khisanth, he had invited a new dragon to fly wing. Remembering the last time the high-lord had made such an offer, something inside the ever-wary black dragon snapped.

Khisanth clawed her soul mate's face to shreds, while Salah Khan watched.

At least that's what Takhisis told her when she pulled the insensate black dragon into the Abyss one last time. The Dark Queen was true to her promise: Khisanth did not fare well in her second meeting with the queen. Takhisis was most displeased by the murder of a highlord at so crucial a time. Unlike the last time, Khisanth didn't even try to explain herself. She knew there was no point.

I seldom give second chances, Khisanth. Never a third.

The black dragon held her breath, readying herself for the killing blow.

Don't force me to regret making an exception now. You'll wish I had slain you here.

The Dark Queen had sent her post-haste to Xak Tsaroth to guard the blasted staff for Verminaard. A sentence that, as time wore on and nothing of consequence happened, seemed more punishment than reprieve.

Heaving an enormously bored sigh, Khisanth leaped back onto the stone altar and reclined on her haunches. Spotting the ancient spellbook, she picked it up in her talons and began to thumb through the musty brown pages. At least she could improve her skills in this wretched hole.

The horns on Khisanth's head suddenly quivered, sensing vibrations from the upper levels. Ears tilted, the dragon held as still as black marble, listening. Something, or someone, was definitely walking above in the Plaza of Death. It was neither gully dwarf nor draconian; she knew that for sure. Khisanth's heart began to hammer in anticipation. She had waited so long for someone to come.

The dragon sprang from the altar and began her ascent the thousand feet to the ceiling of the underground city. Halfway up, she passed the north falls, but kept climbing to the bottom of the well. Knowing she would need more than ordinary speed to ascend through the well shaft, Khisanth concentrated on the words of a haste spell. She gave one last upward thrust, clamped her wings to her sides, and shot up the shaft at twice her normal speed.

Khisanth burst from the mouth of the well and into the sunny Plaza of Death. Pivoting in air, she saw her first human in years, bent over the fallen form of a young elf girl. The man was a dark-haired, well-muscled barbarian, wearing only wrist bands and a loincloth over fringed leather leggings. The dragon's red eyes abruptly grew wide.

In the barbarian's hands was the wooden staff.

Khisanth's weathered lips drew back in a smile of anticipation. The barbarian was obviously of little importance, but he would be easy enough to slaughter.

At long last, things were turning around for the black dragon. Khisanth could feel it. She would soon fulfill her destiny.